TEASE

TERRAWAY
BOOK SEVEN

MARY E. TWOMEY

MARY E. TWOMEY, LLC

TEASE

BOOK SEVEN IN THE TERRAWAY SERIES

By

Mary E. Twomey

COPYRIGHT

Copyright © 2016 Mary E. Twomey
Cover Art by Crowe Covers

For information:
http://www.maryetwomey.com

DEDICATION

For Kevin Winningham

My ambition is to one day be as organized,
lovingly kind and gracious as you.

(I know that's not possible, but if I don't shoot for the moon, I'll
never get anywhere)

NOT BURIED YET

I was afraid to dream when I fell asleep that evening. I didn't know if I'd see Von or Philip, and dreaded meeting either in my subconscious.

My brain tripped on the mistake I made without thinking. *Not Philip.* There never was a Philip. The man with white-blond hair who came to me in my dreams was named Sama. We'd slept together in my imagination because I'd been lonely and wanted something fun to distract from the unending stream of exhausting work that Terraway never tired of throwing at me. So I'd conjured myself up a fake boyfriend. I would say that's pathetic, but it's not like everyone else doesn't do the exact same thing. Most other people choose Ian Somerhalder or David Duchovny as their fantasy hottie. I thought I'd made Philip up. But it was Sama, the dude with a surfer's body who wanted nothing less than all the power in Terraway, and an heir to share it with. He couldn't get a girl pregnant in real life, due to his remote location, so he'd found a way to possibly dreamwalk into my uterus. It was anybody's guess who the father was: Von or Sama.

Von had been gone for three days, and I think at this point only Mariang was holding out hope he'd be back. Gotta love the girl for her sweet heart and total optimism. The engagement ring Von had given me was tucked in the drawer of my nightstand, taunting me with beauty I couldn't bring myself to look at.

"I made you some tea, Lady October," Graham offered as he came into my bedroom. He and Alton were the two brothers sandwiched in the middle of the Vandershot birth order. They had been brought in to pull for me with Boston, and to guard the house I hadn't left in days.

"Thanks, Graham. I'll be out in a minute."

My room had once been my sanctuary, but now it was my man in the woods cabin with a "beware all who enter" invisible sign. Graham respected the charade that I had some say in my life, and kept the tea in the kitchen, which I appreciated.

Boston and Alton were both wolfing down a salad bowl full of scrambled eggs. They were practically starving from pulling all night long for September and me. "Sorry, guys," I offered, but they waved off my apology. Boston didn't even look up as he reached around in the air for my arm to rest his hand on it. He pulled from me while he shoveled in as much as he could swallow.

Graham plated me some eggs and slid them in front of me on the table – a gentleman amongst boys. "I hope you're hungry, your grace. There's plenty."

I didn't have it in me to ask him again not to bother with formalities. Alton and Graham were polite and proper around me. It bespoke of how much I'd changed that I didn't care enough to correct them after the second reminder that a formal address wasn't necessary. "This is perfect. Thanks, man." I ate my food like it was my job, taking no pleasure or time to wonder whether or not this is what I wanted, or even if I was hungry.

None of my life was what I wanted anymore. I was living with strangers and a married couple. I was sure Danny and Mariang would rather be living somewhere fun, and not with a jilted pregnant woman.

I wore my pajamas like a uniform, since I couldn't perform my soul-sucking job anymore, what with both my Reapers nowhere in sight. I hadn't showered in three days, but this was only partly due to the depression I could feel seeping into my pores. The other part was because if a Duwende wasn't touching me, I had not even a five-minute window before I went into labor. The contractions were no picnic, and took a long time to subside. My master plan to compensate for this was to simply stop showering. It was a solid plan. None of Von's brothers had seen me naked so far, so you know, I was winning at least on that front. As fast as I could shower under the gun if I had to, being in my last month of pregnancy made everything take a little longer than it used to. I was scared to go into labor – but more scared of what might come out of me when the D-day finally came.

When I finished, I made to take my plate to the sink, but Graham swept it away and washed my plate. I liked Graham.

I sipped my tea made from the dried *himila* weed that Mariang and I shared to keep our babies healthy. Boston held tight to my hand to keep up a steady pull. I couldn't even be proud of how far I'd come that I'd kicked so much of my OCD to be able to indulge in handholding. This, however, was no indulgence. It was necessary, so I decided it best to form no opinion at all on the claustrophobia I was engulfed in. I was grateful that the three guys didn't need me to be social as they ate and discussed how weird it felt to drive on the wrong side of the road here.

Graham waited until I finished my tea and then carefully helped me up out of my chair. "It's a lovely day for a walk, yeah?"

Graham motioned to my big picture window, and sure enough, there were birds who were looking at me like, "What the crap does she look like garbage for?" I didn't have an answer.

I shrugged noncommittally. "You should go enjoy yourself. No reason you should be chained to me. I can sit with Boston and Alton till you get back."

Boston spoke with a mouthful of food. "Ee means oo should get ow of the house."

Graham nodded. "Indeed. Couldn't have said it better than if he'd been raised with actual manners."

Boston pumped his fist in the air that he didn't need such boring things as manners to communicate effectively. "Go on, 'Tober."

"A walk? I dunno. I was thinking of going back to bed."

Graham let out a quiet sigh, Alton shot Boston a look, and Boston spoke for those too polite to do so after he swallowed. "It's ten-thirty in the morning! You can't live in your bed, October. You have to get out and move around. Von will come back when he's ready. He always does."

"I don't care about that," I snapped. "Von's doing what he wants, which is fine by me. I'm tired because I'm pregnant. That's normal."

"Is not showering normal, too?"

"It is when I can't be alone long enough to take one without going into labor. Do you want to help me in the shower, Bos?"

Boston geared up to say something pervy, judging by the crook in his eyebrow and the smarmy smirk he conjured out of thin air. Alton stood, saving his brother a black eye, adjusting the gold-rimmed circular frames on his nose as he spoke. "You've got three weeks left, yeah? I can't imagine you'll be comfortable not showering for that long."

Graham held his elbow out to me to walk me to the bathroom. "I can fix that. If you're worried about something, you're supposed to tell us. We can help." He opened the bathroom door with a practiced smile of calm he tried to bestow upon me. Graham had chocolate-hued hair that was cut short to his head, showing off his kind blue eyes and nonthreatening smile that never seemed to have any agenda. He was taller than Boston, but not as bulky, reminding me of a professor who worked out just enough to have biceps that were useful in a bar fight, but not quite so intimidating as Danny. He had a freckle next to his left eye that somehow made his smiles that much more sweet, with no note of Boston's locker room humor. Boston could make anything dirty, but Graham was calmer, older. He was twenty-seven, and treated me like I was eight.

Graham led me into the bathroom and leaned against the sink. "I'll wait right here. Every few minutes, just reach your arm out, and I'll pull from you while you're behind the curtain. No problem at all."

My spirits lifted slightly at the idea that I might not have to spend the next three weeks without a shower. "Really? You're sure you're okay with that?"

He shrugged, my hand pinned between his elbow and his ribs. "Why wouldn't I be? Ezra brought us here to keep you safe and see to whatever you needed. You underestimate your beauty to think any of us would think it an inconvenience to wait here while you're in the bath."

The first smile I'd found in days teased my lips as I batted at his charming sweetness. "Oh, hush. Seriously, though. I know this is weird, and I really appreciate you being so cool about it all. I mean, you guys left your jobs and your homes for this."

"For the most prestigious and well-paying job a Duwende could ask for, you forget. It surprises me how little you know about our culture, that you constantly think you're inconveniencing us. We never get to see Danny and Vo—" Graham stopped himself short of finishing the name of the brother they were careful not to mention too often around me. He cleared his throat. "After Bishop dying, it's a good thing for us to be able to be together as a family. Though Mum's in a state with all of us over here. I half expect her to show up any day, demanding to join the party."

My anxiety climbed at Von's mama showing up at random. "She wouldn't come unannounced, would she?"

Graham smiled at my nerves. "Let's go get you some fresh clothes, yeah?"

I was getting better at holding hands, thanks to no one in my life giving the remnants of my OCD any kind of space. Graham linked his fingers through mine and walked with me to my bedroom, letting me fish out my first outfit in days that was not pajamas. The fitted cotton light green shirt and maternity jeans felt like the first step to putting my depression on a shelf.

My movements were jerky and swift in the shower. Each time I had to reach out and touch Graham's hand, I wished showering didn't have to be done so very nakedly. We both survived the awkwardness, due in large part to

Graham's kind and gentle demeanor. He was meek, but unafraid of taking charge when I needed someone else to take the lead. His temperament reminded me a little of Allie's, which was most likely why I didn't mind him taking up space in my home.

Alton knocked on the door after I finished dressing. He handed my phone to me as I emerged from the bathroom with Graham's fingers twined through mine. "Phone for you."

I pursed my lips, wishing Alton hadn't answered my phone while I was in the bathroom. "Thanks." I put the device to my ear tentatively. "Hello?"

Judge's voice came over icy and laced with an edge. "Is that the clown who got you in trouble?"

"Who, Alton? No. Alton's his brother. And I'm not in trouble. I'm pregnant. Big difference." I desperately wanted privacy, so I could talk Judge down without an audience, but knew I'd get none. Judge had been my world once upon a time when I was a little girl. Now that I was all grown up, I could see clearly the distance that had been birthed and grown between my unofficial big brother and me over the years. "What can I do for you?"

The doorbell rang, which brought Danny out of the bedroom he'd been "resting" in with Mariang. Boston moved to answer the door, revealing none other than Judge on my front doorstep. He spoke both to my face and into the phone at the same time. "You can tell me what happened to your life!" He pocketed his phone and jerked his thumb at Boston. "Is this him?"

"No. That's a friend." I wanted to be mad that Judge showed up unannounced at my house. I knew I should read him the riot act for butting in and trying to oversee my life too many years too late. I should be so many shades of pissed at him, but all I could feel was relief. Judge was part of my normal life, while everything else felt too fantastical. I missed normal with all my heart. When I opened my mouth to yell at him, all that came out was an unsteady inhale that revealed a quivering lip I couldn't control.

Judge made a beeline for me without so much as blinking, ignoring the posturing of the Vandershot brothers, who weren't keen on strangers in the house. "I'm here, and I'll take care of it, baby girl." He pointed to Graham with a scowl. "You don't hold her hand. I don't know you."

Graham released my hand with a look of warning to make this quick. I wasn't sure the storm inside of me could be rushed or contained. I fought back tears in Judge's strong arms as they coiled around me. When I was little and not so inhibited, I remember seeing him down the street and running to him, not caring about the passing cars as I flew to his embrace, jumping up into his arms with laughter and abandon. Life had been so simple back then. Though I wanted to push him away now, the lost part of me anchored myself to the spot where he stood. After a steadying, indulgent breath, I withdrew from his arms, standing next to Graham as serenely as I could manage.

"Where's the father?" Judge asked with a tensed jaw. "You quit your job at the prison, so how are you making money? How are you supporting yourself and the baby?"

I tried to compose myself, and smiled sweetly up at him. "I thought I'd get a job working for you. You got room on the payroll for another dealer?"

Judge scowled at my poignant jab that beamed like innocence wafting off my face. "Which one of these guys is the father?"

"Oh, none of them. The father is great. You'd love him. He wants to open a topless bar, and call me a romantic, but I'm all about supporting my man and his dreams. I'll be his first investor."

"Knock it off, October."

"We're pretty serious. I mean, he even asked me to cosign on a loan for him. I was thinking of hopping on the back of his motorcycle and heading off to his mama's place. That's where he lives, of course. There's something poetic about a guy in his late forties who still lives with his mama."

I could practically see the steam billowing out of Judge's ears. "I said that's enough."

"You'll watch how you talk to my sister," Danny postured, taking a step toward me to stand on my other side. His hand rested on the small of my back – a thing Judge did not miss.

Judge's nostrils flared. "She was *my* sister long before any of you moved in here and messed up her life. She was doing fine before she got involved in whatever you've all got going on." He narrowed his eyes at me. "I've been watching the house for a while now. Tell me what suicidal future eunuch knocked you up. If it's not one of these jokers, then who?"

"You haven't met Bubba yet?" I blinked up at him, pushing all of his buttons. "I'm thinking of taking out a mortgage on the house to help out with his new business. It'll be my money and his know-how, but what's money when we're in love? Bubba said I'd be a terrific dancer. So you don't have to worry about me making money. I've got it covered." I looked up at the ceiling in thought. "Or *un*covered, now that I think about it."

"I don't have the patience for your humor today. Where's Ollie? He would never stand for this." Judge looked around at the unfamiliar faces with an impenetrable glare.

"He's out of town." That part was true. Ollie was still in Sakuna with Prince Langgam, helping him get the country back on its feet.

"Let's go. You're coming home with me. Ollie can come pick you up when he gets back."

Danny, Graham, Boston and Alton postured. "October has to stay here until the baby comes," Danny ruled.

Unbidden emotion swelled up inside my chest, easing my temper. I'd wanted to be welcomed into Judge's home for years, but not like this. I wanted to pal around with him, like the old days. I gazed up at him, wishing so many things hadn't gone so very wrong. Confusion and hope that felt like hurt formed a knot in my throat, making my voice squeak. "You want me to come to your house?"

"Absolutely not. Who even is this guy?" Danny was livid that a stranger came in that he didn't give the all-clear on. He kept giving Ollie's door furtive glances, and I knew he was trying to lock Mariang in the bedroom with his mind.

Judge kept a stern face, but his midnight eyes gave away how much he regretted sending me, Ollie and Allie away all those years ago, telling us never to come back. "Of course I'd let you stay at my place. I'd do anything to keep you safe."

I took a tentative step closer, searching for answers. "Your home is a safe place?" I knew the answer to that, but wished for a beautiful lie that would save the day. Oh, how I longed for Judge to be my safe place.

Judge hesitated, unable to fib to cover the hard truths of his life. "I have security."

"So do I." I motioned around the living room to the guys. "They're watching the house for me while I'm pregnant."

Judge rubbed his forehead in frustration. It was a rare thing to see him so without a plan. He valued control and power, but he'd walked straight into my home, knowing he'd have none. In that simple gesture, I knew that Judge loved me. "Jeez, baby girl. What kind of danger are you in?"

"No danger," I lied. "My new stepfather's the overprotective type. So's the father of the baby. He's out right now, but these are his brothers, so you don't have to worry."

Judge sneered at the guys, whose fingers were all itching to grab at their knives. They had knives, but Judge had a gun. "No. Just... no. You're coming home with me right now. I don't like the idea of you living with a bunch of men I haven't vetted. This isn't safe." He leveled his finger in Danny's direction. "Get your hand off of her. You're too close to my sister."

Of course Danny didn't obey, nor did he bother with a retort.

"I wish I could come with you, Judge. Believe me, some days I want nothing more than to run straight to you," I admitted, letting the barbed wire I kept around my heart fall into disrepair. "But you handle your problems, and I'll handle mine."

"I can help you."

Danny was in no mood. "She's got all the help she needs."

"Are you still touching her?" Judge barked with too much aggression in his bite.

I shook my head, talking over Danny's acerbic reply. "You can stay with me around the clock? I'm on bedrest, Judge. These guys are helping me until the baby comes."

"Is this you laying down in your invisible bed?" His

black eyebrows furrowed. "Get in your bed right now, if that's where you're supposed to be!" He snapped his fingers at the guys, livid. "You're supposed to be watching her? Make sure she follows the doctor's orders, understand? What's wrong with the baby, October? Do you want me to hire a nurse to watch you?"

Danny stiffened, his snarl pronounced at someone telling him how to do his job, but he said nothing.

I tried to keep my chin up to appear convincing. "The baby's alright. You don't have to worry about me."

Judge drew me in for another hug, knowing we both needed the comfort. Also, I think he wanted to tug me away from Danny. "That's the thing about us. I never stopped worrying about you, just like you never stopped caring about me, hoping I'd do the right thing and turn my life around." He cleared his throat. "Don't make me tell you twice to get in that bed right now."

I nodded into Judge's crisp white shirt. The pressed material contrasted with his dark skin, and as much as I knew he didn't like his shirts to wrinkle, I couldn't let go. When I didn't end the hug with a brisk brush-off, Judge felt my vulnerability. He cupped the back of my head to steady me against his shoulder, giving me a portion of his strength that I was too prideful to ask for. It was nearly half a minute before I pulled out of the embrace I tried not to need. Judge was the home I'd been kicked out of, but never stopped wanting to return to. I didn't expect him to follow me into my bedroom, but there we were, with Graham holding tight to my elbow, and Danny in the doorway, watching like a hawk.

"Aren't you going to introduce me to your friends?" Judge asked as he took my trembling hand and helped me into my bed.

"Guys, this is my oldest friend, Judge."

"Do any of your new friends have names?"

"No," I warned before Graham could open his mouth to introduce himself. "None of them have names. Thank you for your concern, but I'm handling my situation, and myself. I don't need help."

Judge pulled the covers up around my belly, tilting his head down at me curiously. We no doubt were having the same flashback, of him tucking me into Mama McCray's bed. Every now and then, Ollie, Allie and I decided to stay late at the McCray house when Bev was too drunkenly violent to go home to. Judge would tuck me into his mama's bed and make up bedtime stories about a princess who slayed dragons. Judge always gave me beautiful dreams. The princess had a protector who kept watch in the background, ready to intervene when the inferno grew too dangerous to handle on her own. "You're not so little anymore," Judge mused. "Don't be stubborn, October. Come stay with me if anything comes up. I mean it. Call me, and I'll come get you."

I nodded, and then bunched my hand in the front of his shirt, pulling him down so I could wrap my arms around his neck. I clung to him, despite my usual proclivity for space. It was a true testament to how much I'd grown, and how scared I was that I reached for Judge to anchor myself to the universe. "I know you would. Thank you. I really am fine, though. Honest." Then I turned my cheek to whisper in his ear. "Remember when you sent us away? Well, now I have to do the same thing to you. My world is getting... I don't want you involved in what I'm buried in."

Judge squeezed me, holding me tight to his chest for a few beats while we both relished how rare a thing it was for us to both leave ourselves unguarded enough to be human and scared. Judge kissed my forehead and laid me back down, his eyebrow creased with worry. "I don't like this. I worried enough with you working at the prison, pretending danger was no big deal. That you're scared now? Promise me that you'll call when you need to get out of whatever it is you're trapped in."

"I promise. Now I need you to go, and to stay away until things blow over for me, understand? I can't worry about you getting hurt."

"That's not how this works. I'm the older brother. *I* worry about *you*."

My smile was weak, but it surfaced all the same. "The guys have the house guarded twenty-four hours a day." I didn't pull away when he clutched my hand. The two notes of our skin looked beautiful together, and wish as I might, the little girl inside of me missed Judge every day. When he was around, I didn't have to have all the answers. Lately it felt like my whole life had turned into one big question mark. "I love you," I admitted, softening further when he kissed my knuckles and then held my hand to his chest. "Now you have to go. I need you safe, Judge. So stay away until I come see you again."

Judge's lashes swept shut through a wince of pain. "You're killing me, baby girl. This is what I did to you? Because it hurts."

"And I'll do it again and again if it keeps you alive."

Judge hugged me once more before he exited, pausing to stare down Danny in the doorway in silent threat.

I wasn't fine by any stretch of the imagination, but I wasn't buried, either.

No. I wasn't buried yet.

2

FATTY

After a day where I was actually clean, wearing fresh non-pajamas and went for a long walk with Graham and Alton, I felt like I could breathe again. Judge had been worried about me, which meant I needed to get my act together, lest I lean on him when I knew I couldn't. The ache in my chest never went away; being abandoned took a certain skillset to deal with. Unfortunately, I was well-versed in that particular talent.

When Danny and Mariang got home from a day of reaping, it was decided we'd all watch a movie, now that they weren't afraid of making noise that would disturb my mourning.

"How about *Love in Pieces with Johnny*?" Mariang suggested, smiling hopefully at the title she'd picked off my streaming movie channel.

Graham and Alton sighed quietly through their polite

smiles, but Boston didn't feel the need to hold back. "No and never. Danny has to sit through the boring love movies, but I'm not married to you. The only movie I want to watch is if Johnny gets ripped into pieces, his guts splattered by some kind of home-fashioned rusty weapon, or an alien of some sort. I'll also accept zombies."

Mariang deflated when Graham and Alton chimed in with their preference that was more in line with Boston's than her emotion-filled flick. She tossed the remote to Alton, who fumbled with it before holding it the right way and selecting a movie that looked awesome – just the right amount of gore and non-plot. It was my poison of choice. It didn't have Bruce Campbell in it, but every movie needs a flaw, I guess.

It took a few starts and stops, but I eventually stood up from the couch and moved to the kitchen to pop some popcorn for everyone. After about two minutes, Danny found his way next to me, his hand on my back to pull from me so I didn't go into labor. "You shouldn't wander off like that."

I didn't answer, not wanting to fight over the fact that I'd simply stepped into the next room, not driven to Toledo on a whim. "How's Mariang holding up, reaping by herself?"

"She's amazing. Like you were before you got knocked up. Strong, young. Barely tired after reaping six souls."

"Six? She only needs to do two to keep things afloat."

The corner of Danny's mouth angled upward. "We

were thinking of going on a ten-day cruise for our belated honeymoon. She wants to make sure you won't have to reap until September's a month old." He looked down at me with too much hinting in his tone. "Not a bad consideration, if you ask me."

"That's real nice of her. And yeah, when I'm back to work, I can make sure she has a nice, long maternity leave, too. You know me; I always work to the max when I can."

"I do know that about you, yes." We listened to the popcorn dance and crackle in the microwave, filling the kitchen with the tease of buttery goodness. "You're out of bed," he commented.

"You should be a detective. Nothing gets by you."

"That's good. I know I should be mad because you're on bedrest, but it's nice to see you with a little life in you. You're being funny and you're not hiding under the covers. Maybe I should thank that Judge friend of yours for stopping by. You've seemed more yourself since then." Danny lowered his voice. "Any more dreams about Sama?"

"No," I answered quickly. "No dreams at all." I let that statement hang between us, cluing him into the fact that either Von had been awake while I was asleep, or we weren't in love anymore. Oh, how quickly it all devolved. I rubbed my belly to remind myself that I had to keep it together for September.

"That's good, but it sucks. I'm sorry Von's being a wanker."

"You warned me." I sighed, getting out a big bowl from

under the counter. "You know, if the whole detective thing doesn't work out for you, you could be a legit shrink with poetic empathy like that."

Danny chuckled, his hand on my back wrapping around my hips to pull me into one of the hugs he was getting much better at doling out. I shrugged away from the comforting touch. "What?" Danny asked of my sudden shunning, affronted.

"You can't hug me. I don't know why, but I can't take it. It's like you squeeze the tears out of me, and I'm doing better today."

"Mariang hugs you. So does Boston. I'm trying to be more... you know, better at stuff like that. You told me to be nicer! You said the babies would be happier if I was nice," he accused. Now he wore a solid frown that replaced the smile that had been more readily at the surface lately.

"They will be, and you're doing a great job. It's not you, it's me. I'm an emotional basket case, and you're one of the few people I actually feel kind of safe around. When you hug me? I feel all the things I can't fix."

"Me? You feel safe around *me*? I make you be able to break down?" He was stunned, as if I'd just told him he held the key to the magical land of Narnia. "No one's ever told me that besides Mariang."

I shrugged and pulled the bag of popcorn out of the microwave by the edges. "Well, you can't be nice to me today. It'll make me remember that Von's not here, and that Ollie's still not home. I'll remember that I'm alone, and I can't go there right now." I shook my head, my mouth in a tight line. "Don't look at me like that. You're being nice with your eyes."

"Man, your mood swings are hard to follow."

"That's good. Now call me fat or something, so I don't want to break down and sob whenever you're around because I know you'll be good to me. Be mean to me, or I'll cry all over you," I threatened.

Danny chuckled at my logic. "I'm not calling you fat."

"Call me fat, or I'll cry right now. I'll do it, Danny. I've got a bucket of tears on standby."

"Okay, fine. You're fat as a cow. You should start auditions to become a sumo wrestler. Now do you feel better?"

Mariang entered the kitchen at the tail end of our exchange. "Danny! October is not fat! She's pregnant, and she's carrying the baby like a graceful lady of dignity. Don't ever say anything like that to her." She flitted over and hugged me, forcing me to hold my breath so I didn't dissolve into tears at her tender affection. "You are not fat. You're perfect. Absolutely perfect."

Danny spluttered. "But I... I didn't mean... She made me do it! I give up." He threw out his hands in exasperation. "Now I'm taking *all* the bloody popcorn, so make your own bowl, fatty!"

A laugh burst out of me, unbidden, as Mariang ramped up a rant to put Danny in his place.

It wasn't perfect, but these were my people, for better or worse.

3

THE OTHER GIRL

That night I went to bed with Graham and Boston. Boston was my constant bedmate, since we'd already built up a weird rapport with each other. Sometimes Boston cried in the middle of the night, and I was decent at calming him down. Alton and Graham rotated, with the other sharing Ollie's bed with Danny and Mariang to give her a double pull, which made her twice as strong for her day of reaping. You know, like the super-woman I used to be.

I missed Mason terribly, and felt wrong sleeping without him or Von, but I made do. I used Boston's leg like a body pillow, while Graham pressed his back to mine, ensuring I was encased all through the night so I didn't up and have the baby in my bed. I don't know when I stopped being weirded out sharing sheets with two grown men, but somehow I was able to fall asleep.

"You!" whooshed a voice I wished I didn't recognize. It was Philip, not Von, running toward me in my dream on the beach where we'd first made love. His white-blond hair was bouncing in the night air, and his beach shorts-clad body looked every bit as muscular as I remembered.

"Get back!" I ordered, conjuring up a long, heavy sword in my hand. I don't know why I didn't dream up a gun or a ninja or a tank or something, but apparently the slasher movie we'd watched that evening had taken up all the good weapons. "Go away, Sama!" I snarled when he stopped short a few feet from me. "Yeah, that's right. I know who you are now, and I don't want anything to do with you."

Philip looked like I'd injured his feelings. The stars shone down in the navy sky, highlighting his pain. "That's a hell of a thing to say to the father of your child."

"This isn't your baby!" I roared, hoping my volume had the power to control genetics. "This is Von's baby. Von loves me, and we're having this baby together. I thought you were fake, but you were just using me so you could try to have a child."

Philip went from hurt to scowling. "You only know what Ezra's poisoned your mind to think. If it weren't for that insufferable Kapre, I wouldn't be in this situation. I'd be able to have children with whomever I wished. Your mind was open, and we were a good fit. You can't deny that."

"Except I didn't even know your real name or who you

actually were! I thought you were pretend." I swished the sword between us when he took a step forward. It was much bulkier than the one I'd ganked off the Mer-soldier in the war on Kabayo's land so long ago.

Philip sighed in exasperation. "Who taught you how to hold that thing? Come here." Before I could stab him through the guts, he was next to me, his hand on mine as he moved the sword through the air with more precision. "Like that. See? And your front foot should point in the direction the sword starts at." He nudged my bare foot with the instep of his, and then jabbed the sword forward again. "See? Now you have more control."

I frowned, temporarily forgetting myself. "Oh, like this?" I tried a sweep, leaning forward as his hand guided mine while we clutched the hilt together.

"That's better. Needs work, though. And this blade's much too big for you. Try not moving with your whole body so much. Keep your hips centered."

"Hello, I'm like, crazy pregnant. I couldn't find my center if I had a roadmap."

Philip pressed his chest to my back. His hips mashed to my body as his free hand wrapped around my belly, so I moved when he did. We practiced a few stabs, and then a couple sideways cuts through the air. "Like that. See how much more natural that feels? You never want to give your enemy the impression they could easily best you, which is what you do when you wave your weapon around like a lunatic."

He stopped moving my arm with the sword around, and I realized he was rubbing my stomach. He lavished me with too much attachment and tenderness to be the evil villain I knew he really was. I stepped away from him, my expression displaying just how frustrating this whole situation was. "Why me? You could've dreamwalked with Mariang or any number of women, probably."

Philip sat down on the sand near the perfect blue ocean, waving his hand to the empty spot by his side for me to join him. I sat across from him instead, my back to the gently lapping waves. Our conversation felt intimate, surrounded by the dark of night as we were. "Dreamwalking only exists with Omens, and Mariang knows what I look like. She would never let me get as close as you did. You practically jumped me the first minute after I came into your mind."

"That's because I thought you were fake! Had I known, I never would've let you near me."

The corner of his mouth lifted to tease me. "You know now, and we're near enough for all sorts of our favorite things."

"Shut up, you. Make no mistake, you're not getting anywhere near this baby. She's not yours anyway. She's mine and Von's."

Philip's glare was sharp. "You think I don't know when you're lying to me by now?"

"Fine. We don't know whose she is, but one thing's for

sure – she's mine. And I won't let her set foot inside Terraway."

Philip waved his hand at my threat. "I can dreamwalk with Omens, having never met you before. I'll dreamwalk with September as soon as she's able. She'll come to me because I can give her a life without the duties she'll be born into as an Omen. I can give her land, wealth, servants – all of it. I can give you *both* those things."

I scoffed. "You don't have land. You're trapped on an island. I'll pass on eternal incarceration, but thanks."

Philip lowered his chin to glower at me. "I own land all over Terraway that civilians exchanged for my rations."

"You can give me land that shouldn't even be yours. Fantastic. If you know me by now, you should know that I'd never take property that people gave up out of desperation." I bristled, and moved to stand. Standing when you're super pregnant is frustrating. Add sand to that equation, and I qualified for a Three Stooges type of physical comedy act. Philip steadied me and lifted me up more gracefully. I took a step back from him, my chin level. "Your army tried to kill me when I was in Silo! You don't give a crap about anything but owning. You want to own me, own September."

A fierce light flared in Philip's eyes. "I didn't know you would come out and fight with Kabayo's people. I assumed you'd be safe inside his stone palace, which is where you should've been. My lieutenant had orders to take out

Kabayo's army if they didn't surrender the stone. You were never meant to come to any harm."

"You don't know the first thing about me if you think I'd let people fight while I sit in the palace, sipping margaritas."

"You're still alive. You're safe. There's nothing to be upset about. You slept with me of your own free will. I could've forced myself on you, but I didn't have to."

I gaped at him. "That's how you're playing this off? You're a jerk! I can't believe how messed up this whole situation is. You really think this'll end well for you? You think this is the way to get me to play your game?"

"I'm not trying to play a game. I never lied to you. *You* named me Philip. *You* made the first advance. I've never had a woman look at me like you do – or like you did. Ask me anything; I've no reason to lie to the mother of my child."

I ground my fingers into my temples. "For the last time, this baby's mine and Von's, not yours."

"Whatever you need to tell yourself."

"Fine, you want to give me answers? How can you dreamwalk with me if we've never met?"

Philip didn't seem surprised that I was cutting to the hard stuff. "Years of practice. A few failed attempts. You're certainly not the first one I've dreamwalked with."

"Actually how, Philip. Jeez."

He sighed, scratching his elbow. "I drank the blood of my master's wife before she passed. She's a powerful

Kapre, just like her husband. Or was, anyway. It was all decades ago. A century, even. It gave me certain abilities that no one else has. I can do a great many things with people's minds. It's how I gained control of my army – taking the mindless undead and bending them to my will. It was harder at first, but it's easy as breathing now. When your mind is the only weapon you have, you learn to use it well."

My mouth went dry. "You can mind-meld people who are still alive, can't you."

"I'm working on it. The rations I gave to the desperate people of Terraway help to dull their minds so I can get in."

"You're seriously telling me all this?"

Philip shrugged. "Why would I hide it? You're my wife, or you will be anyways. Besides, it's not a secret for those who pay attention to the signs. Everyone knows I can control the undead. It was only a matter of time before I tired of them and moved on to the living. And see? You're a good match for me, because you'd already figured most of that out."

I shook my head at the state of things. "I actually told Ezra that this was what I thought you might be up to. You're right; all the signs were there."

"More proof that I won't lie to you."

I chewed this over, tugging on my fingers as I thought. "Okay. So you're saying I'm mindless? That's why you could dreamwalk with me, even though I'm not undead?

It's because I'm mindless as a zombie? I'm gullible? Is that it?"

Philip had the nerve to laugh. "That's got nothing to do with it, though you did sleep with me rather easily, so I can't speak to your gullibility."

"I hate you so much."

He waved off my insult as if it was no concern. "I can dreamwalk with you because you're an awakened Omen. I've done it before, you know. Dreamwalked with an Omen I'd never met. I did it wrong, though. It all works better once the Omen is awakened. I learned how to do it more gently without harming my subject once I figured that out."

"Are you kidding me with this? Who did you hurt? How many girls have you knocked up like this?"

"Jealous, are we?" he teased.

I shot him a simpering look. "Shut up. How'd you hurt them? What happened to them?"

"There was only one other that I successfully grew my seed in, but many I've tried with."

My face soured. "Dude, gross. Way to disgusting up the whole thing. Don't say 'grew my seed.' You sound about ninety when you talk like that."

Philip laughed, though I couldn't tell you why. "I'm well over ninety, actually. I love that you're not afraid of me. There's something truly adorable about your ignorance."

"I thought I told you to shut up." I continued tugging at my fingers to keep from scratching at the backs of my hands. "What happened with the one you got pregnant before? Did she carry the baby to term?"

"She couldn't handle it. Her body wasn't as strong as yours is. I didn't understand what I know now. You need the *himila* weed to sustain the pregnancy. You need it, or you'll lose the baby, and when you do, your life force will go out with the fetus. Or at least most of your life force will, anyway."

My pulse started to race. "Are you kidding me? Your baby killed the other girl?"

"Didn't kill her, but left her brain partially muted. She can't access her body anymore. She wasn't awakened when my spies found her and told me they suspected she was an Omen. I waited a long time for Ezra to find you, to awaken you properly. I covered myself and dreamwalked with Mariang to give her the vision that led the Manauls to you. She still has no idea it was me who put your family's name into her head."

I gaped at this. "What the crap, Philip? That's messed up."

He spoke as if reasoning out which kind of gardening tools would best grow the ripest tomatoes. His finger was pressed to the dimple in his chin while he spoke. "I think the fact that I waited for you to be awakened, plus you ingesting the *himila* weed is perhaps the difference that's helped you to be able to carry my child this long. The other pregnancy didn't last more than three months."

"Oh man, that poor girl. Did she even know about Terraway?"

"No. She didn't need to know. She only needed to keep our child alive, but she couldn't manage even that."

"I hate you so much that you did that to some poor girl. Who was she?" I don't know why I asked. It felt like someone should know the unfortunate girl's name, to mourn the life she'd had no control over. At least I had Ezra to explain things to me. She'd meandered through a psychic pregnancy alone, no doubt thinking she was crazy.

Philip paused. "I'll tell you, but only so you know that I've never lied to you. And by the way, she loved me in our dreams, even more than you did."

"Tell me, then."

Philip shot me a look of pity, like I was stupid or something for not knowing all of his past conquests. "I can only dreamwalk with Omens, and you're genetically set up to be one. So was your sister, Allison."

I stumbled backward, the whole world melting into a sandstorm that I couldn't get ahold of. The beach was suddenly in an uproar, the waves coming from out of nowhere and crashing at our feet as the sand swirled around us in time with my shock, anger and blind rage. I lunged at Philip, not needing a sword to inflict the damage he'd done to my soul with a single sentence. Insults and hurt that came from a long-dormant part of me roiled up to spew at him as I punched and clawed, trying to gouge out his eyes with my fingernails to damage him the way he'd damaged my Allie.

When he calmly pushed my attack away, I ran to the sword, furious that he wasn't more afraid of me. "*Hani*, understand that I loved your sister. We had a great many conversations about you. How do you think I already knew you so well?"

"You were fake!" I shouted as I drove my sword toward his gut. Philip dodged more easily than I thought he should've been able to, countering my rage coolly.

"Calm down. This can't be good for the baby."

"You took Allie from me! You fried my sister's brain? I'll end you!" When my second stab got me nowhere, I took all the lightning and thunder in my soul and conjured up a legit Tyrannosaurus Rex. Rex seemed like the most terrifying thing at my disposal. My monster barreled through the sandstorm toward Philip, who blinked at my new pet with actual fear of the unknown. I guessed Terraway didn't feature a whole lot of dinosaurs.

Good.

"I can show her to you! But if you kill me in your dreams, I don't know what will happen in real life. Kill me, and you'll never see Allison again!"

I held up my hand to Rex. My dinosaur was every bit as fearsome as *Jurassic Park* had trained me to understand his breed to be. Jeff Goldblum would be so proud. "Take me to her now! Take me to Allie, and then you die."

Philip looked up at the scaly creature who dropped a

puddle-sized gob of saliva next to him. Rex grunted with hunger, waiting for my command. "She's in a coma at St. Jude's Memorial Hospital in California. She's there under a false name. Jane Doe or something."

"Good. Now, you die."

Philip help up his hands to stop me from clicking my fingers to my oversized Jurassic puppy. "It was an honest mistake. I didn't know I needed the Omen awakened for the baby to survive. I didn't know I needed to give her the *himila* weed. Look at how well you've carried our child. I'm not the monster you think I am. I cared for your sister, and I care for you."

"Allie didn't tell you crap about me, otherwise you'd know that messing with my family gets you nothing but six feet under." I snapped my fingers, giving Rex permission to unleash on Philip.

Rex let out a bloodcurdling roar that scared even me as the vibrations shook my bones. My monster didn't waste any time bending down to tear Philip's thoughtless head clean off his body, but seconds before he could close his jaws around his prey, Philip vanished into thin air.

4

HOW CRAZY IT ALL SOUNDS

"I'm telling you, I'm going – with or without all of you."

Danny jutted his chin out to match my stubbornness. "And I'm telling you, there's no way. You're a couple weeks away from your due date. Not exactly the time for a cross-country trip."

"Hello, I'm going to a hospital. If I go into labor, I'm sure they know the song and dance of how to deliver a baby in California."

"You need your doctor. You need to rest. Bedrest, kid. That's what you've been prescribed, so march!" Danny pointed his finger to the bedroom with imperious authority.

"I can sit in a car just the same as sitting in a bed. This is my sister, Danny! My sister's lying somewhere in a hospital without me! She needs me!" The thought of her hooked up to life support with tubes and needles all over her choked me around the throat and threatened my sanity. I couldn't bear the thought of her alone in a room for years now with no one to brush her hair or tell the hospital her name wasn't friggin' Jane Doe.

Danny held up his hands to calm me down. "Look, you're getting this information from where? It came to you randomly in a dream? You have to know how crazy it all sounds!"

I chewed on my lower lip, wishing I didn't have to offer up the entire confession. "It wasn't exactly random. Philip, I mean Sama, came to me in my dream last night."

Any traces of friendship that had been blooming between us turned icy by the time my sentence hit the air and crackled between us. Boston's hand in mine turned stony, and Graham, Alton and Mariang all gasped. "He what?" Danny asked in a deadly low tone, his fists clenched.

I threw out my free hand in exasperation. "I can't exactly help it. And I tried to kill him in my dream, but he like, evaporated out before I could end him. He told me I wasn't the first Omen he'd tried to get pregnant, that he'd done the same thing with Allie." My heart tugged painfully. I tried to rip my hand from Boston's so I could scrape at my skin, but the smarty only clung tighter. "Sama got my Allie pregnant, but something about her not being awakened first, or not having the stupid weed fried her brain. Fried her brain, Danny! That's why he's been giving me the *himila* weed. It's how September's stayed healthy."

Danny took a step back and rubbed his forehead as he processed the new information. "But Mariang was the only Omen for years before you came along. We didn't even know you had a sister until you told Ezra that first day we met you."

"Somehow Sama knew Allie could be an Omen before anyone else did, so he got into her mind and got her pregnant before she could be awakened."

Danny spun on his heel and yanked out his phone, calling Ezra from the kitchen. I stood in the middle of the living room, wishing I was standing next to Allie. Allie who hadn't abandoned us. Allie who loved me. Allie who needed me.

Mariang came to life first, standing and wrapping her arms around me. "I'm so sorry! I'll help you get to her however I can. We'll find her."

"St. Jude's Memorial Hospital in California. She's Jane Doe!" I cried, utterly woebegone. "No one even knows that she's loved, that she belongs to a family." I squeezed Mariang as tears started to fall, our bellies dueling for space in our hug. We both felt September reach out to press her hands to Mariang's baby, which made us cling tighter to each other. "Allie needs me, and I won't lie around while she's scared."

"We'll find her. We'll find her. Dad's not going to rest if one of his children is out there and needs help."

I nodded, knowing she wasn't just trying to make me feel better. "Thank you. She needs to meet you. Having you on my side? It's made all the difference. She needs you in her life. She'd love you." I stomped my foot to the floor when Graham's hand rested on my back. "And where's Ollie? He needs to be here!"

Mariang nodded, releasing me. "I'll go talk to Dad, make sure he orders Prince Langgam to bring him home today. They've been in touch, but Prince Langgam's insisted Ollie's been a great help to him down there. The country's in an upset, and Ollie's good in those kinds of crises."

"This is more important. I need him here right now."

5

I'LL BE IN BED, IF ANYONE NEEDS ME

"I don't know why you're looking at me like I'm a human clock or something. He's your brother." Danny had regressed back into his surly self, which was a comfort in its own way – knowing that some things were constant in a world of change.

"I'm looking at you because you're just so darn pretty. Like an ad for fabric softener or something. Downright sunshiny." I was on the couch nestled between Alton and Graham. It was the most adventure I'd had in a while – moving to sit on the couch. Let me tell you a little story about bedrest: it's boring. Making Danny even angrier was a welcome distraction from the monotony of reading medical journals and watching TV on the tablet in bed with everyone except Von.

"Deal with her," Danny groused to Mariang, who was doing yoga in the corner with Boston. Well, she was doing yoga. Boston was drinking a beer while standing on one foot. Not quite the same thing.

"Ollie's on his way," Mariang reassured me, and then sighed dreamily. "I was thinking of Solomon."

Danny's ears perked up. "Who's Solomon?"

"If it's a boy. What do you think of Solomon Daniel Vandershot?"

Danny shrugged. "I feel about as enthusiastic about Solomon as I did with Jeremiah, Kyle and Frederick. Whatever you like is fine. Just make sure when you shorten it, the nickname isn't obnoxious."

Graham's arm was around me while Alton's hand rested in mine. Alton's head was leaning back on the couch, causing his mouth to fall open and a light snore to escape his lips. I looked around at the stir-crazy Vandershots and tried to lean forward without moving Alton too much. "You guys have been pretty good sports about staying inside and being boring with me, but we've got to do something to pass the time, or it's going to be a long couple of weeks." An innocent smile crossed my lips. "Anyone want to play poker?"

Boston clapped his hand to his thigh and drained his beer. "I knew I liked you for a reason."

Danny shook his head. "This is bedrest, not sit at the table and drink beer time."

My shoulders fell. "Seriously? It's just sitting at the kitchen table instead of the couch. Aren't you bored?"

"Bored doesn't matter as much as alive does. It's important your baby stays alive. Maybe not to you, but to me and the rest of the kingdom, it'll be good to have an Omen to spare. Two, if Solomon turns out to be a girl."

My glare was supposed to cut Danny to the quick, but dude was impenetrable. "Fine. I'll be living it up in bed. Call me when Ollie gets here."

"And bedrest doesn't mean sitting up in the bed; it means laying down. Try to remember that, yeah?"

"I'm the nurse, you assjack!" I gave Danny the finger and stomped into my bedroom, knowing one of my constant shadows would soon follow me. What I didn't expect was three minutes later, for everyone to come into my bedroom with cards, the poker chips and chairs. I was so surprised and touched that I almost forgot I was pissed at Danny. Almost.

"Will it shut you up if we play in here?"

"I don't know. Are you bringing your personality?"

Boston looked uncomfortably at the chips. "Just playing for quarters, right?"

I remembered that he'd lost more than he could pay back when he and Von had gone gambling in Dagat. Von had sold himself to pay off Boston's debt, which I'm guessing had given Boston a healthy aversion to any kind of betting. "We don't even have to do that. We can just play for fun."

Boston relaxed visibly, his shoulders loosening as he climbed into the bed next to me and started shuffling the cards. "That sounds more my speed. You ready to lose, little sister?"

"Aw, it's sweet how little you know me. Deal it up, hun. You got enough room?"

Boston situated himself more comfortably on the bed, leaning against the headboard and pressing his shoulder to mine so he could pull while we played. Alton was still sleeping on the couch, but Mariang, Danny and Graham were gathered around the bed, ready for something other than movies and conversation about baby stuff. When Mariang started up about sonograms, I was grateful when Boston came to the rescue. "No way, love. This is poker. There's no baby chatter in poker."

Mariang quickly lost interest after losing her chips, not quite understanding which hands were higher than the others. She kissed Danny and left to go take a nap with Alton in Ollie's room.

With Mariang's sweetness gone, the trash talk picked up. "I didn't know you were also bad at cards," Graham said to me after I purposefully lost a hand so I could solidify everyone's tells. "Bad at bedrest and bad at cards. Utter shame. I believe Mariang's in Ollie's bedroom if you wanted to start a knitting circle. Perhaps you're good at that sort of thing?" His wicked smile paved the pathway to his defeat four hands later. I'd cajoled him into raising past what he'd wanted and took more than half his chips.

Boston was nearly knocked out of the bed when the

front door opened. "October?" Ollie called through the house.

"Ollie!" I scrambled to get to my brother, but only managed to mess up my pile of chips as I fumbled off the bed. "I'm in here!" I ignored Danny's protests that I was supposed to be in bed and ran to Ollie, which is harder to do than it sounds when you're so very pregnant. Ollie oofed when I collided into his filthy body. He had mud and dirt everywhere, but I didn't care. I hugged my brother, the story about Allie spilling out of me before he'd even taken his shoes off.

"Hold on. What?"

I realized the whole long story would have to be explained, with Sama and everything. Danny didn't have the patience for any of it, and barked for me to get back into bed. "I mean it, daft girl. If I see you out of your bed again, I'll lick all your spoons and put them back into the drawer."

My skin started to crawl with all the icks. "Don't you even think about it."

Ollie held up his hands to the living room. "Okay, let me shower and change, and then tell me what I missed, other than September growing to be the size of a water-melon. I mean, wow!" He looked around the room, only vaguely remembering the extended collection of Vander-shot brothers. "Where's Von?"

"He stepped out," I offered before anyone else could tell my brother that I was leave-able, that September didn't have a father, and that I was alone in this. "Go wash up, and we'll fill you in on everything."

After Ollie was safely tucked inside the bathroom, Mariang lowered her voice. "Why didn't you tell Ollie that Von left?"

"Because it's embarrassing. Because I don't want my brother to know that the sister he sacrificed everything for can't even get a guy to stick around the day her fiancé asks her to marry him." I pointed my finger out at the Vandershot audience. "And we're not mentioning the proposal, since Von isn't in the picture anymore. You all got that? Ollie's got enough on his plate."

The nods of uncertain compliance bobbed in my vision. "He'll find out eventually," Graham warned. "Wouldn't it be better coming from you?"

I couldn't bring myself to add more drama to the overflowing plate of pure crap. "I'll be in bed if anybody needs me."

6

STAYING FOR US

Ollie barely heard the whole story about Philip being Sama, and Allie being in a hospital before he was out the door and on a plane with Ezra and Alton. He and Danny both agreed that I couldn't go, and that it would be faster to fly instead of drive.

Each hour that passed stretched out into eternity. I felt awful just lying in bed while Allie was in a hospital in California, trying to call for me, but unable to make her voice heard.

I'd thought she'd written us off. I'd thought she'd left us. The guilt sunk hard in me, like a rock that made my whole gut sour as I turned over the heartache to examine it from every angle.

I spent that day and the next morning trying not to check my phone every five minutes, proud of myself when

I made it to ten whole minutes without diving for the device.

"I don't know how you can make sense of this," Graham said of my book from Finn. I was determined to finish the series, if for no other reason than to occupy my mind so I didn't go crazy. "It's written completely in Mer."

"It's not so bad. Just a code that needs cracking, characters that need organizing. I totally get into stuff like that."

"Will you read it to me?"

I quirked an eyebrow at him. "Seriously? I can't imagine you'd be into love stories about Mermaids and humans."

His arm was slung low around my hips as we sat on the bed together, giving Boston a much-needed break to refuel. "I'm into anything that'll keep me from falling asleep."

"I'm not sure this'll do it for you, but sure." I stopped translating and read only from my notes. They had been meticulously scribed so I could read myself the series that was probably no more special than any other love story. Except this was my mountain to climb, and for that reason, I loved it.

Graham was a great audience, letting me read without too much interruptive commentary. It wasn't until the third chapter that I glanced up and realized his eyes were unfocused, and staring toward the nightstand. "Whatcha thinking about?" I asked, setting the notebook down.

"Truth?"

I shrugged. "Why not?"

"I was wondering what to do about Sama getting inside your mind while you're asleep. Maybe we could wake you every so often so you get interrupted and he can't get to you for very long."

"Huh. It's not a terrible idea, except for the fact that I'll eventually need to sleep a full night. Not to be overly dramatic, but growing a human? Tiring."

"I can imagine it's slightly more difficult than growing a plant." He frowned. "I'm sure you don't want to hear this, but every time Von's gone away, it's always been for a good reason."

I cleared my throat. "As much as I appreciate the pep talk, I don't think I need it. I'm dealing. There are plenty of single moms who pick themselves up and move on with their baby when the guy splits. I never knew my dad, and I turned out alright."

Graham pulled me tighter to his side and pressed his temple to mine. I'd quickly learned that Graham was a sweetie pie. He was the gentleman type, which subconsciously made me sit up straighter and speak softer. "Indeed. Though let's not throw in the towel on Von yet, shall we? Our father was gone, too, and though we grew up alright, I wouldn't wish that on a child. Especially not my niece."

I opened the notebook again, fishing for a change of subject. "I appreciate you guys being here for this to help out. It's a good feeling in the middle of all this black to think of September being close to her uncles."

A genuine smile lit Graham's face. "That's a relief. For all your talk about raising the baby alone, we were worried you'd edge us out, since you're planning on doing this without Von."

I picked up Graham's hand and placed it where September's tiny little butt was positioned. "Of course I want you guys around for her. But I'm not delusional. I know you have lives. You're giving up enough just being here."

"Aw, there's nowhere I'd rather be. I'll stay as long as you'll have me. The IT profession will still be there when I return to the Topsider workforce. And you underestimate how well Ezra pays his employees. He puts a high premium on his daughters' lives. Terraway spares no expense when it comes to protecting the Omens. This is the best job any Duwende can hope for. The fact that it's you and September? So much the better. I'll stay until September graduates university, if that's what you like." He rubbed my belly like a crystal ball. "Alton may have to move home again after September comes because his girlfriend's back in London, but I've got nothing holding me anywhere but here. I'm in it for the long haul."

I kept my head down as my eyes fogged over. "You'll really stay with us?"

"Oh, darling. Of course I will." Graham's lax arm around me coiled and tightened until I was cuddled up to his chest. He even dabbed at my tears with his handkerchief, like a true gentleman. "Oh, there's no need to cry. Unless, of course, you're realizing this means you're also stuck with Boston for the next twenty years."

I choked out a laugh as Graham held me, realizing I wasn't all that alone after all.

When my phone beeped that I'd received a text, I jumped and all but lunged for the nightstand, holding my phone so Graham could see.

My heart thudded unsteadily as I read the message from Ollie. *Found Allie. She's got promising brainwaves, but still in a coma. Bringing her home. Should be there tomorrow night.*

7

MADNESS IS MY SPECIALTY

I'm not sure why my brother assumed I would be patient, or that I'd sleep, but it took Boston and Graham half an hour of steady pulling to drag me under. "But I should be cleaning," I insisted. "Allie's coming home, and she gets nervous when the house is messy."

"Daft girl," Boston said as he shifted next to me, staring up at the ceiling. "Your house is perfectly clean. Annoyingly clean, if you ask me."

"She loves apple pie. We used to bake them on the first Sunday of the month. She said they were too good for us to make them more often than that – it would spoil us." I sat up with renewed purpose. "I should bake her one. We need apples. And cheddar cheese. Ollie only eats apple pie with a slice of thick cheddar cheese melted on top."

Boston grimaced. "Apple pie with cheese? I can't imagine a better way to ruin a good thing."

Graham reached a weighted hand up and dragged me down to lay on my side facing him. "She's in a coma, honey. She can't eat pie yet."

"But maybe the smell! That's what she needs. Just to smell something familiar. The hospital doesn't smell famil-iar. Who would want to wake up to that? She's probably staying so long in her coma on protest because there's nothing delicious to smell in there."

Graham's hand rested on my cheek, his eyes barely open. "Sleep first. I'll bake a pie with you in the morning. If you do it now, the smell won't be near as fresh. You don't want to bring her an old pie now, do you?"

I deflated at his solid logic. "You're good."

"I'm tired, and so are you. Close your eyes."

"But I can clean the house now. She notices dust, and I haven't checked for cobwebs in two days! Two! Do you know how much damage dust can do in forty-eight hours?"

Graham's voice was quiet, but insistent. "Close your eyes, darling."

"Oh, man. I should probably put fresh linens on her bed. They'll take a day to straighten any wrinkles out."

"Close your eyes," Graham whispered, which made me want to lower my voice. "Close your eyes and picture life a few months from now. September will be dressed all in pink if Mariang has any say. It'll be warm out, so we'll take her for stroller walks and show her the different flowers." He paused, scratching his barely there stubble. "What else?"

"I want her to spend lots of time outside. Maybe Ollie and I can put up a swing set in the backyard when she gets big enough to enjoy it."

"Hmm. That sounds nice."

Boston chimed in with, "Von has a thing about swing sets, so you might have a bigger battle on your hands than you realize."

"What are you talking about? Von's afraid of the swings?"

Boston turned on his side and spooned me, his arm draping over my belly lazily as he spoke sleepily into the nape of my neck. "Bish broke his arm when we were kids, jumping off the swings at school. Von carried him in from the play yard all the way to the school nurse. He was always worried when we went on the swings after that. He'd hover worse than Mum. It was funny. We took to doing flips off the swings just to make him panic." He shifted against me, finally resting his nose to my neck as his breathing started to even out. A few minutes later, Boston was snoring like a sweet little kitten. I don't know why that made me smile – perhaps because their quirks were familiar now. We were comfortable enough with each other for him to spoon me and cuddle up to me without even a hint of a pervy joke. As much as I often wanted my space, I was starting to love the Vandershot boys.

Graham's arm draped around my shoulder, encasing me in the bubble of protection. It reinforced Graham's pledge that no matter what, September would have a family who loved her and showed up for her.

Graham pulled harder than usual. He relaxed me enough to go to sleep after a few minutes of fighting the desire to get up and clean the whole house.

My breathing evened, and I was transported to an amusement park I'd been to when I was a child. It was the same one that Bev, Ollie and Allie had spent the whole night fighting at, only they were nowhere in sight as I searched through the night. I could smell the popcorn and hot dogs in the air, making me salivate as I longed for a simpler life. I was alone in the park under the stars, but instead of a creepy eerie feeling, I felt liberated. No one was fighting this time. I could go on any ride I wanted, eat all the cotton candy, and no one would tell me I was too pregnant to do the fun stuff.

I trotted to the Ferris wheel and closed myself inside one of the cars. With the magic of my imagination, the ride climbed higher until I stopped the progression, over-looking the Eiffel tower I'd moved to make the scenery spectacular. In reality, it had been a strip mall as the back-drop for the night Allie had cried and Ollie and Bev had shouted for an hour straight over something I'd been too young to understand.

I smiled and sighed with satisfaction that in the still of the night, I could look at something beautiful while being so high above the ground and away from all of the problems it held for me. The Ferris wheel structure was massive. In my childhood mind's eye, it stretched to the heavens, taking my breath away when not even birds dared to fly this high. There was something peaceful, thinking about the amazing things humans could do without magic.

"I'm glad you've decided to play nice this time."

I turned my head, and suddenly Philip was in the cart on my left. "Get away from me!"

Philip was unperturbed by my complete and total rejection of him. He sat back in the cart, his hands folded behind his head as if we were on a romantic date, and I was happy to be here. I wanted to punch him, but knew I couldn't get much of a windup. Instead I made the Ferris wheel move so I could run away from him. The steady clinks of the wheel brought me one step closer to freedom.

Still, Philip was unperturbed. "I've been here before, you know. Your sister used to bring us here and relive the whole traumatic event, back when I was a comfort to her. You mother was quite the villain." He pointed to a trash can below. "Right there was where Allison was so hungry, she took a hot dog that was sitting half eaten on the edge of the garbage can. Your mother called her fat, though you know Allie's always been thin as a rail, like yourself. Allie was so ashamed that she made herself throw up the hot dog back into the trash can she'd stolen it from. Caused quite the ruckus between your brother and your mother." Philip cleared his throat, seeing the scene in detail. "I took her through the whole park while we ate our fill of what-ever she'd been cheated on in her real life. I lit a fire in the garbage can, and we burned all the things that tormented her." His eyes were very far off as he replayed the scene. "I was good to her. She had no cause to resist me, but eventu-ally she did."

"I don't want to hear how great you were at lying to my sister. I already know you're good at that."

He smiled at me as the Ferris wheel stopped halfway down, still nowhere near being close enough to the ground for me to hop off. I tried to make the wheel move again, but it was stuck. With each jolt that didn't move the giant structure, Philip grew more and more relaxed, if not smugly happy. His wide smile showed off his perfect teeth as he turned his head to grin at me. "Having some trouble, dear?"

"I'm not talking to you. Get out of my dream."

"Oh, but this is *our* dream now. This is exactly how it was with Allie before I gained total control."

"What are you yammering about?"

"Your monster tried to eat me the last time we met. Unfortunate. Each time you try to kill me in your mind and I escape, I only grow more powerful. Each time you lose, I win. It's how Allie was toward the end. She started fighting me off, but each time I lived, she grew weaker. Her mind, and then her body. Eventually she couldn't lift her head or move her mouth to speak for herself. That's how she ended up useless to me. Her body wouldn't respond when I put my seed in her over and over again. She couldn't conceive anymore. But I'm smarter now." He reached over and palmed my belly, smirking at my horrified expression. "You can try to kill me right now, if you like. I'll only come for you more. And trust me, my fantasies are far different than yours."

I gulped with dread at Philip's laughter. "Ollie's bringing her home, and we'll fix her."

Philip's arm coiled around my shoulders. He thumbed at my face, as if I was being childish and told him I wanted to live on the moon and eat green cheese. The laugh I'd once thought charming was only evil now as he looked on me with amusement. "Of course you will."

"Tell me how to get Allie back. Ollie said she's still in a coma."

"And she'll stay that way until I set her free, which I have no intention of doing."

"What's she to you? Let her go. She needs me, and I need her."

"You've gotten along just fine without her." He shook his head. "She knows too much, so you can move her body as often as you like. I gave you her body as a gesture of goodwill. I told you I wouldn't lie to you, and I didn't. But she's not waking up until I say so."

I wanted to push him off the Ferris wheel. I wanted to conjure a knife and gut him right then and there, but I was afraid. If I missed, he'd be more powerful and haunt my dreams until I was only a shell.

I wouldn't be a shell, so help me.

Philip laughed again at the conundrum that was so obviously displayed on my face. "Oh, *hani*. You're so easy to read. You want to kill me, but you know that would only bring me closer to getting everything I want from you whenever I feel like it." He traced the modest V-neck dip of my shirt, smirking at my disgusted shiver. "We can have a whole castle filled with children. My master tried to curse me so I would always be alone, but I found a way around it. Then Allie tried to send me away after she lost our first baby, but I found a way around that, too. I'm smarter now. You won't kill me *because* you're a fighter. Because you'll do anything to stay in control of your mind, even if it means losing a little of your say-so." He sucked my earlobe into his mouth and chewed, which would've driven me crazy before, but now only sent a chill of cold death through me. He released my earlobe with a pop and nuzzled me from my ear down my neck so he could press a kiss to the top swell of each breast. "Couldn't have picked a better woman to mother my children."

I hated myself, my body and the world as I uttered the next words that tasted like vomit in my mouth. "I want my sister back. Give me Allie, and I'll give you anything."

He tsked me, taking his time teasing my body that was no longer responsive to his ministrations in the way he wished me to be. I was rigid and repulsed, but he didn't seem to mind. "You'll give me anything because you have no choice and can't fight back. You can have Allie's body;

it's useless to me anyway now. But I'm keeping what's left of her mind." He touched where he wasn't allowed, laughing at my scream as I shoved him back.

"Get off me! My body doesn't belong to you!"

Philip gripped my face and tugged me close, mashing his lips to mine almost as if in punishment. "I think I'll keep your body until you lose your control and give me your mind, as well. I'll have you as I wish, as often as I wish."

My blood ran cold as I fought to stay sane through what I hoped would be the worst moments of my life. I couldn't kill Philip. My mind ran through the short list of possibilities, flipping through dead ends like a Rolodex, searching for the right fit that would get me out of the nightmare.

Von. My brain settled on Von trying to wake himself up after we'd met in our dreams when I'd been held by the Manas in that awful basement. He'd needed to get out of our dream, but couldn't until I'd punched him across the face.

Maybe I couldn't kill Philip, but I could sure do some damage to myself. Years of self-mutilation had trained me for just such an occasion. In a motion that had more control than I felt, being scared as I was, I swept Philip's hands from my body. Before he could magnetize them back on me, I gripped the iron bar that held us in place and cracked my forehead down on it.

Philip shouted in surprise and grabbed at me to stop

the madness. Little did he know, madness was my specialty. "Stop! You'll hurt yourself and our baby!"

I was strong enough to get in a second bash.

The first one dazed me. The second one brought me home.

8

EZRA'S PROMISE

I awoke to my own screams, which is probably the worst alarm clock a girl could ask for. Arms were everywhere, and I fought them off with punches and kicks as I rolled haphazardly in the bed, unable to see my foe to get a good look at his face.

"Stop it, October! Calm down!" Boston's voice was clear in the dark, but I didn't understand why he was holding me down.

"Danny, help!" Graham called as he wrestled with my arms to pin me down.

Fear lit me up like a quick-burning fire, heating my veins and reigniting my terror afresh. I let out a scream that scared even me, not knowing why Graham and Boston had turned on me, and were now holding me down for who knows what purpose. "Let me go! Let me go! It's *my* body! It's mine!"

Danny barreled into the bedroom, hair askew and no shirt on. He flipped the light on and tried to assess how best to be helpful. "Stand back, mates," he ordered his brothers, wiping his hands off on his pajama pants.

Graham was distraught as he held me down as best he could. "We can't! She woke us up clawing at her body like she was having some sort of fit. She's going to hurt herself, Danny!"

"Trust me on this, Graham. I know her. Let her go."

The moment Graham and Boston released me, I went from screaming to trying to catch my breath. My eyes were wild as I scrambled to the head of the bed. I needed to put as much distance between myself and them as possible.

Danny held his hands up as a silent promise he wouldn't touch me. "Tell me what happened. Just a nightmare that got out of control? Do you need that medicine in the needle Ollie gave you when you were touched in the head?"

I clutched my shirt to my chest to ensure it was still there. As the world became clearer, I looked at Boston and Graham's scared expressions, realizing that they would never pin me down unless I actually was hurting myself. I covered my chest as much as I could and whispered a terrified, "Sama."

Danny's shoulders tightened. "He's still visiting you?"

I nodded. "He knows how to heal Allie, but he won't tell me. She's got dirt on him or something." I pulled the comforter tight around my chest to add one more layer of protection, feeling as if Philip's hands were burned on my skin. "I tried to kill him in my last dream he showed up in. Come to find out, that only makes him stronger. It's how he was able to put Allie in a coma. She tried to kill him so much that he started to be able to control her dreams, and then he got so powerful, he could tell her body not to move anymore. It's how she has brainwaves but can't get up."

Danny rubbed his forehead, trying to catch up. "So he wants you to try and kill him so he gets more powerful?"

I nodded. "He knows I won't try to kill him anymore, so he's having a little fun." I swallowed hard, unable to look at any of the men in the room as I clutched my shirt tighter to me. "Could I just have a minute alone? It's been..." I wished for Ollie to be there. He would know what to do.

Danny nodded in understanding. He shooed his brothers out, sending Graham to sleep with Mariang, and locked us in the bedroom together. He moved slowly and deliberately, making sure I knew he was safe. He went into my dresser and pulled out one of Von's hoodies, laying it on the bed so I could put it on and cover myself with something comforting. The material felt like armor and a hug all wrapped up in one. Though I knew I couldn't count on Von, his scent was a balm to my body. I looked around my bedroom, feeling like something was missing, but as I took stock of my modest possessions, everything was there.

But Mason wasn't here, and neither was Von. I'm not sure at what point it was a given to me that they belonged here, but now that they were both gone, my home felt empty, and I felt hollow along with it.

I looked up at Danny, lost and without that crucial hope that someday things would all work out. "My home doesn't feel like home anymore."

Danny seemed to understand, motioning with a jerk of his head for me to get under the covers. "It's going on three in the morning, kid."

"Could you just go?" I asked through my tears. "Seeing Philip was... I just need some time by myself to sort it out."

"Believe me, I wish I could, but you know we can't let you alone more than a couple minutes before you go into labor. Even though it'd probably be safe for September to come now, we're not in a hospital, and Von's not..." Danny cleared his throat and rubbed the back of his neck. "Pretty soon you'll be able to get a little space. But for now, I'm nonnegotiable." He turned off the light and moved to the side of the bed, sighing as if gearing himself up before he slid in under the covers. He situated himself on Boston's pillow, his hand finding my back as I sat next to his supine body. Danny's voice was quiet, without the edge of antagonism he'd been doling out. "So Sama forced himself on you this time?"

I didn't want to answer. I closed my eyes and wished for anyone but my sister's fiancé to be in the bed with me. "Is Ollie back yet?"

"Not yet. He's settling Allie in at the hospital here. I imagine he won't be home for another day or two."

"I won't be able to see Allie until September's here because of the whole stupid bedrest thing."

"Lay down, kid. I'm tired, and I know you are too."

I shook my head. "I can't fall asleep. He'll come for me. Sama isn't going to let me keep September. He wants her in Terraway. Then he wants more children." I gulped. "A whole castle full." I started tearing at my arms when the angst grew to be too much. The fear welled up in me. "He's going to rape me and knock me up over and over again, Danny!"

Danny sat up, blinking and forcing himself to wake up so he could be on his game. "He said that?"

"That was pretty much the gist." I shook my head and hugged my belly as I rocked maniacally back and forth, wishing I knew for sure September was Von's. "Danny?"

"Yeah, kid?"

"I can't do this!"

Danny's arms banded around me, drawing my head to his bare chest in the dark. He swore a few times, no doubt working through possible solutions that would get Philip out of my head, but coming up empty-handed. "We'll figure this out. I don't know how yet, but we'll set this right." He reached over and turned on the lamp to give his skin a slight glow. "Until then, try to stay awake."

I couldn't have slept right then if he paid me, but I knew eventually I'd need to sleep. I scraped at my hands, the healthier skin not tearing as easily. Eventually I broke through, sighing with relief as pinpricks of blood dotted my arms.

"Okay, you have to stop this." Danny leaned against the headboard and separated my hands, holding one so it didn't misbehave. He squeezed my fingers and leaned his cheek to the side of my head. "This stuff worries me more than Sama. You tearing yourself up? You're bent, and I don't know how to set you right when you do this." He reached for my phone on the nightstand, calling one of my speed dials. "Ezra? Sorry to wake you. We've got a bit of a situation here." He explained the problem as best he could before handing the phone to me.

Just hearing Ezra's voice brought about a sense of relief I couldn't find otherwise. I spent the next ten minutes letting Ezra comfort me, tell me he'd find a solution so I could sleep, and that of course the baby was Von's. Of course Von would be home soon. When Ezra started groveling about trying to eat September and morphing into a ginormous lion, I cut him short. "You didn't know what you were doing. I know you love us."

"I do!" Ezra insisted with a note of pleading. "I'll never forgive myself for losing control like that. I'll never be able to apologize enough. I only hope that one day you let me see my granddaughter."

"Oh, jeez. I was never thinking of keeping her from you beyond that first month you asked me to."

His outpouring of relief made me smile. I waited until

he was finished, and as I was tucked in Danny's strong arms I whispered, "Ezra?"

"Yes, darling?"

"I'm so scared."

There was a promise in his voice that made me rally. "I will fix this. Try and stay awake for the night, and perhaps take a nap mid-morning. He's not likely to stay asleep during the day. Rest up, and I'll make it better. I won't close my eyes until you can rest without fear of him coming for you."

"Dad?" I whispered.

I heard the softness of joy in his voice that came whenever I claimed him as mine. "Tell me how I can help you."

"Do you know where Von is?"

"I wish I did. I'll send out some notices to bring him home straightaway."

"No. Don't. He shouldn't be here if he doesn't want to be. I was just curious. I haven't been able to find him in my dreams."

Ezra's voice was grave. "Let's not give up hope, shall we? Give me the day, and I'll find us a solution, so Sama never comes into your mind again."

"Thanks, Dad. I love you, you know." As I said the words, I realized how true they were. I did love Ezra, and trusted that if he promised a fix, he'd deliver on it.

"Oh, darling. I love you too, and I'll make this better for you. I'll make it all better."

I ended the call and handed the phone back to Danny,

expecting him to release me from the hug so at least he could get some sleep. Instead he held me tighter, his hug mutating into a shield of protection from the outside world. We were somber and silent a few minutes before he worked out a quiet, "So tell me about Allie."

9

THE LABOR OF LOVE

*D*anny and I spent the rest of the night telling childhood stories and talking about the future we hoped for our children while he held me. In the solace of the night, we realized that we had actually started to become friends at some point in our strange arrangement. When morning came, Danny was grumpy, but not surly. I felt terrible for him, but he didn't complain about having to go to work on half a night of sleep to reap with Mariang.

Mariang was a ball of emotion, excited to meet her new sister, scared for me, and on and off tearful that Sama's plans for me were only just beginning. Girlfriend hugged me no less than a dozen times before she left with Danny, who cupped my head to his hip in lieu of a hug before they left for work.

I ended up taking a nap with Graham, who held me

protectively in slumber. The uneventful sleep was exactly what I needed, and I awoke in the evening refreshed.

Graham and I made dinner for everyone, moving easily around each other in the kitchen while the others played video games and read out in the living room. Danny didn't even get on my case about the whole bedrest thing. We all ate without talking about the thing that had kept everyone up, and tried to enjoy what little of life that was still permitted to be enjoyable.

After dinner, Danny sent me back to bed with Boston, who talked on his phone with a girl from London, subjecting me to nearly twenty minutes of "What are you wearing?" and sexy talk that devolved from there. I entertained myself by dramatically pretending to barf all over him.

I sat up straight when the front door banged open and the voice I didn't expect to hear wafted through the house. "Baby? November, I'm home!"

I wanted both to run to and away from Von, so I compromised and stayed put. Boston hung up the phone and stood, wincing when he heard the sound of fist on flesh, followed by a steady stream of Danny shouting. "Shite. Danny's defending your honor." Boston cracked open the bedroom door, letting the voices in more clearly.

"You left that poor girl, you waste of space! You walked out on your responsibility, just like Dad!"

"What are you on about? I've been searching for the man who gave her the *himila* weed. Finn's soldier, Thad.

Finn and I found him and brought him to Ezra for questioning. Why would you think I left her?"

Danny was incredulous. "Because you left her! No explanation, no word on where you were or when you'd be back. Nothing!"

Graham joined in the argument. "She could've had the baby while you were gone. Were you planning on missing that?"

"Of course not! I was planning on eliminating Sama's access to my fiancée. If Sama's got a man in Finn's army in his pocket, he can get to October more easily. I have no plans to leave October ever. I asked her to marry me!"

Danny was livid. "And then you left her. Some husband you're turning out to be. She's been crying for days! It's all we can do to keep her from going into labor. We're cleaning up your mess, taking care of your girlfriend, your baby."

"The least you could've done was told us where you were," Graham offered, frustrated.

"I'm here now, mates. No need to be sore about it. We found the mole."

"I don't care about the mole!" Danny roared, and I heard a commotion that sounded like wrestling. "I held your girlfriend while she took off her engagement ring. I was there when Sama got back in her mind because you weren't around. He tried to force himself on her because you weren't there in her dreams. Did you even stop to think that when you're gone, Sama's got an in? Of course you didn't think! I was there when you weren't! Typical Von. Flashy promises with no substance. You can't behave like this when you're a father. Irresponsible pile of shite."

"She took off her ring? October! I didn't leave you!" Von shouted in earnest so his voice carried. "*Hani*, I'm here!"

I heard more fists on flesh, and shot Boston a look of fear. "I'll handle it," Boston assured me, running out to the living room to break up the fight. There was shouting and fighting and too many minutes of a brawl that only confused me.

Mariang snuck into my bedroom and shut the door, climbing into the bed with me. "Don't worry. Danny'll sort things out. Von's back!" She held my hand with hope shining in her features, but I couldn't feel it. I couldn't feel anything.

And then the first contraction hit me. *That* pang of reality, I felt. I swore in the middle of Mariang's pep talk, trying to keep my pain as private as possible. After two minutes of "I knew Von wouldn't leave you," a more powerful one I couldn't keep quiet through grabbed my uterus and shook it with a punishing force. "What... Are you in labor?" Mariang asked, wide-eyed.

I nodded, afraid and in pain. "Get Boston!"

Mariang ran to the door and flung it open, yelling to the brawling bears for help. They were too tangled in their fight to pay attention to her, so by the time Graham ran into the bedroom, my third contraction was in full swing. I clung to the sheets, breathing through my teeth with my back braced against the headboard. It wasn't just pain; it was fear that shook me. We were at least twenty minutes from the hospital, and I couldn't go two minutes without a contraction.

Boston ran in, his shirt disheveled as he sized me up with a wild look about him, only slightly less scared than I was. I didn't want to have September in my bed, and I really didn't want the guys here for the whole show.

Graham stood at my bedside, motioning for Boston to sit next to me in the bed. I kept my mouth closed through a scream while my body arched of its own volition. Mariang backed away so the guys could do their thing and stop the labor. Boston was afraid to touch me too much while I was in the throes, so he simply held my hand, crying out when I squeezed too hard. Graham was bent over me, one arm around my back and the other palming my belly like a basketball.

Mariang ran out of the room and shrieked in surprise. "Danny! That's enough! You two are finished. Absolutely finished! We've got a woman in labor in the next room, so stop your fight and focus on the baby. September's coming tonight if we can't get October's contractions to stop."

Danny barreled through the door, pushing up his sleeves as if he expected to deliver the baby himself. He had a bloody lip and a surly expression that was determined as he met my eyes. He nodded to let me know that he was here, and somehow that meant that everything would be okay. He shooed Boston out of the way, who was more than grateful to vacate the room and get as far away from me as possible. Danny slid in next to me and mirrored Graham's hold so I was completely encased in the brotherly strength. Danny pushed a long breath out through pursed lips, reminding me to breathe in between the searing ripples of pain. He caught Mariang's eye. "Time the contractions, hun."

Mariang snatched my phone up off the nightstand and found the timer app, dropping the device twice as she tried to manage both technology and her nerves. She watched me howl and struggle for breath as she held her own belly with one hand. Fear was etched all over her face, and I couldn't tell if she was more afraid for me, or because she was seeing what grand treats were in store for her when her time came.

"Look at me. Nothing else," Danny demanded when I started panicking at the contraction that went on far too long. He jerked my chin so our noses were only inches apart. "Look at me. Don't I look calm? This is nothing. We'll get this under control, but you have to trust me."

I shook my head, scared and in too much pain for too long. "They're not slowing down!"

"That's because I just got in here. Now that I'm here, everything will be fine." His voice sharpened. "Say it."

"Danny's here. Everything will be fine." The contraction eased up, giving me a moment to collect myself.

Von limped into the bedroom, taking my breath away

with how beaten and disheveled he looked. "I'm here. I can help."

Graham relinquished his spot and moved to my feet, pulling by holding onto my ankles. I studied Von while still trying to control my jumpy breaths. "What happened to you?"

"Ran into a bit of trouble trying to find Sama's mole in Finn's army. Turns out, my charm only works on you, not military men."

"You have a black eye. You're limping."

Von leaned down and kissed my stomach. "Let's not think on that now, love. Even like this, I'm the most dashing man you've ever laid eyes on." Von's arm coiled around the small of my back as he drew me from Danny's chest to lean on his. His lips were dry and the left side of his mouth had a trickle of blood coming down from it, but most of his bumps and bruises were days old. "I didn't mean to be gone so long. I was detained."

"By who? What happened? You said you were going to fix it, and that you were stepping out, and then you didn't come back!"

"In hindsight, I should've left a note or something with Ezra. I knew if I told you, you wouldn't let me go. I needed to keep you safe, Peach. I can't have Sama finding ways to bring you presents. If he can send you good things, he can certainly find ways to send you bad ones. So Finn and I went to Dagat to bring Thad in."

"Thad's here now?"

"He's at Ezra's, locked in my cell in the basement." Von's nose crinkled. "I do hope he doesn't mess my cell up. I have things just the way I like them in there."

As confused as I was, when the next contraction hit, I didn't have anything else in my mind other than agony, and what I could do to get it out of me quicker. I gripped Von's neck and screamed into his shirt. Though I could tell Von's arms were weak and something was wrong with his ribs, he held me as tight as he was able. "You left me!" I wailed as I pounded my fist to his chest.

Von was earnest, his hands gripping me as my body tried to puzzle through how to push out a baby when my brain was telling it not to. "No, *hani*. I didn't leave you. I stepped out for what I thought would be an hour or two. I was going to tell Finn to bring his man in, but it got more complicated. I should've left word with Ezra. No, no. I promised you I'd never leave you again. I wasn't running out on you. I was trying to make you safer, to be sure Sama didn't get his hands on our baby."

The contraction left me, making me emotional. "I'm sorry I had sex with him in my brain. I didn't know he was real! I don't want the baby to be his. I want September to be yours!"

Von kissed my cheeks with a note of urgency that made me swoon. "No matter what the paternity comes about as, September is *ours*. But Sama won't care about DNA results. He'll want her. I have to stop him from getting to you."

"You didn't run out on me?" I asked hopefully. I was so

turned around in the moment that very little resonated with me, but that solitary note finally did. It rang in my heart and set me spinning.

Von closed his eyes, in pain at my words that cut too deep for him to admit in front of Danny. "Never. I told you I was all in. I'm sorry I made you worry. We were supposed to be in and out, back by supper. Where is your ring?"

I pointed to my nightstand, and Von yanked it out of the drawer. He picked up my hand and kissed my ring finger in supplication for forgiveness.

"Please," he whispered, holding the ring at the tip of my finger, waiting for my permission before sliding it on.

I permitted a pregnant pause to rest between us before I nodded. "Please," I agreed, exhaling when he fitted my finger with the ring that belonged attached to me, reminding me every day that Von loved me.

His lips brushed mine, and despite our audience, I indulged myself in the fresh air of Von's kiss. It sucked us both under like letting the water out of a drain, immersing us in shimmering gold and blue that infiltrated our lungs. I breathed in pure gold and Von, and couldn't recall a sweeter scent.

We were ecstatic to be together again, making up for lost time as quickly as we could. His lips were full and needy, and I couldn't get enough. Though he was tired and worn, he devoured me as our park materialized around us, sealing the fate that we were still very much in love.

I lost track of the time, losing myself in the lips I'd been for too long without. I felt the twinge of discomfort in my abdomen, but pressed on, my fingers feeling Von's ripples of abdomen muscles as if his body were made of Braille.

"Marry me," he begged between kisses, thumbing the ring on my finger.

"Yes," I breathed. There was only one answer, and I knew it like a well-rehearsed song only my heart could sing.

There was another twinge of discomfort a couple minutes later, but I couldn't be bothered. Von was home, and finally, so was I.

10

DANNY'S LOVE

After the labor faded from screams to kisses to nothing at all, the others pried Von off of me long enough to give us both a moment of clarity. The park faded, and in its place was my bedroom, filled with the brothers and Mariang, who were all a little war-torn from watching a woman lose herself in the throes of labor. I'm sure I looked like I'd been tossed around inside a dryer, but I wasn't exactly vying for beauty pageant queen or anything.

"When Von kissed you, did you feel your contractions?" Mariang asked before anyone else could speak.

I thought it through as I blinked the world back into focus with both Von and Danny's hands on my back. "I don't think so. I mean, twice I felt an annoying twinge in my belly, but it wasn't painful. Just uncomfortable."

Mariang lit up like she'd just won the lottery. "Danny, when I go into labor, you have to kiss me."

Danny raised his eyebrow. "If you insist."

"October, you had two contractions while you and Von were kissing. I mean, we could see your belly tense up, and your breathing hitched, but you didn't cry out. You really didn't feel them?"

I shook my head, still breathing hard from the labor and the kiss. "Dude, get out of jail free."

Von finally collected himself, rubbing my belly protectively. "I've got you," he promised. "I'm sorry I made you worry." He looked around the room at his family. "All of you. This one's on me. I should've left word. I'll not take off again."

Danny muttered under his breath several disparaging remarks as he stood up off the bed.

Von turned to Boston. "Could you stay with November for a few more minutes, mate? I haven't showered since I last saw you, and I might actually need to call a doctor, or at least clean myself up for the sexy nurse." He gave me a wink, but some of the effect was lost due to his other eye being swollen.

"Sure."

Mariang left on Graham's arm. Before Danny made it to the door, he swung his finger in my face. "Don't you dare let Von off the hook for this. Take him back if you want to, but don't pretend like this was all okay. I'll not go through this again."

I hooked my finger through his and surprised him by pulling him down for a hug while Boston made himself comfortable next to me. My arms wrapped around Danny, and as much as I could feel he wanted to resist, he let me hold him. "You love me," I declared. "Thank you."

"Oh, shut it," he groused with a palpable chagrin that only made him more irritable. Then Danny sat on the edge of the bed so he wasn't leaning over me, deepening the embrace so he could wrap his arms around me, too, and actually participate in the affection. He let out a dramatic exhale. "You're my sister. Of course I love you. Now stop going into labor. It's terrifying."

"Yes, sir."

Danny released me and left for the living room with the others. Boston chewed on his nails, his hip pressed to mine to keep the contractions from starting all over again. "That was something," Boston commented, his eyes wide from the events of the evening. "Danny being... I don't want to say 'nice', because it was more frightening than that. Whatever that was, Danny loves you, that's for certain."

"I love him, too. I love all of you knuckleheads."

"Yes, but that's to be expected. You're a good person who has a heart. Danny isn't, and he doesn't. That's a rare thing, that is. He took a swing at his own brother for you."

I nodded, swallowing hard. "I don't want you guys fighting."

"I know. It's just odd to see him care about anything

other than Mariang, is all. If you could use your advantage to teach him to smile more or to like the rest of us, that would be amazing."

I looped my arm through Boston's. "Danny loves you."

"*Von* loves me. Danny tolerates the world."

"Well, *I* love you, Boston."

Boston shot me a sideways smile. "I love you, too, little sis."

HORMONES AND HOPE

on was the perfect cure for keeping Sama away from my subconscious. It also gave the brothers and me a break from each other, which we all desperately needed. Von was pretty banged up, but he still slowly stripped for me as seductively as he could manage so I could examine him after he returned from his shower and kicked Boston out. I swore in astonishment when I saw the injuries his clothes had been hiding. He had bruises coloring his body everywhere in puffs of black and purple, wreathed in red.

His eyes never left me as I pressed my fingers to various parts of him to test if any ribs were broken, or if the damage went deeper than his skin. "I thought I was over-selling how amazing you look pregnant in my imagination, but I was spot on."

"I missed you." I looked up at him, wounded. "You

shouldn't have left like that. You just took off. I could've had September without you even in this world!"

"I honestly thought I'd be back in a few hours. Turns out Finn's men don't take kindly to one of their own being accused of being in league with Sama."

"I can't picture you and Finn working together on anything. Is he alright, or does he look like you?" I pushed two fingers to his fourth rib, noticing his sharp intake of breath that told me he was in pain he wouldn't admit to.

"Nah, they wouldn't lay a hand on him. They didn't know we were working together on this. Finn got me out of that mess, and then we both snuck into Thad's house when he was alone and stole him out. Ezra's questioning him now." Von winced when I touched on another sore spot, but didn't cry out. "So if this whole Reaper thing doesn't work out, I could make my fair living at performing middle of the night abductions, I'm certain."

I grabbed some kinesio tape from my bathroom and taped up Von's side so he didn't move it so much and injure it more.

We stared at each other for a long minute, and then Von attacked. We stumbled into the bed as his lips crashed onto mine, savoring the taste of me and begging for more – always more. He was eager to make us both feel united, separate as we had been. I welcomed my fiancé with open arms, and legs that tangled through his.

We rolled around in our park, smearing the multicolored grass on our backs and letting it streak our hair. Blue and gold dust was hung around us, suspended and motionless until we rolled over and knocked the particles out of the way in a gust of frenzied motion.

Our clothes were easily ripped and discarded, letting us be Adam and Eve in our own personal Eden. We made love for what felt like hours, but it was still never enough. Though injured, Von was athletic and limber, not caring to be gentle to his side or anywhere else that he'd been hurt.

In our park, in the grass, in his arms, in our world I felt the first traces of a hope I'd been pretending it was fine to live without. I felt safe, at home with the man I loved.

There was a banging sound, like a fist on a wooden door in the heavens above us. Von tore his lips from mine to look up, irritated someone was interrupting our reunion. He bent down and kissed me some more, cherishing my body and all the things that made me the woman who was carrying his baby.

The knock came again and again, but we ignored it, lost in each other. It wasn't until Von was ripped off of me that the real world slowly reentered my vision, the park vanishing in slow drips that made me reach out for the haven to return. I blinked in confusion, coming to and finding Danny and Boston in my bedroom, holding back a frantic Von who reached for me with heartbreaking zeal.

In that moment, I saw how desperate he was for me, and knew he hadn't really meant to walk out on us. He was here, which was exactly where he wanted to be. "Let me go, Bos! This is our room, and we're making good use of it."

"Calm down, mate!" Boston worked out through gritted teeth. "Ezra needs to talk to October."

Danny shoved Von backward with a hearty thrust, and I knew Von was pissed, as well as hiding how much pain his ribs were in at the sudden movement. "Snap out of it, Von! Give us five minutes for her to talk on the phone, and you can go back to your makeout place."

Von breathed through his nose like a bull, not bothering to conceal his lust or his frustration that we'd been interrupted. I looked down and found to my surprise that I was fully clothed, thank goodness. I reached out an unsteady hand and took the phone from Danny, who glowered at me.

"Hello?"

"October?"

The voice that greeted me wasn't Ezra, but one that made my heart tug in my chest. I sat up straight and made to stand from the bed, but Danny gently shoved me back, reminding me that bedrest was a nonnegotiable. Emotion was thick in my voice when I finally answered. "Mason?"

I could hear his smile that was affection mixed with indulgence. "Yeah, it's me. I'm at the mansion with Ezra. He needed some help guarding the place, so I stepped in."

"Oh, I wish I had the superhuman ability to climb through the phone so I could hug you right now. I need to make sure you're okay, and see if your smile crinkles the corners of your eyes, the way it should." I paused to rub my belly. "As it is, my most impressive superhuman ability is to get randomly knocked up by psychic sperm, which really isn't all that helpful in this situation."

Mason barked out a laugh, which sounded good on him. "Oh, *hani*. How I've missed you. Only and exactly you."

"How long have you been back? I've missed you, too," I admitted, not caring that I had an audience. "Are you alright? Are you hurt? How was Sombi?"

Mason's gentle low chuckle warmed my heart so much that my hand migrated to my chest to stem the swell. "I'm just fine. I'm relieved now. I'm glad you're not upset with me about how I had to leave. I really didn't mean to bite you."

I waved my hand in the air. "Oh, I don't care about that. I just care that you're alright. I hated leaving, thinking you might be hurt or scared with no one there to help you. I'm so sorry I had to leave when life got confusing for you."

"You're the only person I know who'd apologize for *me* attacking *you*. I've been sick about the whole thing. Are you alright? How's your leg?"

"My leg?" My nose scrunched until I remembered the slice of Mason's wolfy teeth in my calf and winced. "It barely hurt at all. You're such a puppy."

"Now I know you're lying. I really hurt you. I'm so sorry, *hani*."

"It's all fine. I'm just glad you're okay."

"I'm okay, and I have questions for you."

I straightened in the bed, trying to ignore the three sets of eyes that were on me. "Hit me."

"I've got Thad locked in Ezra's cell, and he's finally started talking."

"Please tell me you're not hurting him."

Mason hesitated, and when he finally spoke, his voice came out light and innocent. "Of course not. I've been using good conversation and honest reasoning with him. Nothing gets criminals talking faster."

"Ugh. Don't give me the specifics. And please stop torturing people. Total lack of imagination and a giant step down for all of humanity."

"Do I need to remind you again that no part of me is human?"

"No. You just need to pacify me with some response that tells me anything I said got through to you."

"Sure, *hani*. I'm reformed already. All it took was a two-minute phone conversation."

"I remember missing you. I forget why now."

"Because you love me," Mason stated with certainty, and I adored him for the bold declaration. Then he cleared his throat. "Thad's been saying there are factions of Ekeks who now know that Sama's possibly reproduced with you. It seems like his spies are trying hard to get help to you to make sure the baby lives."

"Um, am I bonkers, or does that sound like good news?"

"Yes to both questions. But the drawback is that most

of the Ekeks and Manas are like us, and they hate Sama. So if word leaks out from his loyalists that he's gotten you pregnant, then they might try to intervene."

"Intervene?"

Mason swallowed. "Stay inside with the Vandershots. Stay away from windows."

"Okay. I can do that."

"I want you to remain Topside, alright? No matter what, Sama and hopefully most of his spies can't get up here. It's the one thing keeping Ezra moderately sane, so stick with the Vandershots and stay Topside no matter what. Understood?"

"It's like you're telling me to eat ice cream for dinner. I've got no problem staying out of Terraway."

"And take it easy. This whole thing about you always going into labor? I don't like it. Stay with Von until your due date. I mean it. Don't let a stupid fight break up a good thing."

I smiled, wondering when it was that we became the kind of friends who knew how to fight for what was best for each other. "I love you, you know." I waved off Von's dramatic sigh.

I could hear the grin in Mason's voice. "I know. And I love you enough to tell you to stay with Von no matter what."

"Thanks, Mason."

"And to stay out of Terraway."

"No problem. I already said that'd be fine." I shrugged,

rubbing my belly. Von got his libido under control and situated himself next to me on the bed, leaning back against the headboard so he could pull for me and September. I rested my shoulder to his chest contentedly.

"That's good. I told Danny to keep you out of Terraway, too. Because you're going to want to go back after I tell you the next thing, but you can't. Promise me."

"I super promise."

"Like, an actual promise, October."

I stiffened. "What's wrong? Where's Ezra?"

"Ezra's here. We got some information out of Thad on how to wake your sister up from her coma." Mason paused for my reaction, but I had no words. I was completely motionless, so tensed with nerves, Von's hand stilled in my hair. He pressed his cheek to mine to listen in. Mason continued. "We have to go to the Baluki forest to pick some *sigla* flowers. That *might* bring her back. Might, October. Might. I don't want you to go flying off the handle about this. I've never heard of the root being used for this kind of thing, so it's a very long, long, long shot."

"Who's getting the flowers? I should go with them. What do the flowers look like?"

Mason blew out a loud gust of exasperation. "Hand the phone to Von."

"I'm serious, Mason. I should go."

"You're the one person who can't go. The only place the *sigla* flowers grow is in a remote province of Hayop."

"So? That's good. Then we go to Hayop. No big deal. You've always wanted to show me your home country."

Mason paused, and I wished for anything other than the next words that tumbled out of his mouth. "You can't go to the Baluki forest. It's where Sama served his apprenticeship."

"So?"

"My people won't even venture near it. The forest is riddled with curses and dark magic left over from all the experimenting Sama and the other apprentice did. It's where they made the elixir to turn themselves immortal. Plus, Hayop is the last place a pregnant woman should be. It's a land filled with Matruculans. You'd be a walking pot roast. You wouldn't last five minutes."

My heart sank. "Crap. I guess that makes sense. Okay, I promise I'll stay Topside. Probably shouldn't let September near any freaky curses or baby-eating folk."

"Look at you, thinking like a mother. Tell September her Uncle Mason will find a way to bring her Aunt Allie home."

"Be careful, Mason."

"Oh, *hani*, I'm only ever careful with you."

12

EVERYTHING WAS CHAOS

One week out from my due date, and Allie still remained in the hospital where Ollie had moved her. She was twenty miles away from me, but there might as well have been an ocean between us, since she couldn't get to me, and everyone had a cow whenever I got out of bed for any reason at all.

Von was stuck to our bed like glue, proving to me and September that he wasn't going anywhere. He never once complained about how boring bedrest was, and went out of his way to make the experience a fun one for the three of us.

"Just once more. I promise I'll get it right this time."

"You've got terrible aim with these things." I laughed at him, my belly shaking the cereal bowl I'd precariously perched atop my baby bump as I lay back in the bed.

"They're not weighted properly."

"They're cotton balls! They're not weighted at all." When he threw the next cotton ball at the bowl on my belly and missed, the white fluff bounced off my nose and rolled onto the pillow. "Face it. You suck at cotton ball pong."

"Now, now. I'm just warming up. No need to get snippy."

"Can't we go outside for just a little bit? I'm starting to miss the feel of real air. Danny won't even let us unlock the window to get in anything fresh."

"Fancy letting me paint your belly again?" he offered. "I was thinking a giant castle with September waving from a window in the top tower."

I rolled my shirt up to reveal the globe he'd painted on my belly that morning. Instead of the continents, he'd done representations of the countries of Terraway, so I could see them all laid out from a bird's eye view. "But I like this. You did such a good job. Makes me feel like a work of art."

"But darling, you are."

I was expecting Boston to come home with the pizzas they were pretty much mainlining by this point. I was expecting his cheery, "Who loves Boston?" which would accompany Graham and Von shouting out that they loved him most, and therefore should have all the pizza. Then Danny would gank the box off the top without participating in the game.

I was not expecting a crash, nor Mariang's scream of

distress, followed by the sounds of man grunts and shouting. I bolted upright, and Von grabbed the knife he had atop my dresser. It had gone unused for days. We'd been safe with no upset for days. Blissful days.

Von pressed his finger to his lips to tell me to keep quiet. He motioned for me to get in the closet, giving me a hard pull before he moved to the bedroom door and cracked it open. I heard the ominous wak-wak whirring sound that sent chills up my spine.

Manas.

Serena had marked me with a bat-shaped scar, and I felt the sting anew, even after knowing she was dead. She was gone because Sama had killed her. I'd thought my imagination was just telling me what I wanted to hear, but now I knew that Sama had been protecting his child.

Von's child.

I tiptoed out of the closet and slid the large balisong blade Finn gave me out of the nightstand drawer. I tried not to breathe as I shut myself back inside the closet. I breathed through the claustrophobia, trying to push out the awful things that crept in on my psyche when cramped in a small, dark space.

Now couldn't be the time for a freak-out. I'd have a good meltdown when I had a Puller with me and no monsters. I closed my eyes and dreamed of a life with no monsters as I heard the chaos banging around in my house just feet away from where I stood. I held my breath and prayed for a break in the drama.

I heard something that sounded like the lamp Allie had picked out crash with purpose from the living room. I cringed as I wondered which of the brothers had weaponized the appliance. The Manas screamed, but the wak-wak sound of her wings only multiplied. Then there were three. Then there were four.

Then I lost count.

My heart exploded in time with my bedroom window, shattering glass all over my room, and flinging who knows what sort of staining outside elements all over my white carpet. I clawed at my hands and tried to conjure up Ollie's old mantra that never failed to ring true: *Life is messy, and that's okay.*

I ripped the skin open on the backs of my hands as Von stabbed and lunged, fighting the Manas who were clearly on a mission. "We don't want to harm the Omens. It's just the baby we want!" Their leader's words were delivered in a "there's nothing to see here" kind of way. The casual nature of her telling Von she'd come for mine and Mari-ang's babies made me grip September tight, my upper lip curling in a snarl.

"Over my dead body!" Von roared, and something breakable smashed. Yet another lamp bit the dust. I cracked the closet door so I could see through the folding vertical slat.

Lamps are replaceable. This whole house is replaceable. People are not.

The head Manas screamed, but soon another set of

wings joined the fray, coming in through my window and ripping out a chunk of Von's hair from his head. She had a purple corset with pockets that zipped shut on her half a body that was detached from her hips and legs. She had orangy red hair and a mixture of fear and a sneer on her face. She pocketed the stolen black hair she'd ripped out of Von's head, like she was holding onto a souvenir or something of value. "We're not here for you, Reaper!" she shouted at Von, who punched her. Then she flew back out the window, leaving her sisters in arms to fight, while she escaped with her treasure.

"Susa, get back here!" the lead woman called after her friend who ditched her so quickly.

Von sneered at the woman who appeared to be in charge, her long nose and ears making her stand out slightly. "If you came for my daughter, you've come for me." Von's perfect lips curved into a snarl that made me rally.

"We won't hurt your Omen if we don't have to. We just want Sama's baby. He can't have an heir. He can't have an offspring!"

"He doesn't, you crazy witch! The baby's mine! She's mine! September and October, both mine!"

There was some sort of scuffle, and I stayed motionless inside the closet, for once obeying instructions. I wanted to fight. Oh, how I wanted to end anyone who thought it was a good idea to threaten September in my presence. But I knew that I was very pregnant and on bedrest. I couldn't fight like I knew my non-pregnant body could, and even that might not be enough.

Von's howl of pain lit me from the inside with panic, but I remained in the closet, a ghost on the edge of the fight. When I heard Mariang's scream of distress, I bit my lip and dug my fingers into my biceps. I crossed my arms over my chest, the pain anchoring me to the spot.

Relief coursed through me when I heard one of them say to her batty troops, "That's not her. She's Ezra's rightful daughter. We want the new Omen, not Mariang. Leave her and her baby be."

Mariang's screams turned into scared sobs while Danny, Boston and Graham roared and crashed like rhinos through my house, ripping at random and slicing at will.

My home and my life had been in order before Terraway, and now everything was chaos.

I did what they asked me and stayed put, going against every instinct to never be the victim, to fight for the people you loved and for the life you wanted. I put my trust in my friends, my sister and my fiancé.

I kept my scream inside my lips when the closet door was flung open by a filthy Manas. She had matted black hair that looked like it hadn't been brushed or washed in months. "I found her!" she called to the rest of the house, yanking me out with force I was too clumsy to resist with any sort of clarity. Finn's jagged balisong blade was clutched in my steady hand, and before the disheveled but determined Manas could do what she wanted to

September, I sliced her across her throat. My knife cut true, as it had when I'd fought off the army of zombies with Finn. Though Finn was in his own world now, I felt him with me, slicing and gutting the half-women who'd left their legs elsewhere, so their torsos could fly around and wreak havoc on my house and my life.

The Manas who'd yanked me from the closet flapped haphazardly and then collapsed. I knew it wouldn't be over until we salted or burned them, but going out of the bedroom would only flood me with more Manas I might not be able to overtake. Flashes of them lifting Bishop and me and flying us beyond where Von could find us terrified me to my very core.

I stepped over the dormant body of the Manas I'd temporarily killed and ran to Von. He had three determined Manas on him and four in that limbo of temporary death at his feet. He fought valiantly with knives and his teeth, biting and slashing with purpose and desire. Bloodlust was plain in his wide eyes, so I stabbed one of the Manas in the back and dragged the blade sideways so he could have some breathing room and some lunch.

"Get back!" Von warned, but the Manas turned from attacking him to raising their razor-like claws at me.

I didn't hesitate, but flashed my knife across the torso of the one on the right. This only seemed to piss off the others. My body wasn't as flexible as it had been nine months ago, and didn't take to being slammed on the bed when several of them ganged up on me. My back twinged, and I felt the beginnings of a contraction coming on, of all things. The mark on my arm started to burn, hopefully communicating to Kabayo to get the crap up here and clean house.

The half-women didn't look angry or like they wanted to kill me. Instead they shushed me as the bedroom door burst open, and more Manas flew in to fight Von. "Don't hurt him! Don't hurt the baby!"

"I'm coming, October!" Von shouted. "Hold on!" I heard an "oof!" and felt fear like none other as I thrashed unsuccessfully on the bed, pinned down by four, five and then six flapping Manas.

"Stop! The baby's not Sama's! She's Von's!" I cried, fighting for both our lives.

The one in charge looked down on me and pulled a pouch out of her jacket pocket as she hovered next to my head, her bat wings flapping to keep her aloft. "Yeah? Well, I can't take that chance."

Danny burst into the bedroom, his crazed eyes locking in on mine before he jumped into the air and grabbed the nearest Manas. He flung her clear across the room like a Frisbee, knocking her out. Von was working his way through the swarm that was on him, and Boston did his best to attack the nearest thing that kept us apart.

There was so much going on. I braced myself against the fistful of light brown ground up spices that was shoved into my mouth. I didn't know what it was, so I tried to spit out the mouthful that tasted like mulch at the Manas who held me down.

"Almost there, sisters!" the one near my head shouted. She crammed the spices back inside and held my mouth shut while she pinched my nose. She lowered her head so I could only see her black eyes and pale skin. Her long nose twitched as she cut off my air. "Just swallow, and it'll all be over. We'll leave right now and never bother you again. We don't want to hurt you or your Puller. We know you need to reap. It's only the baby we want. You and I both know this child can't live." Her determination was calm, trumping my terror as the seconds that I went without air ticked by.

"No!" Danny and Von both cried in unison, slicing and punching to get to me. Each time they killed one Manas, two more took her place.

A contraction hit me, making me suck in, the herbs tickling my throat and causing an involuntary swallow as I tried to work out a scream. I choked, my eyes watering as she held her hand over my mouth and maintained her pinch on my nose long after the first swallow. "A little more," she urged like a gentle mother figure.

I was determined not to cooperate as the contraction rippled through me. My body rebelled, seeking air when there was none. It was searching out relief, when I knew by now there never would be any.

The woman had the gall to kiss my forehead as I

thrashed on the bed. When she pulled herself up, she let out a shrill whistle. "It's done!"

With that, the Manas left their fights mid-swing and flew out of the house as if they were fleeing a fire. Leathery bat wings flapped with purpose as they flooded out of my home through whatever entrance they could find or make for themselves.

13

———

A GOOD RUSE

I was still spitting the herbs out of my mouth when Danny and Von descended on me. They turned me onto my side as Von shoved two frantic fingers down my throat, triggering my gag reflex. "No, no, no, no!" he cried over and over, fear taking over the bloodlust as he forced vomit to thrust out of me all over his hand and onto my formerly white carpet. "Get it out of her!" he shouted to his brothers, and I could hear tears in his command.

Graham ran in with a canister of salt, sprinkling it on the dead Manas so they would stay dead. "What is it?"

"It's the *patayin* root! They force-fed it to her. If we don't get it out now, September will die! Hurry!"

Graham swore and ran to my side, holding my hair back as Von forced me to puke over and over. Von gripped the back of my head to keep it from bucking backward when his fingers dove to the back of my throat over and over. "It'll be okay, *hani*. Just get it out of your system. It hasn't had time to work its way through yet. Right?" Von asked Danny, and I knew he was trying to will his words to be true.

Danny was grim, his voice unsteady with a waiver that made me nervous. Danny was never uncertain. "Don't do any pulling. Our best bet is to let her deliver the baby right now. Get September away from the poison."

"Wha-?" I worked out before I barfed again on Von's hand. "Gross! Von, I have to breathe for a second."

Von wiped his hand off on my comforter as another contraction hit me like a wrecking ball. He looked up and gusted out a greeting of, "What took you so bloody long? I thought your mark was supposed to be some kind of insurance for her."

Kabayo's voice made me turn my head so I could see his giant horse head and neck entering my bedroom. "I came as soon as I could. How can I help?"

Danny briefed him on the situation, ending it with the nonnegotiable, "We don't have time to muck about. She's going to deliver the baby right here, right now."

Kabayo took in my fear and narrowed his eyes, giving a snort that told me to get over it and rally already. "My wife gave birth without a doctor just fine. You're made of sturdy stuff. I've seen your quality."

I felt a trickle run down my legs and swore loudly. "No! Von, I think my water just broke! I need to get to a hospital!" A contraction hit me again, and I doubled over on the bed, gritting my teeth through the pain that forced a scream out of me.

Graham was on the phone with Ezra, his voice scared as he watched me like I was an alien on the bed. Danny let out a petrified bleat of distress before coming to himself. He straightened and got in my face. "Alright. The baby's coming. Those last two contractions weren't even a minute apart. All this stopping and starting of your labor's going to make for a quick delivery, apparently, which is exactly what we need. This is a good thing, so get focused and let's do this."

"What? No! I'm not ready to give birth! I'm not having a baby in my bed! This is the twenty-first century!"

Kabayo called over his shoulder to the living room. "Finn! Get in here and help me."

"What? No! I don't want this! I don't need a horse and a fish! I need a doctor!"

Danny paid me no mind. He snapped his fingers at his brothers. "Boston, Graham, salt and move," he said, indicating the Manas' carcasses. "Toss the bodies in her garage to make some room. Mariang, turn on the kettle and boil me some water. Then get me as many clean towels as you can find."

The three sprang into action, scattering and working as fast as they could. I could tell they were all grateful to be out of the room that would soon have one more person in it.

Finn stumbled into the room, his eyes wide as he took

in my sweaty face and the fear I didn't bother hiding. "How can I help?"

Kabayo rolled up the sleeves of his beige button-down, as if gearing up to slay a zombie army. "I've done this a couple times, but never with a human, and certainly nothing like an Omen. I don't know what to expect, so stay right here to help me."

Finn met my eyes and nodded once, giving me his best impression of a calm smile. "It'll be fine. I'm right here."

"I'm scared," I admitted. "This wasn't how it was supposed to be."

"I told you from the start, if you needed me, I'd be there." Finn was earnest, almost poetic in his devotion to me. Here I was about to give birth to another man's baby, and he was still by my side.

Speaking of the other man...

"I swear to you, if I didn't need as many hands as I can get right now, I'd knock the dreamy look in your eyes straight off of you. Make yourself useful and give her something to drink to rinse out her mouth." Von was on the left side of my mattress, and Danny knelt on the right.

Finn sidestepped my towel-covered barf on the carpet and cupped his hand to my lips. "Don't swallow. Just swish the water around in your mouth and spit."

I obeyed, cringing as I spat onto the towel on the floor.

My perfect white carpet. My perfect home. I spat on my perfect home.

Kabayo set the tone of speaking quietly between my

contractions in hopes of calming the atmosphere in the bedroom. My screams were the only thing that rose above a respectful whisper. I squeezed Danny and Von's hands for support when the countdown to the next contraction came faster than I anticipated.

Danny locked his eyes on me, giving me his best "let's do this" face. "This baby's coming out of you now, so don't wuss out on me."

"No, Danny!" I whimpered. "I need a real doctor and a hospital! I need Ollie and another week and a... and a..."

Danny and Von gently laid me back and held my hands while I screamed through a contraction that made me feel pressure where I didn't want it. "I don't want to push yet!" I shouted to my traitor body.

My mouth still tasted a little like vomit and my body was acting without my consent. Kabayo was saying something to instruct me, but I couldn't hear anything other than the sound of my own screams. When the contraction passed, Finn helped Boston drag the last Manas out of my bedroom and shut the door with only Danny, Von, himself and Kabayo inside with me. Kabayo gave me a calm, reassuring look as he worked off my soaking and bloody leggings, gasping as he took in the damage. "Were you cut by the Manas? Did they hurt you?"

I worked out a breathy, "No. I don't think so," between contractions.

Kabayo waved Von and Finn down toward my feet, and I wanted to kick them both. Finn pointed with dread and shook his head. "Is there supposed to be this much blood?" It was the first time I realized Von had been breathing through his teeth instead of his nose.

Von's jaw stiffened while Danny held my hand and tried to make me comfortable with pillows. "Let's get September out now."

As if on cue, another contraction hit seconds later. With Kabayo running the show, the four moved quickly, doing whatever they could to help my horse doctor deliver my baby. "Finn, rinse her off so I can see what I'm doing." Then he instructed Danny and Von to each take one of my bare and bloody legs, and drape it over their shoulders. They obeyed without hesitation, angling their heads towards mine so my legs were bent with my knees inches from my chest.

Finn migrated toward the money shot, a controlled tight line to his lips that I knew was hiding his internal terror. "It's all okay, *hani*." In a brotherly move I didn't expect, Finn put his hand on Von's back. "Von, are you doing alright with the blood? Do you need to step out?"

Von spoke through gritted teeth. "I had my fill of Manas blood earlier. I couldn't be hungry right now if you paid me. Just worry about her. I'm fine."

Kabayo shut everyone up so I heard only his voice. "Push only when I tell you to, and stop when I say. Are you ready?"

"No!"

Kabayo narrowed his eyes at me and nodded once. "Okay, now!"

I don't know for how long I pushed, but an eternity of searing, ripping agony wasn't too far a stretch. I sobbed between pushes. I was in so much pain; I knew there was a reason medical advances had gone to such leaps and bounds to ensure no woman had to go through this experience without medication, should she elect to have it.

Von's eyes were my focal point. When Kabayo told me to push, I did. When he told me to stop, I obeyed, never once taking my eyes from Von. "You're doing great. You're amazing! You're doing it!" Though Von was scared, he pretended we were in control of this situation. He pretended everything would be okay. He pretended the pain would go away and that everything broken was fixable.

It was a good ruse.

WHEN THE TIME CAME FOR THE FINAL FEW PUSHES, VON WAS instructed to come near my legs so he could catch the baby with Kabayo, who most certainly hadn't anticipated a home birth in his schedule that morning. Finn took Von's place, holding my left leg back. Kabayo was calling out instructions, but I could barely see through my tears and mind-numbing pain. His horse face blurred in my vision as he ordered me to push one more time.

It was with a final scream of agony and triumph that September broke free. I flopped back on the bed with so much relief, I could barely feel my limbs. I was weightless, floating as I waited for the sweet sounds of my daughter's first cries to greet me. The sound that she knew I was near, and that I would be good at quieting her fears. Something in her would know that I was her mama, and that I'd never leave her. I'd never let her know what it was to be alone and scared.

I waited.

When I finally heard the soft sounds of a sob, it wasn't September, but Von. "Why isn't she moving?" he asked, helpless and scared.

Kabayo started calling out commands to Finn and Danny, moving September to a clean towel so they could work on her.

I waited for her cries as my body delivered the afterbirth on autopilot.

I waited for the sweet sound of my daughter as I bled.

And bled.

The world shifted unnaturally and blurred, and I felt everything in slow motion crash over me.

Terraway.

Bev dying.

Ollie bringing a lifeless Allie home.

Terraway.

Then I felt nothing. I heard nothing. I saw nothing as the world faded to black.

14

A LITTLE WHILE LONGER

I awoke to my bedroom in shambles, and was surprised to find that I didn't care about that anymore. I was disoriented, and my tongue was fat and fuzzy in my mouth. I tried to unstick it so I could form words. The world had a black furry halo around it. I tried to get my peripheral vision to work, but it had apparently gone to lunch.

"September?" I croaked out.

Mariang came into my vision with a glass of water, tipping it to my lips as her tearstained face tried to make out words. I drank the cool beverage, feeling a little better as the haze around my vision started to clear a modest amount.

"Can I hold her? Where is she?"

Mariang shook her head, her lips pursed together

through a sob as she tried unsuccessfully to communicate something to me.

I tried to sit up, but Danny came to my other side, his face red and sweaty as he lowered me back down. "You lost a lot of blood, so you have to stay in bed a little while longer."

I felt the bed beneath me, but there was no wetness or blood anywhere. "Did you change the sheets? How long have I been out? Where's September?"

Danny sat down on the side of the bed and picked up my cold and limp hand, sandwiching it between his meaty ones. "September's..."

Mariang's bark was angry, which was uncharacteristic of her dealings with her surly husband. It seemed that while I was out, they'd switched roles. "Don't you dare, Danny! She just woke up. Let her rest a minute." She faked a smile down at me and switched her tone to the one Allie used to use when she was trying to will something to be true that just plain wasn't. "Von's with September now. You can see her in a little bit."

Danny glared over at his wife, unwilling to bend to her. "You're not doing her any good. Go try and help the guys with Von. I'll handle this."

Mariang left the room, though I sensed it wasn't because Danny told her to, but because something bad was about to happen here, and she needed to flee from the scene of the impending crime.

I looked down at my significantly flatter stomach. I felt

like a deflated balloon beneath the sheet I'd been draped in like a corpse. "What happened?" I was barely coherent. Every breath brought me a smidgen more lucidity until I was able to look up at Danny and squeeze his hand. "Where's September?"

Danny addressed my hand that was squished between his as he spoke, afraid for some reason to look at me. "The Manas forced you to swallow the *patayin* root they'd ground up. Do you remember the whole drama with the women in Sakuna losing their babies?"

"Yeah. How awful."

"They lost them because King Geon poisoned the river with *patayin*. A faction of the Manas were afraid of Sama reproducing, so they snuck Topside to force the *patayin* on you."

I stared up at the ceiling. "I guess my spontaneous labor was a good thing. Thank God we got her out right then."

Danny shook his head, still fearful of meeting my eyes. "We got her out of you, but it was too late. The *patayin* is powerful, and works quick."

I didn't understand what Danny was trying to say. Impatient, I shifted uncomfortably on the bed. "Can I just have my baby already? Is she sick from the *patayin* or something?"

Danny cleared his throat and held my hand tighter as dread painted his monster of Frankenstein features. "September isn't sick, hun. She's..."

I saw Danny's lips move, but my ears felt like they had cotton in them. "What?"

"She's...."

"I can't hear you." Each time he tried to tell me, my hearing deserted me. It was the strangest thing.

Finally Danny let go of my hand and held my face so I was inches from him and could see his lips move in slow motion. "September's dead." He leaned forward and rested his forehead to mine. "I'm sorry. I'm so sorry. We did everything we could. She came out without a pulse. There's nothing you or anyone could've done. The *patayin* works fast. She was probably gone the minute the herb touched your tongue."

"What?" I asked, confused as the insane information mangled my brain and refused to make sense. "She's not dead. She's my baby. She just came out of me! I just had her with me a second ago!"

Danny shook his head. "She's gone. Kabayo even worked on her for half an hour. She didn't make it. After the *patayin*, she didn't stand a chance."

The earth shook as I shouted in Danny's face. My body was too weak to sit up, so my voice tried to compensate. "Stop it! You're lying to me! You know she's fine!"

Tears welled in Danny's eyes while he tried to make sure there was at least one sane person in the room. "She's dead. They pronounced her a while ago. Then Von lost himself. He took her into the kitchen and won't let us near them. He bit Graham when he tried to take September from his arms. Then he bit Finn when he tried to take her away after that." He waved his hand like he was clearing the air of a bad smell. "That's nothing for you to trouble yourself with, though. I'll take care of it."

I had no words or concept of time as the seconds passed, giving my mushy brain a moment to process as much as it could of the chaos. When I finally spoke, a whisper was all I could work out. "Bring them in here. Von and September. I want to see my baby."

Danny shook his head, swiping at tears that trickled down his cheeks. "No. You don't need to see what you lost. It's bad enough you lost her. No need to put a face to the nightmare."

A low rumble started in my disoriented guts and echoed out through my body like a war cry. "Bring me my daughter!"

It was a thing of mercy that Danny obeyed me for once. I wasn't sure what kind of inhuman damage I might do if he didn't. It took some time, but finally a wild-eyed and disheveled Von inched into the room. He was clutching a swaddled blanket in his arms like it was a treasure he was afraid would be stolen right out from under his nose. "I... I can fix this," he promised, his wet eyes like saucers, and his movements stiff and unpracticed.

"Come here. Let me see my daughter." I patted the space next to me on the bed, waiting with bated breath to get a look at the person who'd changed my life the most thus far. Von climbed into the cleaned bed and laid his head down on his pillow, resting September between us.

I gasped with fear and wonder as the most beautiful creature I'd ever laid eyes on was unveiled next to me. I shook as I studied every curve and crevice of her sleeping face, wanting more details, more of everything that had to do with her. I never understood the whole love at first sight thing, but in that moment, I did. I loved her. Deep in my bones, her tiny curled fingers wrapped around my heart and held it, squeezing the tears straight from it like an overfull sponge, refusing to let go. "She's gorgeous," I whispered.

Von's voice sounded unbalanced and a little insane, but I let him woo me with his crazy. "I can fix her. I've been feeding her a little of my blood to see if it'll transform her into a quarter-vamp. I know traditionally only a full vampire can change someone, but maybe that's just because no one like me's tried it before. Just give her a little more time and keep her warm, yeah?"

"Okay, Von." I agreed because it meant I got to keep my daughter a little while longer. She had thin cheeks and a button nose like mine. "She's got your chin," I remarked, tracing with trembling fingers the arc that was precious to me. In truth, it could've been my chin. Philip's chin had a cleft in it, and September's didn't. It was one drop of hope in my ocean of bleak nothingness, so I clung to it.

Tears flowed out of me as Von kissed her temple and

then mine. "She's our girl. Sama's got hideous white-blond hair, but September's is darker."

I didn't tell him that since my hair was auburn and September's had a bit of color to it, that it didn't actually confirm paternity. He was too in love for me to burst the bubble with logic. "She's perfect, that's for sure. Do you think she'd be able to talk people into stupid things, like you can?"

A hint of a smile touched Von's lips. "I have no doubt. She's got your ears, which I'm guessing means she won't listen when she's told no."

I smiled through my grief that I could see coming like a giant boat-smashing tsunami. "That's my girl." Von swallowed uncomfortably, and I knew he could smell my blood. "Why don't you go drink from one of the Manas in the garage? I can tell you're thirsty."

"I'm fine. I won't leave her."

"You're not leaving her. You're going into the next room so she can lay next to her mama."

Von shook his head. "I'm not ready to blink yet. I'm afraid if I do, they'll take her away from us. I can save her. I can fix this."

Danny cleared his throat, alerting us to his presence in the room. "I brought you this. Take some time together and say goodbye." He reached over me and handed a blood bag to Von, who gripped his brother's arm in gratitude.

Von lowered his voice to a whisper when Danny left

the bedroom. "I'm not saying goodbye. Let's give my blood time to work its way through her system."

September didn't have a heartbeat, so nothing would work through her system, no matter how powerful the fictional antidote may be. But I wanted to believe Von because I wanted the lie to be true. I wanted to know that life would be kind to us, that after all the horror, it would give us something good to hold onto. "How much more time?"

"I don't know. A little while longer."

"Okay, Von. We can keep her a little while longer."

Von met my eyes and nodded, tearing a slice with his incisor through his already scabbed wrist. Then he dripped his blood into my precious daughter's mouth.

I closed my eyes against the image that would forever be seared into my brain. Now I knew that life would continue on as it always had, doling out breaks for others, but keeping us wrapped firmly around the throats.

15

THE LIFE VON ALMOST HAD

When Danny drew the short stick again and braved our grim family picnic, Von was in better spirits, now that the three of us were together, and I seemed to be on his side. "Perfect timing, mate. I want a picture of the three of us. My phone's somewhere."

Danny's mouth dropped open as dread pulled at the features I knew he preferred stoic. "I... Von, I can't take a photo of you guys. September's dead. I'll not have you posing with a corpse."

Von's sneer was instantaneous as his hackles rose, scaring me with his conviction. "September's not dead! She's not! Get out if you can't be useful. Send in Mariang."

I was afraid to touch Von, but knew I was the only one who could bring him back to earth. "Von, honey. It's alright."

"What have I asked for lately, huh? What have I ever

asked you for, Danny? All I want is a photo of my daughter, and you can't even manage that without a fight! It kills you to see me happy."

Danny shook his head, for once backing down from a fight. "You're not happy, Von. You're in shock. But I'll take the photo, if that's what you want. No problem. Mariang's not here anyways. I had Boston take her to a hotel, in case the Manas come back."

Von settled down in the bed, his arm wrapping around our stiff baby to hold my elbow as he nuzzled his nose to her frozen cheek. "We have to keep her warm," he reminded me.

Danny could barely look at us as he took the photo, blanching when Von instructed me to close my eyes so it looked like we were taking a nap together. Danny took a few shots of September and Von, and then a couple of me and my daughter, though I couldn't bring myself to open my eyes and admit to the world that I felt haunted and hollow. I didn't want digital proof of the madness that was seeping into my pores, setting in deep.

"Where's Ollie?" I asked, knowing my tether to sanity was fragile at best.

"He's here. He was trying to help in the kitchen when Von wouldn't let us near September. It got a little intense, so he stepped out to get some air. I'll send him in once he gets his stomach back."

"Is he alright?"

Danny shook his head, utterly lost. "Are any of us? He

wanted to get himself together before he came in here." He cleared his throat and pocketed his phone.

I barely paid attention to Danny, instead sinking down into the covers with Von and our stiff baby. "Von," I whispered. "It's been some time, and it doesn't seem like your blood's working."

Von shot me a look like I'd betrayed him. "I told you I would fix this."

"Okay." I swallowed, wishing I didn't have to be sane, that I could check out and live in a world where problems were fixable, and death negotiable. "You have twenty more minutes. If she's not alive by then, Kabayo's going to take her away and bury her for us."

"Fine. Twenty more minutes. We just have to keep her warm," Von insisted, burrowing closer and nudging my rigid daughter against my breast.

"What are you doing?" I whispered, tears streaming down my face as I felt my cold daughter not respond to my sore and overfull breasts.

"Can you try to nurse her? That might help."

My eyes closed against the image of the very maternal thing I would never get to do for my sweet baby. My voice came out in a pinched whisper laced with unfathomable agony. "Von, this hurts me."

Von was in a world unto himself, scared and determined that something in his life would turn out right. That the life he'd almost gotten his hands on wouldn't slip through his fingers. I wanted to save him from the nightmare, but I couldn't... I just couldn't.

When Ollie came into the room, I didn't have words. All I had was a trembling chin that rambled nonsense, hoping my beacon of strength and sanity would have the means to put the fragments into whole sentences of solace. Ollie kissed three fingers and pressed them to September's forehead. Then my brother wrapped his arms around me and gently lifted so I was slumped against him on the bed, giving me some breathing room from my worst nightmare.

"No! Get her back down here, Ollie. We have to keep September warm." Von tugged at my arm, and though Ollie resisted, I nodded my consent, knowing that as lost as I was, Von was even further out at sea.

"Von, I don't want my sister doing this. It's hurting her, and I know you don't want that."

"Just a little while longer!"

I held Ollie's hand tight, silently begging for him to not leave me in my hour of need. "It's alright, Ollie. I promised Von we could try for twenty more minutes. Then it's over."

Ollie squeezed my hand. "Anything you want, kid. I'm right here."

I wasn't delusional. I didn't expect Von to suddenly snap to reason when Finn and Kabayo entered my bedroom when the twenty minutes of mercy passed. Von snatched September up and held her to his chest. A trickle of crimson stained his chin from his last attempt to revive our daughter with his blood.

Danny quietly explained the situation to Finn and Kabayo. They exchanged grave nods and moved to either side of Von with the air of "this is happening, dude" to them. "She's my daughter, and you'll not take her from me!" Von roared. "She's not dead; it just takes time for the vampire blood to go through her." Then he turned to me and yelled, "Tell them!"

I tried to hold it together while Ollie sat me up in the bed and leaned me back against the headboard. My abdominal muscles were all higgledy-piggledy, so nothing worked properly. My voice was quiet but steady. "Von, you agreed that if it didn't work in twenty minutes, then you'd give her to Kabayo so he could bury her."

Von shook with rage, spittle flinging out as he wailed, "I can fix this! You don't trust me! After everything, you still don't trust me with our daughter!"

My heart broke for him – for us. "Honey, of course I trust you, but you agreed. This was what you said could happen if she didn't come back to life by now."

Kabayo held out his arms expectantly, a white towel draped between them to wrap my daughter in. "I promise to give her the burial of an Omen. I'll lay her to rest in my family's mausoleum, where a guard is always posted, if that's okay with the two of you. You can visit her there whenever you wish."

Von clung greedily to our daughter, holding her face to his. His blood that had been dribbled on September's mouth smeared across his cheek as he moved back against the wall like a cornered animal. Von looked positively rabid, hissing and baring his fangs at Kabayo, like he might snap and attack the King of Silo at any moment.

Finn held his hands up to calm Von, but it had the opposite effect. Von drew his knife, slashing it wildly in the air to fend off the friendly advance. Finn shot me a withering look. "I don't think Ezra wants me to hurt him, but he's making it pretty tempting."

Danny drew his knife in threat. "You'll not hurt my brother! He's clearly touched in the head."

"Help me up, Ollie." I swung my legs off the bed, taking my first steps since giving birth. I didn't even realize what they'd dressed me in until the sheet fell off me, revealing bare legs and the rest of me clad in one of Von's button downs that fit me like a party dress. Everything in my body felt bruised, and walking was more of an effort than I wanted to admit. Leaning on Ollie, I made my way to Von, dropping my brother's arm when he tried to pull me back from the blade Von was too fond of brandishing. "Von? Honey? You have to give me September. You promised, and it's time."

"I didn't get to see Penny born," he whispered, pressing the tip of the blade to his forehead and closing his eyes, each breath making his lips tremble. He was stark raving mad, and I was only a hair's breath away from the edge myself. "But I got to be there for September. She's *my* daughter, and *I* say when she's dead."

I reached up slowly and took the knife away from his

forehead, hating the image that burned in my mind. The love of all my many real and imagined lives was truly unbalanced. Von's hand stiffened on the hilt, not letting me lower it all the way. Instead of fighting him on it, I moved the tip of the blade to my chest bone, closing my eyes through my tears as I whispered so loudly, the force shook my insides. "You're hurting me with this, Von. Don't make me take her from you."

Finn hissed at the blade poking me, his body shifting so that at the slightest hint of distress, he could pull me back. Danny crept toward Von's side, making the whole circle claustrophobic and tense. He held up his hand behind Von and wriggled his fingers so I could see them. I knew he was aiming to bliss Von out if he didn't hand over the baby soon.

Von tucked his knife into his belt, still clinging to September. "No," he growled. "I'm not giving up on her. I can't believe you would turn your back on our daughter."

The slam hit me hard, punching me in my mangled guts and deflating my fight. A tormented sob escaped my lips, but I closed my mouth before another could tumble out. I gave Danny a slight nod, and his hand clamped on Von's shoulder in brotherly solidarity. Von postured, but then wavered, his rigid spine relaxing until his eyes rolled back and his arms went limp.

Danny caught Von and lowered him gently to my white carpet that was littered with the bloody stains of my broken life.

I caught September with clumsy fingers and handed her to Kabayo. My horse king wrapped her tight in the clean towel, carefully and respectfully handling her tiny body, knowing it was precious to me.

Finn supported me by holding my elbow as the world crashed and crushed with punishing force. No matter how many times Bev had tried to tell me I was the cause for all the problems of the world, I knew I wasn't responsible for this one. This one was on the world itself, so I decided it was time to check out from my painful reality that only ever teased me with the hope of brighter days ahead. My legs gave out, and Finn swept me up before I could bang my head on the bedframe. Though I felt the heaviness of too many burdens, in Finn's capable arms I was lighter than air.

I watched the ceiling above me change to another, and then we were outside. Somehow I'd been wrapped in a clean blanket. Finn's breath was soft in my ear. "Close your eyes, *sinta*. I'm here now."

16

I LOST MY BABY

I awoke to the smell of a clean room. Not just clean, but sterile. I inhaled deeply, letting the sting of the nothingness fill my lungs before I ventured a peek at where I was. I looked around at the small TV mounted on the wall across from my bed. I had an IV stuck in my hand, and my arms were bandaged to hide my cuts from view.

I tried to sit up quietly, but Ollie roused from where he'd fallen asleep in the stiff chair next to my hospital bed. "October? Are you alright?" He pressed the intercom for the nurse to come in and leaned forward. "How do you feel?"

I shrugged. "How am I supposed to feel?"

Ollie didn't have an answer, and when the nurse bustled into my room, I didn't have an answer for her, either. I'd been out for an entire day, but it felt like a week.

I was sore, but if the dry as the Sahara feeling in my mouth was any indicator, I was on something that was managing the brunt of the pain.

Good. Keep it coming.

The nurse was kind, but I wasn't paying much attention to the specifics. I needed to take it easy, move slow. Take as much time as I needed after the emotional and physical trauma. Blah, blah, blah. "How's Von? Where's Von?" I asked the second the nurse left the room.

Ollie was guarding his words. "He's dealing with it all still. Dealing with it all finally, I guess. He spent the night in Ezra's cell because we were afraid of what he might do to himself or Kabayo when he woke up. But Danny said he seems to be coming to terms with the fact that there was nothing you two could've done to save September." Her name twisted in his mouth, and I could tell it hurt him to say her name out loud. "They let him out of the cage this morning, and he seems to be mildly human again, for better or worse. Boston and Danny are with him, pulling when he gets too worked up. He's half delirious, honestly. He'll be up later today when he gets himself together. Ezra's making him stay in the mansion until he's sure Von's head's screwed on mostly straight."

"I should get going, then. He needs me."

Ollie stood and gently pushed me back onto the bed when I tried to get up. "Nope. Man, I knew you'd say that, too. This is the pneumonia incident all over again. You were a pill then, too. You're staying here for the next few days until the doctor sends you home. Like it or not, you just gave birth. That requires a little downtime."

My voice was quiet as I thought through the trauma that hit me in waves. "I had a baby, Ollie. I had a daughter."

Ollie nodded once, pursing his lips as he searched for the right words. "Yes, you did. You gave birth to a full-term baby with no anesthesia and no doctor! Danny told us all how incredible you were."

I stared ahead at the wall, picturing September's thin, delicate face. "She was beautiful."

"She was. Looked just like you. I don't remember a ton from when you were first born, but I remember that. You were so tiny. I was afraid I might break you if I held you wrong." He paused, examining the hard look on my face that couldn't afford to break down anymore. "And look at you. You turned out real good, kid."

I waited a few beats to make sure there was no accusation in my tone. "What took you so long to come back from Sakuna?"

Ollie wiped his hand down his face in a show of exhaustion. "It started out as me learning about Lang's country, helping rebuild where I could. Then it turned into him helping me, trying to see if I could be taught to shapeshift."

I wasn't sure what I'd been expecting my brother to say, but it sure as Sunday wasn't that. "Um, what?"

"You're an Omen because Bev was human and whoever our dad was is Matruculan. Half of me is Matruculan, kiddo. Lang was trying to bring out the Terraway part of me, but it's just not there. I wanted to be able to protect you and September with some kind of superhuman ability, but it looks like you're stuck with just me."

I gaped at him, floored. "I don't know what to say to that."

Ollie shot me half a smile, his eyes tired. "Say you love me just the way I am, and that you wouldn't want me to change into a python, or something that could be useful in an attack."

I reached out and squeezed his fingers. "I think pythons are stupid, and I love you just the way you are. No place safer than with you."

"Pythons *are* stupid." Ollie nodded once, and then let the silence settle between us while I tried to puzzle through it all. Ollie patted my hand to center me. "Kabayo told me you delivered September like a champ."

I didn't know if I believed him, but I was too weak to argue much. "The nurse didn't say, but can I have children again? That *patayin* didn't permanently mess me up, did it?"

Ollie was serious, leaving no room for questions. "You can absolutely have children someday when the time is right. *Nothing* about you is messed up."

I bit my lip and nodded, looking down at the hospital gown I was dressed in. "I think I'd like a shower. Do I have clothes?"

"You do, but you're not leaving today. Go take a shower

and then come on back here so I can school you at cards. It's about time I taught you how to really play."

I tried to smile at his joke that he could best me at poker, but I couldn't find my sense of humor. Ollie seemed to understand, and didn't take offense. He was good like that.

My shower was careful and slow until something hit me midway through, speeding me up and making me impatient with my body. I fumbled with the soap sliver and did my best to figure out the best way to wash my feet without bending too much.

"Where's Allie?" was the first thing out of my mouth the second I was dried and dressed. "Is she here? I haven't been able to get out of the house to see her, but now I can."

"She's here, but she can wait. You need to take it easy before shouldering another hurdle. Seriously, kid. Deal with what happened before jumping headfirst into another mess."

My chin rattled from side to side rapidly, my eyes too wide for a normal conversation. "I can't, Ollie. I mean, how do you deal with losing a baby? What's the recipe?"

Ollie stared hard at me for a few beats. "I guess that's fair. I just don't want you to get your hopes up about Allie right after being crushed like this. This thing with Allie? It's a marathon that might not end well, and you just got beaten down all the way through one of those and barely survived."

"I lost a baby, Ollie."

My brother's expression softened. I knew that look. He wanted to fix all the problems in the world for me, but he couldn't. Ain't no fixing this. "I know, hun."

I blinked twice. "I lost my baby."

Ollie nodded slowly. "You did everything you could to keep her healthy."

"I lost my baby."

His jaw stiffened. "This isn't on you. I hope you understand that. This is all on the Manas. This one's on Terraway."

My voice died down to a whisper. "I lost my baby."

Ollie gave up on responding, instead nodding to let me puzzle through how the words sounded on my tongue.

"I lost my baby." The words tasted bitter and felt hollow, like an echo of madness I could now add to my growing list of dysfunctions I specialized in. Madness was my specialty, and I was steeped in it. "I lost my baby."

Ollie's arms raised and lowered a few times, debating whether or not he should hug me. He landed on extending one arm to me, corralling me to the hospital bed and lowering me down gently.

"I lost my baby."

"I know, sweetie. Let it all out. How about I deal us a few hands, and you tell me anything you feel like."

"I lost my baby," I reminded myself as I sifted through the hand he dealt. We played round after round, taking no joy in the game, but hypnotizing ourselves in the mindlessness of the ritual. "I lost my baby," I repeated whenever it came into my brain.

I'd lost September, and I'd never get her back.

Finally, the tears started falling, breaking through the logic that had been the only thing that anchored me. They weren't sobs of sadness, uncontrollable with loss; the few tears that birthed out of me paid tribute to the pain I hoped she hadn't felt, and the agony I knew I might always carry. "I lost September."

It was the first thing I'd said with any variation in a while, so Ollie ventured a response. "She was beautiful. Absolutely perfect."

"Do you think she was in pain when the poison root hit her?"

Ollie mulled this over, so he didn't answer with an obligatory "of course not." He shuffled the deck thoughtfully. "Did you feel anything other than the contractions to make you think she might've suffered?"

"No. The contractions were pretty blinding."

"Then my vote is no. It sounds like she passed the second the poison went into your system. That doesn't leave a whole lot of time for feeling pain."

I looked over the nightstand at my brother. The sterile smell of the hospital and the shuffle of feet in the hallway of people carrying on with normal life all faded away. I saw my brother clearly in his response that was both logical and kind. "Thank you."

Ollie nodded in response, thinking I meant thank you

for not blowing me off with something cheery. It was far more than that, though. I hadn't been able to feel much, but with his careful and honest response, I began to feel a small glimmer of something tender. Life had been so very rough with me, but Ollie's gentleness softened each blow into something bearable.

"You gave up your life for me," I said. My eyes narrowed in confusion and something akin to wonder. "I was as tiny as September. I was that helpless. You and Allie... I don't know how you did it. You were both so young." I swallowed as my eyes welled with appreciation for the grand gift that was my brother. "I wouldn't be alive if it weren't for you two." And there were days that I treated the life that had been granted to me as if it was a labor, a chore, a punishment. "You didn't just help me stay alive when Bev forgot about me, you went out of your way to give me a good life."

Ollie was quiet, unsure what to say to any of it.

"I ate because of you two. I went to school and graduated early because of you two. I got a degree because of you two. I have a home because of you two." I shook my head at myself. "I complain about this Terraway thing messing up my life, but I wouldn't have a life at all if it weren't for you." I vowed to stop feeling so put out that the responsibility of feeding nations had been dumped on me. Ollie never complained that I'd been dumped on him. "You were just a kid yourself. I'm so sorry I made you sacrifice your childhood to raise me."

Ollie leveled his finger in my face. "That's where I pause you. I wouldn't have had a childhood even if you hadn't been born. Bev didn't take care of us, so that wasn't in the cards either way. I know what you're doing. You're going to heap guilt on yourself, and I won't have it. I'll take the gratitude. I'll take the you appreciating what a miracle your life is. But me not having a childhood isn't on you. You gave me purpose and direction. You kept me from running off with Judge and getting into some real trouble." He looked hard into my eyes across the nightstand, and I could see emotion sparking on his lashes. "Don't you know, kid? You're the best thing that ever happened to me. That's what I want you to carry around with you in your back pocket when you start feeling like you can't get things perfect, how you like them. You're the best thing that ever happened to Allie and me, and we wouldn't have done anything different."

I smiled, and though my facial muscles protested, lightness slowly began to trickle through my features. "I was just going to say the same thing to you. You and Allie are the best things that ever happened to me. I love you."

Ollie moved to sit next to me on the side of the bed, the muffled shifting of the tall frame accommodating both of us. The thin mattress shielded us from the storm that always seemed to overturn our safest of places. "Oh, kid. You have no idea. I love you, and I'm so proud of you."

In the seclusion of the hospital room, I let my brother hold me like I was his daughter. I allowed myself to be small, instead of always fighting and striving to be big enough, strong enough, smart enough and together enough. I let the mess be exactly what it was, and Ollie didn't try to paint a pretty picture on any of it. The whole thing had been a horror that ended in tragedy, and we both respected the somberness of life's many twists and turns that teased us all too often with a promise of peace.

17

ONE SISTER FOR ANOTHER

Ollie and I went back and forth on the specifics of what "take it easy" meant, and eventually compromised on him taking me in a wheelchair to the ward where Allie was being held. He moved painstakingly slowly through the halls, being extra ginger with the turns. It was sweet, but I needed to see my sister, to make sure she was real. We had to slow down to accommodate a patient pushing their IV drip, the labored shuffle of her slippers on the floor trying my patience. With every passing moment, it felt like Allie might slip away from me yet again.

When Ollie checked us in at the nurse's station, I was scared the universe might implode before I got to actually see my sister for the first time in years. Ollie wheeled me through the door and pulled back the squeaky curtain, revealing a thinned-out version of the woman who'd raised me.

I gasped at the sight of my sister. She was so pale; her pinprick freckles stood out across the bridge of her button nose that matched mine. Her auburn hair was curlier than mine, and lay back against the pillow like she was a sleeping princess, just waiting for the magic to come along and wake her from her eternal slumber.

Her frail fingers that could French braid my hair like a true mama lay at her sides, motionless. Her whole body was still, as if she didn't know we were there, watching her. As if she couldn't hear my heart slamming against my ribcage because part of the missing piece was finally returned to me.

"Allie?" I worked out, the gust of her name powerful in my mouth. I was surprised when the sound I made didn't wake her at all. My voice didn't rouse her one bit.

Ollie fidgeted with the curtain again, tucking the edge to the corner of the windowsill, so Allie could see the world outside when she was ready. There was a vase of yellow daisies on the nightstand, bringing life where there was barely any to speak of. "Allie loves yellow daisies. Are those from you?" I asked, transfixed by the sight of my sister. I wheeled myself closer and placed my hand in hers, thinking that surely if she felt me near, she would wake up.

"No. They're from Ezra. He asked what kind of flowers she liked, and I remember her always stopping at the grocery store to look at the daisies. He has a fresh bouquet sent to her room once a week. He visits, too. Reads her Shakespearean plays. They sound pretty cool when read by an actual Brit. Not a bad dad, that one."

I nodded. "I can't believe of all the things we've lost, that we got to keep Ezra."

Ollie walked to the other side of the bed and squeezed Allie's hand. "I'm sorry I haven't been around much lately. I wasn't sure which of you needed me more. Since you had a whole army at the house, I decided you could spare me, so I could sit with Allie."

I waved off his apology. "I'd rather someone was with her. I wished I could've been here. I can't believe Philip actually had her this whole time. She's been through I can only guess what because of him." I studied my sister's ghostly skin, running through the list of things that wouldn't work to wake her. When the nurse list in my brain came up empty, I switched to the less traditional Terraway options. "Do you think there's an herb or some-thing that could wake her up? Like something from Terraway? Other than the one in the haunted forest in Hayop?"

Ollie started applying pressure to Allie's wrist. His grip moved up her arm to get the blood to flow the way it would if she was swinging her arms as she walked. "Believe me, I grilled Ezra on all of that. There's nothing except that *sigla* flower that only grows in that cursed forest in Hayop, and that's out of the question."

I couldn't stand the sight of my sister so helpless. She'd

given up too much of her life so I could have a future, and now here she was, defeated and motionless. It wasn't fair. I waited a few beats before offering up my plan in a lowered voice. "I know Sama will give us whatever we ask if I go to his island and stay with him."

Ollie's head shot up, his nostrils flaring. "Out of the question. First off, I'll not trade one sister for another. Allie would wake up, and the first thing she'd do is run to Terraway to free you. Then you'd both be right where that jackass wants you. Find another plan. One that's less suicidal."

"Challenge accepted. Give me a few minutes."

Ollie scoffed. "A few minutes? You think you'll be able to solve what doctors and Ezra couldn't?"

"I think I'm far more stubborn than any of you, so yeah."

18

THE B-WORD

Even though I hadn't woken Allie up after the few minutes I'd hoped it would take for me to find a solution, I didn't give up, even after I was discharged and sent home. Having a problem to solve kept me focused on a solution instead of on the shambles my life was in now.

Von had no such anchor. He stayed in our bedroom in the mansion most days, coming down only when I tried to do something by myself. He would sit in a chair facing the window that overlooked the expansive backyard. He didn't talk much – I didn't need him to. I'd hoped the scenery of the spacious grounds of the mansion would do him some good, but it seemed nothing got through to him.

We grieved as any normal couple would after such a tragic event – psychically. I didn't want people to see me carrying on in public; their pitying looks were already more than I could handle. So when we went to sleep at night, Von and I sat under a tall, thick oak tree in our park, not saying anything as we wept and held each other in our misery.

"When we wake up, I'll give you your ring back," I offered quietly, cuddled in his arms that trembled as he cried. His back was propped up against our tree, the purple and blue leaves shaking to the ground, as if nature wanted to weep alongside us.

Von recoiled, horrified. "Why would you kick me while I'm down?"

"No! That's not what this is. I just know you probably wouldn't have proposed if I hadn't been pregnant, so I'm letting you off the hook."

"I'm not on a hook." His nose crinkled in distaste. "Did you only say yes because you were pregnant?"

"Of course not. I want to marry you still. Is that what you want?"

"It's the *only* thing I want." He shifted against the tree, drawing me to sit between his legs so all four of his limbs could encircle me. "Don't leave me now. I'm afraid I can't take it."

I exhaled my relief as I let my body go limp in his arms. "I'm here, honey. No matter what." A swarm of cerulean and violet butterflies fluttered around us, sending a trail of gold glitter through the air, like a puffy cloud left by a jet in the sky. It was a beautiful place we dwelt in, while drowning in the depths of our misery.

When we awoke, I'd hoped the mornings would be

easier, but the crushing weight on my chest didn't lift as the days ticked off on the calendar, piling up to a whole week since the incident. Von was still in his chair in our bedroom, looking out at the world but refusing to join it.

I came back from the bathroom that morning in clean clothes that were not pajamas, making a statement that I would not wallow while my sister was in limbo. I'd tried to visit her a few times, but Von had insisted it was too dangerous to leave the mansion. I cleared my throat to garner his attention. Though he was a few feet from me, he seemed a million miles away. "I'm going to see Allie at the hospital. You want to come?"

Von turned to me, as if seeing me for the first time. "Why are you dressed?"

I pursed my lips, knowing that patience was the only attitude I could have in this situation. "I'm going to go visit my sister. Would you like to come?" I tried not to let any insecurity poke through. "I'd love for you to meet her." While I knew she couldn't disapprove of Von in her current state, there was a part of me that needed her to love him, and needed him to adore and respect her.

Von turned back to the window. "No. And you shouldn't go, either. It's not safe out there. If the Manas got you before, they can get to you again." His cigars had made a reappearance this week, making everything in the room fragrant with the sweet sting of the Von I'd first met. He clutched his cigar and took another puff, letting the smoke waft out without direction, flair or thought.

"I won't go alone. I'll take one of your brothers if you don't want to go."

He looked up at me, blinking his hurt through thick, black lashes. "You're leaving me?"

My eyebrows pushed together in concern at his overly fragile state. It was uncharacteristic of the playboy I loved. "You know I'd never do that. I'm going out for a couple hours. You're welcome to join me. I can't leave my sister alone, Von. She needs me."

"*I* need you."

"And you have me. This is me. I'm not the girl who holes herself up in her room when there's work to be done. My house is a wreck and my sister's in a coma. I don't have it in me to leave those things untouched anymore."

"Give me some time to think about it." He went to staring out the window again, puffing on his cigar to melt his brain a little. "Not today. Maybe tomorrow or next week."

"Okay, sweetie. Take your time. I'll be home for dinner tonight, alright?"

I didn't expect Von to start crying, so I floundered, tripping over my messenger bag and a spare pillow on the carpet as I tried to wrap my arms around him to hold him together. The sobs wracked his body hard out of nowhere. "We were going to be a family!"

I hugged his head to my breast and combed my fingers through his hair as he wet my white t-shirt with his tears. "Von, we still *are* a family. You and me, honey.

You'll be the husband and I'll be the wife. That's a family."

"She was so tiny!"

I swallowed my emotions and did my best to be there for him. The general rule of thumb was that only one person could freak out at a time. Any more than that, and there wasn't anyone to add reason to the chaos. "I know, sweetheart. I know." I ran my hand through his hair and down the side of his face. My fingers caught on his earlobe that felt hot, puffy and abnormal. I looked down and observed that his ear was red and slightly swollen, and wondered how that had happened. "Did you bang your ear on something, hun?" I asked curiously.

Von's response was only more brokenness, so I held him through it, being there when it was most tempting to check out.

It took ten minutes to get Von under control, which meant he went back to staring out the window. I wasn't sure he understood that I was still leaving, so I left him a note telling him where I'd be, and that I'd be home that evening.

The air outside of our bedroom felt like the first breath that ever was. The cigar stench had made me slightly light-headed, so being without it made me feel like I was flying. I leaned against the door and let myself just breathe for a solid minute, permitting myself to be a person instead of a grieving almost-mother.

I was quiet as I toed the carpet down the stairs,

surprising everyone at the breakfast table, who stood to greet me when I entered the dining room. Ezra's hugs were the hardest to get through, because I knew he meant them. He held on tight, and I could barely breathe as it was. My body felt strange now, going from my giant belly making hugs awkward to now having no space to fend off the affection at all. It wasn't a bad thing, but an adjustment. Graham, ever the gentleman, held out my chair for me to sit between him and Alton.

There had been lively conversation before, but it came to a halt as they all puzzled through how to tiptoe around my palpable grief. "Anyone want to give me a lift home? Or can I borrow one of your cars, Ezra?"

Ezra's mouth drew to the side as he considered my request. "What's mine is yours, of course. But your home hasn't been cleaned yet. That's where Ollie is right now, in fact. He said you wouldn't want to see it how it is."

I didn't want to dig in my heels already, but this was important to me. "It's my house, so I should help clean it. I want to go there, and then visit Allie for lunch. Is that alright?"

"Of course, darling. I insist you take Alton or Graham with you, but yes. I'll call Oliver and let him know you're on your way."

"Where's Mason?"

"Still in Sombi, I assume. I called him back, but he hasn't responded. I'll send someone to fetch him if another week goes by and he hasn't returned. He's a hard worker, that one. Difficult to pull him away."

I let the silence fall over the table, and wanted to kick myself for putting a stop to all conversation simply by showing up. "So, what'd I miss?"

Ezra answered, since everyone else was incapable of taking their eyes from their scrambled eggs and bacon. "Boston is staying with Danny and Mariang at the hotel. They send their love, of course. Ms. Vandershot sent flowers for you, along with her love. Alton and Graham have been making themselves useful around the grounds."

"That's nice. When Mason comes Topside, can I go back to work?"

Ezra's fork stilled before it reached his mouth. "Eventually, yes. There's no need to rush back in, though. We're well ahead of the quota, and Mariang is still reaping."

I chewed my eggs in thought. "Give me like, two days, and I'll be good to go. Can you get Mason back here by then? Von's not really up for work yet."

Ezra sighed and rubbed his forehead. "I was thinking more like two weeks."

"I can't lie around and be sad anymore, Dad. I have to move around. I have to do something other than think about all the awful."

"Whatever you like, but please do rest. Mariang is quite healthy, and the daily quota is low enough for her to keep up with for another month."

"Her maternity leave should start soon. She should rest." I gulped the mouthful of food that felt like sand in my mouth. "Maybe she and Danny might want to take a vacation. Be together without all the drama before the b-baby comes." My voice faltered on the B-word, but I steadied myself, chanting the mantra that I could grieve as long as I wanted to in my dreams. "Um, Von's not feeling up to getting out today, so if you guys could check on him every now and then, I'd appreciate it. I told him I'd be back for dinner, but he's kind of out of it."

"Of course." Ezra, Graham and Alton nodded, silently taking shifts to ensure Von didn't fall off the map completely.

19

I GET BY WITH A LITTLE HELP
FROM MY FRIENDS

Graham sat next to me in the car, his hand migrating to my elbow as I drove. "It's okay, Graham. I don't need you to pull for me today."

Graham's hand froze between us before cradling my elbow again. "I know you don't think you need pulling unless it's work-related, but this is the most I've been able to be useful in days for you. Let me take away a little of the heartache. How are you feeling?"

"Fine."

Graham shot me a withering look. "October, come on. It's me. Aren't we past being strangers? You're my sister."

I sighed. "I feel like I got hit with a pillowcase filled with bricks. Every day it's a little less, like one fewer brick in the pillowcase, which doesn't really seem anything to be all that cheery about, but I'm trying. I think I'm down to like, three bricks now. Should be pain-free in another handful of days."

"There. Now was that so hard?"

"Yes." I gulped, keeping my eyes on the road. "Everything's hard. I feel bad leaving Von with only Alton and Ezra."

"Von's made of tough stuff. He just has to remember that. I think he's lost a little of himself lately."

I didn't need to voice my agreement; Von's checked-out status was palpable.

I glanced to the tail of our dead-end street, seeing a smattering of familiar cars lining the road in front of my house. I swore, wishing I'd thought to make sure Ollie locked up so our friends didn't try to throw a party in the middle of the bloodbath.

When we pulled into my driveway, I stopped short of parking in the garage, not sure if that's where the Manas bodies were still being stored. I cut the engine, wondering how I was going to explain away the damage to my no doubt shocked friends. I blinked as I stared at the cars. "It's ten in the morning," I stated, confused.

"It is, indeed. Something wrong?"

"My friends. They like to show up at random and throw parties at our house. But that's always in the evening. I don't get what they're doing here."

Graham gripped the hilt of his knife on his belt, readying to attack. "There's Ollie's car, yeah? He must've let them in. Stay behind me, though, just in case."

I walked a few paces behind Graham, hesitating when we got to the front porch and heard friendly commotion coming from inside. He put his knife back in its sheath on his belt and popped his elbow out to me, like the weapon-wielding gentleman he was. Graham fingered the doorknob and let us in, assessing the mood to be congenial, and not a threat.

My friends were frozen with mouths dropped open, caught in the scandalous act of... cleaning?

I clung to Graham with both hands, staring around the house like I'd never seen it before. The lamp was gone, my end table was toppled over and missing a leg, there were scuffs and streaks of blood on the walls, violent holes in the drywall and too many stains on the carpet. "I... My home!" I whispered, my heart breaking all over again at everything we'd worked for, that was now trashed so thoroughly.

"Now, now. Not to worry, love. See? They'll put it all right again." Graham motioned to a few of my friends, who were still frozen mid-scrub as they gaped at me. Graham lifted his chin at Jordan, who was nearest. "Mate, could you tell Ollie his sister's here?"

"Bait?" Jordan called my nickname as if it was something of reverence, not a group joke. "Everyone, Bait's here!"

Ollie flew out of my bedroom, wearing his beat-up housework jeans and an undershirt. "Hey, kid. Whatcha doing out of bed?"

"I... I... Um, I was going to come clean up. What's everyone doing here?"

Ollie took my other arm and helped Graham lower me to the couch. My whole body was still pretty sore from the whole giving birth thing. The couch had several murderous slashes through it that spilled out the fluffy innards on the other end from where I sat. Ollie patted my hand carefully. "They're helping set the house right after the attack from the break-in."

"The attack from the break-in?" I echoed, unsure of the story we were selling.

Ollie nodded. "The idiots who broke in, hurt you so bad you lost the baby, and tore up our home. I made a few calls, and they all showed up to help. Took time off work, brought over their tools, and pooled their resources." Ollie met my eyes with a kind smile that told me how very worried he'd been. "I didn't want you to see the place like this. No matter what, I want you to stay out of your bedroom. If you need something, Graham can get it for you."

My lower lip quivered as I took in the damage done to my safe place. Glancing down at my deflated stomach, I knew there wouldn't be true healing for a long time. I bit my lip to keep the trembling at bay. "You... You really all did this for us? You showed up to help us?" I asked of my mute friends.

Jordan sat down next to me, his arm draped on the back of the couch. "Of course, kiddo. We trash your house often enough. Figured it was our turn to clean it for you."

I couldn't help the emotion that welled up in me, or tamper down the swelling that threatened to crack my ribs as my heart grew to the bursting point. My understood walls of social distance started to crumble, and I slumped in Jordan's half-embrace, sinking into him as my tears fell onto his shirt. I don't recall ever hugging Jordan of my own volition, though I'd known him for years. "Thank you," I whispered, burying myself in his arms that scrambled to hold me awkwardly while I fell apart.

"Whoa. It's okay, hun." Jordan had tons of practice hugging the other girls, but was a novice when it came to holding me. He was a quick learner, and gripped me tight, rocking me slightly in that comforting big brother way I'd never let him be for me. He pressed his lips to my hair, clutching my head to his chest like a football. "We've got your back. We'll have this place looking good as new in no time."

I indulged in a few more seconds of public affection before righting myself with a rallying inhale. I wiped my embarrassing tears off my cheeks. "How can I help? Give me a job."

Ollie said nothing of my public breakdown, but gave me a strange look, almost like he was proud of me for hugging someone I'd known for years. That was the beautiful thing about Ollie. He didn't mention that I had no reason not to be doling out hugs this whole time to the people who were in my life. He was only ever proud of me, complimenting my forward steps, and pretending the backwards ones weren't there at all.

Ollie smiled down at me. "Your job is to sit here and tell the others what needs to be done." He moved around to stand behind the couch and leaned heavily on Jordan's shoulder. "This one here's your new butler. If you want something hung a certain way, you say, 'Hey butler, a little to the left.' If you're thirsty, he'll get you some water. We don't have much else. Fridge is busted. Beto's picking up the new one from the store now."

"Our refrigerator's broken?" I rubbed my temples. "What else?"

"Nothing you have to worry about. Pretend it's a renovation, not an invasion. It was time for an upgrade anyway. You'll have a whole new inside in just a couple days." He squeezed my hand and stood up straight. "Nick and Darius are helping me with the drywall, so I'm going to get back to it."

"Wait, Darius? Darius is here? He knows? Who told him?"

Darius strolled out of my bedroom, cracking his neck with a tired expression that told me he'd been there for hours, though it was still morning. "I was the first one here. Ollie called and told me you'd been attacked. I came first thing. Judge was here all night helping, too. Just left half an hour ago to see to his business. He sends his condolences." The corner of his mouth twitched upwards.

"He bought you a new appliance to replace one of them that got broken, but he said not to tell you which one, so you couldn't return it."

My hand rubbed my forehead to try and make sense of everything. "That's really sweet of you both. Thank you. I... You really came for us?"

Darius' shoulders lowered. He had a white smudge of drywall dust across his ebony forehead. "Of course I did. You're my conscience."

His sweet declaration tugged at my heart. "I always knew you were a good man."

He watched me with a tender expression. "And I've always had your back. You just forgot how to lean on me."

I looked up at Darius in wonder that after all the cat and mouse we'd played for power and respect, respect and love had won out. "I don't know what to say to that. Thank you, Nefarious."

Darius sniggered at how ridiculous I sounded when I used his street name. "Anytime, Bait."

Ollie pointed his finger at Graham. "I'm serious. Make sure she doesn't get off this couch."

"Sure, give me the impossible job. Anyone want to trade?" Graham joked.

Jordan was sweaty and positively filthy, but I sunk into his embrace again when he tugged me to him with an affectionate grin. I marveled at how much I'd grown that I couldn't feel the germs on my friend. "Hey, Bait. How're you feeling after the..." He apparently couldn't say the B-word, so he mimed a baby bump over his modest beer gut. Jordan wasn't a particularly eloquent kind of sweetheart, but I was grateful for him all the same.

"I'm fine."

He lowered his voice and leaned in so I could smell his musky armpits. "You should've told us. We would've visited you in the hospital. Did you at least get a good look at the guys who messed you up? Ollie didn't say what happened to them."

I swallowed hard. "It doesn't matter. It's done. They're not coming back. My daughter's dead, so that's that." The words hurt to say, but I forced them out so my brain could recognize the pain as truth and deal with it. "I can't believe you're really helping fix all this. I didn't realize how broken it all got."

Jordan squeezed me tighter, as if afraid I might bolt when it dawned on me that I was in his arms. "Don't worry, Bait. You won't always feel this broken."

KATRINA'S GRAND EXIT

Graham leaned on the arm of the couch, remaining by my side while everyone told me everything they'd been up to in the past twenty-four hours, amazing me to no end. "What can I do to help?" I repeated, but they waved off my insistence that I make myself useful somehow.

Graham placed his hand on my shoulder. "Maybe we should go. Let them do their thing."

The front door opened before I could respond, revealing Gabby, Katrina and Rachel with baskets filled with my clothing, all folded in neat little piles. Gabby dropped the laundry basket on the floor and ran to me, scooping me up off the couch in a hug I reminded myself would be abnormal to resist. I would get good at hugging, so help me. Ezra would be so proud if he could see me now. "Oh, kid! We've been so worried about you! Jessica and I were blowing up your phone until the voice mailbox came back full. How are you? Sit down already! You've just been through the worst of the worst."

I didn't have it in me to explain that I'd only stood because she'd hefted me up for the hug. "I'm fine. I can't believe you're all here, cleaning my house. I don't know what to do with the shock of that on its own. It's so sweet of you guys. I'm still trying to wrap my mind around it. Really, you're all wonderful for this."

Gabby pulled me up and hugged me again. "We've been so worried! I mean, how awful, right? Did they catch the bastards who did this to you?" Before I could answer, she called into the bedroom, "Ollie! Could you bring me Bait's hairbrush?"

Ollie worked out a strained, "I'm kinda in the middle of something, Gabby. It's in the bathroom in the second drawer."

"We're going to give you a makeover," Rachel gushed, taking the next hug. "You'll feel so much better when you don't look like death warmed over."

I was overcome with several urges that I knew I couldn't act on. I wanted to punch Rachel square across the face for telling me I looked like death when I'd just had death cuddled up in my arms. I wanted to run from the prospect of a makeover that I knew would involve instrumentation and a whole big show. I wanted to rage against the machine and rant that I didn't owe being beautiful to my own house. It didn't matter what I looked like; I was grieving.

The doctor had warned me about postpartum depression and mood swings and whatnot upon being discharged from the hospital. Maybe I should've paid better attention to him. I'd gone from weeping in public, to hugging Jordan, to chewing on my venomous rage at something that probably wasn't actually all that offensive. Gabby loved me, so I smiled up at her as best I could and simmered my tart response down to a quiet, "Sure. That's real nice of you guys. Thanks."

Graham sat on the arm of the couch next to me and scooped up my hand, pulling hard to keep me from laying out my girlfriends in one misguided blow. "Now, now. My sister's lovely even without her hair fashioned."

I leaned my head to his hip, sighing as I deflated. Despite my aversion to pulling when we weren't reaping, I was grateful for Graham. "Thank you. I needed that."

"I know, darling. Take it one moment at a time." Graham squeezed my hand twice.

"I'm glad you're here. You're a good big brother."

"I wouldn't want to be anywhere else."

Katrina saddled up beside Gabby, sizing up the new British meat. "And who are you?"

"Graham Vandershot, Miss. Ezra sent me to look after October for the day."

"Vandershot, eh? Von's brother? You sure are a handholding kind of family. Bait practically runs away when we try to hug her, but she's got Von's family on a leash. First Von, then Boston, and now you." She let out a throaty laugh that had the edge of bitterness slicing through it. I'd made the capitol offense – gotten close to the new guy without letting Katrina take him for a spin first. The urge to lash out irrationally and punch her flooded me. I'd never felt so unbalanced, so ready to pounce at the slightest provocation. It was a thing of fortune that Graham held tight to my hand.

Graham's polite smile stayed in place. "I'll not argue with that. Boston and I love our little sister. She takes care of us every bit as much as we look after her."

Katrina's simpering smile told me she'd never cared about me, not that I was surprised at that. She'd been nice to me in the past because I was a kid to her – no competition at all. Now that her conquests and future toys looked my way? I was a threat that apparently needed to be neutralized. She was the Queen Bee of the group, and everyone knew to scatter when she pounced. "That's nice. Von's not with you?" She looked around to verify that the guy she'd slept with a few times wasn't there. "I can't say I'm surprised. It's a lot to deal with. Getting engaged because of the baby, and then when there's no baby, he takes off on you."

Gabby and Rachel gasped, looking to my face for confirmation of the horror that I'd been jilted. Jordan threw his hands up in the air. "Jeez, Katrina. Retract the claws. Bait's just a kid. You don't need to pick on her like this just because Von passed you over for her. Your boobs are still amazing, your legs are still smoking, and you know, pretend I said all the other things you need to hear to know you're still the center of the universe."

I didn't feel the need to defend myself or Von to her, but Graham sure as Sunday did. I shifted closer to Jordan when Graham slid down from the arm of the couch to squeeze in next to me. "Von and October are to be married, just as they were before. He didn't ask her to marry him because she got pregnant. They're very much in love." Graham held my hand up to display my audacious ring as proof. The square-shaped diamond sparkled, announcing to the world that I was one-hundred percent off the market.

Katrina's eyes bulged, and she actually stumbled back a few steps. She fell off her game momentarily, but pounced again with vengeance. "Nice how they can make cubic zirconia as big as they like without the guy having to put out hardly any extra cash."

Graham's nose crinkled. "It's a real diamond, of course. My brother wouldn't skimp on something as important as her engagement ring." His arm draped around my shoulder, pulling me tight to him as if to shield me from the verbal attack. In that moment, I didn't resist the shelter Graham provided. My head rested against his collarbone, and he held my hand to his chest to keep my ring clearly displayed. "Is this girl actually your friend, darling?" Graham glared protectively out at the woman who verbally attacked me, and the other two women who let it happen. I finally saw clearly why Ollie had never taken that next step with Gabby. Ollie would fight to the death for something he loved. Ollie was a fighter. Gabby was a follower.

I didn't answer. The whole showdown had taken place without me having to say much of anything. Just like the Manas, existing had been enough to warrant an attack, and I was tired of the fight. I remember battling against a zombie army once upon a time. Now I could barely hold my chin up through a catty slice at my morale. I tried to remind myself that I was grieving, and that I'd get my moxie back when I was ready.

Katrina forced out another throaty laugh. "Oh, we're just playing. Bait knows I'm only kidding." She paused, taking in our body language that had me tucked in Graham's arms like a shell-shocked kitten. "Looks like someone should tell Von he's got some competition from the home court."

Ollie barked from behind me, making everyone in the house jump. "Katrina! Knock it off. If you want to have sex with Graham, you don't need to run my sister down to do it."

Graham's mouth fell open that he was the source of Katrina's steady needling. "I... Um... I'm sure I don't..." He clung to my hand now to steady himself, and I was grateful he didn't desert me when his pure intentions were brought into question. "Perhaps we should go out for lunch and come back later." Graham stood, gently tugging me up next to him. He turned to Ollie and jerked his thumb over his shoulder toward Katrina. "When we come back, I trust you'll have escorted this one out?"

"Are you serious? I just got done doing her laundry! Newsflash: if you want to keep Von around, I'd invest in some lacier underwear. I mean, when Von was with me, my panties barely stayed on. But still, for show and all. Might want to upgrade."

"You'll not have a laugh at my sister's expense!" Graham roared, clutching me tight to his chest in the middle of the living room, like I was something precious. I felt used and worn down, like a tool meant to be abused until it lost its will to serve its purpose. But somehow Graham didn't see me like that. In his arms, I was a prize, haggard and beaten by life as I was.

Katrina was astonished, and I understood why. I was the quiet one in the group who didn't make a fuss about much. Now fuss was being made for me, and I wasn't the joke anymore. I was an actual woman. Not a kid. Not Bait. A legit woman who could be friends with a man without jumping in the sack with him.

Graham turned back to Katrina with his chin in the air and his arm around me. "October's the lady of this house. You'll not set foot in this place again after going to such lengths to insult my sister. She just lost her child. All you lost was a casual fling. You'll not trouble my sister again with your foolishness."

Katrina scoffed, looking around at Gabby and Rachel, who had taken a step back from the lightning bolt-sized wrath she was incurring. "Are you seriously trying to tell me what to do? These are my people, you foreigner. This is how we do things. If Bait wants to play with the big girls, this is how low we swing."

Graham kissed my fingers when I tried to offer up a weak protest. "It's really fine, Graham. It's just how it is."

He leveled his gaze at me and said his words like a promise, loud enough for everyone to hear. "You are not a joke, and I'll not stand for you being insulted in your own home. You're a queen." My heart lifted at his grand words that only had sincerity and kindness to them. Then he turned Katrina around, and marched her out the front door. He didn't pause when she scrambled for retorts that were mingled with desperate apologies. For all his gentlemanly ways, Graham shoved Katrina through the front door and locked her out, ignoring her fists that pounded for us to let her back in. "Does anyone else want to make jokes about my sister who just lost her daughter? Or are you all here to be good friends and help the girl you care for?"

Ollie clapped in appreciation, and Darius pointed his finger at Graham. "I like you, man. You ever need a job, you come see me."

"No," I warned Darius. Graham wouldn't go near Judge's empire.

Graham kept his hands pressed together while he

spoke. "While I'm clearing the air, I don't much care for the nickname Bait. My sister's not here for your amusement, nor is she a lure for mindless men. She's a prize, so if you can get onboard with being respectful and kind, you can stay. Ollie would love to have help from people who actually respect all our sister's been through."

My lower lip trembled, and I knew I was seconds away from another waterfall. A solitary tear dripped down my cheek, burning a trail of humiliation for all to see. "I really do appreciate you guys helping fix up the house. You didn't have to do that."

"Are you kidding me?" Gabby said, her smile trying to break the tension. "After all the times we trashed it? It's the least we could do."

I didn't argue with her there.

"Let's let them surprise us with how good they can be to you. How about I take you out for lunch?" Graham coiled his arm around my back as he escorted me out past a red-faced Katrina, who called me all the dirty names she'd been holding back. Each insult stuck to me like an arrow, sinking into my skin and leaving a mark.

SOCKS AND LOTION

Graham shut me in the passenger's seat and went around to the driver's side, choking the steering wheel before putting the car into gear. "I can drive, Graham. You're upset."

"Of course I'm upset! Those are your friends? Truly?"

"That's the crew. They're actually Ollie's friends. I come with the package."

He eyed Katrina's red face, her fist in the air, her sneer in full swing, and he revved the engine. "I could give her just a little tap. It wouldn't hurt her much."

"Now, now. Let's save vehicular manslaughter for Monday. That's a much better weekday activity."

"You're no fun."

"So I've been told."

Graham backed the car out with care. "Fancy lunch?"

"Not really. But thanks for getting me out of there. I

thought I was ready to face the damage, but I just plain wasn't. Mind if we go to the hospital instead? I want to check in on Allie. See if I can't figure out how to wake her up."

"Of course."

I kept my voice quiet. "Thanks for that back there, by the way. Sticking up for me like that. Katrina doesn't normally dig her claws into me. It's the whole Von thing. I usually let the little stuff go, but lately everything feels like too much. Too big, too hard, too unnerving. I think I froze. Maybe I'm turning into a wuss or something."

Graham reached over and held my hand. "I meant every word, you know. You and Mariang are my sisters. I'll not stand back and watch someone walk all over you."

"You're a good guy, Graham. Thanks for being my brother."

We drove a few minutes in silence before Graham squeezed my hand. "We're going to see your sister, but I'm afraid I know nothing about her. Fancy telling me a little so I'm not so lost?"

"Sure. Allie's great. She can make a game out of anything. She sews. Did you know that?"

"I know shockingly little about your family. Just the briefing Ezra gave us on Bev's passing."

I felt him give me an extra pull at the mention of Bev. Graham and I had a good rhythm. "We were poor. Nothing like the life Mariang and Ezra have. When I needed clothes, Allie would go to the secondhand store and buy stained oversized men's shirts for pennies. Then she'd somehow transform them into little dresses for me to wear. When we moved out, she learned how to knit. That year we had so many hats and scarves and mittens, we didn't know what to do with them all. Ollie was sweet. He insisted on wearing all his hats to make Allie feel better when she was having a rough day. He went to work one day with seven knit caps on, five pairs of mittens and eight scarves. Then he came home and complained that he needed her to make him a few more." I smiled at the memory.

Graham chuckled. "That's sweet. Is she funny, like you?"

I blinked at Graham. Cracking jokes felt like a me I didn't recognize anymore. "She's funny, sure. She's kind and selfless. Not many teenage girls would give up their Friday nights to work so we could get ahead. We bought that house, the three of us. We own it outright. When she left for California and Ollie for New York, I promised them I'd take care of our home. It was our safe place." My chin quivered again, but this time I didn't feel ashamed as the tears started to cloud my vision. I knew Graham wouldn't take my pride; he'd given me back my dignity. "I let our safe place get broken. My daughter died in my safe place!" Out of nowhere, a horrible unintelligible sob birthed from my mouth, announcing my agony to the car. I covered my mouth quickly, as if I could shove the sound back down my throat. "I'm sorry." I straightened, blinking away the madness that clawed at my insides. "I told myself I'd be normal today. Spontaneous crying? Not normal. Can you pick a new topic?"

"That's a beautiful ring," Graham offered after a few beats of respectful silence while he waited for me to collect myself. "The only reason Katrina said it was fake was because no man will ever give her a ring like that."

I glanced down at my hand, grateful that after everything, Von hadn't wanted it back. All along he'd wanted me. Just me.

As if on cue, Graham's phone rang. "Yeah?"

I heard Von shout, "Where is she? Is she with you?"

"Whoa! Hold on, mate. October's fine. She's right here." Graham put the phone on speaker so I could talk.

"Hey, hun. How are you feeling?" I asked, trying to keep my voice conversational.

"How am I feeling? Bloody wonderful! I look up, and you're gone! Where are you?"

I made sure to keep calm, so as not to coax Von to fly further off the handle. "I'm on my way to the hospital to see Allie. I told you all this, and I even left you a note on the nightstand. Do you see it?"

I heard rustling and a loud exhale. "Oh. I guess Ezra wasn't lying, then."

"Why would Ezra lie to you? Ezra loves you."

"Come home. I don't like it here without you."

My heart broke for him, but I knew this was the right thing to do. I needed to stand on my own, and Von did, too.

Only then could we stand together when life inevitably tipped us on our heads again and again. "I told you I'd be home for dinner, so that's when you'll see me. Maybe you should go for a walk. Take Alton and move around a little. Get something to eat."

"I can't stop picturing your body in a ditch somewhere. I can't lose you, Peach. I need you to be safe. Come home."

"Of course I'll come home. And I'm with Graham, who's an excellent driver. Do you want me to pick you up anything while I'm out?"

"No. Just come back here in one piece. That's all I want. I'll go back to bed. Wake me when you get back."

I fished for something that would get him out of the bedroom, casting around for any distraction at all from his grief. "Could you do me a favor?" I asked, forcing a smile into my voice that did not appear on my face.

"Anything. What do you need, love?"

"Socks."

"You need me to bring you socks?"

I waved off Graham's inquiring eyebrow. "No, but would you mind making a run to the store for me? I have the regular kind, but my feet keep getting cold at night. Could you pick me up a pair of those really thick fuzzy ones that Mariang wears to sleep? Those look warm."

"Um, sure. You want me to go to the store?"

I nodded. "And pick up warm socks for me to wear at night."

"Okay. I'll put it on the list and have Lynna pick some up when she goes to the grocer's on Wednesday."

I feigned a dramatic sigh. "I was kind of hoping you'd pick them out for me. Something you think is cute. And something for tonight. I don't want cold feet for another half a week." I knew I was pushing the border of being high maintenance, but I couldn't stand the thought of Von lying in bed all day, or staring out the window vacantly again for hours on end. "If you don't mind."

Von paused. "I don't think you understand men if you think we fancy which kind of fuzzy socks our wife wears. If you're asking me, I prefer you in nothing at all."

I tried to ignore Graham's dramatic barfing. I closed my eyes, pushing harder, knowing this was all for Von's own good. "Please? If it's not too much trouble, I'd really appreciate it."

Von waited a few beats, and I could picture him nodding. "Okay. Sure." His tone changed, and I could tell he was exasperated with himself. "Hey, of course I'll pick you up some socks. No problem. Good for you for finally asking for something. Anything else?"

I fished around for anything I might possibly need, grateful for the glimmer of Von I heard crackling over the phone as Graham drove along the tree-lined freeway. "Maybe some hand lotion? My skin sucks lately."

Von sounded wary. "Okay. Be specific. What kind exactly?"

I softened and explained the brand I preferred. We

hung up after a heaping helping of "you're the greatest guy in the world for helping me out," and "I don't know what I'd do without you."

Graham grinned at me. "I see what you did there. You tricked Von into getting out of bed. Well done." He high-fived me. "Before you know it, he'll be back to his old self."

"You really think it's as simple as lotion and fuzzy socks?"

Graham squeezed my hand as he drove us closer to the hospital. "I think it's as simple as you."

THE SKANKIEST OF SKANKS

I shut the door behind us, hoping we wouldn't be disturbed by the errant nurse checking on my sister. Allie looked the exact same as when I'd last seen her: the bland expression of slumber, her pale hands at her sides. She was begging to be kissed by the sun, which was always out of her reach, no matter how wide we yanked open the curtains.

Graham came in behind me to look at Allie, his breath catching as his eyes pored over her face. I led him closer so our thighs were pressed against her bedrail. He had the strangest look on his face. I observed him watch my Allie with something that could only be described as rapture. "I... This is her? Of course it's her. She looks just like you, but not. You've got that way about you, and she's..." I didn't know how he was planning on finishing that sentence, but the tender expression on his face told me he saw what was obvious – that Allie was a beautiful woman, even lifeless as she was. No makeup, no fancy clothing, and my Allie was still a showstopper.

Standing by Allie's bedside tied a knot in my chest as I tried to find the right words to say. As it was, I'd barely said hello before my mouth sealed itself shut.

Graham sat in the chair near the window and pulled out his earbuds. "Feel free to talk away. I'll be properly distracted. I would offer to leave you alone, but I promised Ezra you wouldn't be out of my sight. He said nothing about earshot, though."

"Thanks, Graham." The second Graham closed his eyes and laid his head back in the chair by the window, I slid the bedside chair up to my motionless sister and unloaded, my guts spilling out all over her. Allie had to merely exist for my world to feel somehow anchored. Even though the pieces were smashed and shattered, there was hope. Allie could fix anything, even if she couldn't fix herself just yet.

I confessed the whole story about Philip, and how he was the same guy who stole her away from her life. We'd both fallen for the same mirage. I told her about September, and the horrible birth that scarred me deeper than I liked to admit to the others.

But it was Allie. She could see right through me, even with her eyes closed. I'd never seen much point in lying to her or holding back.

Telling her about Von took longer. I started from the

beginning, letting her in on the ups and downs, the passionate collisions and the separations that were always horrible and without good reason, but then somehow *with* good reason when the full story came out. I showed her my ring, knowing she'd gawk at the rock that still felt obnoxiously big to me.

Since we were in no hurry, I delved into the beginning – my introduction to Terraway, and all of its magic that had only dimmed my world in the end. I told her about my awakening, about Mason and Von binding themselves to me. I took her through each world, introducing her to my friends and enemies.

My version of Dagat wasn't colored with all the sordid details, but I did mention that Finn and I had indulged a little before Von and I got together for real. I tried to make the whole visit G-rated, but after a few almost lies, my conscience got the better of me. I'd never been able to lie to Allie.

"Okay, fine!" I threw my arms up, exasperated that as usual, she could still see right through me with her eyes closed. I covered my face with my hands, embarrassed. "I fell hard for Finn. I let him suck on my toes because he's got a foot fetish. And you know what? It was amazing! But it wasn't always about the physical connection. I didn't realize what a sucker I am for a guy reading to me, but man, I totally am. But it's long over, okay? I was torn, but I haven't been for a while." My voice lowered. "And that's the whole truth. I'm a whore. I let Finn suck on my toes once, so I'm a giant whore! Just say it!" I shook my head at myself. "Okay, twice. Maybe a few times when I was staying at his place. But Von and I weren't together, and I put a stop to things the second it got real. Does it make me a skank if I liked it?"

A low chuckle escaped Graham, making my head shoot up in his direction. He tried to stifle the mistake, but it was clear he'd been listening in. I gasped in horror, standing with heat coloring my cheeks. "You said you wouldn't listen!"

Graham belted out a laugh as I ran around the bed to swat at him over and over. He held up his arms to shield himself from my wrath. "To answer your question, yes. Only the skankiest skanks like their toes licked. You're one filthy vixen!"

I straightened, horrified. "You don't know what you're talking about!"

Graham stood, a wicked grin on his face. "Captain Finn has a foot fetish, eh? I guess that makes sense. Boy, it's a good thing you've got your shoes on. I don't know if I'd be able to control myself." He laughed when I swatted at him again. "Does Von know about your unusual preference?"

I gasped, scandalized. "You'll not mention a word of this to Von. Finn would be so embarrassed if it got out that he... If you value your life, you'll keep your mouth shut about everything you swore you wouldn't hear. And by 'life', I mean 'your testicles'."

Graham turned to the bed and shot Allie a conspiratorial look. "What are we going to do with her? Asking military men to suck on her toes in broad daylight! What'll the neighbors say?"

I huffed, throwing my hair over my shoulder. "Hush, you. Allie, I'll be back without this joker next time. Hang tight, girl. I'll figure this out. I'll bust you out of this hospital in no time."

Graham stifled his laugh and tried to present a sober nod to my sister, which I appreciated. He popped out his elbow to me. "Shall we?"

"Are you kidding me? After that skank crack? You can escort yourself."

Graham bowed his head with a snigger as he opened the door. "After you, Lady October. Until we meet again, Lady Allison."

23

PUT THE LOTION IN THE BASKET

We were home long before dinner, but Von wasn't. I was proud of him for getting out, and grateful Ezra had insisted Alton go with him. The Vandershot brothers were on glorified babysitting duty, but I knew they preferred the boring chauffeuring moments to the harrowing attacks that tore their family down.

I'd stopped with Graham at a store to pick Von up some gum in hopes he'd smoke a little less. I sat down at the dining room table with Ezra, upset with myself that I hadn't helped Lynna in the kitchen at all. I made a mental note to wash the dishes to give her a little break later.

Ezra asked simple questions, keeping it light so I didn't retreat back to my bedroom. I heard the front door open, but only Alton came in to join us at the soup course. He flopped in his chair, pushing his gold-rimmed glasses up on his nose as his dark hair swung into his face. "We're trading tomorrow. You get the basket case, and I get the pretty girl," he said to Graham.

"What's wrong? Is he alright?" I asked, suddenly worried my plan to reintroduce the outside world to Von had gone terribly south somehow.

"He's carrying in his purchases. I'll let that be a terrifying little surprise for you later. If there's ever any doubt that Von loves you, I hope it's cleared up when he shows you all he bought."

I raised an eyebrow. "Oh. Okay. So long as he's alright, that's fine. I don't care what he bought. I just wanted to get him out of the house."

"Mission accomplished. No more letting him make simple decisions, though. He can't handle the stress of it."

I frowned, worried I'd pushed Von too far. "Stress? I didn't mean for that. Is he alright? Is he coming down?"

"After he unloads the car by himself, yes. And don't anyone volunteer to help him. He's got to learn his lesson. He's cracked, Ezra. Absolutely batty."

Von joined us when the roasted chicken and sides were served, scooping me up from my chair with palpable relief. "You came back," he breathed, pressing his lips to mine briefly. "I was so worried."

I'd never been a fan of public kissing, especially since our kisses were more psychedelic than your standard run-of-the-mill makeout. Von's lips captured mine a second time, grateful and filled with relief that I hadn't been stolen away, that my body wasn't lying in a ditch, and that I hadn't up and left him. I heard the tinkle of bells greeting us, and the swirls of blue and gold dripped down the dining room walls like slow-melting glittery wax. I lost myself for a solid ten seconds in the transformation of worlds that happened when Von made me see stars in the home of his lips.

I pulled away, my cheeks pink as I kept my head down. "Sorry about that, guys. Have a seat, Von. You must be hungry. Come eat dinner with us."

Instead of taking the open seat next to Alton across the table from Graham, Von brought the chair next to me, sliding his plate and everything, so his thigh could smoosh to the outside of mine while we ate. He kissed my temple and barely paid attention to the others at the table. He ate a few bites with his arm wrapped around me, holding me tight and checking behind himself occasionally, as if he expected a monster to come flying in and snatch me away from him.

I tried to stay engaged in the normal dinner conversation. I answered Ezra's questions about our afternoon, and accepted his invitation to go to a museum with him on Wednesday – like, you know, an actual social life. When Von opened his mouth to say that he didn't feel up to a trip to the museum, Ezra cut him off with, "You've got a visitor coming on Wednesday, Von. Danny wanted to take you out. He needs your help with something. Alton will be guarding Mariang with Boston while she rests."

"What help does Danny need?"

Ezra shrugged evasively. "He didn't say."

"Just for a little bit?"

"I believe it was only a couple hours."

"Okay, fine. And you'll be with October the whole time?"

"Graham and I, yes. I promise to look after her with my life."

Von watched Ezra as if studying him for false moves. "Okay. I guess that would be alright." Von agreed, but his grip around me tightened. I felt terrible for him. I could see fear beneath the suspicion, and knew that when we'd lost September, it changed him in a way that wouldn't be possible to undo anytime soon.

After dinner, Von wasted no time corralling me upstairs. He shut the door and leaned against it, exhaling with relief. "That took forever. I don't like being separated from you."

"I missed you too, babe." I looked around the room and found ten overlarge shopping bags from the nearest mall. "I guess you needed to hit the store, too. What'd you get?"

"You told me you needed socks and lotion, so I got you socks and lotion."

"Thanks, sweetheart. But what's the rest of it?" I walked over to the nearest bag and peeked inside.

"It's all socks and lotion. I didn't know which kind to buy, so I just kept going."

My mouth fell open as I dug into the bag, revealing

dozens of pairs of fuzzy socks, along with every kind of lotion imaginable. "Are you serious? Von, I needed like, one pair. Two, at most." I gasped at the next bag that was filled to the top with big bottles of various lotions, each a different brand in the same lavender scent. "Oh, honey. This is... Thank you, really, but we have to take these back."

"Do what you want with them. You said you needed lotion and socks, so I brought some home for you. This way you'll never have to leave me to go buy them."

My mouth went dry as I began to see the psychosis seeping into his pores. I moved slowly around the room, opening each bag that solidified what I should've seen a mile away – Von was cracked. "These are my favorites." I picked out a pair of socks at random. For good measure, I selected six more pairs and laid them on the bed. Then I chose three bottles of lotion with the least annoying smells. "The rest can go back to the store though. Sorry I wasn't more specific. I didn't mean you had to buy all the lotion in the whole mall."

Von shrugged. "It's no trouble." His earlobe was still red and swollen, perhaps even more so than when I'd left that morning. Von pulled off his shirt and kicked his pants to the floor. He climbed into the bed and held his arms out to me. "It's been a long day. I need you here. I don't like when I turn around and you're gone."

I quirked my eyebrow at the switch in our roles. Now I

was the one "stepping out", and he was the one feeling abandoned.

"Okay, hun. I'll be right there." I grabbed pajamas out of my drawer and moved to change in the bathroom. I came out a few minutes later, and Von was biting his nails, eyes darting around the room to accuse the shadows of foul play. I sank into the bed with him, though it was barely seven o'clock, and let him gather my body greedily to his. His lips found mine in the darkness. Our bodies were lit only by the twilight that seeped through the edges of the beige curtains. It took mere seconds for him to sweep us away from the mansion and transplant us smack in the middle of our park, the beautiful colors dancing around us to celebrate our return to the fanciful life that was far prettier than reality.

Von was desperate and handsy; it wasn't like him to be so frantic, erratic and uncontrolled. I slowed him down with long, languid kisses, reminding him that I wasn't going anywhere, and we had all night in our dreams.

Right when I'd slowed down his pace to a less harried and fearful romp, Von's emotions crested. He crashed down atop me in a fit of tears that overtook him without warning. It was so strange that I scrambled to hold him, hoping to give him an anchor when he was so very lost. "It's okay, Von. Let it out."

"It's not okay!" he roared into my shoulder. "It'll never be okay. I wanted a daughter who was mine. Penny's brilliant, and I love her, but I know her eyes belong to some other bloke, and that her mum and I will never be together. She's not even mine on paper! But September would've been mine. The first child that's mine, and she's broken! I couldn't save her. What good is vampire blood if it does absolutely nothing when you need it to? What good am I if I can't save a little girl?"

The entire night and the next few days were a lengthier version of that. Von was terrified every time I left the bedroom, so I stayed mostly locked inside to pacify him, since it seemed he was in the throes of a mental breakdown. Then slowly, me just being in the same room as Von wasn't enough; we had to be touching, cuddling, kissing. I left him to use the bathroom (and you know, breathe), and after a minute, he pounded on the door, frantic that I'd cracked my head on the porcelain or some nonsense.

I understood crazy better than most, since I'd been on the brink of it much of my life. I stayed with him for days, locked in the bedroom with no hope of release. Von vented his grief while I held him. I kept my own anguish locked up tight, where no one would bother me about it. It wasn't as if I could lean on Von; he could barely hold himself upright with his own misery. I decided to save my agony for Allie, knowing she would keep my secrets.

24

FRESH AIR AND SUFFOCATION

It was a long debate to get Von out of the bedroom when Wednesday morning finally rolled around. "You need to eat before you go out with Danny. It's important you have some blood in your system. Come on, babe. It's been at least two days since you've had any blood at all. That can't be healthy."

"I'm not hungry."

I harrumphed, pulling on a hoodie that made my deflated body shapeless, so I didn't feel so strange in my own skin. "Well, I am. I'm going downstairs to eat now." Lynna had been bringing our meals up to our room, but I wanted to eat at an actual table this time.

This moved Von off his chair that overlooked the back-yard grounds. "I'll come with you." He hadn't showered in at least three days, and the cigar smoke was practically leaking out of his pores, permeating the room and making me a little nauseous. His swollen earlobe was getting fatter for no reason I could tell, making it look unnaturally elongated, despite the antihistamine I'd been giving him regularly. His hair was matted in parts and stiffly stuck up in others, making him look just as unbalanced as he was inside. His white undershirt had stains on the armpits, but he didn't care. Von was broken.

I'd broken Von.

I held tight to his hand, leading him through the house to the dining room. I sat him at the table, like a doll who couldn't move without my permission.

Ezra and Graham ate silently, afraid to look at the mess that was Von, in case eye contact might make him retreat back to the bedroom. As discreetly as I could, I banded his fingers around the hilt of his fork, silently reminding him that we were here to eat.

Von took a few bites, not even looking up when Danny entered the room, nodding his condolences to both of us. "Are you ready, mate?" Danny asked as he snuck a piece of bacon off the platter.

"Huh? For what?"

Danny looked to Ezra with his thick eyebrows pushed together. "Didn't you tell him I'd be over?"

"I did. October Grace, might I see you in the living room with Danny for a moment?"

Von snapped to life when my chair moved back and I stood to leave. "Wait! Where are you going? It's not safe for you to be running off today."

I placed my hand atop his head. "Hun, I'm not running off. I'm just going to talk to Ezra in the kitchen. I'll be back in like, five minutes. I'm not even leaving the mansion"

"Fine, then I'll go with you." Von stood, knocking his chair back and causing the guys to hold up their hands with "Hey, hey!" kinds of noises. "What? It's only a chair. I turned my back for one second, and she was gone the other day. I blinked and my daughter died right before my eyes. I'll not take chances with October's safety."

My hand slid into his, and I refused to look up at the guys, who would only confirm what I already knew. Von had lost several very important marbles from his brain.

Ezra placed his hand on Von's shoulder and slowly drew him into a hug that started out soft, but tightened gradually. "Son, there's nothing you could've done. You were outnumbered. I've already put in a motion for Mulvano to be removed from his interim throne in Lumipad. It takes time for justice to be served."

"I don't care about justice. I just want..." Von's voice caught, and I could tell by the look on Danny's face that he hadn't expected Von to burst into tears in Ezra's arms in the middle of the dining room. Graham was unsurprised, and drank his orange juice as he watched the scene unfold.

"I know, son. Today's going to be difficult, but I should like to spend a little time with my daughter. October needs a break. Don't you want her to have a day out, where she doesn't have to think about the awful incident?"

Von squeezed my hand while Ezra held him. "I don't

want her to go. I know something bad will happen. I'll never forgive myself if she gets attacked while I'm not there to keep her safe."

Ezra held tight to Von. "Do you trust me with your treasure?"

Von hesitated, clinging to my hand in fear. I could feel his indecision, knowing that he was too lost for concepts as grand as trust. He couldn't find the words, so he stuck with one stiff nod into Ezra's shoulder, followed by more tears that made Danny back away with wide and wary eyes.

I squeezed Von's hand before releasing it. "I'm going to go upstairs and change into something that screams 'museum'. I promise I'll be right back."

"No! I'll come with you."

"I'll only be five minutes, Von. Honest. I'll be right back down."

"No, you could trip on the stairs! You could hit your head on the wall and die easy as anything. Ezra, let go, mate!"

I moved closer so Von didn't fight Ezra. "Hey, I promise I'll be super careful." I kissed his cheek and smoothed his greasy hair from his forehead. "You worry about me too much, Mister. I'm not in any danger in the mansion."

"I don't like it. I know the second you're out of my sight, something dreadful's going to happen. I feel it in my gut."

Danny held up his hand. "I'll take her. You get some air. Ezra, Graham, why don't you take my big brother for a walk outside. Get him some oxygen that doesn't stink of cigars."

"My big brother" was the kind of talk Danny usually avoided. It was sweet and showed affection. I wasn't sure why Danny was being good to Von, but I appreciated the help.

"Superb idea, Danny." Ezra tightened his arm around Von and led him toward the back door. Graham closed the divide to cut Von off from me, casting me a grave nod that told me he would handle his brother.

I knew it was too easy. Von broke away, shoving Ezra and knocking Graham out of the way. Danny shouted for Von to be careful when my fiancé crashed into me, holding too tight. He held me like I was his life raft, and he was afraid of drowning. His chest heaved unevenly. "That was a close one. I saw you tripping and slicing your head open on the banister. No more stairs! I'll bring your clothes down to you."

I winced at how tightly he gripped me. "Easy, Von. I'm not totally bulletproof yet. Gentle hugs, babe. My body's still healing."

Graham raised his hand. "I'll get her clothes for you, mate."

Von cast a sideways glance to his brother. "Cheers, Graham."

I gently extracted myself from Von's manic hold. "Okay. I'm totally safe now. I won't go up any stairs while you're out on your walk."

"What? Not a chance. I'm not stepping a toe away from you. That was too close a call."

Ezra was gentle but firm as he put his arm around Von's shoulder. "Come," he insisted. "Just a short walk. Ten minutes, Von. You need some fresh air." There were a few more false starts, but eventually the two made it out.

Graham leveled his gaze at me. "You can get your own clothes without cracking your head open, yeah?"

"Of course. Go with Ezra and keep an eye on him. I don't want him to lose his temper and take a swing at my dad. Thanks, Graham." The second the door closed behind Graham, I reached out for the wall and used it to hold myself upright. My brave and calm smile ran clean off my face, but I still tried to keep it together for the viewers. "I'll just be a few minutes. Thanks for taking him out today, Danny."

Danny covered his mouth with the back of his hand, still catching up to the drama that had gone on without him. "I had no idea it was this bad. I would've come sooner."

"It's fine. Or it'll be fine. I know you've got Mariang to look after. I wouldn't assume you'd stick around to put my fiancé back together. You don't owe me that." I felt my way along the wall toward the stairs, moving one foot in front of the other, though they both felt like lead.

"You're an Omen. If you can't even get out of the house to do your job, all of Terraway suffers. I'm here now, and

Prince Langgam will come in a week if things don't improve."

I made my way up the stairs, not expecting Danny to harrumph from behind me. "This is exhausting just watching you."

"Dude, I just gave birth. I'm moving a little slower than usual, so chill."

Danny was less antagonistic when he reopened his mouth. "You're right. Let me help you. Come on." His arm went around my back, and he offered his hand for me to grip so I could lean on his strength.

Danny was plenty strong. I used to be strong, but lately I just plain wasn't.

25

THE LAST OF VON'S MARBLES

*D*anny set me down on my bed with a furrowed brow. "Whoa. You didn't fight me on that one. You actually let me help you up the stairs. Now I know you're having a rough go of it. Anything I can do?"

"Put Von back together and magic me a new body. That's what you can do." I fished out a white blouse that had enough elasticity to cover my form, which hadn't quite shrunken back to its original shape. I found a pair of jeans that were comfortable and wouldn't be too annoying. "I don't want you fighting with him today, or any day for that matter. I mean it. You saw him down there; he's gone."

Danny fished through one of the shopping bags curiously. "Why do you have so many pairs of socks?"

"This is what I'm talking about. I asked him to pick me up some socks, and he bought like, every pair in the mall! He can't put things in the right order in his mind. He's totally manic. I have whole conversations with him, and he forgets we even spoke minutes later. So I don't want you to start with him." I frowned. "In fact, maybe you should send Boston to come be with Von." The idea started to sound better and better the more I turned it over in my mind. "Yeah. Boston and Graham can take Von out, and you can go hang with Mariang and Alton."

Danny's eyebrows rose into his hairline. "You're actually trying to send me away? I just got here."

I leaned on the dresser to steady myself. "You and I both know you hate Von. He doesn't need that. Not now. He needs someone who loves him and believes he's not a screw-up."

Danny lowered his chin to stare at the carpet and slowly shook his head. "That's not fair. I came here today because I know Von's hurting. I came to help him."

"The time to help him was years ago, when he took the parenting responsibility because your dad split. The time to help him would've been standing by his side when he got kicked out of the Academy. You've had plenty of time to help Von when he really needed it, and you turned your back on him. Right now, I need someone I can trust with Von, and while I appreciate you're trying now, that's never been you."

"And now that I'm here, not turning my back, you're sending me away? How does that measure out?"

I punched my fist to my chest, probably looking a little crazy. "You lost your chance to be good for him, and right now, Von only needs what's good for him. You don't know the first thing about that."

Danny stood, towering over me with his height and the added bonus of his anger, which was always somehow bigger than mine. "Hey, I was there when you lost September. I stayed with both of you through the whole thing. We're all going through this, here. Mariang's afraid to call you because she thinks you'll be upset to hear her voice."

My nose crinkled. "Huh? Why would I be mad at her?"

"Because she gets to keep her baby, and you didn't."

It was like Danny slapped me across the face. I leaned against my dresser to brace myself again, counting to five before opening my mouth. "That's a helluva thing to say to me. Do you really think I'm that petty?"

"No, but I do think it was that dreadful. I don't care what you say, I'm here for my brother now. I'm taking him out for the day."

"Where are you going with him? I don't want him drinking. Not when he's lost like this."

"Fine."

"I swear to you, Danny. I used to treat criminals. I know the good places to stash a body. They'll never find you if you wreck him more."

Danny popped open our window, sticking his head out to breathe in something fresh. "How can you live in this? It's awful!"

"I'll forgive you just about anything if you can break him of his cigars."

Danny brought his head back in and stared at me, scowling. It was as if his face knew his mouth was about to be nice, so it had to compensate somehow. "How are you holding it together?"

"I'm an amazing actress," I deadpanned.

"Any appearances from Sama in your mind?"

I shook my head. "If Von's in my head, Sama can't hijack me. So it's a good idea for us to go to sleep together. Not a permanent solution, but a good enough Band-Aid so I don't take a screwdriver to my temple." I said it as a joke, but the visual was one I'd been tempted by before. I swallowed the lump in my throat. "I've got to change, so you know, scram."

I shut Danny out of the room and pulled on the outfit that had fit me just fine a few months ago. Now it made me look like I was at the end of my first trimester. Just enough of a bump for strangers to comment on. I tried sucking in my stomach, but it was no use. My body was a beacon for the worst moment of my life.

Von burst through the door, wild-eyed and filled with terror. I backed up, instantly fearing an attack on the mansion. "What is it?"

"I told you not to go up the stairs without me!" Von didn't bother shutting the door, but ran to me, sinking to his knees and sobbing into my thighs with actual tears. "I don't want you to go to the museum! It's too dangerous!"

"Seriously? We're still on this?" I knew I shouldn't be exasperated, but the clingy thing did nothing for me. I brushed my hand down his cheek as Danny inched back into the room, mouth agape. "I'm only going out for a few hours. I promise not to leave Ezra's side, okay? I love you, but this is unhealthy. You have to let me leave the house without throwing yourself on the floor at my feet!" I'd wanted a boyfriend who stuck around, but the opposite swing of having one who wouldn't let me leave the house was a steep drop-off.

Von stood and ran to the door, barring the exit by using his body like an X to keep me from going. "I have a bad feeling about you leaving today. Stay, *hani*. Stay and make love to me all afternoon."

Danny buried his face in his hand. "Stop. You'll put me off my lunch."

"You know I can't do that. The doctor said we had to wait six weeks." I shook my head. "And you wanted to wait until our honeymoon for the real thing."

Von gripped the doorjamb like a bull holding himself back for the kill. "We don't need the real thing."

Lust flared up in his eyes, and I took a hesitant step back. "Von, stop! No! Don't kiss me!"

It was too late. Von launched himself at me, holding my face and mashing his lips to mine, dunking me under and immersing me in our surreal life. The colors flew at me too fast, and I started to feel seasick. I tried to push at his chest, but he was determined.

Just as quick as he descended on me, Von was ripped away by Danny, who threw his brother into the opposite wall. Von barred his fangs, seething and readying to attack his brother.

"Stop, Von! Look at yourself!" I shouted through my tears. He'd torn open the top button of my blouse, revealing nothing but my shame that somehow I'd ended up in a relationship like this.

Danny held up his fists, ignoring Graham, Alton and Ezra, who ascended the stairs at the commotion. Von was seething, spittle flying out of his mouth as his focus turned to Danny. "I knew you wanted her for yourself. Couldn't stand to see me happy. Well, she's mine! *I* bought the ring. I'm the one who wins this time! I get to keep something good for myself finally! I've died enough for our family. It's *my* turn to live!"

Danny was poised to fight, though I could tell he didn't want to. "Do you hear what you're saying? When have I ever looked at a woman who wasn't Mariang? Why would you think I'd go in for your girl? You're mad!"

"You're jealous! Why else would you be here when we're clearly trying to be together?"

"You attacked her! She told you to stop, and you practically forced her into the bed. Who are you? This isn't you."

Von was out of words, so he took the first swing, popping Danny across the face. I gasped, and Graham and Ezra shouted for Von to stand down. Von whirled on them, taking a swing at Graham, who luckily dodged.

Danny turned as if in slow motion to Von. I was worried about the years of resentment culminating into a bloodbath all over my bedroom. "You're lucky I just promised your girl I wouldn't lay into you. Enjoy that punch, Von. Try it again, and I'll beat you into the ground."

"I'd like to see you try, little brother." Von raised his fists again, squaring off for round two.

Alton was horrified at the sight of his superman devolving so thoroughly. "No, Von! You love us! This isn't you."

"Don't do this, guys!" I cried, running to stand between the seething Danny and the volatile Von. I kept my back to Danny, inching until my shoulders were pressed against his chest to keep him from swinging out at the guy who used to be the man I love. I pleaded with my eyes for Von to see clearly through his haze. "Please, honey. Don't you see that this hurts me? I need you to keep it together, because most days, I'm barely upright! You can't lose it on me like this. You're hitting Danny now? You love Danny, even when he doesn't deserve it. That's one of my favorite things about you."

Von blinked rapidly, like he was trying to get something out of his eyes. His shoulder started twitching, but he kept his focus on me. "You want to leave me."

I shook my head, tears welling in my eyes. "No! Of course I don't want to split up. I tell you what, if you leave Danny and Graham alone, I'll go with you wherever you want. Just you and me."

Ezra opened his mouth to protest, but Graham held up his hand to stop him. I heard two sets of footsteps pounding up towards us, and knew that whoever it was would surely set Von off.

Von had almost relaxed his fists, but tightened them again when Kabayo and Finn came running into our bedroom. "You called Finn?" Von accused. "How could you? I knew you still had feelings for him!"

"I didn't..." I eked out, and then screamed when Von's fist flew out at me.

I'd been punched before, but there's something about the man you're engaged to clocking you across the face that takes you by surprise.

I didn't see what happened after that. I hit the ground, holding my cheek as I sobbed uncontrollably, hurt just as bad by the emotional trauma as the physical assault. I heard fighting as the men descended on the stranger who used to be Von. I didn't watch, but crawled over to the corner and held myself as I wept in my hopeless abyss.

26

MY DARK FAIRY TALE

"Get away from me." I was embarrassed and scared, my cheek throbbing with betrayal and the beginnings of a nice shiner as I knelt in the corner of my bedroom. I tried not to lose my cool, but I was barely hanging on. Ezra, Kabayo, Alton and Finn had taken the blissed-out version of Von down to his cell in the basement. They left me with two Duwendes, who I wouldn't let within three feet of me. Graham tried to rest his hand on my shoulder, but I batted at him like a caged animal. I didn't want to hurt him, but needed the message to be clear: Don't touch October.

I clawed at the backs of my hands, my face red as I tried to find a reason why it was a good idea for me to stay sane. I couldn't come up with anything, so I sought to remove the skin from my arms one layer at a time. Pain made sense. Von hitting me didn't.

"Come on, love. Let me take a look at your eye. Danny brought you an icepack."

I tried not to yell, and kept my voice quiet, so I didn't give in to the screaming I wanted to do. "I don't want it. Just leave me alone." I could feel that I was rocking back and forth like a maniac, but I let my body do what it needed to. "I want to go home."

Graham's voice was quiet and sad. "You can't go back there. There's not even windows put in yet. This is your home, too."

"My boyfriend would never hit me in my own home. I wouldn't let that happen. I'm not one of those girls who lets that happen." With all the pain of a knife slicing off my finger, I slid off Von's ring and dropped it in Danny's outstretched hand. "It's over. It's done. I won't put up with an ounce of that."

"Okay. I get it. Just breathe for now." Danny tried to maintain some semblance of control as Finn reentered the bedroom.

"I'm fine, so you can go. I want to be alone."

"You're hurting yourself!" Danny pointed at my hands that were set on destroying my skin one shred at a time.

"I'm sad, which is normal to feel in a situation like this. I'm normal!" I declared, rocking in the corner, holding myself so I didn't claw off my skin with so many witnesses.

"Clearly. October, you have to calm down. Ezra's going to handle Von. Something's cracked because you're right, Von would never hit you, especially in your own home.

Von would never hit me, either. I don't know what's going on, but that wasn't Von, just then. Kabayo's here, and together they'll sort it out."

"Sort what out? There's nothing unclear to me. Everything I love breaks. My home is broken. Bev is broken. Allie is broken. My baby is broken! My fiancé is broken. Everywhere I turn, my life is breaking, and you want to tell me to calm down?" The agony of being a homeless orphan with a black eye from her boyfriend shot through me, piling misery on top of grief that I couldn't reason my way through. Maybe I was being dramatic, but I'd flipped a switch or something. Too many days of being calm so Von could fall apart had stacked up into a wall of crazy. The punch to my face had toppled the wall all over the place, and now I was stumbling hopelessly through the rubble, not caring who I crashed into.

Danny tried a different tact. "You don't want us in your space? Fine. But Ezra ordered that medicine Ollie used on you when you lost your mind before. If you can't settle down, I'll go get that needle. Don't make me do it, kid."

I turned to look up at Danny, livid and seething with betrayal. "You touch me with that needle, and I'll end you. You're not my doctor."

"What medicine?" Finn inquired, watching the scene from a few feet back.

"Stuff for when she loses her mind."

"This has happened before?"

"There's no 'this'. All I want is for you to get out of my room. Can't a girl get some privacy?"

Danny threw out his hands. "Fine! Far be it from me to keep you from hurting yourself. I'm such a monster. I've got a black eye too, you know!" Danny stormed out, taking his anger with him.

Graham tried to put his hand on my shoulder again, but I shoved it away. "I said don't touch me. Go help Danny. Go help Ezra. I want to be alone."

Graham stood, tapping his heart. "It hurts you when Von clings too hard? Well it hurts me when you push us away like this. I want to be your friend."

"You want to be my friend?" I sniffled, trying to think a little more rationally, now that there was one less person in the room and on my case. "You are. I just want some space. I freak out less if people leave me to deal. It's a lot to take right now."

Graham nodded. "I can get onboard with that. Is there anything I can get you while you take some time for yourself?"

"No, thanks. But could you make sure someone visits Allie? I told her I'd see her today, but I don't feel up to driving."

"Of course. If Ollie can't step away, I'll go myself."

I breathed, feeling the difference immediately as oxygen and just a little bit of space helped to clear my head. "Tell Ezra not to give Von any more of the antihistamine if he's going to have him locked up for more than a day or so. I've been giving him a daily dose, but his ear's not getting any better. Maybe he's allergic to the medicine or something, because he started getting super nuts right around then. I'm grasping at straws." I shook my head at myself. "I don't even think it's possible to have a psychotic reaction to an anti-histamine."

"His ear?"

I turned back to my corner, so I didn't have to look at anyone. "It's swollen. He should have it looked at."

"I can do that. Anything else?"

"Just a little quiet. That's all I want."

"Of course, little sister." Graham left, and I closed my eyes, letting the tears flow freely, now that I didn't have an audience. I kept my body cuddled into the corner of the room, my eyes shut as I clawed at my arms slowly. I needed to feel the deep pain that made me focus on the physical and not the emotional. Physical could heal. Physical pain was fixable.

"I really wish you'd stop that," Finn said from behind me.

I straightened and whirled on him, furious that he'd been watching me and hadn't vacated the room like I'd asked. "If you don't like it, then you can leave."

But he didn't leave. Finn walked over to my dresser and pulled out one of the books he'd given me. "I can't remember where we were. Do you?"

"Where we were what?"

"In the story. Had Lissima's parents killed Ricardo by ripping his heart out of his body yet?"

My mouth dropped open in shock. "I can't believe you just did that! Of course we haven't gotten there yet. Are you serious? Did you really just ruin the ending of a series I translated by hand?"

Finn cracked a smile at me. "I'm only kidding. I know where we are." He took the book, shut the bedroom door and locked it. Then Finn grabbed a blanket from the bed, covered my shoulders with it, and sat down two feet from me, leaning his back against the wall. He didn't look at my face, and part of me appreciated that he knew me well enough to understand that I didn't want anyone to see me so broken. He didn't address the assault, but made a show of breathing deeply in and out, setting the tone for the level of tranquility he willed into the bedroom. He wasn't going to treat me like a victim, which for some reason reminded me that I was stronger than crying in a corner. "Now, where were we? Are we to the part where we find out Lissima's really the daughter of the wicked sea king?"

"You make jokes now, but you'll be the one eating that book if that turns out to be the case."

"Let me read to you," he offered, rolling his shoulders back. "I've had a long day."

I chuckled, which I didn't think myself capable of doing. "You poor guy. All that surfing grow tiresome?"

"Shut up and relax. Let's deal with life another day."

I looked over at his face finally and saw sleeplessness

etched into the corners. I could tell he needed the break just as much as I did. I shifted my body and held myself on the floor, my knees pushed to my chest, cuddling into the blanket he was kind enough to get for me.

I closed my eyes and rested my head against the wall as Finn began reading, drenching us in the details of another world with fictional problems far more complicated than ours. After he flipped the page, he kept reading, but reached his free hand out between us, palm up in invitation. I didn't know what to make of the offer, and let it rest a few paragraphs before tentatively stretching my arm out to lay my hand in his. It wasn't flirty or laced with the blush-worthy tawdriness our non-relationship was famous for. It was kindness – pure and simple. Beneath the attraction and the intention that never went anywhere, Finn and I had a friendship that was worth holding onto.

I thought I knew how much I appreciated Finn's offer to be there for me through a pretty confusing time. I thought I'd reached full velocity on my emotional rollercoaster where he was concerned. Then my palm grew damp, and I realized that Finn was washing my hand for me while he read. He didn't say a word as he washed away the germs that clawed at my flesh; he simply rinsed away my demons and held my hand until the madness passed. Tears welled in my eyes, and each one that spilled was a tribute to my gratitude for our budding friendship. I don't know how I got so lucky that after all the shake-ups and fights, I somehow got to keep part of Finn in my heart, and got to hold him tight in my hand.

Finn read an entire chapter before resting the open book facedown over his shin. "How's your eye?"

"Feels awesome. My whole life feels awesome," I deadpanned.

Finn chuckled at the bitter note in my voice. "I admit, I never thought Von would lay a hand on you. Maybe you'll feel better once you're back in your home."

I took a steadying breath. "I don't have a home. That was supposed to be my safe place, and my daughter died right on my bed."

Finn took a chance and pulled me and the blanket closer, so he could loop my arm through his. "My home is always yours. Nothing romantic. Just while Ezra sorts Von out. I really can't believe Von would hit you in his right mind. When he came to Dagat to find the mole in my battalion, I saw it."

"Saw what?"

"I saw how much he loves you. I love you, make no mistake, but Von? That's a whole other level of devotion." He shook his head and scratched his chest. "This whole conscience thing is rough." He cleared his throat. "I promise not to make a move on you until you and Von figure out where you stand. That being said, I want you to come stay with me for a little while. I'll keep you safe."

I kept my voice barely above a whisper. "I was molested right outside your house. And if you remember, you blacked my other eye once upon a time in my dark fairy tale. I'm not safe anywhere."

Finn winced. "I'm different now. *We're* different. You broke my curse and gave me the chance at growing a conscience."

I shook my head, too messed up to think clearly. "You have to stop. I'm barely a person anymore. I can't process more than this. Thanks for the offer, but I need to stay Topside. You and I are dangerous together, and I've had enough danger in my life."

Finn held me tighter. "Okay. Maybe I shouldn't have said anything."

"Sometimes nothing is the perfect thing to say."

Finn looked down on me with too much love, too much adoration. My heart broke that I was never in the right place at the right time, that I wanted something simple, but the options were messy and crumbled when I got too near. I stilled as Finn brought my fingers to his lips, kissing each one slowly, lacing each blessing with a silent promise that not everything broken would always be thus. His full lips brushed the burgeoning bruise on my cheek. "I love you," he whispered, "and I want more for you than this."

"How can you look at me like that?" I marveled, staring up at him in confusion. "My body's all messed up, I'm gross from crying, and..."

"I see you," Finn answered simply. "You're still in there, even if you can't feel it. I see you."

I swallowed, wishing I could see the me he did, that I could be the girl worth looking at like... like that. "You shouldn't be nice to me. I'm a wreck."

The corner of his mouth tugged up in half a smile. "I know you. You've got miles to go before someone like you's wrecked."

The sweetness of his declaration pinged in my fragile heart. Of all the things we'd whispered to each other during our alone time, I prayed for that one note to ring true.

MANGKUKULAM

The knock on the door couldn't have been better timed if Jiminy Cricket himself wasn't right outside the door, orchestrating the whole thing to make sure Finn and I stayed friends after he let me lean on him so beautifully. "October Grace? Might I have a word?"

Finn kissed the back of my hand, and then stood to open the door for Ezra. "She's resting."

"She needs to hear this straightaway." Ezra moved into the room, sizing up my expression to see if I was already cheating on Von. "Has anyone taken any of Von's hair, fingernails or saliva?"

"Huh?" I listened as Ezra repeated himself, but even the second time around, it didn't sound any less weird. "When?"

"Right before Von started devolving. Think hard. Anything at all would be helpful."

Finn gasped. "You don't think Sama…"

"What?"

Ezra nodded at Finn gravely. "That's exactly what I think. He'd need the blood of a queen, though, and Sylvia died long before this. She's the only queen in Terraway."

The image of the purple corset Manas with the orangy-red hair stood out in my mind. "Well, in the fight where the Manas broke in and fed me that poison, there was one who flew in, ripped out a chunk of Von's hair and flew right back out. I thought it was weird she didn't stick around to actually fight. One of the other Manas even called after her, but she didn't come back. Susa? Suzie? I'm not sure. Would that count?"

Ezra hung his head. "Yes, dear. Thank you. That confirms it for me. Sama's a Mangkukulam, which is our version of a sorcerer. He'd need the hair of his victim, the droppings of a sigbin and the blood of a queen. I don't know how he got ahold of Sylvia's blood, but I'm willing to go to the mat on this."

I swallowed hard. "He didn't take Sylvia's blood. He sent out his spirit and had Serena killed. He had her carved up for what she did to me. That's who got to her and killed her before you found her, Ezra. If Serena was in charge of Lumipad after she killed Sylvia, then wouldn't she be the queen?"

Ezra pressed his hand to his forehead. "That would be good enough for the spell, I believe. I mean, clearly Von's being controlled, so however Sama managed the magic, it's done."

"Wait, controlled? By Sama? And you're saying it's done? Von's stuck like this?"

Ezra rolled back his shoulders and straightened. "No, darling. We can set him right. It'll take a few days, and I'd rather you weren't here for it. It can get messy, and I'm afraid you've had enough of that in your life. I insist you go to your home, or to the hotel with Mariang."

I stiffened. "I think you know me better than that by now. If Von's being messed with, I'm not leaving him."

Ezra moved over to me and pulled me up off the floor. "Von can sense you in the house. He can feel that you're nearby. Sama's bewitched him to crave you. He'll try to break out of the cell to get to you. Undoing the magic takes time, and it'll be easier for Von to focus on healing if he's not worried about getting to you."

"Can't I just kiss him?" My mouth drew to the side when I realized we'd been kissing for days, and he was still like this. "My kiss is supposed to break curses, right?"

"This isn't a curse, dear. It's simply magic. But thank you for offering your help."

I nodded, unable to place my feelings in the right category. "Do I have time to take a shower? I kind of want to wash this day off of me."

"Of course, darling. Quickly, though. I'll have one of the boys pack you a bag. I'll send someone with you, of course, to watch the house and pull for you."

I shook my head. "No, thanks. I don't want pulling."

Ezra tilted his head to the side. "You need it. You need it in spades."

"Everyone needs something like that. I can handle myself. I've always been able to deal, so that's what I'll do. Besides, it sounds like you'll need all the help you can get here."

THE FIREFIGHTER AND THE FIRE-BREATHING DRAGON

It turns out that Ezra was almost as stubborn as me. Almost. He consented to no pulling at my insistence, but ruled that I still needed someone to watch the house. "I've summoned Mason again, letting him know that he's to drop whatever's distracting him from his duties and come Topside straightaway. Captain Finn will stay with you until Mason relieves him." He turned to glower at Finn in silent warning. "Which I pray will be any moment. I'm sending Captain Finn instead of one of the boys because, safe as I pray we are, if anything should arise, he's to port you down to Silo first thing." He narrowed his eyes at Finn. "Silo, not Dagat."

"Yes, your majesty."

"Thanks. You sure you don't mind?" I asked Finn, hefting my duffel over my shoulder. I'd taken a long shower, washing myself three times, just the way I preferred. I felt a little more clarity, now that I was clean and dressed in comfortable clothes that hid the shape of my body.

"Of course I don't mind. The council's duty-bound to make sure the Omens are safe and can do their job. Without you and Mariang, we all starve. Besides all that, we're friends, right? Friends are supposed to help out when the other's knocked down."

I nodded, glad he was being cool about it all. Though it was probably unwise to be alone with Finn, I knew if I took Graham, he'd keep trying to pull the stress from me. I knew I couldn't run from the awful feelings forever. I needed to deal and move on.

Ezra cuffed Finn's bicep on the way out. "You'll conduct yourself like a gentleman around my daughter, or I'll see to it the council hangs you for every one of your crimes. Do not underestimate my temper. The lion in me is nothing to the man, once provoked."

Finn said nothing to this, but nodded once.

I hadn't driven in a while, and was grateful for the opportunity to give Terence the Taurus a go. I'd spent a lot of time with Terence, and I knew the only pulling he did was the organic stress relief of speeding slightly on the freeway. I loved going a solid five miles over the speed limit. There was something a little rebellious in me that smiled at bending the rules just enough for a thrill, but not enough to get caught.

Finn was watching me, leaning back in his seat with

his too long legs sprawled open next to me. He was dressed in his standard military black pants and black t-shirt, looking every bit himself. "I'll tell you what, I'll teach you how to swim if you show me how to drive."

I glanced over at him, noticing that he loved the thrill of the high velocity, too. "I can teach you to drive, sure. But I have no desire to learn how to swim. I don't plan on getting back into the water ever again."

Finn's jaw tightened. "But it's my world, and I want to share it all with you."

"I don't belong in Terraway, Finn. You and I both know it. The last time I was underwater, it didn't go so well."

"I can teach you in a pool or something, where there're no Mermen at all."

"I'll keep that in mind." That was my polite way of saying, "Thanks, but never. Not ever. Quit asking."

We reached my house that still had too many cars parked in front. I don't know why I'd thought the work would've been done in a day. "Um, so in there are a bunch of Ollie's friends. You'll have to wear your scarf. They're doing us a solid and helping clean up the place. It might not be all that restful here, but we can give it a shot. I kind of want to help, too."

"You're the boss."

I smirked, feeling one-tenth more myself. "I'll remember you said that." I got out of the car and moved toward the back to retrieve my duffel, but Finn already had it slung over his shoulder. We walked into my house and I let out a gasp, stopping two steps in. "Whoa! What happened here?"

Jordan and Beto looked up from the paint pans. Their rollers were dipped in a light silverish lavender color they had been spreading on the living room wall. "Bait's here!" Jordan called through the house, clearly forgetting that Graham had asked him not to use that nickname ever again. He dropped his roller and came over to give me a sweaty fist bump. "You like the color?"

I nodded, surprised at how good it looked. "You guys even fixed the holes in the drywall? That's awesome! Who knew you were so handy?"

Jordan flexed his muscles before shaking Finn's hand. "Do I even want to guess at who this is? Another guard from your mysterious paternal benefactor?"

"Finn's my friend. Finn, this is Jordan and Beto. Hi, Gabby. And that's Gabby, Jessica and Rachel." I noticed the absence of Katrina and relaxed. Finn gave a perfunctory nod, but offered nothing in the way of conversation.

Jordan thumbed my face, so I batted his hand away on instinct. "Whoa, is this new? Who kicked in your face, Bait?"

"Work," I explained. I wasn't sure if they knew I'd left the prison, and prayed that succinct explanation would suffice. It had served me quite well in the past.

"Rough. Good thing he's already behind bars, or I'd have to mess him up for ya." Jordan pounded his fist into his palm to demonstrate just how down and dirty he was prepared to get on my behalf. I knew it was all a joke, but I was so upside-down on my emotions that I took the front as truth and threw myself into Jordan's sweaty arms. "Whoa! Hey, you alright?" Jordan took the small window of me silently admitting that I was falling apart and hugged me tight, his hand rubbing in circles on my spine. When I didn't answer, Jordan lowered his voice. "I've got your back, kid. Maybe I go with Ollie to talk to the warden this time. See what I can't straighten out."

"Is Ollie here? I need to talk to him."

"Brother of the year's out getting more paint for his bedroom, so prepare yourself for his oncoming freak-out when he sees your eye."

I pulled back, clenched my fists across my chest and squinched my eyes shut as if readying for a monster task. "I'm prepared for the wrath of Ollie."

"Are you sure? I could yell at you now to give you a preview, if you like. It'd go something like, 'This job's too dangerous!' and 'I want his name so I can make sure the warden throws his loser butt in solitary. No one hits my sister!'" Jordan's fist in the air demanded vindication.

I chuckled at the joker being an actual threat to anyone. "That was a decent Ollie impersonation. You were almost intimidating."

Darius came out of my bedroom, sweaty and filthy. "Someone say something about Bait getting hit? What happened?"

I shrugged it all off like it was no big deal. "Work. It's fine. I've had worse."

Jessica tried to be helpful with a chipper, "I've got some foundation that'll cover that right up for you."

"I'm fine. Thanks, though. Sweet of you."

Darius mopped the sweat off his brow and came closer so he could examine my face. "I didn't know you were back at the prison. Which inmate?"

"It wasn't Terence or Fender, of course."

Darius rolled his eyes at me. "I know my guys wouldn't lay a finger on you. Give me a name, Bait. Who hit you?"

I shook my head. "It's really fine."

"Pistola," Darius ruled. "I know it was him. T told me Pistola was the one who stabbed you in the thigh. I'll make a few calls. It's taken care of. Clearly he didn't listen the first time I sent the message that you weren't to be messed with."

Finn pointed to Darius, finally deigning to speak. "I like this one."

My friends all gasped at the injury I'd tried to keep a secret for years. I palmed my forehead when Finn joined my friends in the line of questioning I refused to answer. "Aw, jeez. That stabbing was a secret, Darius, and it was a long time ago. Ollie doesn't know about it, and neither did these guys."

Darius thumbed my cheek to turn my face, so he could examine my eyes more closely. "Man, Pistola really nailed you. He didn't..." Darius looked pointedly at my crotch, making my ears turn pink.

"Sheesh, it wasn't Pistola, and everything's fine. I'm fine. I appreciate you being all terrifying on my behalf, but it's not necessary. I can handle my life."

"I'm sure you can, but Judge is going to hear about this."

I blew out a disrespectful raspberry. "If Judge could actually help me, I'd be begging on his doorstep."

Darius eyed me curiously. "What sort of trouble are you in that not even Judge could get you out of?"

I shook my head, trying not to let my melancholy get the better of me. "Nothing. Everything. Don't tell Judge. I'm really fine."

Darius gave me a hard look. "You're too stubborn for your own good."

"Don't I know it," Finn mumbled.

"Who do you think taught me that? Was it your stubborn older brother or mine?" I waved my hand to clear the air. "Too much serious talk. I'm really fine. Thanks for the concern, but I'm alright. The house looks amazing. I mean, if one of those home makeover shows is looking for a new crew, you guys are seriously top of the list. Wow!" I looked around with a smile that couldn't help but creep onto my face. "Y'all are incredible for doing all this. The place looks amazing."

"Oh! I knew you'd like it!" Gabby clapped her hands together as she sidled up beside me, all too willing to change topics to a happier one. I could tell Ollie had given her free reign with his bank account to refurbish the place. She had that retail therapy high about her that made her voice extra squeaky.

There were new end tables made of blonde wood, and a silver lamp that somehow matched the crazy new paint on the walls. The couch was new – a welcoming lavender with sporadic diamond shapes in white spread across the fabric. It was in a slightly different place than the old couch had been. Now it was a few feet to the left when you first walked in the door, instead of a straight shot. Somehow the small difference made a huge difference. I couldn't picture Manas' bodies littering my living room. I couldn't see the blood painting the walls. It looked like... a home. A cozy, welcoming home.

"Whose idea was it to hang those pictures? And where did... Is that me?" I moved over to the one wall behind the TV that was a cream color to contrast with the silver to brighten the room. In silver frames were blown-up pictures of Ollie, Allie and me in three separate matching rectangles.

Finn moved quietly beside me, unsure how to assess the danger in the space, or if there even was any. "Oh, is that your sister?" he asked, studying Allie at my nod.

There we were – a real family. I touched my heart to stem the swelling and took a step back before the emotion could infect my tear ducts. They were all pictures taken with cell phones at various parties in our house. The one of Allie had her frozen doing the Running Man, color in her cheeks and a giant smile on her face. Ollie's picture was of him flexing and shouting something hilarious into the camera.

The one of me I didn't even remember posing for. My hair was longer, so I knew it had to be a couple years ago. I wore my hospital scrubs and a long-sleeved thermal to cover the scars on my arms. I had my hand up to the person taking the picture with a polite smile that said, "Welcome to my home," and also, "Get that thing out of my face. Here's your pose, now leave me the crap alone."

"These are incredible. You seriously did all this?"

Gabby bounced on the balls of her feet, overjoyed that I was happy. Her spindly black curls bounced with glee. Despite everything that kept me mildly distant from her over the years, I always knew she had friend potential in her. "Wait until you see the picture in your new bedroom."

"My new bedroom?" I quirked my eyebrow at her silly grin that came when she was too excited about something. "I can't wait to see the makeover job you guys did on the rest of the place. You're blowing me away, here."

The front door opened, and I intuitively knew it was my brother before his greeting sounded across the living room. "October? I didn't know you were coming home today. Everything alright?"

I turned, revealing my swelling cheekbone that told enough of the story. "I decided to come sleep here tonight. Is that alright?"

Ollie's jaw was tense as he tempered his words. I could almost see him biting back the angry versions of "Who did that to you? I'll kill him!" Instead he swallowed. "Come for a walk with me? Too many paint fumes."

I nodded and moved out of the house, feeling Finn behind me. He'd been quiet during the whole exchange, for which I was grateful. It was nice to be out in the open spring air that felt like life to my pores, seeping through to my innards with restorative power.

Ollie waited a solid fifteen seconds to make sure we were out of earshot from the crew before he let loose. "Who blacked your eye? Another Manas?" He clenched his fists. "For all the power everyone claims Ezra has, dude cannot keep you safe!"

Finn put his hand on Ollie's shoulder. "I'm watching her now. You don't have to worry about anyone snatching at her while I'm around."

My voice was quiet as I explained the descent of Von into madness. I watched Ollie's shoulders rise with "I'll kill that idiot" vengeance, but then fall with a "Crap, I wish I could kill that idiot, but poor guy didn't stand a chance" droop. "Ezra sent me away for a few days so they can deprogram Von. Apparently, that process is a whole big, brutal thing. Finn's here to make sure no flying monkeys snatch me out of the sky." I meant that last one as a joke, but flying bat women wasn't too far a stretch.

Ollie rubbed the back of his neck. "I really, really wish we could have like, a solid month of nothing bad happening. Every time I see you, it's like you acquire a new injury. I never thought there'd be a job more dangerous than working at the prison, but you sure found it." He pointed to his ring finger, indicating my naked one. "So is this it for you and Von?"

I didn't answer for several paces, looking around at the few trees that lined our dead-end street. There were a few birds whistling, as if nothing horrible could ever dampen their spirits. I wished I had a little bit of that magic in me. "No, but I'm taking a little space for now. I can't really make heads or tails of anything. He takes off on me, but I understand the reasoning. He punches me, but I can't really get mad because he was possessed. He's like, a normal boyfriend and the worst boyfriend all rolled into one. Hard to say which way's up. I think the few days apart is a good idea. I have to know how much of him is the guy who would never hit me, and how much of him is the guy who decked me. I'm giving myself a chance to breathe and figure things out."

"Breathing's a good thing. I highly recommend. I do it habitually."

Finn cut through the feelings aspect of our conversation and got down to business. "Is the house ready for us to stay in tonight?"

"No, and there are parts I still don't want her to see yet." Ollie slung his arm around my shoulder. "I'm trying to do a total transformation on the place, so it doesn't remind us at all of the attack."

My arm wrapped around his waist as we walked. "Ollie, you don't have to do all this. You look like you haven't slept in a week. You need downtime. You've been through too much. Let me help with the repairs. It's my house, too."

Ollie shook his head. "I'm firm on this one, kiddo. I can't fix Allie, but this one I can fix. I need to be able to make something better. I need this for me."

I mulled over his reason and finally nodded. "If you get overwhelmed, will you call me?"

"Of course," he lied. "But a big project like this helps me to not get overwhelmed, if that makes any sense." He gave me a squeeze. "Go to Mariang's hotel for a few days. The house is almost done."

"You're the best brother in the whole world. In all my lives, you're my favorite version of you in this one."

Ollie smirked. "What about the life where I was a firefighter?"

"Well, I was a fire-breathing dragon back then, so we were at odds more often than not."

"Ah. The eternal struggle." He walked Finn and me to my car and opened the door. "I've got work to do, kid. Try not to get banged up anymore before I see you next, okay?" He cast a silent warning glance at Finn, who returned the unspoken promise that he'd look out for me.

29

WONDER WOMAN

"Okay, brake! Brake!" I shouted, my pulse racing a mile a minute, even though we were only going twenty-five miles per hour on our dead-end street. "Now put the car in park before I have a heart attack. No, P is for Park! Not R, P!"

"What'd I do wrong?"

I was gripping the door, and looked up at the roof to rein in my response. "Nothing. Nothing at all. I needed a good life-flashing-before-my-eyes moment. I've been living too safe an existence."

"You said to put my foot on the right pedal, so that's what I did."

"Yes, but you can't keep your eyes on the pedal. You have to watch where you're aiming the car. See?" I pointed to the mailbox he'd almost hit.

Finn deflated at my valid point. "Oh. Well, now I know.

Let me try again. How do I back this thing up?"

"Ho, no. Boston can teach you. I'm too young to die like this. We're switching."

Finn glared at me and got out with a frustrated huff, slamming the passenger door shut when he flopped into his seat. "You're a terrible teacher. Made me nervous with your little terrified hisses every five seconds. I was going slow, just like you told me."

"I guess I don't realize how many things you have to pay attention to. It's good you were focusing on which pedal you were pressing, and great that you were watching the speed limit. But you also have to watch where you're going. It's hard. You did a good job for your first time."

"Don't patronize me." Finn crossed his arms petulantly and stared out the window with a frown.

I don't know why his pouting struck me as funny, but I couldn't help the chuckle that escaped my lips. "You're adorable when you suck at something. Never thought I'd get to see you actually be bad at anything, but it's cute."

"Shut up." He shifted in his seat. "I hope you brought your swimsuit, because I'm teaching you how to swim the second we find a lake."

"The hotel's probably got a pool, but I don't want to learn to swim. I don't plan on ever going into the water again, so I don't need to know how."

"That's weak," Finn said, calling me out with no room for mercy. "That's not you. Be afraid all you want, but don't you ever tell me fear's stopping you from doing something important."

"Hello, swimming's not important in my line of work."

"What if someone you loved was drowning?"

I chucked his shoulder while keeping my eyes on the road. "That's why I have you to save the day in such a situation."

"I won't always be here. I'm sure the second Von comes back to himself, you'll send me on my way." He raised his hand when I opened my mouth. "Don't bother with the denial, or the charade you fed Ollie that you're taking some space from him. I'm a big boy. I know it'll be him. I'm just enjoying the time I get while I have it. I told you I'd be your friend before, and I haven't changed my mind on that." He cleared his throat. "But I'm firm on you learning how to swim. I'm here to keep you safe, so let me do my job."

"Well, I don't own a bathing suit, so that's that." I kept my eyes on the road, maintaining my silence as best I could until we neared the hotel. I checked us into a room on the same floor as Mariang's, and went straight to her room instead of unloading my bag into ours. The cleanliness of the lobby and hallways put me at ease. This was easily a five-star hotel, and the difference in room price meant more Lysol was used, the sheets were washed regularly, and the vacuum was run more often. My shoulders relaxed at the heady feeling of comfort the non-germy environment gave me.

Mariang let us into her room with a hug that threatened to force emotion out of me, so I ducked out of it five seconds in. "I missed you, too," I admitted with a smile. Her belly was big and round, making her tiny frame look unstable. I ignored the stab of pain I felt at being around a pregnant woman, and chose to focus on my sister going into the tail end of her third trimester. "How are you feeling?" I asked, rubbing her belly without asking permission. She didn't have the hang-ups about touch that I did, and reveled in the glory of pregnancy.

"Great! Bored, but I feel fine. So ready to meet little Anastasia Grace." She grinned at my eyes that went wide.

"Grace? Like, after me?" I was stunned. It dawned on me that no matter how much I adored Mariang, she would always find a way to be more generous with her love. "Are you serious?"

Mariang nodded quickly, finally backing up to let us all the way in after she shook Finn's hand. "I'm so in love with the name. It was Danny's idea, actually."

I shot her a withering look, getting the familiar feeling that she was trying to force me to like Danny by putting nice words in his foul mouth. "I can't picture that. Hey, Boston," I said to the brother who was texting on his phone from the chair by the window. He didn't bother to stand up to greet us, which only added to Boston's brand of charm.

"Hey, sis. Miss me so bad you just had to come visit?"

"Something like that."

Mariang held her hand up. "Honest! It was Danny's idea. He wanted to name her after a strong woman, and said he didn't know any who were stronger than you."

I winced. "Yikes. I almost feel bad for yelling at him before I left. He really said that?"

Boston nodded. "I remember because I made him repeat it. I mean, strongest woman? I nominated Wonder Woman, but he turned it down. Anastasia Wonder Woman Vandershot. Has a certain ring to it."

I chuckled and bent slightly to kiss his forehead, mussing his hair. "Missed you too, Bos." I scribbled down our room number on the pad of paper on the desk and flopped onto the bed next to where Mariang sat, rubbing her belly like it was a crystal ball. "So tell me about my niece. What've I missed? Kicking a lot?"

Finn excused himself to go do a few rounds to inspect the grounds, and put up charms to reinforce the ones Boston already had in place. Mariang and I talked animatedly about her pregnancy while I brushed her hair and braided it for her. With every question I asked her about her baby, she grew more and more overjoyed, relieved that I didn't hate her for being able to keep her baby when I couldn't have mine.

I loved her, plain and simple.

30

BOYS AND BIKINIS

"**C**ome on, you yellow chicken!" Boston jeered with a playful smile from the deep end of the pool.

"The water's warm, hun. You'll love it." Mariang waded in the shallow end, laving water over her arms.

"I don't want to do this," I gulped, standing at the edge of the pool. I peered into the chlorinated water, my arms crossed over my stomach. Of course Mariang had multiples of everything, including swimsuits. This one could hardly be classified as a suit; it was pink and skimpy, and I felt so exposed that I couldn't leave the hotel room until I'd pulled a tank top over the barely-there swimsuit. Though I didn't have my scars anymore, I didn't need the whole world seeing me in what was basically my underwear. Come to think of it, my underwear covered a lot more than this pink number did. While I was shorter than Mariang, my breasts were heaping handfuls larger than hers, and my butt was a little rounder than her size two frame. Pregnancy had only enhanced the areas I tried to keep off the map. Trying to stuff my body into the smaller bikini made me painfully aware that I was a woman. I was wary of a wardrobe malfunction if I moved my arms too much.

Finn held his arms out to me expectantly. He was the only one in the sparsely populated pool who wore a scarf. "Come on in. I won't drop you."

"Yes, you will. You're a soldier. You're a tough love kind of guy, and I'm not ready for that. You'll let go, and I'll sink to the bottom and die. This was a bad idea. Let's just go back to the room."

Finn waded to the edge and touched my toes with his wet fingers. "I won't let go."

I shook my head, panic tight in my eyes. I remembered vividly the feeling of almost drowning. The brutality I'd witnessed under the water forced me to take a step back. "I... I forgot something upstairs." I spun on my heel and deserted Finn, Boston and Mariang in the pool. I ignored Finn calling my name and the splash of water that meant he was coming to join me. Of all the things I'd been through, this was a torture I didn't need to subject myself to. "Finn, just leave it alone."

Finn didn't say a word. He simply scooped me up like a bride and charged toward the pool, ignoring my muffled scream as he cannonballed into the deep end. Despite the fact that I wanted to punch him, I clung to Finn as the water enveloped me. He pinched my nose and pressed his open mouth to my scream, forcing air into me so I could remain in my nightmare even longer. When he spoke, I heard him clearly through my whimpering and begging him to take me up. "This is my world. I'll not have you afraid to stick your toe into it."

As the water pushed at my pores and seeped into my psyche, I fought off the panic with everything in me. I would not lose my mind. I would not think about Garrick being ripped apart. I wouldn't picture wolf Mason holding his arm like a chew toy. I wouldn't feel the fishy Mermen trying to tear off my clothes. I wouldn't feel any of it. Though the pool would disguise my tears in an act of kindness, I kept them tight inside me. Instead of losing my mind, I clung to Finn, who only held tighter to me. He sat us at the bottom of the pool, my legs straddling his waist as the pressure from the water, his grip and just plain life squeezed me for all I was worth.

I would not break.

My fiancé had just given me a black eye, but I would not break.

My other Reaper was nowhere to be found, but I would not break.

September, Garrick, Bishop and Bev were dead, but I would not break.

Allie was in a coma, but I would not break.

"I feel you bracing yourself," Finn whispered in my ear. He breathed for me, kissed my temple and then pressed his cheek to mine. "I'm keeping you anchored here until you calm down."

My teeth were gritted against the softening he tried to bring about in me, and the emotions that threatened to shatter my fragile grip on reality. "Why do you care?"

"Because I love you. I won't let you cower while I'm around. I make you stronger. That's who we are to each other. Isn't that what friends are supposed to do?"

Finn's promise swelled in me; I couldn't believe anyone could love me that much. He stood up to me and wouldn't let me punk out. Though I was a mess, he didn't see that part. He still believed I was strong, even when I couldn't feel it.

I closed my eyes and tried to find the strength he swore was there. My chin looped over his shoulder for a few seconds while that extreme devotion sunk in. "You don't know how hard it's been."

Finn didn't argue; he simply gave me more breath to hold in my lungs, to sustain me another quarter of a minute while he held me. His hand trailed down my back and lifted my tank top so he could touch my bare skin, his fingers tracing lazy circles around the base of my spine. "Then tell me. No one can hear you under the water."

I considered his offer to actually be there for me during a pretty confusing time. I wanted to confess everything, to tell him the horrible hand I'd been dealt, but I knew that would only tie me closer to Finn, which wasn't fair to him. Instead I turned my head, inched his scarf down with my chin, and pressed my lips to his gills, placing a kiss on the ripply skin. "Some other time. I'm too upside-down to make sense right now."

"But I'm your friend. You're supposed to talk to me." His hand trailed from my spine down over the curve of my backside, his thumb looping in the string of the bikini at my hip. He smirked at the goosebumps I couldn't fight off, and the tightening of my thighs that, I swear, was inadvertent. He bit his lower lip when my hips slid closer to the edge of danger, welcoming his firm body when I knew I should've been pulling away.

But I slid closer, letting him kiss the underside of my jaw, fondling my neck like it was made of a foreign texture he couldn't get enough of. "We're not supposed to do this," I warned us both, though the guilt only seemed to work like an aphrodisiac. He sucked on my shoulder while he pulled the straps of my tank top and bikini down, kissing a sensual line along the horizon of my breasts. Finn made it so easy to forget myself, forget my life, my responsibilities. His hands were experienced, and every sensation was the dawn of something I was too new at to evaluate with any sort of clarity. My heart thudded in my chest, and I'm sure he could hear every traitorous beat.

"If we're not supposed to, then why aren't you pushing me away? Maybe this is just how our friendship works." He breathed for me again, this time tugging at the clasp that held my top in place.

A breach of the water just to the left of us broke the

trance that was growing too heated too fast. Boston's curled body had done a cannonball right next to us, breaking the mood with his goofy "Nyah! I got you" face. When my bikini clasp sprung open, I yelped and clung to Finn to keep my bathing suit in place, so Boston didn't get the wrong idea.

Or you know, the spot on totally right idea of the very wrong thing I shouldn't have been doing.

Boston went back up to the surface, and Finn followed behind, deciding we could no longer ignore the others without arousing suspicion. My head broke the water and I grasped for the fresh air, pulling gallons of it into my lungs. Finn was sweet as he kept his pep talk quiet in my ear. "It's alright. See? I told you I'd get you to relax in the water. Another couple of minutes and I could've gotten you to forget all kinds of things."

"My bikini came undone!" I whispered through my thumbs up and smile at Mariang, who was paddling over to us.

Finn winced. "Oops. Take a breath." He gave me three seconds to comply and then plunged us back under, his hands making quick work of putting my swimsuit right again. He lingered, as I could've guessed he would, cupping the outer swells of my breasts and then kissing my scowl with an impish "look what I just got away with" kind of face.

He floated us back to the surface, his arms tight around me. He swam us toward the shallower end, where Mariang was still making her way toward us. "That's so amazing! Did you truly breathe for her that whole time?"

Finn nodded, rubbing my back in concentric circles. "Of course. That's easy. It's getting her to trust me that's the hard part."

"Oh, that'll come in time." Mariang made a few nervous faces with a squinched nose and gritted teeth before speaking what was on her mind. "Can you breathe for anyone like that?"

Finn's face split into a grin, and I was proud of him for shedding his Captain Finn: Tough Guy demeanor temporarily for my sister. "Only for the beautiful women who tell me I'm the king of the seven oceans."

Mariang blushed and shook her head. "Never mind. I was silly to ask."

Finn walked a few more feet until I could touch the ground on my own. Slowly he let his grip on my legs go, but I still clung to him with all four limbs. I'm pretty sure my legs had frozen in place. He softened and squeezed me, and I could practically feel his heart swelling that I'd reached for him this time – that I was now the one who couldn't let go. He smiled into my hair and pinched my backside under the water. Then he slid his thumb along the inside of my bottoms, just to feel me rock against his body. "Hey, I'll be right back. Promise. Nothing will hurt you while I'm around."

"Boy, are you going to be sorry if I drown in this pool."

Finn chuckled, took a chance and kissed my cheek in

full view of Mariang and Boston, who stiffened. "I'll be right back, *sinta*."

Finn lowered me so my feet touched the bottom, the water lapping at my ribs and making me feel unsteady. He turned and offered his hand to Mariang, who let out a slow, nervous giggle at her daring. "Danny would never let me do something like this."

Finn raised his dark blond eyebrow at her. "Well, Danny's not here, is he? It looks like you get to make the decisions. Do you want to go for a swim with the Captain of Dagat?"

Mariang had that look of wild daring in her eyes that made me all of a sudden turn into an adult. "Go slow, Finn. I mean it. She's super pregnant, so however gentle you think you're being, double it."

Boston scratched his elbow as he talked to me over his shoulder after the two disappeared below the water. "How much are we trusting him? I mean, Ezra sent you over with him as your guard, so that's something. But should I be worried he's taking my charge under the water?"

"I think it's a little late for worry now, man." I laughed as Boston sobered, paling at the possibility that he'd just handed over his sister to a dangerous Kataw. "Nah, I'm only kidding. Finn's fine. He kept me alive through Silo and Dagat. He knows the Omens have to be safe."

Boston exhaled. "Okay. How about we keep this little adventure to ourselves, yeah?"

"Alright."

Boston didn't meet my eyes as he spoke, but watched the pool's surface for Mariang's head. "So, any news on them undoing the spell Sama put on Von?"

"I think it's too soon to tell."

"That sucks."

I waded to the side of the pool and held onto the ledge to keep myself from floating away. "See? That's what I like about you. Your eloquence."

"What? It does suck. I don't like the idea of someone coming along and addling my brother's brains. I was just getting used to the idea of having you for a sister, and then Sama goes and mucks it all up."

"'Mucks it all up?' Watch your language, sailor." I tried to make light of the situation, but I was pretty sure my eye was nice and purple by now, leaving no room for denial. "I just need to know how much control Von had over himself when he hauled off and hit me."

"None of it," Boston answered, resolute.

"You're sure about that?"

"Absolutely. I mean, Danny explained it to me. And seriously, it's Von. You're truly not sure if it was him in there who hit you? Really? He's never... I know how he sorted out Dad when the lowlife raised a hand to Mum."

"You do?"

"Yeah. Bish told me. Von wouldn't stand for Mum getting knocked about. I can't imagine what must've snapped in his brain to make him do that to you. I've seen Von in all sorts of states, but I've never seen him love a woman the intense way he does you. You have no idea the way Von can sacrifice himself when he loves. I can tell you for certain that none of the man who hit you was my brother."

I met Boston's eye with a quiet understanding. "I know the sacrifice he made for you in Dagat."

Boston stiffened, staring ahead to make sure he didn't take in any more of my sincere gaze. "Does he ever talk about his time there?"

I nodded, swallowing as I remembered holding Von while he broke down in my arms in the quiet of my bedroom. "Only to me, and only when he can't take the torment anymore. It gets to him still."

Boston closed his eyes, quiet for a few seconds as I let him peek in on a vulnerable part of his Superman big brother that was usually kept concealed. "I haven't gambled a quid since that day. He said the only way I could pay him back was to graduate and make something of myself. So that's what I did."

"Von's proud of you. Says so all the time. Brags about his baby brother who can set people on edge while putting them at ease." I smirked as I pictured the crinkle Von got in the corner of his eye when he bragged about his brothers.

Boston lowered his chin, and I could tell the emotion of the moment was getting to him. I linked my fingers through his under the water and squeezed. "He's a good man, my brother. He'd give anything for the people he loves. Von always finds a way to do the right thing, even if it looks all wrong when it comes out." He shook his head, frowning. "I know none of the tosser who attacked you was him."

"You *know*, eh? I really hope you're right."

31

IT'S A DATE

Mariang's cheeks were still pink as we walked down the hall to our respective rooms. She couldn't look at Finn and darted into her hotel room quickly with a "don't ask about it" wave goodbye.

Finn's grin was telling after we dropped Boston and Mariang at their room and traveled down to ours. "What happened when you took Mariang under the water? I've never seen her cheeks so red."

Finn shrugged, but his impish smile couldn't be masked. "What? I was breathing for her. It was an honest slip."

I gaped up at him when the pieces slid into place. "You kissed her? You kissed a knocked-up, married woman? You kissed an Omen?" I shook my head at his bravado. "You're one slippery fish, Finn."

He held up his hand to declare his innocence as I

swiped us into our room with my keycard. "It really was an accident, but boy, did that spook her. She spent nearly half the time we were down there apologizing and begging me not to say anything to Danny."

"If you know what's good for you, you'll keep that promise. Danny's not all that understanding."

Finn couldn't stop smiling. "I know. Two Omens, though. Who can say they've kissed two Omens?"

"Well, Danny, I guess. He's the only one besides you." Then I had to explain my awakening, and Danny's errant kiss that had earned him a punch in the face. "It wasn't exactly romantic, or two-way." I gathered up fresh clothes and took a shower, coming out with wet hair and clean skin from the never-ending hot water and soap the hotel supplied us with. The thrum of the air conditioning unit distracted me while I flipped mindlessly through the channels on the television. I hadn't watched TV in so long; I had no idea what any of the shows were, so I turned it off after only two minutes of channel surfing.

When Finn came out from washing up, I was already making myself comfortable on the bed, sitting against the headboard with the comforter tugged over my lap. "Tired already? It's barely four o'clock in the afternoon."

I tapped my temple. "Gotta try and stay out of Sama's reach. Since Von's not going to be there to protect my mind, it's best I sleep when Sama's not expecting it."

Finn's look was filled with pity as he studied my black eye. "I forgot about that." He swore as he recalled we weren't on a lovers' vacation. "I don't know how to keep him out of your head."

"It wasn't an issue when Von and I were together." I tried to be matter-of-fact about everything to cover over my broken heart. My phone chirped, so I distracted myself with answering one of the dozens of texts Danny had sent while we were in the pool. No sooner had I pressed send to my "What crawled up your butthole" response to his "Where is everyone? Call me immediately" text did Danny see my activity and call. I rolled my eyes and answered, knowing it was best to let the guard dog do his thing than let him get himself all riled up. "What's up, Danny?"

"What's up? What's up? I've been calling you all afternoon! And Mariang hasn't been picking up either. I'm on my way to the hotel, is what's up. Where have you been?"

"Oh, jeez. In the pool. Nowhere harrowing. Just going for a swim. Mariang's probably in the shower. She's alright."

"Do you want news on Von or not?" Danny was hostile, which meant he was hungry, or just that he was awake and it was a normal day.

"Not."

That stopped him short. "What do you mean? Of course you want to know what's going on at the mansion."

I threw out my hands as I cradled the phone in the crook of my shoulder. "Seriously? Why do you even ask?"

"You pick the oddest times to be stubborn. Sama's been controlling Von."

I laid back on the bed, staring up at the stucco ceiling. "I thought we already knew that."

"We suspected, but we didn't know. It probably started shortly after... you know, the incident."

Somehow people calling it "the incident" made it all feel clinical. My daughter deserved to be remembered, so I didn't skate over it for comfort's sake. "Ah, you mean my daughter dying. Yes. I recall *the incident*."

I could practically picture Danny flinching when I refused to PC the worst moment of my life. "Yes, well. The control gets stronger over time. We're drawing out the poison now. Ezra and Kabayo, actually. They made me leave after my part."

"What was your part?"

"Blood donor. Has to be family blood for the undoing."

"Why'd they send you away after your part?"

Danny gulped audibly. "I'm not meant to see Von that way. No one should. He's... It's bad. I've got your ring here if you want it back. I didn't show it to Von, so he doesn't know you took it off. I thought you might want the chance to make an informed decision, now that you know it wasn't him that slugged you."

I swallowed, keeping my eyes on the ceiling. "Yeah. Thanks. I guess not telling Von I didn't have faith in him is a good idea."

"Hey, kid. Stop it. It's got nothing to do with your faith in him. He punched you. You had every right to take off the ring. And you don't have to take it back now. I just thought you'd like the option."

"I do. Thanks." I fished for a change of topic. "Any word from Mason yet?"

"No. He's not with you?"

"Nope. And you know how you get anxious when you're not with Mariang? I'm starting to get that same itch, being without one of my Reapers for this long."

I could hear the frown in Danny's reply. "That's troubling. I'll touch base with Ezra about that. Then I'll do an extra lap around the hotel to make sure security's in place."

"Thanks. Can I go back to the mansion and see Von?"

"No way. Undoing magic like this involved a fair amount of torture. He wouldn't want you to see him like that. You're best where you are. Maybe I can take you back tomorrow, yeah? They seem to've caught it early on, so it's not in him terribly deep."

I ended the call with Danny while Finn paced the floor, casting me intermittent glances. "You sure you want to try sleeping?" I could tell by the creases in his forehead that he was worried I would get dream raped on his watch.

I sat up against the headboard, weighing the pros and cons. "I guess I can hold off. Mainline some caffeine until Von's himself again. Danny didn't seem to think it would take more than a day or so. I can stay awake until then."

Finn exhaled with relief. "Good. I honestly wasn't sure what to do if Sama got in your head while you were asleep. I mean, it's not as if I can tell by looking at you."

"Well, how about we go visit Allie instead of hanging around in an empty room?"

"Sure. Can I drive?" Finn asked hopefully.

I cast him a withering look as I shoved on socks and shoes. "Not in this lifetime."

Finn caught my eye with a note of sincerity I wasn't expecting. "Well, then how about the next one, or the one where you're a dragon, and Ollie's a firefighter? Think I'll make it into your life then?"

The corner of my mouth lifted with the levity I found absolutely precious. "You want to be in my next life with me?"

"Whenever you'll have me, I'll be there."

I touched my heart, letting him know he brushed over my tender spots. "The next life, then. I think I played it a little safe this time around, so something with a little adventure."

Finn snorted. "Sure. Because this life is so dull."

"It's settled. You can drive the getaway car if I decide to take up a career as a bank robber."

Finn's hand rested on the small of my back. "It's a date."

We caught Danny on the way out, where he surprised me by wrapping me in an awkward hug I could tell he wasn't well-practiced in. He slipped the ring onto my finger, giving me a small smirk when it looked like he was the one proposing to me, instead of delivering his brother's ring.

Finn dried my hair with his hand while I drove the car.

He kept his hand in the tresses long after the need had passed. When I pulled into the hospital parking garage that I'd been to what seemed like a million times by now, Finn kept a hand affixed to me still. He tucked me into his side like he was the boyfriend, and I was the lucky girl on his arm. It was the most I could give him, and for the moment, it was enough.

Allie. Allie was my focus. She trumped the black eye, the Von drama, the Finn confusion and everything else.

I was expecting her quiet room with Ezra's staple yellow daisies in the vase on the table. I was not expecting Graham to stand suddenly when we interrupted the one-way conversation, nor had I anticipated the bouquet of pink and yellow roses clutched in his hands. "Oh, um, hallo, October. Captain Finn."

"Hey, Graham. I forgot I asked you to check in on her."

Graham nodded, relieved. "Yes, you did. You asked me to come here, so I did."

"And you brought Allie flowers? That's thoughtful of you."

"Seemed appropriate."

I glanced to the book on the table. "You're reading to her?"

"Just a biography of Margaret Thatcher. I didn't know what she'd like, so I brought along what I've been reading. You want I should give you two some space?"

"Could you and Finn give me just a few minutes? I wanted to talk to Allie about some private stuff." I cast my sweet brother a smile. "Thank you for reading to her. That's above and beyond. You're a good guy, Graham."

Graham looked like he wanted to debate me on my slice of alone time with my sister, but finally consented. "Of course. Captain Finn, perhaps you and I can find a coffee machine. I'm starting to nod off."

I waited until the two left and then started in on the nurse aspect of things. I checked her vitals, which hadn't changed, and then tried a few non-traditional methods of waking her – i.e., shaking her, begging her to open her eyes, and poking her side in the way I knew she'd get annoyed by. "Allie, come on. I need you to open your eyes. I need you for so many things. I mean, what's the point of having you back if you're not actually back? Is Sama in your mind? If you could just let me know how to help you, I'll do it!"

Twenty minutes of desperation gave way to me laying in the bed beside her, cuddled up the way I always did when life got too confusing or harrowing to go through alone. She used to welcome me into her bed or into her sleeping bag, and hold me while I confessed the things I didn't understand and couldn't fix. Allie would comb her dainty fingers through my hair and help me puzzle through the parts that didn't make sense. Either we found a solution together, or I'd fall asleep in the safety of her arms.

Though she couldn't brush her fingers through my hair anymore, I draped her arm across her body to rest on my ribs. It wasn't perfect, but it was the best I would get. As much as she could be, Allie was there for me, and I was there for her. I told her all about the war inside of me I couldn't make peace with – that Von was a great guy who occasionally did things I couldn't reconcile. I told her about my black eye, and how much I hated Sama for turning something so beautiful against me. "I want to go down to Terraway myself and kill him with my bare hands, so I know the job's good and done, but I know Ezra won't let me down there again."

Allie's skin was so fragile, her face too thin. "I don't like you unguarded here. Graham's with you now, but what about when he goes to sleep?" I wasn't sure if Von's paranoia had rubbed off on me, or if I'd been through too much to have an unjaded view of the world. I closed my eyes and rested my forehead to my sister's temple, wondering if she'd even recognize me when she opened her eyes. I'd changed so much; some days I barely recognized myself. "You know I'd give anything to get you back, right? Anything in the world to keep you safe." I sighed, knowing what I had to do. "I'll even put aside my pride to make sure no one snatches at you ever again. I love you, Allie. I'll take care of you."

I kissed my sister's cheek before I sat up, knowing exactly where I needed to go tomorrow night.

3 2

RED PAINT

*L*a Luna was full the next night, but I knew there would be a private room that was held every week for Judge and his entourage. I scratched at the nape of my neck after I parked in the lot. Finn watched me hesitate, and spoke to me even after I'd explained the very firm "don't speak at all" rule. "I get the feeling we shouldn't be doing whatever it is you're about to do."

"What are my rules?"

Finn ticked them off on his fingers. "No talking. No stabbing anyone. I know, I know. It's your show. Is Ezra going to be mad to find you here?"

"Ezra won't know about this. Mason and Von came with me here before, and it was all fine." I didn't tell Finn that Mason would in no way be cool with me meeting up with Judge ever again. But Mason wasn't here, so I got to call the shots.

We walked in together, Finn's hand on the small of my back. I mentally repeated Ollie's mantra of *keep your chin up, take it slow*. I clutched the package and kept my gaze forward, though my descending pride tempted my head to tilt downward. We were escorted to Judge's table in the secluded backroom, and I was glad to see Darius all cleaned up from working with Ollie to help rebuild our home. He was nothing as impressive as Judge, but not many were. The two wore pressed collared shirts and dress pants, like the Kingpin and Junior they marketed themselves as. I was surprised I hadn't interrupted a meeting with the assorted unnamed criminals they usually dined with. "Good evening, gentleman," I greeted them, hoping I came off as confident.

But I wasn't confident, and I knew Judge could smell an easy takedown a mile away.

Darius stood to greet me with a kiss to my cheek, and then snapped his fingers to the hostess to bring a chair for me. Finn stood behind me, as the sentries always did. He was a guard, and nothing more than that for this exchange. Big Mike moved toward Finn to pat him down, but I saved him the trouble. "He's carrying a knife, and you'll let him have it. He wouldn't come in with nothing. I tried, believe me. He's my security, Michael."

Big Mike frowned, but when Judge waved his hand to permit it, Mike stepped back behind Judge's chair.

Judge sat back in his seat, his ankle crossed over his knee as he watched me set the package on the table. "What do we have here? You're not returning another one of my gifts, are you?"

"I am, though only because it's a baby gift, and I'm not pregnant anymore. Didn't seem right to keep it. If my daughter had made it, I would've sent you a thank you card and kept the gift. But she didn't, so it's not right of me to keep the presents. Thank you, though. I can't actually picture you at a store picking out a breast pump."

"I had Sherita pick it out. You didn't have to return it, though, and certainly not in person." Judge's jaw was tight as he took in the scope of me. "I see your new job isn't any safer than your old one. What happened?"

"Oh, you know, flying monkeys came in through my window and attacked me. Lost the baby. Just another day."

He pointed to his eye. "That shiner's fresh. Who did it? I hope it's not the clown who put that obnoxious ring on your finger." Judge glowered disapprovingly at my engagement ring.

"It's no one you need to worry about."

Judge's tone was firm. "You'll answer me, October."

I stiffened in my chair, eyeing the red wine the waitress poured for me. I knew it would be my favorite kind. Judge didn't bother with flaws, so his taste in wine was always spot on. "It was your drug dealers who blacked my eye. All of them, in fact. You should punish them by firing your entire organization."

Judge squinted one eye at my sass. "I want a name."

"Charles Manson. Wild in bed, that one. Sex maniacs have all the good drugs."

"Seriously, baby girl. Tell me who knocked you around."

"My pimp, actually. Johnny McHerpes-Penis. He's got a thing for mouthy women. When he hits me, I know it's true love. I call him 'No! Johnny, please!' and his pet name for me is 'Shut up, skank'. Ah, young love."

Judge's eyes flared with barely contained rage. "Tell me who was stupid enough to hit you, before I lose my temper."

"Get used to disappointment. I'm not here to talk about the problems I can handle. I'm here to talk about the one I can't."

He folded his fingers over his stomach after he waved the waitress away. He waited until the door closed before he proceeded. "Tell me which problem is so big, you'd come here to talk about it."

I lowered my voice and scooted my chair in, though I could still feel Finn at my back. "It's Allie," I began, noting Darius' intake of breath. "Allie didn't leave for California a couple years ago, she was taken. We only just found her as a Jane Doe who's been laid up in a hospital all this time."

Darius swore, leaning forward and forsaking his stoic cool guy demeanor. "Which hospital? Where is she now?"

"She's in a coma at St. Martin's General just a little ways from here. Ollie got her transferred out of California as soon as we found her."

Darius leaned back in his chair, his hand over his mouth in shock. Once upon a better time, he'd been smitten with Allie. It had broken his jaded heart when she up and left us all. "Whatever you need, it's done. Medical bills? Is that what you need help with? Give her some cash, Judge. I mean it. Whatever it takes. Can I visit her?"

I chewed on my lower lip to keep it from quivering. "You loved her. I always suspected you did."

Darius didn't answer, but I saw it there. That bold determination to bust through walls and tear down whole worlds if it would make Allie breathe a little easier. "What are the doctors saying?"

I drew on what I knew from Philip's confessions. "She was raped. I don't know how often. She got pregnant, but lost the baby, like me. The guy who... he messed her up. She's got brainwaves, but her mind can't connect with her body. There's hope, but not much."

Darius' hand on his mouth stifled a noise of distress. "Who is this guy?" When I didn't answer, he stood, towering over me with his knuckles on the table. "Don't you dare play games with me, Bait. I want a name! I want an address, and I want his head on a platter!"

I don't recall Darius ever yelling at me before. It was a testament to how much he cared for Allie that he would raise his voice to me to get closer to her.

Finn's hand on my shoulder acted as a pillar for me to lean on if I needed it, but it also served as a beacon to Darius that nobody was allowed to yell at me.

I swallowed, patting Finn's hand on my shoulder. "I only just found my sister, Darius. Don't you think if I knew who or where this guy was, he wouldn't already be six feet under? Everything I know is from the medical reports." Yes, that was a lie, but I couldn't very well tell Darius about Sama without him checking me into the Loony Bin. "Allie's the only one who can tell us who did this, but she's stuck in her coma."

Darius sunk back down, his hands shaking with rage and heartbreak. "All this time?"

I nodded, my face stony. "All this time."

Judge was still sitting back in his chair, watching me with feigned stoicism. "Why did you come here?" he asked quietly, and with no trace of anger. He knew that the only thing that could make me toss my rules and my pride out the window was my family.

I didn't think I could feel any lower, but as I sat at the table with the brothers, I felt a whole other layer of degradation weighing me down. "I'm here because I need a favor. The flying monkeys who messed me up? Well, they're pretty ruthless. I'm not the safest person to be around, but I can't sleep knowing Allie's alone in the hospital. To be honest, it's only a matter of time before the people who are after me start gunning for her." I closed my eyes to stave off the mental image of the miscellaneous residents of Terraway who operate on Sama's orders coming for Allie. What would they do to her body? I swallowed down my anxiety. "Ollie and I are doing our best, but we were doing our best to keep my daughter safe, and we f-failed." I froze, horrified that I might cry in front of Judge. I waited until I could stuff my emotions back down before opening my mouth again. I balled my toes inside my shoes until I felt the avalanche of tears recede. "If you could spare a couple guys to watch her room for us, that would be a tremendous help. You don't have to, of course. I just didn't know who else to turn to. I'm sort of running out of people who I know can get the job done."

I shook my head, my chin still pointing toward the ground in defeat. I couldn't believe it had come to this – that I was here, asking Judge for help. The sudden stripping of my pride made me feel bereft of dignity. I felt as if the people outside our private backroom, clinking their water goblets and shuffling their truffle-laden, rich people food with gold forks, could see that I'd lost everything. I felt naked, and very much aware of my imperfections.

My voice was small, and I felt diminished along with it. "I can't fail this time. I already lost my daughter to these guys. I can't lose Allie, Judge. Whatever you want, I'll do it. I can deliver messages to your guys on the inside, if that's what you need. I don't care anymore. I just need my sister to be safe."

Darius waved off my offer and pulled out his phone. "It's done. You don't owe us anything." His eyes turned threatening as he cut over to his older brother. "Not a thing. You shouldn't hesitate to come to us with this stuff. You've got enough to worry about. You'll stay with one of us." He held up his hand to stave off my protest. "I don't want to hear it. You were attacked, lost your daughter, and now Allie's in a coma? No." When I started to speak, Darius barked at me. "I saw your house, Bait! I saw your bedroom, and the massacre that happened there. There was blood everywhere! I can't believe you survived!"

My head darted to the side, hoping the red walls were decently soundproofed. "Will you stop shouting 'blood'? I get that I'm in deep, but it's too late for me. I'm in it." I was an Omen now; Terraway had me until my body decided I couldn't keep up with this life anymore. Then I'd move onto the next life, where I could be a high-stakes bank robber, with Bruce Campbell as my sidekick. Good old Bruce wouldn't mind that I'd been super damaged. He'd have faith in me. He'd look into my soul and call me "sweetheart", and somehow the blackness that had set in deep would remember the sweetness I'd long given up on.

"What is 'it'? What game are you in that we don't know about?" Darius' eyes drifted up to Finn with a silent threat.

I hung my head. "I need help watching Allie. That's all. I came here because I know you won't take chances with her safety."

Judge was silent. Too silent. He watched me debase myself, offering up my services and what was left of my pride to save my sister. He watched me while I wrote down Allie's hospital room number and slid it over to Darius, who didn't waste a second. He made a single phone call that absconded with thirty percent of the stress in my life. "Thank you, Darius. Truly. I didn't know where else to go."

"You should always come to me with this stuff. I'll go see Allie tomorrow first thing, and in the next half hour, there'll be guys posted there around the clock until she wakes up. I don't care how long it takes."

I gusted out my relief. "Thank you. That's all I needed." I took a drink of my wine before gearing up for the big blow. "So, what's this going to cost me?"

Darius waved off my assumption that they only did favors to get favors, but I knew better.

Judge drew a circle on the white linen tablecloth with his dark brown finger. "You'll let my men put a tracker on your car, and you'll keep it there until I say so. I'll send you a phone tomorrow that you'll use instead of the one you have now."

I nodded, taking my punishment without a fight. I knew Judge. I knew him before he was the great man on a throne. I knew him when his mama taught me how to make applesauce in her kitchen. I knew him when I'd caught him washing blood off his hands with the garden hose behind his house. He'd been a teenager back then, and I was barely five. "You told me it was paint," I said quietly, finally meeting Judge's penetrating stare.

Judge quirked an eyebrow at me, letting me know my comment had caught him off-guard. "What was paint?"

"When I saw you washing the blood off your hands behind Mama McCray's house. You told me to go back inside with Darius and Ollie. You told me you'd spilled red paint. I knew what it was, but I never told anyone." I held his gaze, unable to hide my sadness. "Maybe I should've."

"It wouldn't have changed anything. And I told you that to protect you, not so you'd end up here with a black eye." His jaw tightened every time his gaze fell on my shiner.

I hugged my middle, forlorn and completely without the pride that I'd needed so badly before this moment. "I've spilled a lot of paint lately. Don't bring more of it to my doorstep. I'm begging you."

Judge stood slowly, and with too much menace. "You're begging me?"

I paused at the acrid medicine that I wanted to resist. I had no choice but to swallow it down with a wince. "Yes, Judge."

"Are you a beggar now? That's who you've become?" He held my gaze as he motioned for me to move toward the back exit with him. Darius remained in his seat, turning his head from me.

I knew that exit let out into the alley. That was Judge's alley, and there was red paint all over it from years of taking too many meetings exactly like this one. I swallowed hard and followed him, my head down and my shoulders tight. *Judge wouldn't hurt me*, I told myself, forcing truth into my fear. I don't know why my hands were clammy. I don't know why my legs were trembling as I looked down at my shoes when we made it out into the crisp night air. I saw cars breaking the speed limit on the street at the end of the long alley. The drivers spent a good few seconds honking at each other to fight over who could be the biggest jackwagon on the road. The brick buildings that sandwiched us in made me feel claustrophobic. I could smell urine, and there were several fresh blood stains on the concrete.

Finn stood beside me, keeping silent, but making it clear that no one was going to hoist my lifeless body into the dumpster on his watch. It's a good friend who doesn't let you get thrown away. Big Mike stood behind Judge, waiting for the command to let loose on me.

I shifted hesitantly as I stood before Judge, hugging my middle and trying to simply stand under his intense brand of scrutiny. He'd always been able to see through my raised chin and forced confidence, so I didn't feel the need to put on the show of bravery this time.

Finn hissed when Judge tucked his finger under my chin and lifted it so he could see my shame under the solitary light of the moon. His dark eyes were hard, angry and menacing. His voice was low, and he spoke through gritted teeth. "I don't ever want to hear you beg for anything ever again. Do you understand? You'll break what's left of me. I raised you better than begging." He kissed my cheek and brought me into his embrace. Judge was tall, solid and hugged exactly as one might expect – like a man who didn't do it often. He didn't use to be this unpracticed at it; his arms used to be my safe place. One by one, life had ripped my safe places away, until I barely recognized the bones of a structure that used to feel like home.

"What is this? What's happening?" I asked, confused and rigid.

Finn stiffened, his hand on my shoulder to rip me away if the need arose.

Judge snarled at Finn, but kept his voice low to me. "This is a hug, and it's all that's keeping me from yelling at you, and turning your friend's hand into an ashtray." It took him a solid four seconds after Finn removed his hand from me before the embrace softened into something tender. The familiar motion of holding me came back to him the longer he permitted himself the indulgence. "The trackers are so I know where you're at. I saw your house. You were attacked, lost a baby, and you're still getting knocked around. The trackers are because I love you. If things had been different... You were a sister to me before things started changing in my neighborhood. I turned you guys away that last time Ollie brought you by because it was too dangerous for you to come to my street anymore. The trailer next to ours had been lit up in a drive-by the night before. All I could see was your little body splayed out on the concrete. I knew I couldn't let you come back." He shook his head, as if he was trying to clear his imagination of the mental picture that still haunted him. "I've always been looking out for you. You just stopped learning how to let me."

I remembered that last day we visited the McCray

house. It was burned in my mind as the last time I'd been able to see Mama McCray. Judge had told Ollie to get lost, that there was no more food for housework available, and that if he saw us again on his property, he'd make sure no one saw me ever again. I couldn't help the confusion in my eyes that shone up into his. "I didn't understand how you could let us starve like that. I still don't."

The catch in his voice tripped up his usually stoic deportment. "You should know me better by now. There's always more to me than what I say. I sent you away because you're precious to me." He kissed my forehead, and I could feel the regret and emotional turmoil that still wrecked him.

My hand climbed up between us so I could hold onto his crisp, unwrinkled shirt, keeping him close before he inevitably pushed me away again. The information swirled around in my psyche, spinning my worldview on its end, and painting Judge in a less damning light. It wasn't quite a halo that beamed on his brow now, but it was a degree of difference I desperately needed. Part of me probably could've worked out his true intentions, but the hurt rang deeper than reason could reach. "You should've told me the truth, Judge. You broke my heart."

I could feel Finn's penetrating glare. It was as if he was dissecting how Judge got me to admit I had a heart, and then got close enough to break it, while still managing a hug out of the deal. I had no answers for him; Judge and I made little sense to anyone, least of all me.

"I had to push you out, baby girl. Just like how you're breaking my heart now, giving me the bare minimum information. You're keeping me away from whatever danger you're up against, because you love me. No matter how much you hate me, you're trying to protect my family by keeping us at arm's length." He held tight to my hand, placing an earnest kiss to my knuckles. "You don't have to do that for me, baby girl."

I gazed up into his midnight eyes that always seemed to see right through me. "I'm scared," I admitted in a whisper. "I'm trying to fix it all, but it keeps breaking the more I touch it. Everything I love gets broken."

Judge leaned down and pressed his cheek to mine, and I could hear the vulnerable pang of emotion in his lengthy inhale. His free hand rubbed my back to warm the parts of me that had grown cold over time. He cleared his throat when a car alarm went off down the street. "The phone's so you can call me if there's too much red paint, and you don't know what to do."

I was confused that he wasn't lording his newfound power over me. "Be real with me, Judge. What do you want for this? I'd rather know now."

Judge swayed gently, rocking me slowly from side to side as he pondered. The cars cruising by on the street at the end of the alley didn't notice my heart thudding, but it felt like the organ rattled around in my chest with all the subtlety of a gong. Judge's embrace invoked nostalgia that was painful; I tried never to remember how much I'd once trusted him; how much I'd adored Judge back when I was a child who didn't know any better. "You used to dance while standing on my toes. You probably don't remember that, but I do. You wanted to learn how to 'waltz and mango'. Took me forever to learn the waltz and the tango, but Allie taught me the basics enough to dance with you. Patience of a saint, that girl."

A soft smile played on my lips. "'Waltz and mango'? Dang, I don't know how you ever said no to me. That's adorable."

"It was." He surprised me when his body straightened, his shoulders rolled back, and he held my arm out to the side. Without knowing how, I fell into a slow, three-count box step when his right foot moved with purpose. I glided back when Judge stepped forward, and parried with his steps without having to look down. His grin was wide when he took in my stunned expression. Something inside of me knew how to dance, as if my heart had suppressed a memory my muscles still clung to. "See? Part of you remembers. From day one, you had me dancing like a fool, just to make sure you smiled. It kills me to see all my hard work flushed down the drain. You don't look like you've been happy in a while."

Finn cleared his throat, bringing me back to the present from my haze of childhood bliss. "Let's wrap this up, October."

I lost my footing, and stopped the dance. I expected Judge to release me from the hold, but he fell back into the soothing hug I didn't want to admit I still needed. He drew my head to his chest, proving beyond a shadow of a doubt that he did still have a heart, jaded as it now was. His voice was quiet, but had that steady power to it that warned me not to argue. "I want you to call me every time you go back to the prison. If you're going there, you'll deliver messages for me, and you'll do it without a fight until Allie wakes up."

I swallowed the bitter pill. "Okay. If I'm already going there, sure."

"Second on the list is that if we need a nurse, you'll come when we call."

Finn shook his head. "No. You negotiate one favor for one favor, not an endless litany of requests."

I stiffened in Judge's arms. "I can help you and Darius, sure. And of course, Terence, once he gets paroled. But I have no interest in cleaning your victims up so you can drag out the fun. Not enough gauze in the world for the sadist I know you are."

The corner of Judge's mouth lifted. "See that? You're being stubborn again. I thought I'd lost you forever."

I shrugged. "I guess I'm still in here. Good to know. It's been a long one."

"The most I've ever enjoyed fighting with anyone's been with you. Watching you surrender like that? That's not the scrappy little kid in pigtails I knew. If you need help, we can help. But I don't have the stomach to watch you beg for anything ever again. I've seen what happens to people who waste their time begging instead of planning." He clutched me tight to his firm chest. Though he seemed in control of the situation, I could feel his quickened heartbeat. I couldn't trust his words, but his heart? Judge was scared for me. Judge didn't do scared, but he bent his armor for me. He looked down on me with a tightened jaw. "Promise me. No more begging."

My face tilted upward to look into his dark, foreboding eyes. "The next time I need help, I won't beg. I'll hold your head underwater until you give me what I want, like the good little girl you love."

Judge laughed, and the levity finally touched his eyes. "That's my girl, right there. You're right. I do love you."

Judge kissed my good cheek and then gripped me so tight, it squashed the air from my lungs. I yelped when he gave my bruised eye several hard flicks. Pain ricocheted through my face, and I panicked when I found I couldn't get away from it. His backhand didn't have space for a windup, but the smack stung me on too many levels when his knuckles cracked across my purple cheekbone. I cried out in confusion and pain, wondering how I'd gotten so comfortable in the viper's arms.

Finn could only be expected to be decoration for so long. He ripped me out of Judge's embrace, drawing his knife as he put himself between us. "And now you die."

Big Mike drew his gun, and I knew no good would come from this. I held up my hand to still Finn's temper, my fingers touching his fingers over the hilt of his blade. "No, Finn! I've got this under control. Please."

Finn glowered down at me. "Clearly. Wrap this up, before I lose my patience. You stand right next to me, and don't take a step closer. He touches you again, he loses a hand."

With angry swipes, I rubbed my face as I turned to Judge. "Ow! What'd you do that for? That hurt me, you jag!"

Judge reached for his gun to fend off Finn's temper. I inched between the two alphas, hoping for the best when Big Mike finally lowered his gun on Judge's command. Judge held his weapon at his side, but I knew he could aim and fire without warning. His voice was clear, and not apologetic, as I thought he should be. "Whatever you're a part of that's wrecking your life? You should get out now. Remember that sting from me smacking your eye, and get as far away from it as you can. Anything that bangs you up, run the other way."

I scowled at him. "That's not the advice you'd give Darius. You only bring him closer to the danger."

Judge shrugged, letting me know that he didn't need to explain himself any further. "Goodnight, baby girl. I'll be in touch."

33

BEATEN DOWN AND TIRED

Though it had been a full two days since I'd left the mansion, I hadn't slept. Ezra finally deemed it safe for me to return to the mansion, and I couldn't get there fast enough. I felt unanchored, ungrounded and totally out of my skin. I'd gone to the McCray brothers for help. Clearly, I was off my rocker.

"Ezra?" I called through the vast home. When he didn't answer right away, I panicked. I ran through the main floor of the mansion, scared that while I'd been gone, someone had ripped my lifeline away. "Ezra!"

The hurried footsteps pounded up the steps from the basement, and Ezra met me in a borderline violent hug we both needed. "I'm here. I'm sorry, dear. I was cleaning up the basement. Are you alright?" He winced when he took in my face. "Oh, it's quite purple now. Do you need some ice?"

"I'm fine. I barely feel it."

Finn guffawed from the doorway. "She's lying, I hope you know. She's lying and she's crazy. I don't have it in me to tell you what kind of company your daughter keeps." Finn was exhausted from staying up with me to make sure I didn't fall asleep. "If everything's set here, I'm heading back to Dagat. Is Mason back yet?"

Ezra shook his head. "No. No word from him, either. But go on home and rest, Captain. I'll handle the Omens and Reapers from here. Thank you for helping us."

Finn nodded, and cast me a tired smile, jerking his chin to the door so we could say goodbye without my father's watchful eye. "We did it," he said quietly. "We made it through that whole time together without kissing. I think this means we're actually friends."

I nodded, covering my mouth to stifle a yawn. "You only get to kiss one Omen per weekend, and I guess it was Mariang's turn." I giggled deviously at his wide, mischievous grin. "I'm teasing you. We totally did it. I feel like we climbed a hurdle or something. Look at us – two grownups. Thanks for being cool. I wasn't doing so hot. You being good to me? It really helped. And thanks for not stabbing Judge."

Finn's smile dropped into a frown of dismay. "I thought when we got to this point, I wouldn't still want you, but I do." He tapped his heart, as if the steady organ pained him with its betrayal. "How do I make it stop feeling like this?

You've had a free will and a shiny conscience longer than I have."

My hopeful smile at our budding friendship fell into disrepair. "It might feel like that for a little while longer. It's my fault. I clung too hard in the pool. I see something safe, and I squeeze too tight. It's my perpetual downfall, and I'm sorry I clung too hard to you. It's unfair, what I've done." I shook my head at myself. "That pain in your chest? I did that. It's *my* conscience that was defunct in all of it. I can do better the next time I see you."

"So, the goal is for me to stop loving you?" His face twisted into a grimace. "How is that better?"

"Maybe it's not, but it's necessary." I let Finn kiss my unmarked cheek, his lips lingering on my skin to feel the heat that rose at his touch. I stepped back, trying to be firm with both of us. "I'll see you at the next council meeting. Thanks for keeping me safe."

Finn's eyes bathed me in too much tenderness. "Don't you know? 'If you live, then I breathe.'" Before I could respond, Finn up and vanished into thin air.

That's right. I made it through a whole weekend with him and didn't kiss him once. I rock at self-control now. Like, I rock with rocks that rock.

I'm so freaking tired.

I wandered into the kitchen, where Ezra was waiting with a tightness to his posture. "Von?" I inquired. "He's back to normal?"

"He's himself again, though slightly less so. The

process of undoing what Sama did to him was quite grueling. You might want to save the important talks for tomorrow. He's quite under the weather."

"Okay. Thanks, Dad. I'm safe up there with him?"

"I daresay Von's the safest man in the world for you to be around right now. He's quite beside himself with what he did while he was being controlled." Ezra's hand on my back directed me toward the stairs. "Von's in your room washing up."

"You alright? You look pretty beat yourself."

Ezra nodded, the bags under his eyes showing off his exhaustion that matched mine. I wondered when the last time he'd slept was. "Take it easy with Von, darling. See if you can get him to eat, and then the two of you get some rest."

I turned and engulfed Ezra in a hard hug that had the last of my energy and too much emotion laced into the embrace. "I love you, Ezra. You're the best dad a girl could ask for. Thank you for putting Von back together."

Ezra was startled at my sudden declaration, and then softened in my grip. He squeezed me, tucking my head under his chin. "I love you too, my dear. Now run upstairs and get some rest. And be gentle with Von."

I nodded into his chest, silently relieved that Ezra confirmed Von had no control over his meltdown. I tripped twice on the way up the stairs, and stumbled into my bedroom just as the shower turned off. "Hallo?" Von called from the bathroom. "Is someone in the room?"

"Just me and the Abominable Snowman. I figured you missed sleeping as a threesome, so I brought in a wild monster. That's okay, right? He's cold now, sure. He's made of snow. But wait until he warms to you. Absolutely melts, the puppy."

The silence that greeted me wasn't all that reassuring. "You're back, then?"

"Of course. I live here, apparently. Come on out. I want to run something by you. I had a little talk with Judge that I think might fix a few things for now." I locked our door so we could have some privacy, and flopped on the bed that called out to me.

I stared up at the ceiling, my body jittery from all the coffee, but I was still exhausted because, let's face it, coffee can only be expected to do so much.

I heard the bathroom door open, but was too tired to get up, so I waited for Von to come to me. I addressed the ceiling as I spoke. "And no matter what I say, your job is to be like, 'October, that's the most amazing plan I've ever heard. Brilliant. Pip-pip. Cheerio. Bangers and mash.'" My impression of his accent was slightly less than stellar, but I made no apologies. When Von didn't laugh, I turned my head toward him and gasped at the sight that greeted me. "Von! Oh, what happened to you?"

My exhaustion took a backseat as I sat up and swung my legs over the side of the bed. I stumbled toward him, my fingers finding welts and bruises peppering his face. I tried to make sense of the drastic change he'd undergone in a weekend. Most shocking of all was his hair – or lack thereof. "You cut off your hair!"

Von closed his eyes and dipped his chin downward as my fingers fluttered over his face and half-inch long black hair. He inhaled the scent of my palm with torment painting his features, as if it pained him to have me this close. "Never thought I'd miss a smell this much. Your hand sanitizer. Smells just as I remembered it." He seemed to recall himself and took a step back. "You shouldn't be here."

I stiffened. "I should be exactly where I want to be. I want to be with you, so that's where I am."

"But I blacked your eye. I must've seemed completely mental! Please tell me you're back because you understand that I was touched in the head. Tell me you have more self-respect than to come back to a bloke who hits you."

"Of course. Ezra and Danny explained it all to me. Sama was controlling you. I'm not mad at you for something you didn't mean to do."

"Tell me you left me," he whispered, the pain in his closed eyes spreading across his face. I hated when Von was in pain. He was so much better with a smile. "Tell me I know your strength."

I nodded, my forehead pressed to his. "I gave your ring to Danny, but he brought it back once they figured out you were being controlled. I don't want to break it off if it wasn't you who hit me. It wasn't you, was it?"

A tear dribbled out from the corner of Von's eye and

drooled down his cheek, his lower lip trembling. "On my mum's honor, I would never raise a hand to you. I'm so sorry my hand raised itself and struck you. I saw myself doing it all, but I couldn't stop it! I love you, November. I would never..."

I pressed a closed-mouth kiss to his repentant and trembling lips. "Shh. I know the rest. Now what happened to your face? Who do I have to pound on for beating you so badly?"

"Oh, most of that's just me again. Sama must've realized he was losing his hold on my mind, so he made me start to trounce myself. Tried knocking myself out on the jail cell bars in the basement."

"That's horrible!" I kissed his face all over, slowly and gently so I didn't press too hard on any of his bruises. "Sama made you cut off your hair, too?" I led him to the bed and sat him down, leaning his forehead to my chest as I stood between his legs and held him, rubbing soothing circles into his back.

"No, I did that. The Manas snatched my hair to give to Sama. Thought I'd keep this from happening ever again. My father hits women, not me! I don't do this!" He clung to me, his tears falling into my shirt. "Tell me I'm not that bastard."

"Of course not. I knew it couldn't be you." I held him tighter, my heart breaking for his inner turmoil as he cried silently into my breasts. "When was the last time you ate anything?"

"I bit Ezra. Does that count?"

"No. He probably only tastes like tea and crumpets." That earned a humorless snort from him, which I considered a small victory. "Let me get you something. What do you want?"

"I don't want to eat. I couldn't stomach a bite."

"Well, you're going to stomach several bites. You're shaking. I'll be right back."

Von held onto my hand, holding me in place for a moment longer. "I would've understood if you'd left me. And you were with Finn, too. If you kissed him, I understand."

I smiled with pride that made me stand a little straighter. "Thanks, but I didn't kiss Finn. I only kiss vampires now. I'm engaged, after all."

Von kissed the ring on my finger, his lips damp from his own tears. "Hurry back, Mrs. Brady."

Leave it to Von to say the perfect thing.

I returned a few minutes later with a plate of cut up fruit, cheese, crackers, bottled waters and a blood bag. "You miss me?" I asked in lieu of anything else to say that might cut the tension.

"You shouldn't be here. You should go to your house for a while. I hit you. You're letting me off the hook too easily." Von was in gym shorts and a green t-shirt, still sitting on the bed and looking like a wild animal who'd been coerced into domestication.

"Oh, I plan to punish Sama right good when I get my

hands on him. You didn't do it, Von. I know who to punish. Had you been the one behind the wheel, it would've been you catching my wrath. Now you get to help me plan his inevitable demise."

Von snorted. "I can get behind that plan."

I pressed a strawberry to his lips, softening when Von looked up at me through thick lashes as he reluctantly let me feed him. "Scoot over. I'm exhausted. What do you say we eat and then take a nap?"

"You're just saying that because I'm tired. You don't have to do this. You're being too nice to me."

"*Now* who's being too nice? I'm barely upright, Von. I haven't slept since the last time we were in bed together. I could use a nap where I'm not afraid Sama's going to infiltrate my dreams. And I need food, come to think of it."

Von picked up a grape from the plate in my hands and fed it to me, a flicker of longing crossing his features. He pulled the covers down and moved to sit on his side of the bed, patting the empty spot beside him, and looking like the sexiest man on earth with an invitation like that. His back pressed against the headboard while his eyes danced over my form. "You really trust me after what I did?"

I snuggled in beside him, tugging the comforter over our laps, and setting the plate across my thighs, so I could feed him a piece of cheese. "I really do. If you say it wasn't you, then it wasn't you. Honestly, after all we've been through, I feel like we need to take a little time to be normal. After we sleep, could we try being boring for a while?"

He picked up a strawberry and fed it to me. "I long for nothing else lately. I still can't believe I hit you. And Danny, too. And the days leading up to that were wonky, as well. What must you have thought when you came home to bags of socks and lotion? Why didn't you send me packing for the Loony Bin right then and there?"

"We were grieving. I think that's the time to be a little irrational. It was sweet. Sama was controlling you back then?"

"He was starting to. Thought he could turn you against me by making me all clingy and manic. He knows you well, Peach. He wanted you to leave me of your own voli-tion. When that didn't work, he resorted to force." Von winced. "I could feel his emotions toward the end. He didn't like the idea of hitting you. Whatever else he's up to, he wants a baby, and he wants you. I didn't think the bastard capable of actual feelings, but he's got them for you, sure enough."

I shuddered and pulled the comforter to my chest. "Oh, good. I was hoping to be creeped out right before bed."

We finished off the plate of food, the water and the blood bag, and then settled into the mattress. Von looked foreign to me with bruises on his face and his head shaved. I'd loved his wild hair, and cursed Sama for making Von cut off one of the things I adored about him.

Von was reluctant to hold me, but after a few minutes

of polite handholding under the covers, our bodies found a way to bridge the gap between the things we wanted to be true and the things that were. Our legs tangled in the sheets, craving the solace we knew would be waiting for us. As we sought comfort in the one failsafe we always came back to, I realized that no matter what life handed us, Von and I would always find a way to tease and tangle ourselves in the beautiful web of each other.

34

OUR ODD LITTLE FAMILY

After a few days of resting and recuperating, Von and I decided it was time to go back to work. Mariang was in her final month, so we decided to give her an extended maternity leave with Danny, reaping so she didn't have to. Graham joined us, since Mason still had not come home. While Graham couldn't reap for me, he pulled as we walked through the hospice to give Von a little break. Our faces were back to normal, but our spirits were sufficiently broken. When Von suggested we call it a day after five reaps, I didn't even argue. Ollie had given me the all clear to come home that evening after work, and I couldn't get there fast enough.

I wasn't sure what to expect, but perhaps I should've anticipated the whole crew would want to be there for the unveiling of the house they'd worked so hard to redeem and give back to us. Their cars were lined up down our street, and I knew they were all patiently waiting inside.

I stood on the porch with Graham and Von, admiring the porch swing that looked handmade, facing out at the street. It was gorgeous, and could fit three easily. "I can't believe this thing. It's incredible. Someone made this, for sure."

Graham tapped the back of the swing. "The top plank has a message here for you."

I came around, shifting close to Graham to read the inscription that had been burned into the wood. *For my wife to rest her weary head upon. With much affection, Prince Langgam.*

My intake of breath couldn't be helped. It had been a year ago that Lang had fake proposed to me, promising to build me a porch swing if I delivered the stone to his land first. I'd forgotten all about the promise, dismissing it as a joke until the tease materialized as an actual porch swing in front of my house. "I can't believe he did this. That's the sweetest thing."

"Can I say I'm not thrilled with princes from foreign countries calling you their wife?" Von jabbed, only half kidding.

"You can say whatever you like, but I'm keeping the swing. It's perfect." I looked to the guys. "You ready to see the house?" The three of us held hands on the porch. I inhaled a steadying breath and plastered a lively smile on my face before opening the door.

We were greeted with hugs, kisses, music, beer and pizza as everyone took turns squeezing me around the ribs, and slapping Von on the back. No one mentioned September, or the fact that Allie was still lying in the hospital with no end in sight. That evening was for celebrating – my friends had given me my home back, and for that, I loved them.

Even Darius came for the unveiling – he'd done more than his fair share of the work. He nodded to me when I came in, tapping a brand new cell phone with a hint of meaning before hugging me so he could slip it into my pocket. "Just to keep you safe," he assured me. I had my doubts, and made a mental note never to talk Terraway business on that phone.

Ollie was in his element, and couldn't stop grinning. He took his time going through the house and pointing out who fixed each part that had once been so very broken. "This one's not your room anymore," he informed me, pointing to my bedroom door. "This is my room now. I thought since Von and your dog would be staying here, you three should have the bigger bedroom."

It was Ollie's sweet way of making sure I didn't have to sleep in the same room I'd lost September in. The tour stopped right there as I sunk into my brother's arms. "I love you for this."

"As you should. I'm nothing if not loveable." When I didn't let go at his shtick, he squeezed me tighter, smiling when Gabby flitted by and smacked my backside.

Graham was busy gorging himself on half a pizza in the kitchen, while Von and I perused Ollie's new room. It barely looked like the place our worst nightmare had unfolded. Ollie's headboard was pressed up against the window, and behind the wood, I noticed thin black bars across the glass. My smile sank when I realized I now lived a life where bars on the windows were necessary. Ollie seemed to understand the sad song my deflated shoulders sang. "It's temporary. Until everything settles down. This way we can sleep without worrying about anything crashing through our windows."

"It's smart," I complimented him. "I'm just sorry this is your life."

Ollie raised his chin, elbowing me so I did the same. "I'm not sorry. Reeses don't fall to pieces, remember? If you're in it, so am I. Best of luck to whoever thinks they can go up against us."

I found my smile again and wore it for Ollie. He showed Von and me to Allie's room, which had been given a fresh coat of cheery yellow paint and new linens with daisies on them for when she awoke.

When, not *if*.

The bathroom had been refurbished with new fixtures that were brushed steel – the kind Ollie wanted when we first moved in, but had been too expensive way back then on our much smaller budget.

"You ready to see your brand new room?" Ollie asked with too much excitement in his voice. The others were milling about the living room. Gabby was trying to start a dance-off with Rachel and Jessica, while Jordan was halfway to losing his third hand of poker at the kitchen table with a few of the guys.

I don't know why I was nervous, but I held tight to Von's hand when Darius flung the door open to Ollie's old bedroom. My jaw dropped as Ollie ushered us inside, not registering a word my brother said as I took in the giant king-sized sleigh bed with a dark wood head and foot-board. "How did you... Is this..." Half-sentences raced through my head, but no whole ideas sprang from my mouth.

"When did you have time to do all this?" Von finally worked out, just as shocked as I was. "Did you build a bookshelf into the wall?"

Ollie slung his arm over Von's shoulders and lowered his voice. "We did. I figured you and Mason could use a few shelves for your stuff. Make it feel like your home, too, which it is."

Von was touched. He turned into Ollie's half-embrace to seal it into a whole hug of unfettered affection. "Cheers, brother. This is incredible. Truly."

Ollie held tighter to Von, clapping him a few times on the back in that unshakeable dude way that choked me with emotion. "You *are* my brother, Von. I always wanted one of those."

Two lavender walls were accented by two cream walls, and on the wall opposite the one our bed was pushed up against was a large framed picture of the three of us. I studied the image of Von and me sitting on the old couch in our living room, with wolf Mason's maw resting protectively on my thigh. My fingers were tangled in his thick gray fur, and his eyes were closed contentedly. I don't even remember anyone taking the picture, but there we were. Von was grinning with his eyes closed, while his lips rested on my temple with the smirk I loved. I looked... It was the strangest thing to see myself with a contented smile on my face. My happiness wasn't forced, and neither was Von's. It was our odd little family, and in the middle of my home, I found us there.

I tangled my fingers through Von's, and he squeezed my hand. "I know. I miss Mason, too," he whispered to me.

"He should've been back by now."

Von looked down at me and kissed my temple the same way he had done in the picture. "I'll see what I can do about bringing him home. Let me talk to Ezra."

"Thank you." I turned to examine it all, taking in the TV mounted to the wall above the desk. "What do you think of our new room?"

A smile I hadn't seen on Von in what felt like ages breezed over his lips, reviving so many things that had for too long been dormant. "I think that bed looks a bit too new. What's say you and I break it in when your friends are gone?"

"I love you," I breathed, missing the grin I'd lived too much of my life without.

"Oh, yeah? You might have to prove it. I'm not sure I believe that dreamy look in your eye when you gaze up at me like I'm your hero."

"You *are* my hero," I echoed with a shy smile.

A low rumble of desire started in Von's chest. "I don't think I can wait until your friends leave us, love."

Ollie didn't need to be asked to give us some space; he shut us in the bedroom so we could acquaint ourselves with the new bed, and the lock on the door.

35

DANCING WITH DANNY

"I don't understand why I can't go. I mean, it's Sombi, which is basically deserted, except for zombies."

Ezra was frustrated with my stubborn streak as we sat around the dining room table in the mansion. "And you don't see the problem with that? I'll not send my daughter into a land filled with zombies."

"Hello, I fought just fine against an army of them with Finn and Kabayo."

Clearly this was the wrong thing to say. Ezra narrowed his eyes at me and set his fork down. "Rethink your argument, young lady. This isn't something you simply waltz into. If Mason's not back yet, there's a reason. I've never known him to dawdle when there's work to be done."

Von sat back in his chair, his arms crossed over his chest, as if the whole conversation bored him. "You want to help me out, here?" I asked him. "Mason's ours, and you're just going to let him keep being lost?"

Von shrugged, and then started tapping his fingers on the table lazily. "Ezra's the boss. Sooner you learn that, the happier you'll be. This is what it is to have a dad, love."

I scowled at Von as Graham, Alton and Boston made plans with Ezra, discussing where they would go searching for Mason first. That night, Von insisted we sleep at our house, not the mansion, which was probably best. I didn't appreciate being "you tiny little woman'd" out of the search party. Being in a different house kept me from shooting daggers at Ezra, who couldn't have cared less that I was pissed.

Von was distracted that night as we got ready for bed. The search party consisted of his brothers (all except for Danny), and they were to leave in two days when Kabayo had time to port them down into Terraway and escort them through Sombi.

When the doorbell rang at ten o'clock at night, I was expecting maybe Gabby, and a group ready to mess up the house they'd just put back together. Instead it was Danny, hands in his pockets and scowl on his face. "You got an extra room I can stay in?" he asked gruffly.

"Um, sure. Everything alright?"

I'd barely stepped back from the doorway when Danny brushed past me. "It's fine. What, we're the perfect couple? We're not allowed to have a row?"

"Well, you're not allowed to leave her unattended. That

much I know. You want me to send Von to take your place for the night and watch her?"

Danny scoffed. "Please, I didn't leave my charge unattended. Alton is staying with her. And I didn't *leave*-leave her. I just want one whole night where I don't have to hear her complain that I won't learn how to dance for the fake wedding we have to have in Terraway. One entire night is all I ask." When I opened my mouth, he shot a sharp, "And I don't want to hear any of it from you, either! I keep her safe, and I'm the best Reaper there is. I don't need to dance around like a fool on top of it just to prove something to her."

I held up my hands. "I was only going to say that you can have Allie's room until she wakes up. So long as Mariang knows where you're at, my house is yours."

"Just for tonight would be good. And she knows I'm here. Cheers, October. It's been a long day."

I texted Mariang that Danny was staying the night with Von and me, just to make sure, knowing I would worry if Von stormed out in the middle of the night. She answered back with a glib, "Best of luck to you and Von. He's in a mood."

Von came out of the bathroom, his shoulders falling at the company. "Oh. Hallo, Danny. Didn't realize you were staying here tonight."

"I don't dance!" he belted out as the reason he was allowed to be surly.

Von scratched his head in confusion. "What did I say?"

"Never mind. Just go back to bed. I'll stay out of your hair."

"Mariang's angry because you won't dance with her?"

Danny nodded. "At the reception in Terraway. I wanted to marry her, not have a giant party where I'm trussed up like a Christmas turkey, parading around in front of Terraway like a bloody muppet."

"Oh, is that all? Danny, dancing's no big deal. It lets your woman know you'll be good in bed."

"Huh?" I quirked my eyebrow at Von, never having made this connection before.

Danny groaned and rolled his eyes. "Mariang already knows I'm good in bed. Dancing's got nothing to do with that."

Von searched through his phone for a Rat Pack song with just enough bounce in it. Then he held his arms out to me with a more serious expression than he usually cared to wear. "Now, watch. Bring your stomach tight to hers." He demonstrated for his brother, using me as the visual display. "This does two things: It shows her you're not afraid of her body, and it'll make her suck her stomach in and push her breasts out, giving you more to look at."

I looked down and realized that's exactly what just happened. "Oh, whoa. That's freaky. How'd you know I'd suck in my stomach?"

"Darling, I'm very good in bed." Von's natural response oozed out of him, coating me with his charm as he started swaying to the music.

Danny groaned. "I came here to escape all the dancing, not get a private lesson in my own personal torture."

"Boy, are you in for a surprise if you ever do get legitimately tortured. It's nothing at all like dancing with a beautiful woman."

I beamed up at Von, who soaked in my smile at the compliment. "You think I'm beautiful."

"If you gaze adoringly like that at me for stating the obvious, then I'll just keep doing it. Your eyes are stunning, you know. And your lips..." Von tugged my lower lip between his, giving us both just enough affection to invoke the swirl of colors and sounds that made us sigh with elation.

"Okay, okay. I'll just go to the mansion if you two nutters clearly need this much privacy."

Von reached out and gripped Danny's arm. "No, no. Come on, mate. I'll teach you how to sweep Mariang off her feet. Worked on this one before she even knew she fancied me."

"It's true," I nodded, stepping out of the dance so Von could instruct Danny. "I thought he was ugly and gross, and then he danced with me, and it scrambled my brains. Now I have all these weird sexual fantasies about Fred Astaire and the guy who does Riverdance."

Von narrowed his eyes at me. "Hey, now. Don't oversell it. He'll never buy that any woman thought I was ugly and gross." He stood across from Danny. "Nearly every song either has a three-count or a four-count. It's basically two steps you need to learn, and everything else falls into place. Easy enough."

Danny set his bag on the floor, his hands over his face. "I don't care how easy it is! I don't want to parade around in front of Terraway like a monkey."

"Well, if you dance like a monkey, you're doing it all wrong." Von dropped his bravado and gripped Danny's shoulders. "Look, Mariang puts up with a lot from you, and she asks for very little. This'll be good for you to learn, yeah? Just because you landed the girl doesn't mean you ever stop auditioning for the role."

I could tell Danny wanted to argue this point, but his shoulders drooped in defeat. "Fine. Show me enough to get by and fake that I know what I'm doing, and then let's turn in."

Von smiled at his younger brother and gathered me up in his arms again, swaying gently to the beat without any fancy steps or twirls that would only scare Danny. "See? It's just counting until you get so familiar with the steps, your brain doesn't need to count any longer."

Danny studied Von's feet with his monster of Frankenstein eyebrows pushed together, as if the more serious his expression was, the better he'd be at mimicking the simple steps. "Fine, but if word gets out that I came here for dance lessons, I won't waste a moment pounding you both into the ground."

"No one would believe you can be sweet, so don't worry. Your secret's safe with us." I let Von twirl me out and then pull me back in, our matching smiles growing at the intimacy and flirtation we could have in plain sight.

Von released me and motioned for Danny to take his place. Danny glowered as he stood across from me, as if this was all my bright idea. He gave a few false starts of holding up his arms in different poses, unsure which was the correct one. Finally, he slumped. "I don't know what to do with my hands."

Von was patient, and I noted his lack of sleazy comments that would only make us both uncomfortable. He positioned Danny's hands, one holding mine out to the side, and the other loosely around my waist as the music played a nonthreatening ditty. "Well, start!" Danny growled at me.

"I don't know how to dance," I admitted. "I just do what Von does, and somehow it works out."

Danny harrumphed and moved back from me. "Are you having a laugh with this? You're giving me a partner who's even more clueless than I am? How does that measure out?"

Von was unperturbed at the setback. "It doesn't matter if the woman knows how to dance. You lead, so if you know how to do this properly, she'll learn to fall in step. Didn't you see how incredible she was when I danced with her? It's because I knew what I was doing. Rally, soldier. You can do it."

Danny glared at me in silent warning not to mess him up. I gulped, nervous before we'd even began. Danny was finally trying to be sweet for Mariang, and I was determined not to make the kindness evaporate before she could benefit from it.

"Just side to side to start," Von instructed. "Danny, what'd I tell you about holding the girl close? How's she supposed to know where your body's going if she can't feel it?" Von gently moved me closer so my hips pressed to Danny's. My surly older brother's eyes widened as a look of alarm crossed his features at our close proximity. Von was in charge, which finally relaxed us both. "Easy, Danny. Dancing will be simple for you once you give it a few tries. You're good at anything physical, and this is just one more problem you use your body to solve." Then Von leaned in and whispered to Danny something that made his eyes turn to saucers when they fell on me.

"Seriously, guys. This is embarrassing enough. Keep the secrets for another day," I groused.

Danny swallowed hard and tightened his arm around me, trying to communicate strength and know-how so I'd follow him. He stood straighter, and this time when his foot moved to the side, mine slid out at the same degree. We were basically shuffling from side to side, but we were doing it together, which was a first. "Am I doing it?" Danny asked, perplexed that his feet were puzzling through the invisible maze.

"You are. And what's more, November's moving with you. If you can get a willful one like her to follow your lead, you'll have no problem with Mariang."

After a few more minutes of the mindless shuffle that Danny was so proud of himself for, Von introduced a simple waltz step. As it turns out, the waltz was far more complicated when I was paying attention to what I was doing, rather than just following Von's or Judge's lead. It took a few false starts, but eventually we started moving to the song like we actually knew what we were doing. We were stiff and unpracticed, but we were dancing.

I smiled up at Danny, who scowled at me to make sure none of my softness leapt into his personality. He didn't want me to pollute his storm clouds with my ponies and unicorns. "You're dancing, Danny! I'm so proud of you."

His arm tightened around me in silent threat. "Shut it. You'll make me lose count."

I pretended to faint in his arms, my southern lilt ramping up to full force. "Oh, your charm! It's just sweeping me off my feet! Whatever shall I do?" I righted myself and cast him up a scolding look. "This is the part where you don't spend the whole time counting in your head. You're supposed to make flirty chitchat with Mari-ang, so make sure you can do this without counting out every beat."

"I'm not worried about romancing you. Of course I'll talk to her when we're..." He sobered and looked over hopelessly at Von, who tried to hide his smile. "But if I talk, I'll lose count!"

"Not to worry. A little more practice, and your feet will

know what they're doing without your brain having to tell them."

We danced for a little while longer until Danny started getting confused, overthinking everything and messing up the parts he'd already mastered.

Von ran his hand over his face, and I could tell he was getting tired. "I'm thirsty. Carry on, and I'll be back in a moment. Danny, you're brilliant. The quicker you realize that, the sooner your surly mug stops tripping your feet. You want a beer?"

"Will a beer make me better at this?"

"Couldn't hurt."

"Cheers, Von. Whatever you've got."

Von left the room, ensuring that Danny started counting out loud, which for some reason tripped me up even more. We had devolved to eighth grade dance stance – where a whole person could fit between us. "You're doing real good, Danny. And hey, this is totally sweet that you're learning all this to make Mariang happy. My guess is that even if you end up sucking at dancing, it won't matter – she'll be so romanced that you tried, that she'll think you're fresh off the cast of *Rent*."

Danny paused, suddenly forlorn. "You really think I'm still rubbish at this?"

I took in his slumped shoulders and dejected demeanor. "Hey, not at all. I just mean you don't have to be so hard on yourself. You're great at this," I lied. "I can't believe this is your first time. Maybe you could try not looking at your feet, though. That might help."

Danny straightened and pulled me flush to him, like he was supposed to. He waited until he caught the downbeat and locked his eyes with mine as he started the waltz. "Like this?" His stare was intense as he tried to get everything perfect; he looked borderline psychotic, with too much intensity.

"Um, could you look nicer maybe? Just a little less like you might murder me in my sleep."

"Oh, sorry. You're like, the third person to say that to me today." His gaze softened, making him appear younger, kinder, and without his signature surliness I was accustomed to.

"Much better." My heartrate started to pick up as the intimacy of the close proximity mingled with such focused eye contact. "Yeah. Exactly like this. Mariang will love it." My hand naturally slid up his bicep to touch his shoulder. I'm not sure why it made me blush, but now I was the one who had a hard time keeping track of the beats. I could feel Danny's heart thudding against mine, so to break the weird vibe that was settling between us, I crossed my eyes while we waltzed. "Do you think I'm sexy when I look into your eyes like this?" I asked, drawing out a small smile from him, which counted as a win for me.

"It's the most attracted I've ever been to you. Maybe it's the way you're doing your hair." Then Danny broke the waltz to muss my hair beyond a two-second tousle. He put me in a headlock and frizzed the top of my head until I twisted myself out of his grip. Instead of letting the razzing end at that, I jumped on Danny's back and messed up his hair, laughing when he looped his arms around my legs to give me a piggyback ride. He carried me into the kitchen, actually smiling the whole way, knowing he was being fun, and that the privacy my house provided was the place he was free to do just that.

Von's eyebrows rose in surprise. "Ho! What'd I miss? Did you buy yourself a smashing new horse, Peach?"

"I did. Isn't he pretty?" I took the opened beer Von handed me and tipped it to Danny's lips, who drank with only a little dribbling down his chin.

"Absolutely stunning. Tell me, do you think your horse can dance well enough for our princess yet?"

"I think Danny can do just about anything he puts his mind to." I took a chance and pressed a kiss to the back of his head, smirking when the nape of his neck turned rosy.

Danny's head shrunk down into his shoulders. "Okay, okay. Stop it with the cutesy girl stuff you always do. I'm not your dolly."

I hugged him around the chest, resting my cheek on the back of his head. "Yes, you are. My little Prince Danny doll who never sasses me. Such a little love bug!"

Danny rolled his eyes and shot to Von, "Does she come with an off button?"

"She does, but not one you're allowed to go fishing for. I was thinking of turning in. You guys tired yet?"

Danny had only just turned on his personality, and I was keyed up at having Von back in one functional piece. "Movie night first? Just one movie, not a marathon. Please?" I begged with my beamiest smile. "Danny never gets to watch the violent movies. We have to save him!"

"Nothing with a deep plot or anything where there's a higher point," Danny demanded. "I want nonsensical blood and guts."

"Like there's any other kind. I know just the thing."

"Okay, but then I go to sleep," Von ruled, too pleased that his brother was being playful to rain on our parade. He followed us into the living room, turning on the TV and spreading out on the couch that was too new to have comfortable divots yet. Danny dumped me onto the cushion next to Von, unlocking my giggles as Von and I wrestled for the remote. We were a family, and it was the very best kind of night.

36

SNEAKING OUT

The movie was the kind of gory where too many extras die, and you don't feel a thing for a single one of them. It was my favorite kind of bloodbath. Danny fell asleep on the couch, his head tipped back as he snored softly beside me.

"Do you want to know a secret?" Von asked quietly with a coy smile.

"You're kind of adorable when you look at me like that. Is your secret that you like to dress up in my underwear and dance around in the moonlight? Because I've got to tell you, I already knew that one."

"Oh, you. My secret is that while I've been entertaining myself prancing around in your knickers, I've been completely blood-free for three days."

I froze next to him, trying to keep the alarm off my face.

"Um, is that okay? Isn't blood kind of one of those vampire non-negotiables?"

Von shrugged. "Your kiss breaking the curse of me craving it so often opened up my mind. I started wondering if I'm only drinking out of desire rather than actual need. People ditch meat and go vegetarian all the time. What if this is no different?"

I chewed on his words. "Well, how are you feeling?"

"Strong. Clear-headed. Sexy. Missing you."

"Well, I'm right here."

"Yes, and so's my brother." He looked into my eyes in that earnest way that let me know he was busy cherishing me in his mind. "I adore you. I hope you know that."

"I do, but only when you tell me, Mr. Brady. So never stop."

Von opened his mouth, as if he wanted to confess something, but then closed it again with a gentle smile. "I adore you," he repeated, with a brush of his lips to mine before he pulled back. "That was decent of you, helping Danny learn to dance."

"Decent of you to teach him. Von?"

"Yes, love?"

"Promise me you'll be careful with this whole blood thing. I mean, I think it's great you're experimenting with this. I just want you to be safe."

"Ah, but that's not the man you love." He tucked me closer into his side to end the conversation.

The movie was a great distraction.

After half an hour, Von wasn't really watching the movie anymore, but studied the label on his beer with too much concentration. My eyes drifted shut as I leaned against him, the movie drawing to a close without me witnessing the unmasking of the villain. Bruce Campbell wasn't the star of this particular slasher, so I didn't much care who won. Bruce always wins, because he's the man.

I felt Von lean me back against the couch so he could stand. I kept my eyes closed and my breathing steady, but peeked when I heard him shoving on his boots. He checked a text on his phone and then picked up a pen and paper, scribbling a note that he left on the coffee table before sneaking out the front door.

The silence roared in my ears, and I wished beyond anything that I could chase Von down and make him stay in one place. I'd overlooked a lot, but sneaking out on me now in the middle of the night felt like a new low. When he exited out the front door, I fingered the hastily written note that said, "Be back in a day or so. Not to worry."

Fury flooded my veins as I crumpled the note in my fist. I stood and stormed to the front door, flinging it open and shouting into the night, "Von Vandershot, get back here right now!"

Von's fist was on the handle of my car door, and he froze like the guilty son-of-a he was. "I thought you were sleeping."

"That's all you've got to say to me? You thought I was

sleeping, so you snuck off in the middle of the night? In the middle of the night! After everything we've been through, this is what you're still pulling?"

"It's not what you think." His shoulders slumped as he turned to face me. "I've got an errand to run. I'll be back tomorrow night. Danny's with you. You'll be safe."

"You'll be single if you keep this up!"

Von's eyes widened. "Calm down, love. I didn't tell you where I was going because I knew you'd want to come along, and this is dangerous stuff."

I glared at him, arms akimbo. "I'm tired of you and Ezra and everyone treating me like I can't handle a little danger. You all throw me headfirst into the pile of broken glass, but then act like I'll fall to pieces if I break a nail. You haven't earned the amount of trust it would take for you to sneak out of the house in the dead of night."

Von scratched his scalp and sighed. "Fine. I'm going to Sombi to bring Mason home. He's the Boy Scout, so if Ezra's been calling him home and he's not come back yet, something's off. You can understand why I don't want to take you to a land where something is for certain wrong, especially if the whole country's filled with zombies."

I blinked at him, not having expected a non-toolish response. "Oh. Well, then let's go. If you think something's wrong, then I'm coming with you."

"See? That's exactly what I didn't want to happen. Sombi's actually dangerous if you don't know what you're doing there. It matters to the kingdom if you live or not."

"Hello, an Omen's nothing without her Reapers. You really think I'm going to just sit back and lose both of you to Terraway? Fat chance. And I know more about killing zombies than you think. I've killed a few dozen. How many zombie bodies exactly do you have under your belt?"

Von frowned in confusion, and then threw his head back. "I forgot about the time you snuck off with *Finn*, no less, and fought in a war you had no business being in."

"Oy! Get in here and wait until I pack a bag," Danny called from the front porch. "If you're going to find Mason, I'm coming with you."

Von threw out his hands in frustration. "I could've been gone already by now."

Both of us grumbled on our way back into the house, saving the arguing for when Danny was finished leaving a cryptic message for Mariang. He slapped his palms together, looking excited for the fight. "Okay, how are we doing this? Who's taking us down to Terraway?"

"Prince Langgam was going to meet *me* and port only me down. The two of us were going to find Mason and bring him back."

I gaped at Von. "Seriously? How could you have this whole plan without me? I know Mason. I can find him."

Von shot me a dubious glance. "Truly? How do you expect you can help us find him in a place you've never been before?"

"Well, smartass, I know how Mason disguises and lays his traps, so I can help you avoid those. I've killed zombies before, so I'm not exactly dead weight. And I know of a few spots he might be, the ones he likes to escape to when he's lying low."

"How do you know where he might be?"

"You know all those nights you spent at Katrina's, sneaking around while I was knocked up? Well, Mason and I spent them talking. Mason confides in me. He pretty much told September everything about his world when he'd talk to her every night before we went to sleep."

Von was livid. "Are you never going to stop throwing that in my face?"

I shrugged, unperturbed that I'd swung low just to smack some sense into him.

Danny pulled his backpack over his shoulder and grabbed a few bottles of water from the fridge, while Von shook his head with a definitive air. "You're not going. Danny, I can't shake October without her thinking I'm stepping out on us, but you've got responsibilities here."

"Responsibilities Graham and Alton can keep tabs on. Mariang can't reap anymore until the baby comes anyway. I left her a message, and if we hurry, we'll be back tomorrow night, just like you said. Does Ollie have a winter jacket I can borrow?"

"In the hall closet. You need one, too, Von."

"Langgam's bringing one for me." Von glowered at Danny while I shoved on my winter boots and fished out a pair of Ollie's for Danny. "I don't like the idea of putting my kid brother and my fiancée in danger."

I moved past him to the bedroom and packed my backpack with a change of clothes, my balisong blade from Finn, and a little food and water for the journey. I jangled my keys to let the guys know that we were leaving, and I was driving.

FATHER AND MOTHER

Maybe I shouldn't have been surprised to see Ruiz and Klark with Lang, but when I saw them, I forgot my game face and ran to the trio, throwing my arms around each of them and kissing them on their dirty cheeks. I'd come a long way from the OCD queen who couldn't shake hands without running for the bathroom to wash the germs off. Blame it on the healing waters, and a steady dose of pulling. "I missed you!" We were in the middle of a parking lot Von had arranged to meet up with them previously. There were two flickering lights shining down in the vast lot, and only the chirping of crickets to distract us. We were surrounded by abandoned concrete buildings and dying shrubs, making us feel like the only people in the world. "Lang, I can't believe the porch swing. Did you make it yourself?"

He cast me a bashful half-smile. "Of course I did. I told you I would. It just took longer than I'd hoped. You like it?"

"I love it." I glanced around at their fur-lined jackets and weatherproof boots. They were usually dressed for the steamy atmosphere of Sakuna. I hoped the winter jacket and thermal layers I wore were enough to weather Sombi's frozen landscape.

Lang shot Von a baleful look at my unexpected presence in the mix as he held onto me. "I didn't realize you were coming. Does Ezra know about this?"

"Of course he doesn't. So let's do this quick before he can throw a fit."

"Have you even been to Sombi before?"

"No, but I thought with one of my Reapers missing, it was high time for me to make the trip. You guys ready?"

Lang sighed. "Well, if Sombi doesn't kill us, it's nice to know Ezra will finish us off for stealing his daughter." He handed me his backpack. "We were going to deliver the last stone ourselves while we're down there."

"But you can't touch it!"

"I know, but you *shouldn't* touch it. It warps your mind. We were going to be careful."

My eyebrows furrowed as I removed the backpack with the baseball-sized remaining bit of the stone from Lang. I wadded the pack up, and shoved it inside my backpack of supplies. Then I hefted the whole thing over my shoulders. "Careful? Careful you don't turn to stone? Give me a break, Lang. This is my responsibility. I can't believe you were going to try and deliver something so dangerous without Ollie or me. How'd you even know where it was? Ezra hid it."

The corner of Lang's mouth twitched upward. "He hid it in Sakuna with me. A decision I'm sure he'll regret soon enough."

I watched Ruiz reach out and hold Danny's hand while Klark gripped Von's. Lang brought me in for another tight hug. Without a word, the parking lot dematerialized, and we were sucked down into the freezing midnight of Terraway.

The smell of Sombi was awful – like rotting eggs and rancid chicken. The stark difference the two parking lot lights made in my world was never clearer than Terraway in the dead of night. The moon was dim, like it was only lit halfway. The stars were also turned down a notch, and I wasn't sure how we were going to find our way to Mason if we couldn't see more than a few feet in front of us.

Lang clapped his hands twice and whispered to the group, "First things first: find some *baga* root so Lady October can breathe." He pointed to his right where there was a smattering of snow-covered trees that were taller than your average redwood. We jogged to the woods, dropping to our knees and digging in the dirt beneath the foot of snow, scavenging around complicated brush and branch systems to find the janky root I needed to survive in Terraway.

Lang's fingers lit up, casting just enough illumination

so I could tell that what I was putting into my mouth wasn't something useless, but something that would help me breathe. I choked it down, grimacing through the used gum feeling, while I pocketed a second root, just in case. "Okay, I'm good now. Let's find Mason. Be on the lookout for trees in groups of three with Y formations to their trunks. He likes to lay traps covered with snow and leaves between them."

Von's head swiveled toward me, surprised I had actual useful information. "What kind of traps?"

"Not the break your leg off kind, but usually a net that'll slow us down. The break your leg kind's around where his house is, which is in the northeast end of Sombi." I looked around, unsure where I was, and how far we were from the northeast end. I was grateful I hadn't zoned out when Mason had been explaining the ins and outs of Sombi to September.

Danny held up his hand. "I know where his house is. Shortest path is through the woods." He pointed straight ahead. "I've only ever gone there with Mason, so I didn't have to deal with his traps. What other kinds does he have down here?"

"Mostly nonlethal this far out. The closer you get to his house, the traps get more dangerous. He doesn't like to hurt anyone who's just coming to Sombi to find their dead so they can bury them." I stood beside Danny and nodded. "You lead the way."

Danny postured, his knife drawn as he stomped

through the night with Lang's fingers barely lighting the snow, bramble and crispy leaf-covered ground. I tried not to let my mind dwell on how cold it was as I crunched through snow that was easily a foot deep.

"So what'd I miss? How's Sakuna?" I asked Lang, my breath leaving a fog of chill when I spoke. My tone was light and conversational, but my eyes never left the area before us.

Lang answered for the trio. "The rebuilding's slow, but we're moving forward. We lost father's army to Sama. They've been using his rations the longest, so when Sama sent a puppet to our land a few months ago, he snapped his fingers, and our army went marching to his command. Didn't even pack bags. Just left the palace in droves and marched out of Sakuna. The western territory wasn't too far behind them."

Ruiz made me jump when he stabbed into the ground after veering off the course a little. He came back with a lifeless black cat in his hands. "Dinner for the Duwendes and Omen," he clarified.

I blanched inwardly, hoping we'd find Mason soon so I didn't have to eat a kitty cat. I cleared my throat and turned my attention back to Lang. "Man, that sucks. You lost so many people to the famine. You'd think that once that was on its way to being fixed, you'd stop losing people. I'm sorry, Lang."

Lang gave me a "what can you do" shrug. "Aranya doesn't know what to do with himself without an army. I gave him a few projects to oversee, but he doesn't have much interest in helping the people. He wants to rule, but he's got no one to enforce his commands."

"How's everyone doing with the army being in Sama's pocket now?"

"We're focusing on building a wall between the deep forest that separates Sombi from us. It won't do much, but it gives us all a common goal. They need purpose, to feel like they can overcome Sama somehow."

Danny's whisper came out irritable, which was no great shock to anyone. "Can we catch up some other time? We're mobile chum, here, with all our organs walking about. The zombies will hear us coming if they don't already smell us, and I don't fancy being torn apart for my vitals."

"Oh, Danny. Always the practical one." Von slashed at a low-hanging needly branch that proved problematic. "I say we make as much noise as we can. Sama's been gathering more zombies into his army to replace the ones he lost in Silo. I want him to catch word that his lovely prize isn't afraid to traipse around Terraway as she pleases. And I want Sama to hear of me in my right mind, storming through Terraway, slaughtering his potential recruits with *his* heart's desire by *my* side." Then Von lifted his voice to a shout. "You should've killed me, you cowardly witch! Possession's so classless. It's like you can't get a life of your own, so you glom onto mine, trying to make it yours. Pitiful!"

Danny groaned, and I looked up to see his head was buried in his hands. "Let's not taunt the most formidable, yeah? I say we let him never hear of us coming into Terraway. We don't know what's been detaining Mason. It might take us more than a blink to get him back Topside."

"I guess that's a fair point."

Ruiz trotted off our path and stabbed another cat. Seeing the lifeless eyes reflect off the light from Lang's fingers made my stomach roil. "I'm getting a pretty decent meal together. Hope you're hungry, your majesty."

"You're the sweetest," I cooed, hoping I wouldn't be hungry throughout the entire trip. "Thanks, Ruiz." In the dark, I wanted to pinched myself, to punish the skin on my arm because I couldn't punish Sama as I wanted to. The gloves made this problematic. "Don't call me Sama's heart's desire, Von. It's nothing as romantic or grand as you're making it sound." I pushed at a branch that swung low toward my face after Klark moved it out of his way. "I'm his idiot. He doesn't want a great love; he wants a dummy who doesn't know any better, otherwise he would've told me who he was in the first place."

"You're no one's idiot," Von offered as we trudged in a single-file formation through one of the thickets of trees that only seemed to increase in number. Our feet couldn't be as quiet as we wanted as they crunched atop the dried leaves and crisp snow that was packed deeper and firmer as we trudged onward. There were no birds, only the deafening silence of boots on snow.

"He made a joke out of me, invaded my head and tried to… If we come across him, he'll rue the day he thought I could be his little toy. That I'd sit back and be afraid every night to fall asleep. That I'd let him have power in any way."

Von reached behind him and grabbed for my hand that didn't have Finn's long balisong blade in it. "You don't have to be afraid to sleep; I'm here. So long as we don't lose each other or throw each other away, he can't get inside."

I squeezed Von's hand to assure us both that we were stronger than Terraway, than Sama and all he could cook up for us.

I heard Klark's feet in the lead with Danny stop suddenly before I heard the reason why. In the distance, there was a faint cry. At first it sounded like a wounded bird, but as the cry continued, I realized it was a baby wailing. I gasped and turned off our line through the woods. I moved quickly toward the sound that stirred maternal instincts I didn't realize I had on tap. Apparently, part of me was still a mama, with or without my baby to make it all true.

"October, no!" Danny called after me, but it was no use. Someone had lost a baby in the icy woods, and I wasn't about to turn my back on that.

Von's gloved hand never left mine, his fingers twining through and clasping as his chest puffed. In the dark of the forest, he was a father, and I was a mother. No matter the urgency we felt to find Mason and restore our duo to a trio, knowing there was a baby out in the frozen woods who was scared and without comfort triggered us both to abandon everything else.

We ignored Danny, Lang, Ruiz and Klark, who called after us, warning us to come back to them. Our footsteps picked up as the baby's cry amplified, ringing in my ears. There was no mother's calm shushing to comfort the child. There was no other sound at all but the crying. I didn't realize I had an unending supply tears, but suddenly they were running down my cheeks, chilling my face. I was a mama without a baby; I couldn't imagine the agony the baby in the woods must feel to be a soul without a mama. "Hurry, Von! It sounds like the baby's hurting!"

"Don't let go of my hand, *hani*. We'll find her."

It made me rally to hear the concern in Von's voice that was quickly growing to desperation. As we ran toward the baby who was lost or abandoned in the woods, I knew with everything in me that Von would've made a fantastic father.

I wasn't expecting the arms that wrapped around me – so thoroughly engrossed was I in finding the baby. "Stop!" Lang whisper-shouted in my ear. He yanked me backward to pause my flight toward the baby, who obviously needed me.

Danny did the same to Von, only the two devolved into wrestling in the snow on the forest floor, while I stood straining against the prison of Lang's arms. He smelled of mud, and his forearms were thick and immoveable. "Lang, we can't just leave a baby in the woods! Help me find her!"

Lang tightened his grip around my torso, his voice low and deadly in my ear. "It's not a baby. What you hear is the sound of a Tiyanak." When this did not deter my struggle, he explained with all the patience of a much older sibling laying out the way of the world. "Tiyanaks are babies who died in the womb. Their spirits come here to roam the forest of Sombi. Something about the transition from womb to death, instead of life, twists them. They're not the babies they might've grown up to be – instead they're evil. They cry from deep in the woods to lure people to them. Then when you get close, they mutate into a horrific monster and kill the person who tried to help them. The Tiyanaks eat their victims' organs so they can age a few months."

If I thought I understood the creepiness of Terraway, it was nothing to the horror Lang's explanation bathed me with. "Are you serious?"

Lang nodded. "I wish I wasn't. Mason usually traps and drowns them. When father poisoned our women, Sombi was filled with Tiyanaks overnight. He's no doubt had his hands full since then."

I heard the insistent wailing of the baby. She was growing desperate, calling out for anyone to save her. My face drained of color. "Is September here? Is my daughter a Tiyanak?"

Lang loosened his grip on me so he could rub my back. "This is where her spirit would go, yes."

The whispered ambiance was broken by a cry so horrible and anguished, I could scarcely believe it birthed from my mouth. I broke free from the group and ran full-stop toward the wailing. "September! I'm here!" Tears blurred my vision as I bolted through the snow toward the awful cry that my whole body yearned to quell.

I could comfort my daughter. I didn't care what kind of monster she was now; she was mine. I loved Mason when he turned into a baby-eating monster. I loved Von, and he would permanently be half a monster. I could love my daughter, no matter what Terraway had done to her sweet spirit. "September! Honey, I'm coming! I'm sorry! I'm sorry! I would never leave you alone in the woods!" My heart thudded at what a horrible mama I was – to leave my daughter alone in the snow of Sombi. How many zombies had she seen already? My whole body yearned to get to her and save her from the nightmare.

I heard the men running after me, so I hurried my own footfalls through the dark. I made good use of my smaller stature by ducking under branches and shimmying between trees they couldn't maneuver as easily.

"Stop! October, you'll get yourself killed!"

I ran as the crying grew clearer, my heart feeling like it might burst in my chest. I was sobbing audibly now, matching the baby's wails decibel for decibel. When I reached the source of the commotion, a strangled cry escaped me.

It was a toddler, a little boy with dark hair and chubby hands. He had tears streaming down his face as he reached for me, his beacon of safety in the darkness.

BOBBY BRADY

The crush of thinking I might find my daughter in the darkness, only to lose her so suddenly all over again, tore at my insides. The raw emotion pushed a mournful cry from my lips that was so painful, I winced at the sound of my own torment. Terraway was cruel, and I had been an idiot once again to think I would get anything other than a harsh slap in my sore spots from the land that had given me nothing, and demanded my everything. I shook from head to toe with grief, barely able to see the little guy who was clothed only in a dark scrap of fabric that fit him like a loincloth.

"It's okay, sweetheart," I worked out as I bent down to reach for him. "I'll help you. You must be freezing out here. Where's your coat?"

He was helpless and innocent as he blinked up at me with his big, round brown eyes. I couldn't believe he'd ever done a naughty thing in his little life. "What's your name?" He didn't seem to be able to talk, so I made up a name to add a little humanity to the Jungle Book vibe he had going. "How about Bobby? Bobby Brady is a good boy. His mama loves him and takes care of him."

Bobby's crying stopped as he reached for me, and I felt that cozy warmth Allie must've felt when I cried for her when I'd been a kid. Though I didn't have a baby anymore, something in me was still a mother, and it could calm a child that wasn't even mine. It felt like finally being able to use a superpower I'd given up on and labeled as useless.

"Stop! Don't touch it!" Lang and the others started to form a circle around Bobby and me, weapons drawn.

I scowled at the men, but my mouth fell open at Von's attack stance and focused, yet tear-stained face. "Von! Put that knife away! You'll scare him!"

Von met my gaze with a pained expression. "Listen to me, Peach. Don't touch him. This is how they lure you in. Come to me right now. They're right, and I should've realized it sooner. It's not a baby. It's a twisted spirit. It's a Tiyanak, darling."

"His name is Bobby Brady, not 'it'." I wanted to scoop up the little boy, at once protective of his trembling, brown-skinned body. "We can help him, Von. He needs us!"

"It's not..." Von let out a bleat of agony that came from something scraping at his tender innards. He stared at me, like I was the culprit that caused him such torment.

Lang's voice was steady in the dark, "Everyone, hold your positions. Did anyone bring garlic or salt?"

Various "no"s echoed around me. Ruiz and Klark caught my eye as they took their jackets off and turned them inside out, shoving their arms back through them.

I couldn't help but address the weirdness. "What are you doing?"

Klark answered with a slight waver of fear in his tone. "It's rumored to turn Tiyanaks away. Everyone turn your clothes inside out!"

I cast Klark a withering look, pacifying him by tossing my backpack to Danny, taking off my jacket and turning one of the sleeves inside out while I spoke. "Seriously? Bobby's a little kid, and you're all scaring him. You should be ashamed of yourselves." I couldn't bother with my coat anymore when a fat tear dribbled down Bobby's cheek, his lower lip trembling. I felt powerful in my femininity as I dropped my jacket into the snow and scooped the little guy up in my arms. I knew this was what he needed, and I could give it to him.

"No!" Danny shouted with fear I didn't often hear in him.

The chubby arms clung to me, afraid of the Frankenstein monster with a knife. I couldn't blame the kid. "I've got you, babe. I'll take you someplace warm and safe." I brushed the dark hair out of his eyes. "You don't have to be afraid anymore. I'm a good mama," I promised him, vowing that if I couldn't save my daughter, I could at least help this poor, lost boy.

Then, as if in slow motion with strange sudden purpose, little Bobby Brady turned his head to look up at me. His teary eyes turned into determined slits as he gripped my shoulders and leaned his head to my breast. I rocked him gently through a shiver, and I swear I could feel him smile against my thin shirt atop my thermal, his cheek dragging up the material. I was shivering in the cold winter of Sombi, but I didn't care. Bobby Brady knew that I had true warmth in my soul, and that would be enough to get us through.

September would never feel the warmth that was her mama holding her. She would never fall asleep on me, her little baby breath tickling my neck. I was a mother without a baby – and then suddenly a baby without a mother found me in the woods. What were the chances?

It was fate; it had to be. The world had finally been kind, doling out a sweet bit of mercy after taking too much from me.

I felt nothing but calm as I held the sweet little guy, ignoring the panicked shouts of the others. The toddler turned his face to hide in my breast, like a tired little sweetheart. Then opening his mouth, Bobby shocked a scream out of me when he bit down, sinking razor sharp teeth into my skin. He started at my chest bone and ripped a bloody line down to my breast.

THE THINGS YOU'RE DESTINED TO SAVE

My arms released the boy in shock, but he clung harder to me, his body dangling off mine as I tried to push him without hurting him. "Ow! He bit me! Bobby, no!"

The noises of distress from the men told me something freaky was happening, beyond that of a toddler biting into my breast with all the joy of munching on a juicy apple. Bobby's legs started to elongate, and enormous black wings sprouted from his back as the rest of his body mutated. I nearly vomited when Bobby grew to a size that was more Andre the Giant than toddler. His giant mitts gripped my biceps, squeezing as his fangs grew into long knives that would've fit in great in any number of horror flicks. His smooth brown Sakuna skin seemed to thicken and stretch over his cranium. His skull bulged into a misshapen oblong mass that pushed his left eye out further than the right.

The guys didn't hold back, now that the monster was fully formed before me. They stabbed and pummeled, but were thrown back by the giant who had too much strength, and an endless supply of organs he could now feast on. I'd led my friends right into his well-laid trap.

It wasn't fate that led me here; it was the hunt, and we were the lost kittens who would be served up as dinner.

Bobby screamed when Lang pierced through his kidney from behind. The sound was still boyish and frightened. I cried out for my monster, my sweet little Bobby, who was hopelessly outnumbered. He swung a too-heavy fist and knocked Ruiz into a nearby tree. Then he grabbed Klark's arm to take a tasty bite from the bulging muscle.

Von took advantage of the distraction and ripped me away from Bobby, flinging me behind him as he growled with feral teeth bared. Bobby didn't like me being hidden from view behind Von. I could tell by his frustrated growl and furtive glances in my direction, that he wanted me to see his fighting abilities, almost like a show and tell.

Danny was a force to be reckoned with. He was mostly bulk, while Von was a combination of bulk and agility. Danny focused on the wings, stabbing into the black webbed skin with no hesitation. The ripping sound that hit my ears was a mixture of spilling water and something almost metallic as Danny sliced clean through one of the wings. My surly brother let out a roar at finally letting his barbarian self out to play. He'd been opening doors and learning to waltz, stuffing his zombie-slaying desires away to feign civility for Mariang. Danny put the romance movies on a shelf and let loose.

Lang was wrestling with Bobby, who let out alternating noises that switched between toddler cries for help and roars that sounded like a bear trying to attack its meal. His razor teeth chomped down on Lang's shoulder, ripping the skin with a growl of savory triumph. Lang howled, which rallied Klark and Ruiz. The two threw themselves at Bobby without thought of their own safety. They tried to stab, but Bobby guarded his sturdy core with agility they could not best. The monster watched my face, gaging my emotional response to his fighting prowess. Again, like he wanted my approval.

I shook my head at Bobby, letting him know this wasn't what I wanted. He seemed to grow confused at this, and lost his grip on the upper hand of the battle. Bobby was soon becoming overwhelmed with the sheer number of determined knives that stabbed toward him from every angle. He growled as he flapped his one functional wing, trying to lift himself off the ground to no avail. His head swung in my direction, letting out a mournful cry that seemed to say, "Mama! How could you let them do this to me?"

I didn't have an answer. "Bobby Brady, you put those boys down right now!" I roared in my best I-mean-business voice. I moved from behind Von to stand at his side, angry, shivering and glaring as my chest dripped with my own blood.

Bobby's eyes locked in on mine, and it seemed that with me as his focal point, he was done with wrestling time and wanted the toy he'd originally set out to trap. He flung Lang, Ruiz, Klark and Danny off of him, as if he'd been merely tolerating their antics this entire time.

Bobby ran for me, hungry and crying with that urgency of longing for a life that wasn't filled with loneliness. I knew that feeling. I lived in that longing. Von lunged forward with his knife, but Bobby whacked him sideways in the temple with one hard blow from his battering ram fist, sending Von flying into the nearest tree. I winced at the smack my best friend's body made against the bark, and the snowfall that rained down on his body. I held my finger up to Bobby and shouted, "Young man, don't you dare try anything like that ever again!"

Bobby slowed, as if confused that I wasn't cowering or fighting. I don't think he'd been scolded much in his life, and the anger my finger pointed at him gave him pause.

"Run!" Lang bellowed, jumping on Bobby from behind, his knife poised to slit the beast's throat. Bobby turned his head and gnashed his teeth at Lang, coming dangerously close to slicing through his handsome tattooed face.

"Bobby, I told you to mind your manners! I need all these guys alive, and you'll calm yourself down about it." I motioned for Ruiz to come to me, my palms sweating as a stupid plan began forming out of sheer desperation. "Ruiz, hand me the cat you caught. The one on your belt." Ruiz shouted for me to run, but I paid him no mind, instead extending my hand for the roadkill. "Just do it!"

Ruiz tossed the cat's body toward my feet, making Bobby jump. I held my finger up to steady him. "Now, that's quite enough, young man. You can have the whole thing if you let my guys go." It was a joke, really. I mean, he was far stronger than any of us. He could've just taken the cat. But there was something in his bulging eye that softened me. I saw that he wanted to dominate, to win in some way other than a quick killing. Otherwise we'd already be dead. He loved the fight, just as I did. My eternal struggles with Judge were proof of my addiction to that particular dysfunction. Bobby was a monster, sure, but he was sentient, which meant he cared about how he killed his prey. He had opinions, and some part of him existed that wanted to please the viewers while he won a duel. The way he'd watched me while he fought wasn't strictly to keep an eye on his dinner, but rather to make sure I was noticing how awesome he was. I recognized that same insecurity in the inmates who had a little pride left in them.

I pretended I was back in the prison, lifting my chin to communicate bravery and a certain "deal with it" charm I'd had to ooze on more than one occasion to keep my virginity intact, along with my life. I looked into Bobby's wonky eye and forced a smile, which I'm sure he didn't get a lot of in his current physical state. "If you want this, then you'll have to leave my guys alone." I clicked my fingers over my head to garner everyone's attention. "Ruiz, get Lang out of here. He's bleeding pretty badly."

"I won't leave you with a Tiyanak!" Lang bellowed, angry he'd been wounded.

I kept my voice light and a bland smile on my face as my torn chest burned and oozed. "You'll do as I say and let me handle Bobby. You guys are getting nowhere, going how you are." It was true; Bobby had stopped out of sheer curiosity, not defeat. Everyone was frozen in the middle of the fight they'd been losing, scared to start back up and continue the battle they were nowhere near winning.

Von slowly stood, making his way to my side with his knife drawn and fangs ready while he hissed. "Back up and let us handle him."

Bobby was not thrilled with being put on hold. He roared at Von, vying for my attention like a true two-year-old who needed to be the star. Von and Danny started circling him while Ruiz helped Lang off to the side, so he wouldn't be more appealing to Bobby than the offering of the cat. It made no logical sense from a predatory standpoint why Bobby wouldn't go for the bigger pieces of meat all around him. Why he was so fixated on the cat, which was far smaller and not nearly as fresh.

But I knew it wasn't about food at that point. It was about figuring me out, toying with his inherently human need to please, and the more monstrous desire for the Darwinian need to be the cunning predator. It was anybody's guess which of his two natures would win out.

Bobby let out a baby-ish cry to poke at my weaknesses so that when I fell, the victory would be sweeter, worthy of a longer savor. He kept his eyes on me, experimenting with varying pitiful cries to see how much he owned me.

I let his wails pull the corners of my mouth into a contorted expression to show him that I cared he was in pain, or at least that I understood he wanted me to think that. Danny stabbed at his wing again from behind, and Bobby roared, whirling and batting at Danny irritably. I ran forward, putting my smaller body between the two. Only instead of protecting Danny, I braced my back to Bobby, my arms splayed as I shouted for Danny to stand down.

"You're mad! Get back, daft girl! He'll eat you as soon as look at you!"

"Then it'll be only me who gets eaten. Back up! I mean it, Danny. I'm working on a solution, here. I won't let you get hurt, do you hear me? Give me a few minutes, and then if it doesn't work, you can go nuts. Trust me in this."

Von's voice from behind Bobby was angry, and my teeth set against his vitriolic tone. "He's not your pet. He won't sit and roll over simply because you ask him to. You're bleeding!" he whined, and I knew the scent of my blood was torturing him, making him that much more unsteady.

I was calm, my breathing even as I reached around to place my hand atop Bobby's massive fist. It was nearly as big as my head. I thought of my favorite inmate, who was only slightly smaller than Bobby. Terence the Taurus had been named after him. Darius and Judge's brother, Terence, was inmate number 43732. While I didn't remember everyone's number, I knew everything about Terence, having hung out with him when I'd been a child.

Terence was tall, broad shouldered and had dark, ebony skin. He would have been beautiful, were he not marked down the left side of his face, and several other places on his body. He had a long scar from his temple to his chin that had been patched on the fly in his late teens. The rest of his body was peppered with other poorly healed abrasions from years of running headfirst down the wrong side of the tracks. I'd treated him several times for yard fights, though his bulk had always put him on the winning end of brawls, so he was never too bad off.

Terence didn't talk much. Never had, even when I'd been a kid and he'd been a teenager. The gang that formed around him in lockup was not of his choosing; he didn't care about territories or grudges. Terence wanted peace and quiet. You had to respect that. He was so quiet that people thought he was stupid. Granted, his IQ wasn't anything to brag about, but he was capable of learning. When I'd been learning to read in kindergarten, he'd tried to help me, but wasn't much more adept at the skill than I'd been.

In the first grade, we'd reached the point where I was tutoring him on how to read, so he learned to help me in other useful ways. When the brown, rusty bike Ollie had found for me in someone's trash finally broke after a summer of abuse, Ollie couldn't get the chain back on and was ready to call it. Terence didn't say a word, but silently fixed my bike one night while I was sleeping. He was ten years older than me, but he never grew frustrated with my childhood limitations. Because he was huge, and unable to stop scowling, people assumed he was mean. I'm sure if you asked all the dealers whose arms he'd broken over the years, they'd concur with the general popular opinion. Terence was never vicious to me, though. He was quiet and calm. I saw him as a person, and not a terrifying monster. Thus, he was never a monster around me.

I gulped, praying the same principal held true with Bobby Brady.

Terence didn't speak much at all, except to me. I kept a paperback copy of *The Swiss Family Robinson* on my desk in the infirmary, and casually read aloud to him whenever he came up. He thanked me politely after each encounter, never using my first name in mixed company – yet another way of keeping me safe. Though everyone else feared him, he was a safe place for me. Always had been.

Pistola was quite the opposite. Horny from birth, Pistola couldn't be around anything with boobs without causing a problem. That's the beauty about working in a prison – though there's danger, they're all behind bars or heavily guarded, so you're always aware of the danger, but after a while, it's not so scary. Pistola often picked fights in the yard. When he'd come up to get patched, my skin crawled with his under-the-breath grossness. Pistola loved and hated women, which wasn't all too uncommon in the prison populace. It was his shiv that was responsible for the scar that had marred the inside of my thigh and my arm.

It was a thing of luck he'd picked a fight with Terence that day. Brenden was working on Terence, while I was disinfecting Pistola's arm. Pistola was shorter, skinnier and didn't look like much of a threat, but after a few weeks in lockup, he proved that you don't have to be big in stature to be a giant problem.

I didn't see the shiv, though maybe I should've. Pistola said something with his hot, foul breath about me being a tease (you know, in my shapeless scrubs that were a uniform I had no control over), and then he attacked.

I still remember the feel of the blade slicing my tender inner thigh after my block deflected his arm downward. Pistola turned me around, cuffed my mouth and held the shiv to my throat, demanding all the things a desperate and unstable man would when he doesn't have a prayer of parole.

The guards surrounded us, following protocol and trying to use words before force, but Terence had little patience for such things. He wanted peace and quiet, and Pistola was mucking up what could've been a sunny afternoon. Terence ignored the guards' batons and ripped me away from Pistola, punching him hard on his temple, and sending him to the ground in a pile of limbs. I was shaking and bleeding when I was hoisted up in Terence's arms, so high off the ground that I clung to him.

I didn't get many times in my adulthood where I felt truly safe. Ollie had moved to New York, and I'd been living alone. Most days I'd felt the isolation in my bones. In that moment, suspended above the fray, I knew that, despite Terence's many violent crimes, I was safe. I knew as sure as breathing that he wouldn't hurt me – *couldn't* hurt me. He'd saved me, and I held tight to the truth that you can't hurt the things you're destined to save.

It's what allowed me to forgive Von and Mason, time and time again.

Terence was my friend, my sometimes hero, and it had broken my heart to watched him get cuffed. He was led off to puzzle through the simple books he'd checked out from the library; he still couldn't quite grasp the higher concepts. He needed me to help him understand them, but I wasn't there anymore. No one else in Terence's life cared if he knew how to read.

But *I* cared. I wanted whole worlds of possibility, education and inspiration for Terence.

I couldn't think of a better person to name my Taurus after. Even naming my car "Mr. Brady" didn't have the same ring of the deep breath "Terence" did, and that's saying something.

Bobby Brady wasn't as harmless as Terence, but through the falling snow between us, I saw in him a similar desire for understanding. It wasn't his fault that he survived on organs. He didn't put that into his makeup. It's why he was toying with us. He wanted to play like a human, instead of conquer in one fell swoop, like a monster.

I offered up the cat with a pleasant smile on my face, ignoring my own blood that made me sticky. The bite on my breast stung like his teeth were still in me, but I was practiced at smiling while under duress. I slowly drew out my knife, tsking Bobby's roar of indignation. With careful hands, I sawed off the cat's ear, feeling like the worst kind of criminal for mutilating the pet so cruelly. Bobby was breathing through his long razor teeth, assessing with confusion why I hadn't attacked him with my blade. With a calm expression, I offered him the kitty's ear, which was truly the smallest gift I could've provided. I mean, it's like having a Christmas ham hand you a hard-boiled egg and expect you not to want a bite of the juicy ham.

Yes, I just called myself "juicy" in that analogy.

Bobby was drooling big gobs of desire down his chin, which was still streaked with my blood and Lang's. He took the cat's ear from me, grazing my palm with his too-sharp nail, drawing blood so he could taste it again. Flavor his kitty with a little October Grace sauce. I preferred honey on my chicken, but to each his own.

I tilted my head to the side in scolding. "I know you did that on purpose. Knock it off, or I'm not sharing with you." I took a step closer, knowing that humans and animals alike could smell fear, even when it was properly masked.

Since Bobby Brady was neither human nor animal, I hoped my in-control deportment fooled him well enough. I was a swipe away from being horribly disfigured, a bite away from losing a hand.

Danny's low voice was instructing me to step back, but I knew the second I did, the fighting would start back up, and my guys might lose.

I watched Bobby swallow the cat's ear in a single gulp without chewing. He stared at me the whole time to see if I would betray him. When he finished, I sawed off the other ear, taking a step closer so I could study his naked and muscular form in the light of the dim moon. His skin was tough, like an alligator's, and I began to see the problem of why my guys' knives weren't piercing him through in many places other than his webbed leathery wings.

But I had an advantage they didn't. I was close enough to the monster to see that between the top of his pelvis and the bottom of his ribs, his skin wasn't as tight, and not nearly as armored. It moved as he drew breath, contracting and lightly expanding, while the rest of his skin remained motionless armor.

I had one shot. One small window where the others didn't. It was only a few inches I had to work with, so I knew my aim had to be perfect.

I swallowed bile and remorse as I broke and sawed off the cat's arm, still working up the courage to do what needed to be done. My next step forward landed me half an arm's distance before him. His hot breath wafted down on me, smelling like old feces and ripe compost. This time, instead of letting him take the meat from me, I waited until he extended his hand, asking instead of taking.

I smiled up at him, knowing I'd won. He could be taught. He could be reasoned with. He wanted to please me with manners more than he wanted to conquer.

"That's a good boy," I cooed, placing the small, furry arm in his hand. He devoured it with a loud slurp, hair and all, and whined for more. I leaned forward, slowly placing the rest of the cat in his hand. In an act of daring, and I'm sure insanity, I leaned my head to Bobby's sternum in a show of trust. The men were roaring as they circled us – too afraid to make sudden moves, for fear of Bobby taking my head clean off. I didn't know if my monster would hurt me more than he already had, but I knew for certain he would tear apart the guys as soon as he realized I had no more meat for him.

A tear dripped down my cheek as I clutched the emerald hilt of Finn's jagged balisong blade in my fist. I waited until Bobby was mid-chew before I let the dagger do what it was intended to. It was almost as if Finn was with me, pushing the knife up with more force than my torn conscience could muster. I knew the stab wasn't enough, so I ripped the knife sideways, slicing through his abdomen and cutting through essential organs along the way.

I shot back from Bobby as he roared, touching his stomach and looking at me with the same shock of betrayal I'd worn when he'd bitten me in his toddler form. His free arm flailed as he doubled over to nurse his side. He howled, bent over as he was, betrayed and bleeding. Before Danny could lunge from behind, and before Von could descend on him from my left, I flung my weapon forward and drove the tip of the blade through Bobby's wonky eye, piercing without pause and twisting with a jerk before yanking it back out.

Bobby didn't possess many areas of vulnerability, but I'd managed to hit them both, including his insecurity born of a will to somehow reason with society. I stumbled back as I let the guys finish him off. Now Bobby was isolated from my protection, affection and kindness. His gut-wrenching howl rang through the woods, announcing that I was a bigger monster than even he.

I turned from the horror of my hands, sobbing as Bobby's cries turned more childlike, with less amplification. When I glanced over my shoulder to make sure the guys were winning, I let out a fresh sob when I saw that Bobby was no longer a monster, but had devolved back into a terrified toddler, bloody and mangled as Klark drove his knife through Bobby that final time.

40

THE TRAP OF GRAVITY

I'm not sure how long it was that we walked through the frozen woods. I trusted the others to lead the way, since my brain had taken a vacation. Danny had stopped lecturing me I'm not sure how long ago, realizing that I didn't stand a chance of basic comprehension. I'd helped to murder a little boy. I didn't know what sort of redemption had been in store for me previously, but I knew none existed anymore. I didn't even want my deep cut tended to, such was the state of numbness that descended on me, weighting my shoulders and dragging my feet. I'd killed Bobby Brady, and now I was dead inside.

I wasn't paying attention to anything, which was why I didn't even blink when Ruiz walked right into one of Mason's traps. The three trees formed Y-shapes near each other in a triangle, which was where Mason liked to lay his snares. The net scooped up our man in the lead, suspending him fifteen feet above us with a cry of surprise.

Surprise, not pain. The guys spent the next few minutes assessing Ruiz to make sure he wasn't hurt, but I already knew he was fine. Mason tried his best to make humane traps, in case family members came to Sombi looking for their loved ones. While the guys went back and forth on the best way to get Ruiz down, I started climbing up the trunk. I actually made it halfway up the towering tree before they noticed I was already working on getting Ruiz down.

"Be careful!" Danny called to me, reaching for my feet to offer stability if I needed it.

When my knee scraped against the bark of the tree, I heard Von groan. "If you could try not to cut yourself, I'd be appreciative. You're walking around with a succulent feast smeared all over your glorious breasts. Adding more blood to the mix isn't helping me not devour you whole, yeah?"

"Oh, right. Sorry. You holding up okay?" I asked, perching on a sturdy branch and sawing at the rope that held Ruiz in place. My gloves were necessary, but problematic when it came to doing a speedy job.

"No," Von admitted. He'd maintained a healthy distance from me since the toddler-murdering incident. I think it was dawning on him that abstaining from blood altogether wasn't the way to go. "If you could try to be less delicious, that would help. Perhaps you should start bathing in water with rotting fish heads."

"I'll make a note of it. Ruiz, can you reach through the netting and hold onto the branch? I've almost got you free, but I don't want you to hurt yourself on the fall."

"I think so. Give me a second." Ruiz worked his fists through the netting over his head and grabbed onto the branch, giving me a nod when he was secure. I chopped through the rope with a final slice, grateful that Ruiz didn't crash to the forest floor and break his leg or something. Klark and Lang caught Ruiz with minimal bumps, while I tried to assess how I'd get myself down.

"Just jump down," Klark offered. "I'll catch you."

It was a tribute to how much blood had soaked through my jacket that Von did not offer to catch me, but kept a healthy distance so he didn't, you know, murder me. He was good like that. I gazed at the ground below, assessing how and where would be best to fall. Though I'd encouraged Ruiz to do the same thing, I was having trouble putting my trust in Klark or Lang to make sure I didn't break anything. They were capable, I'm sure; I was just being a giant chicken.

I suddenly realized how high up off the ground I was, and how small everyone looked. I felt the sting on my breast and on my palm. The pain of everything started flooding me, weakening my right arm and making me nervous as to how the crap I was going to get down.

Danny met my eyes and raised his hands. "I'm right here," he assured me. Danny wasn't normally one for reassurances. He wasn't the one to care much about what scared me or didn't. He wasn't my Reaper, but somehow even in the dark that was lit only by Lang's fingers and the moon that filtered in through the evergreens and redwoods, I could see that Danny was trying to be kind. He could sense my nerves that were starting to creep in over my shoulder at being so high up off the ground, and wasn't bothered that he had to help me.

I closed and pocketed the balisong blade, and then climbed down onto a lower branch. I met his eyes with a look that told him I didn't want to give my fear a voice, but that it was very much there. Oh, it was there.

Danny nodded, seeming to understand everything I wanted to say, but couldn't and wouldn't. "I won't let you get hurt," he promised.

My hands shook as I lowered myself down to hang off the branch, my feet still far out of Danny's reach. Lang stood across from Danny, his good arm outstretched to offer his couple of superior inches to help. I dangled for too many seconds, afraid to let go, even though I had no other option.

I'd had to let go of so much in life. I'd looked the other way when Bev didn't want me. I'd let Allie go to California, and Ollie to New York. I'd let the countless crass comments about my body ricochet off me when the inmates were bored and wanted to mouth off. Now here I was again, clinging to something I couldn't let go of, but knew I would have to if I wanted to move forward.

There were some days I was tired of forward. As I hung off the branch, I realized I wanted a whole lifetime of Bruce Campbell movies, naps and blissful stagnation. I wanted to rest, not move on to the next thing that would surely test me, and that I might never be ready for.

I couldn't hear Danny or Lang shouting their encouragements to me. It was Von's voice that finally broke through the panic that was quickly mutating into an inability to move. "Close your eyes, Peach. Listen to my voice. Don't think about anything else."

I let out a whine of distress as my fingers started punking out. "I don't want to be here!"

Von was mature and spared me the "I told you so" I knew I deserved. "Where do you want to be?"

I closed my eyes and tried to picture myself somewhere safe. My house, though lovely with the remodel, didn't feel like that place anymore. I didn't exactly feel unsafe there, but it wasn't the haven it once was. Like me, it had been through too much. We were still standing, but only just. I tried to think of somewhere I wanted to be, but all I could think of were all the places I didn't want to have to travel to anymore. "Somewhere safe. Somewhere with a bed and books and the Brady Bunch. Somewhere no one can find us. Somewhere I can eat soup and drink hot chocolate and not be attacked."

I couldn't see Von, but I heard the small smile in his

voice. "I know just the place. Let go, and I'll take you there when we get back."

"I can't!" I knew my body was about to let go for me, whether or not I was ready. That's the thing about life; it has a way of pushing you forward, ambivalent of the care it takes to pick yourself up after a crash. It doesn't care about your struggle – gravity is gravity, and can't be reasoned with.

Von's voice was warm, and I longed to be near the sound that comforted and cradled me, even though I was so far from it. "Those are two words I never thought I'd hear you say. My wife can do anything."

With a final gulp and a prayer, I let my fingers say their final goodbye to the tree branch, slipping and letting gravity win, as I knew it inevitably would.

41

HUGGING THE MONSTERS

*L*ike most hurdles in life, the anticipation of falling was worse than the actual feat. Danny and Lang caught me with nothing more than a disarming bump when my feet hit the ground. Lang clumsily patted my back, but Danny clung to me, holding me tight when my knees buckled. There was something about the earnest nature of the hug I didn't expect that squeezed the truth out of me. Before I could stop myself, I whispered the confession that had been building in me since the Tiyanak went down. "That's two babies I killed."

At my horrible admission of guilt, Danny's arms tightened, crushing me to him so I couldn't run. He didn't say anything at first, but simply held me through his shock. Lang's hand on my back rubbed sweet circles, and I hoped he hadn't heard what a wretched person I was, though by now, we all knew. Danny kept one arm around me and put the other on the back of my head, anchoring my cheek to his shoulder so I could rest my burdens on him for a minute. Danny was showing public affection, and I felt terrible for making him be so nice to me. Never had it been clearer that I was a train wreck than when I stood in the middle of the dark forest, letting Danny comfort my crazy. Danny was saner than I was.

It was a hard blow.

"Shh," he whispered in my ear as he pulled some of the heartbreak out of me. "I don't want to hear that sort of rubbish from you, yeah? It's not true. The Manas killed your daughter, and what we killed back there was no baby. Tiyanaks aren't truly babies."

I didn't know which way was up, only that my soul felt heavy with gravity and guilt. Maybe Danny was right, but it didn't erase the weight I couldn't shake. Danny waved the others to move on ahead and held onto me, giving me a moment of privacy in a world where I'd been granted none. When we were alone, Danny lightly scratched my scalp and whispered, "Go ahead. Let it out."

Tears welled in my eyes. I hated myself one degree less since there wasn't an audience around to watch me degrade myself. Danny was being kind because I was fragile. I knew what fragile got a girl, and despised myself for the weakness I couldn't seem to escape. I didn't tell Danny any more of the awful things I felt, but I let myself cry in his arms, holding onto him as much as he held onto me.

It wasn't until my sobs subsided that I realized he'd

been talking to me, making sense of the madness I specialized in. "You're a soldier, just as I am. You did what had to be done back there. You were brilliant. I've never seen a Tiyanak act even remotely human before. They're usually just irrational monsters, programmed to kill and eat. But you got him to drop his guard. Only you could make a monster hug you." Then he stopped, examined his words and gave me a tight squeeze. "I'm a monster most days, yet here I am, hugging you because I know you need it, and your boyfriend can't." He pressed his cheek to mine and whispered, "You're a good person, and I'm sorry life is hard."

I don't know why this made my tears dry. Confused as I was, I let Danny wipe my tears with the sleeve of Ollie's jacket. I was grateful for the simple act that preserved my pride; he knew I didn't want to look so wrecked when we rejoined the others. "Thank you." I gripped his gloved fingers and held them to my cheek, using his warmth to anchor me when I felt so hopelessly lost and disconnected from reality.

He rubbed his thumb down the length of my cheekbone while he held me with his other arm slung low on my waist. "Let's find Mason and get you home, yeah? I bet Von's already making plans to take you on your glorious holiday of soup, hot cocoa and American television." He snorted out half a laugh at my idea of paradise. "Can you keep a secret?"

"Hello, my whole life is a secret these days. Shoot."

"After the cruise, I booked us a trip to Costa Rica for part two of our delayed honeymoon. Mariang's always wanted to go to the rainforest, and now she's finally healthy enough for some adventure."

Danny's happiness was just the distraction I needed. "Oh, Danny that's great! She doesn't know?"

"Not a clue. She thinks we're coming straight home after the cruise. She's too wrapped up in the wedding part of things to worry about the honeymoon. It'll be after the baby comes, of course, and after the circus of the ceremony in Terraway, but that's the plan."

"I love it! She'll be so excited. That's a great thing, booking a surprise for the two of you. Totally romantic. Good for you." I smiled up at him, hoping my face didn't look blotchy and tearstained. "You'll have to take her dancing when you get there."

"Ha," Danny replied tonelessly. "I think we all know what a fool I look like dancing."

I pulled my head back and stared up at him. "All you need is more practice. You're good at anything you put your mind to; dancing's no different."

Danny studied my face for a few seconds, debating something in his mind. Finally, he held my hand and slowly moved it out to the side, his arm tightening around my waist. His chest puffed out, and I could see him counting to three in his head. My foot moved back as his moved forward, and before I could analyze the situation, we were waltzing through the snow. Though my body was exhausted from anxiety, getting torn up, and not sleeping, somehow we moved gracefully under the stars. The moon seemed to look down at us with a wink, telling us that even though things were hard, there was still beauty to be enjoyed. Life gave us pure moments to cling to, so we had enough hope to lift our heads. I was covered in blood, waltzing with my almost brother, and somehow, without any magic at all, this became our fairytale.

Danny stepped on my feet four times before he grew frustrated with himself, though I never called him on his missteps. He dropped his arms and broke the rhythm of our dance, rubbing the back of his neck. "I was dreadful still, yeah?"

"Not terrible at all. Dashing, at the very least. Danny, you're getting better at dancing the more you do it. When we get home, make sure you practice all the time with Mariang. It's romantic as anything, and she'll eat it right up."

"You think?"

"I know. You're not bad at the whole romance thing. Quit selling yourself short."

Danny extended his hand to me to take, so we didn't trip in the dark. "You know, I think I just might take your advice on that."

I blame the waltzing on why I didn't hear the footfalls that trampled too near for a quick escape. "Danny?" I warned in a whisper, flipping open my dagger and crouching as I braced myself for whatever was coming.

Danny did the same, his arm stretching in front of me as a shield. His protective instinct was too precious an offer to push away. "It's a zombie. Let me handle it."

I didn't want to stand down, but I was already injured and unsure of my strength after the whole dangling from a tree thing. I heard growling when the feet came closer, crashing through the woods. I heard the gurgling of too much saliva, and the stink of rancid chicken, mixed with hot garbage in motion.

Then there were two sets of footsteps.

Three.

Seven.

"Von!" I called out when the monsters came into view, their jaws slack and their eyes unblinking. I hoped my voice carried to the others for help, but didn't count on the cavalry arriving in time. I moved off to the side to draw out a few of the zombies, so Danny didn't have to be the target for all of them.

"Stay behind me!" he warned.

I think we both knew I wasn't going to listen. I didn't wait for the zombies to claw at me first. I leapt forward, slicing and ripping with my blade as best I could. My conscience was too torn to make lucid decisions, so I killed on autopilot, using Danny as the thing that kept me fighting. I couldn't let Mariang not get to see Costa Rica. I bet it was gorgeous. Danny *had* to take her there, to waltz with her and romance her, the way a great girl like Mariang was meant to be swept off her feet. I ripped through one throat in the name of my new sister, knowing I would stop at nothing to make sure she had a good, long life.

I was scared of reanimation happening mid-battle, so I spent probably too much attention on each zombie, mutilating more than was strictly necessary, just to be safe.

We were down to the last two, and Danny was focused on the one before him. The zombie was a tall and broad-shouldered reverse centaur that made me feel small in comparison.

I never much cared for feeling small.

The Tikbalang zombie looked more freshly dead than the others, who'd had chunks of flesh missing on their faces and arms. This one looked healthier, stronger, though his jaw was still slack and his movements rigid.

I used one of the fallen bodies as leverage, running and jumping off it to fling myself at the tall one who was zeroed in on Danny. My blade glinted in the moonlight before it sunk into the side of his thick horse neck. He let out a howl mixed with a whinny, and then surprised me by sinking his long maw into my right wrist, coming down hard on the bone and ripping through my skin like it was a fruit rollup.

My scream was interrupted by Von, who flew in from out of nowhere, tackling the zombie. I expected him to latch onto the monster with his fangs and drain the life out of him, but Von resisted. He was firm that somehow he would kick this whole vampire thing.

I stumbled back, tripping over a body and falling,

catching myself with my wrist. It made a horrible cracking sound and sent agony up my arm to my brain. I prayed nothing else would come for me while I was down.

And then somehow I wasn't down anymore. I'd been scooped up by something hairy, strong and tall. "Let's get back to my place."

Mason's voice made me swoon. It was his hairy animal furs that he wore like armor, his strong arms and his presence that distracted me from the pain in my wrist. "Mason?"

"I'm here, *hani*." His words were gentle, almost like a song that soothed what ailed me. "This way!" he ordered, carrying me in his arms and leading the way to safety in a run.

42

TAKE ME HOME, HONEY

The way to Mason's house was still pretty far from where we were, but Mason didn't stop running. He didn't slow until he'd crossed a bridge, darted through a frozen tunnel, and ran us through yet more twisted trees with agility belying the icy darkness before he stopped.

"Wait!" I requested, motioning with my good hand for Ruiz to give me my backpack. Mason slowed near an unceremonious stone well near his log cabin in the woods. "The sagrado stone."

Ruiz unzipped the backpack and handed me the wadded-up pack that held the last bit of the stone. Mason steadied me when my feet touched down on the snow, but gave me a fair amount of space when I jerked open the bag using my good hand and my teeth. Without conversation or ceremony, I chucked the stone into the well, exhaling with the last bit of the magical burden off my shoulders. "It's done, then. We did it."

Mason kissed my temple, and then hoisted me up again in his arms, carrying me to the wood cabin. "*You* did it. Thank you for making sure Sombi wasn't forgotten."

Mason didn't let me down until he undid a latch at the top of the doorframe, plus one on the side, and kicked open the door, marching straight to his bedroom and laying me down on his bed. It was covered in long, cozy animal furs. "What are you doing here?" he demanded, his eyes wide. "Did you get shot? What happened to you?"

"Tiyanak," I mumbled, cradling my wrist to my chest. "I'm okay. Are you alright? Where've you been? We came here to bring you home."

Mason poured water from a pitcher into a basin on the nightstand, while the others filtered into the main room of his small log cabin. "I've been setting traps and trying to get a handle on Sombi. It's been a while since I was here, and things needed tending to. I would've come back. I was going to in the next day or so." He said it all like it was no big deal.

"Well, I didn't know that! I was scared you were being held by Sama or something!"

Mason's face contorted as he lit the oil lamp that hung on the wall. "Sama?" He threw a few logs in the fireplace in the corner of the bedroom and lit the kindling, blowing on the embers until the room glowed with a gentle warmth to quell my shivering. The log cabin glowed with amber and flickers of pink as the fire danced, illuminating the sparse wood furniture and fur rug that was stretched out in the middle of the floor. Mason stood, the flames lighting his features with an angelic luminescence. "Why would you be worried about something as crazy as Sama holding me hostage? What could he possibly want with me?"

Von came into the bedroom, but then stepped back out, bracing himself on the doorjamb to keep from getting too near my blood. "Because Sama went after me to hurt November. He's getting creative in his desperation, so we wanted you with us to make sure he didn't get his hooks into you." The firelight revealed drops of blood staining Von's shirt from the Type-A Kool-Aid he'd resisted drinking from the tall zombie. My blood was no doubt permeating his nose, but it seemed barely a distraction from the pain in his eyes as he looked at me from across the way. I could tell he wanted to be at my side, but was unable to trust himself. "Let's get home so we can patch her up. A Tikbalang Amalanhig bit her pretty bad."

Mason nodded, but eyed my still bleeding wrist with a skeptical eye. "That's fine. Let me bandage up her wrist first. I still need to close up the place." He slowly helped me work off my bloodied jacket, and looked down with a serious expression at my body. "This shirt is ruined, right?"

"Yeah."

I yelped in surprise when Mason pulled out his knife and sliced the bottom two inches from my shirts off in a long line, exposing my belly. "What? Did you think I was going to stab you or something?"

"No," I lied. I didn't know which way was up anymore.

Mason took his time bandaging the bite so my wrist didn't move as much, a small smile playing on his lips beneath his half-inch beard. "You came to my house. I've pictured you here a thousand times, but never once were you bleeding."

"Of course I came. I was worried about you. It was Von's idea, actually."

Mason turned to toss a smile up at Von, who was still gripping the doorframe. "You came to get me."

Von nodded in solidarity. "Of course we did. We're a team. Sama's targeting the people October loves. I wasn't about to leave you to fend for yourself."

"I figured the two of you might want some privacy, so I took my time coming back." Mason pried off my left glove, playing with the ring on my finger. A mix of emotions washed over his face. "That's... That's a nice ring," he said to us both.

"We're a team," I echoed. "You can have Allie's room until she wakes up, so you don't feel so uncomfortable. But I won't let Sama get his hooks in you like he did Von. You're coming home. You belong at my house with me."

Mason rested my right wrist to my chest and gathered me in his arms like a child. I leaned into the warmth of his gentle pulling; I'd missed it sorely. He looked like the wild mountain man I adored, having not shaved in who knows how long. He smelled like pine and patchouli, and I sucked in his scent greedily. I could feel his utter acceptance of all the weird things I was, and all the good things I wasn't. "I'm so sorry you lost your baby."

A pang like a hot knife sliced me through the chest. "How'd you even find out about that?"

"Ezra. I got the news and stayed here to make sure... You know."

My eyebrows drew together as I rested in his capable arms. "What?"

"To make sure September didn't... You know."

Von's intake of breath told me he was a few seconds ahead of figuring out the thing that eluded me. "Is that even possible? September's an Omen! She was buried properly by Kabayo in his crypt."

"The body doesn't matter. It's a twisted spirit." Mason shook his head, his tone grave as he held me, rocking gently to soothe the ache in my chest. I could feel him steadily pulling some of my stress, and loved him for it. There was nowhere to wash my hands, and they'd been crawling with germs. "We don't know if September died inside of October or shortly after she was born. If a Terraway baby dies in the womb, its soul twists and births into a Tiyanak. Then it appears in the forest of Sombi. I figured with Sama's involvement, he'd send his spies to search for September's spirit here. I found a few battalions marching through, but they stopped coming around a while ago." His voice lowered. "I haven't found your daughter. All the Tiyanaks I've killed recently have either been boys, or girls that were the wrong age. I'm sorry," he offered. "It's mostly why I haven't returned Topside yet."

My whole body went white as I pictured my perfect daughter chomping down on strangers in the frozen woods. "W-we have to go find her. Let me try. Maybe she'll recognize my voice."

Mason shook his head, holding onto me to make sure I didn't go off on my own. "No. If she's here, she isn't your daughter anymore; she's a twisted spirit. She wouldn't know you from a random stranger. You're a meal to her, and nothing more."

"But I was able to reason with Bobby! I got him to calm down."

"Who's Bobby?" Mason asked Von.

"Bobby Brady!" I answered, frustrated that no one understood the urgency of the situation.

"What?" Von's head tilted to the side. When I explained that I'd named the Tiyanak Bobby Brady, Von's shoulders deflated. "Oh, love. No. You were able to reason with Bobby, sure, but it didn't make him not a monster. If September ended up here, she wouldn't be the girl we love. It would be a violent, twisted spirit. Mason's right."

Anger flared up in me as I struggled to free myself from Mason's embrace; it had been my safe haven mere seconds ago. "I can't believe you'd give up like that! She's our daughter!"

Von flinched, blinking like I'd slapped him. He stepped

back, stumbling into Danny, who glared at me. "You're talking rubbish," Danny growled. "If Mason couldn't find her, then she didn't turn into a Tiyanak. She was born Topside, so perhaps that spared her spirit from coming down here. Either way, you'll not put that kind of guilt on Von."

I deflated, lowering my chin at the scolding I knew I'd deserved. "You're right. I'm sorry, Von. Mason, are you sure she's not here?"

Mason nodded. "As sure as I can be. It's been weeks, and I've been searching every day." He called over his shoulder to the others. "You can start porting back to October's house now. I'd like a word with her, then I'll bring her back."

Danny was hesitant, but eventually went along with anything that got him closer to Mariang. When the pops of porting sounded from the main room, Mason exhaled that we were finally alone. "You alright?" he asked.

"I honestly don't know how much that even matters anymore. It's been a rough... night? Week? Year?"

He cleared his throat, gearing up to say something he'd clearly put a lot of thought into. "I bit you before I went away. I would ask your forgiveness, but some things are just... I don't know how to apologize enough for it. I'm so sorry, *hani*. I should've left sooner, and not assumed I could handle being around you when you were so very pregnant. We were doing well, and then I went and attacked you." He gulped. "Attacked you *again*. The first time, I tried to break your back; the second time, I pinned you down and kissed you; and now this? I can't tell you how sorry I am that you got stuck with a monster like me as your Reaper. That's one of the other reasons I've been reluctant to come back to you."

I reached up with my good hand and placed it over his mouth. "No more. It's all a hundred years ago. You're Matruculan; we both knew it would be tricky. My leg's fine. You don't have to give it another thought. I don't look at you and see a monster."

Mason cast me a dubious look. "Well, you have a terrible radar for that sort of thing. You're engaged to a half-vamp, your new father's Matruculan, and your fiancé's family are all Duwende. You're literally surrounded by monsters."

"Mason, I couldn't be upset with you if I tried. I'm just so happy you're okay. I was worried something bad happened that was keeping you from coming back. And the thing is, we need you."

Mason's eyebrows raised at my declaration. "I need you, too. This Reaper-Omen bond makes it hard to stay away. There's this emptiness." He touched his chest and shook his head. "I don't like being separate from you."

The corner of my mouth tugged upward. "I love you, too, Mason. Let's never be apart for this long again."

"Deal."

I leaned up and kissed his scruffy cheek. "Take me home, honey."

43

TWO CREATURES

Mason was quiet when he ported me Topside. He didn't put me down, but held me in his arms. "I'm alright to stand," I told him. "I only hurt the top of me."

Mason touched the outside of my thigh with his thumb, smirking at my sharp inhalation. "Yeah, it's all going to start hitting you now. Your leg's bleeding, *hani*. I don't want you putting pressure on it. And your wrist needs a doctor to look at it." He cast around my living room, his eyes falling on Von, who was the only other person in the house, apart from Danny. "Can you drive us to a doctor?"

"Sure. Set her down on a chair so you can wash up and change into civilian clothes first. Then we'll take her in."

I exhaled, wishing I could set my wrist myself, if indeed it was broken. Mason gave me another pull before he sat me down on a chair in the kitchen, retiring to the bathroom while Von brought me a clean tank top. "You don't have to be in here, you know. I know all this blood can't be easy for you."

Von forced a light smile. "'Easy' is my middle name, darling." He worked quickly, cutting off my bloody and torn shirts, running a wet rag over my torso to clean up the blood I was coated in, and working my tank top over my head.

I quirked my eyebrow at my boyfriend. "Not a single pervy comment? You're losing your touch."

"I'm breathing through my teeth. If you hadn't kissed me already and broken the curse part of being a vampire, I would've bitten clean through your... But I'm in control. I'm pretty sure," Von admitted, putting my torn shirts in a plastic grocery bag. He paused a moment to smell his fingers, his eyes rolling back. "When you're all bloody like this, I honestly can't decide which part of me wants you more – the fiancé or the vampire. I hate that I'm two creatures." He tightened his fist. "I can do this. It's the same as quitting smoking. Just self-control."

"Are you sure? Maybe with me all oozing isn't the time to test your limits. We have blood bags for a reason, Von."

Von's smile was tight as it spread across his handsome face. "I can still see you, you know. Before you broke my curse, my bloodlust would cloud out the details of why I loved you. I'd start to hear only your heartbeat and smell only your blood. But I can still see you now. I'm beating it, Peach."

"If anyone could, my money would be on you."

Von's gaze softened, and I could feel his adoration. "I love that you believe in me." His eyes fell. "I hate that I'm two creatures. I hope you see I'm not the monster right now."

I tugged on the front of his shirt and pulled him down to plant a kiss on his lips. "You're my fiancé. No matter how good I smell, you're always that guy."

"You should be careful what monsters you invite into your bed, young lady. Positively scandalous." He was joking again, which I took to mean as his thirst was past him now.

"You should kiss me again. Like you mean it. Like you want to make me forget how bad my wrist hurts." I looked up at him through my lashes. "Kiss me like a vampire trying to seduce me into dark corners. We just survived Sombi. I think I deserve a little seduction."

Lust was visible in Von's eyes. As he chewed on his lower lip, I could tell he was very much my fiancé, and not so much the vampire. "You're playing with fire, little Omen."

I gave his shirt a yank with my good hand, so I could press my lips to his ear. "Then make it hurt."

Von groaned, his hands roaming my torso as his lips stroked mine, finally introducing the colors that made me swoon. I'd missed the taste of his mouth, the trumpets and glitter of gold that took me away from what ailed me, and put me on a higher plane of existence. In between kisses, Von's tongue migrated down to my flushed skin just above my bra. I thrilled at the sensation that was both in our fantasy world and in reality. There was no Sombi, no monsters and no responsibilities. There was the kiss, our park and our own little world where we could escape to.

...Until a sharp pain jerked me out of our bliss. "Ow! Oh, that hurts!"

Von stumbled back drunkenly, shaking his head while trying to assess which world we were in. "What happened?"

"Nothing. Something scraped me." *Your teeth.* I realized that maybe I was flirting with danger in the very bad way one should never flirt at all.

Von's nostrils flared, and before I could brace myself, he pounced. My boyfriend knocked my chair back so he could yank my tank top down and nip at the long cut. The slice stretched from my collar to my breast, and wasn't quite closed yet. My head hit the floor, my wrist jarred uncomfortably, and a cry of distress sounded from my lips as Von's teeth grazed my cut, opening it further so his tongue could sweep across the swell. His feral grunts broke my heart. "Help!" I cried to anyone who might hear me. I twisted and struggled to get away, but I couldn't bring myself to punch Von to knock him off me. "No, Von!" I tried to push at him with my good arm, but he was in a world unto himself, his hand cupping my chin so he could pin my head to the floor and get a better angle. It was sensual. It was painful.

It was terrifying.

Danny ran into the kitchen, his eyes wide as he tried to figure out what was going on. When he heard Von's animalistic slurps, he ripped his brother off of me and flung him into the wall. "No! Von, get ahold of yourself." When Von lunged for me again, I scrambled out of the chair and crawled with one functioning arm away from the battling brothers. Danny slammed Von back again, knocking some sense into him with the second blow. "You need blood, but you can't have hers."

Mason ran into the kitchen, wet, and clad in only a pair of pants. He pinned Von to the wall while my boyfriend gnashed his teeth and growled to get at me. Danny ran to the fridge and grabbed a blood bag, twisting off the lid and shoving the lip into Von's mouth. With every pull, Von seemed to come down from the frenzy another notch, his eyes widening and drooping over and over as he tried to get ahold of himself. Then he threw the blood bag down in disgust, the crimson pooling on my clean kitchen floor. "No! I don't want to be a vampire! I'm in control!"

I was useless, curled in a ball in the corner between the counters and the trash can, shuddering at the scene I'd caused. "I'm sorry!" I choked out. "It's my fault. He's been off blood, going on four days now. I shouldn't have kissed him all bloody like I am. Von, I'm so sorry."

Danny was livid. "*Off* blood? How exactly does a vampire go off blood?"

Von swallowed thickly. "Like a person giving up meat and becoming a vegetarian. I'm a person, Danny! I can do this! It's just a setback."

Danny's shock came in the form of shouting. "This is nothing like going off meat! Humans can survive without meat. You're trying to survive without basic sustenance! You're mental if you think this is helping you. You're only going to be more dangerous to October if you keep this up."

Von reached out and clutched Danny's shirt in his fist, shouting his words through gritted teeth. "I'm a person, Danny! I don't want to be a vampire anymore!" There was anger, and beneath that was a desperation that tugged at my heart. "I'm a man! I don't want my bride to marry a monster!"

Mason's restraint mutated into a rough hug, engulfing Von in the embrace I wished I could give him. "Easy, brother. I've got you. Settle down."

Von struggled against the kindness for a few seconds, but finally gave up his fight. "I can be stronger," he worked out, his tone laced with self-loathing and doubt.

"You're plenty strong, Von," Mason assured him, like the good friend he'd learned to be. "It has nothing to do with that. You are who you are, and we all respect you. You don't have to put this on yourself."

"I'm sorry, Von," I managed. "This was on me. I'm a

nurse. I should've done a more thorough check on you to make sure you could actually survive without blood. Danny's right. It's got nothing to do with self-control. Finish your blood bag."

"I don't need it!" Von raged. "You said you believed in me!"

"I do! But what you're doing is starving yourself. Of course I believe in you. I wouldn't be alive still if you didn't have stellar self-control."

When Von slowly calmed, Mason finally released him from the hug. He clapped Von on the shoulder a few times, keeping his hand there, just in case.

Von sneaked longing looks at his saving grace that was leaking on my floor, coating the tile in red. When words finally came to him, they were filled with regret. "Get her to a doctor. I'm sorry, *hani*. I can't go with you. I'm sorry. I'm so sorry." The self-loathing was radiating off of him in waves while Mason kept him in place. "Just go." With a cry of agony, Von collapsed onto all fours and started licking the blood off the floor like an animal. "Go, October! I can't stop, and I don't want you to see me like this!"

I tried standing, but as it turns out, my leg wasn't as strong as it needed to be. None of me was. I don't even remember hurting it. The long slice that caught my eye on my thigh was no doubt the work of a zombie.

Danny bent down, his hand cuffing Von on the scruff of the neck. "I'll watch her for you. Go easy on yourself, mate. Drink until you're full, so you don't hurt her again."

His fingers gripped harder, and his next words came out pained. "You can't transition, Von. I need you to be my big brother."

Von paused his feast and grasped Danny in a tearful hug. He didn't have the words, but I could see the raw emotion on his tear- and blood-stained face.

Danny finally released his brother and helped me to my feet. "I'll take her right now."

I yelped through the pain of my wrist being jostled as Danny lifted me up in his arms. He marched through the living room, snatching up my keys on his way out.

The warm air greeted me, almost surprising me with the fact that it was midday, and you know, not the frozen tundra. Danny was gentle as he lowered me to the passenger's seat, and careful with every crack in the pavement as he drove down the street and pulled out onto the main road.

Finally, I broke the tensed silence. "I'm sorry. I know it was bad. You don't have to bother with the lecture."

"Good. You don't seem to listen when I talk anyway. Von's dangerous, kid. He's a vampire, no matter what degree it's taken him over. I'm just glad Mason's staying with you again. What if we weren't around? Then what do you suppose would've happened? You would've died, or at best, you would live, but Von would've drank enough blood to turn. Then we'd all lose him completely and forever. You have to be more careful than this!"

I nodded, unable to argue the very valid point. In

Danny's frustration, I saw that he did love Von, and cared if his brother was taken from him for good.

My tank top was stained with gooey red, and my hands were shaking from the blood loss. I cursed aloud when I realized I'd left my wallet at home. "We have to go back. I need my information if they're going to treat me at the emergency room."

"We're not going back there. Von's not in control yet. Think of a better option. I can take you to Ezra's. I'm sure he could call a doctor to the mansion."

"No. I need a legit x-ray machine." My brain flipped through a number of roadblocks before I let out a heavy sigh. "Can I borrow your cell phone?" I knew the number by heart. I mean, I only had a handful of contacts, so it wasn't too difficult to remember. I waited three rings, clearing my throat to reassemble my bearings when the male voice answered. "Hey, Brenden. I'm in a bit of a situation."

After that phone call, I knew I had one more that I should make as an act of good will. I closed my eyes as I waited for the other side to pick up, wishing I'd made better choices in life. "Hey, Judge. I'm heading over to the prison. Do you need me to drop any messages for you?"

44

NEVER COME BACK HERE

I kept my head down as the guard at the front desk checked me in with a healthy amount of chitchat I tried to smile through. Luckily, I'd stashed my old work ID in my glove box, back when I had foolish hopes that one day I could return to my regularly scheduled program after the Terraway show was over. I used my old ID (and Brenden's written request to let me up) to get myself past check-in, while Danny used just enough pulling to make it through each checkpoint, the sneak. It didn't dawn on me until then that Mason and Von had most likely used that same maneuver to get past security when they'd gone in with me on my last day. I'd been so turned around that I hadn't questioned it then.

I had too much blood on me, and worried Danny's blue and red flannel shirt would only cover my injury for so long. I'd discarded my tank top in the car in exchange for

Danny's less stained offering. "Just stopping by to pay a visit to the doctor. He needed my consult on a patient," I lied, producing the fib Brenden had instructed me to use.

Danny put his visitor's badge on his sweat-stained white t-shirt, hovering close to quell his nerves. He was used to keeping Mariang safe from monsters, but these were the monsters of my reality, not his. "I don't like this. Are you quite sure there's nowhere else I can take you?"

"Without ID? No. This'll be quick." The guard waved me through without an escort, knowing I knew the prison well enough to get around without supervision.

Danny's hand fell into mine. It was sweet, but had that note of concern to it. He pulled a little of my anxiety that had peaked from the sting of the soreness I still felt. His eyes darted around furtively. "Why on earth did you ever work here? This is so dangerous."

I allowed myself the luxury of a small scoff. "It's a good thing my current job is roses and kittens. I worked where they would hire me as young as I was. There are always guards around, so it's not as unsafe as you're thinking."

"You have no sense of self-preservation."

"That's lucky for all of you, I guess. If I did, there's no way I would've gone along with the Terraway nonsense as long as I have." I led Danny to the infirmary that smelled like rubbing alcohol and felt like a familiar hug I'd missed. Brenden buzzed me into the room with a look of concern marring his welcoming smile. "Hey, Brenden. Good to see you again. Thanks for this."

Brenden scratched the slight cleft on his chin. "Of course. I only wish you came back under better circumstances. Come have a seat on the table. We've got the infirmary to ourselves, at least for now." He was all business, just as he'd been when I'd worked by his side. Fixing the patient had always been priority one, and then we would shoot the breeze over paperwork with our congenial back and forth. His dark brown eyebrows knit together beneath the thick black frames of his glasses. "Tell me about your injury."

"Um, well inju*ries*," I corrected him. "I think my wrist might be fractured, and I've got a few cuts I can't stitch up with one hand."

"How'd you injure your wrist?" he asked, taking the damaged wrist and examining it with feather-like care.

"I fell." It was kind of the truth. I mean, I did let myself fall from that tree after cutting Ruiz down. I didn't think "reverse centaur bite" or "evil baby spirit attack" would go over all that believably.

Brenden unwrapped the bandage Mason had made me from my bloody t-shirt, frowning at the crescent-shaped teeth marks that were clearly not from a simple fall. He pushed his black frames up his nose and squinted one eye at me. "Care to recant your statement? How did you break the skin here?"

I sighed. "It's a long story, and not one I can share. Can you fix my wrist?" I knew he could, it was just a matter of if he would help me, knowing I was lying.

Brenden spoke slowly. "I can. Can you keep something like this from happening to you again?" His eyes flashed to Danny, who was looking around the infirmary with wary eyes. "Are you in some sort of trouble?" He shook his head. "Silly question. Of course you are. Otherwise you would've just gone to the ER."

The buzzer sounded overhead, making Danny even more uncomfortable. "Oh, I didn't realize you had a patient," I said, hopping off the table, and wishing I had my hospital scrubs on to give myself that one degree of professional separation. "Danny, hide behind the partition."

Danny, of course, didn't listen to me. "No need." He held up his palm and wriggled his fingers, letting me know he'd rather pull than leave my side.

Brenden tapped a few buttons on his computer. "I don't have a real patient, actually. But I told the guards I needed you for a consult. It might look suspicious if I didn't have an inmate up here for you to check out." Brenden cast me a dubious look that told me how much he didn't care for having to lie.

"Thank you. And I'm so sorry, Brenden. Really. This'll never happen again."

Brenden's shoulders loosened, and he cracked a small smile. "It's alright. You should always come to me if you have a problem. Just try to have fewer problems that involve a potential fracture in your wrist."

"Duly noted," I said with a nod as Brenden walked to

the wall and pushed the green button to let in the guard with his inmate.

Make that guards.

I turned around to see none other than Terence being escorted in by Jerry and Bryce, instead of the usual one uniform per inmate. Our intakes of breath matched at seeing each other so unexpectedly. The feeling of overwhelming gratitude and the desire to make sure he was okay washed over me, flooding my veins with a maternal tsunami in my chest. I wanted to watch over the towering thirty-three-year-old man like he was my baby bear cub – the way he'd watched over me.

Brenden waved off the second guard. "It's just an exit interview, guys. You know Terence is one of the few inmates Nurse Gracie's actually safe around."

"You've got a visitor in here?" Bryce asked warily, looking at Danny. I didn't know a ton about Bryce, just that he liked his coffee stronger than the breakroom brewed it, and he mostly kept to himself.

Danny shook the hands of both guards, who had been ready to jerk Terence back out of the room at the breach of procedure. I knew Danny would only make such a show of kindness if he had an ulterior motive. I saw Jerry's shoulders relax, and surmised that Danny had pulled the suspicion and protocol straight out of both of them.

"It's my fiancé's brother," I offered, letting them know Danny was fine, despite the cagey looks he kept tossing Terence.

Jerry, my favorite of all the guards because he'd never once called me "kid", dipped his head in my direction as Brenden's eyebrows shot up. "Congratulations, Nurse Gracie. I didn't even know you were seeing anyone. When did you up and get engaged?" His skin was a hair darker than Terence's, and without the scars that littered the second-born McCray boy.

"Not too long ago." I held up my ring that shone with too much audacity and sparkle. "Henry here's brother is quite the charmer." I smiled at Danny, letting him know that his name was now Henry.

Danny nodded to the guard in lieu of speaking a greeting.

"You sure you're okay?" Bryce asked everyone, including Jerry, to make sure he could handle Terence if he acted up. We all nodded, and then Bryce pointed his finger at Terence, who narrowed his eyes at the guard. "Now listen up, T. You get out in a few days. Don't go throwing away your parole now. You behave yourself."

Terence didn't respond in any way, not even with a nod. He didn't much care for being bossed, big as he was. He didn't behave because of threats from guards; he fell in line because he preferred a quiet and peaceful life.

Bryce seemed disconcerted by this, so he swallowed hard and nodded, as if somehow Terence's silence indicated his compliance. "Good. Nice to see you again, kid. And congrats on the wedding. Lucky guy."

I offered up a smile and waved him off, glad there was

one less person to deal with now. My fiancé had almost just killed me because I'd kissed him while nursing an open wound. Images of Von tearing into me during our vows, chomping into my skin through my wedding dress, flooded my mind. The wedding seemed eons away, not that we'd set a date. The well-wishes did little to dispel my inner turmoil.

Terence kept his calculating eyes on Danny throughout Brenden's exam of him, which was fast and clinical. Brenden was taking notes on his clipboard, ready to discharge him when he threw up the obligatory, "What do you think, Nurse Gracie? Is Terence good to go?"

I moved closer to Terence, so I could get a better look. I grimaced through the pain in my leg I'd forgotten about. Danny was my shadow, hovering behind me with a silent threat that I was not to be touched. Jerry watched the exchange with disinterest, no doubt coming to the same conclusion I had long ago – Terence was no threat to me. "Could you stand and raise your arms over your head, please?" I asked, studying the way his left arm wasn't able to raise all the way to a vertical line. "And can you bend down and touch your toes?"

Terence met my gaze with his foreboding dark one, taking a full ten seconds before he obeyed. I could see a million flashes of emotion in the eyes I knew so well. To anyone else, it would have seemed an intimidation tactic, but I could see clearly his worry at me being back at the prison, and what that might mean. His fingers swept toward his shins, but were unable to touch his government-issued shoes. With every movement, Danny watched Terence, in case he breathed wrong. I motioned to a nearby orange plastic chair for Danny to relax in, but he only complied insomuch as he took one step back. "Terence, have you been in a fight recently?"

Terence gave a curt nod, his eyes locking in on mine again to tell me that he was hurt worse than he cared to let on.

Brenden checked his file on Terence, frowning. "He hasn't been up here in a couple months."

"That's because he doesn't like to let on that he's hurt."

Terence opened his mouth to speak – a thing he rarely did without absolute necessity. "I don't like coming up here since you left. Why'd you leave?"

My whole demeanor softened, my shoulders relaxing at the puppy cuteness in his midnight eyes. "It was time for me to move on. I'm sorry you've been hurt this whole time, though. What happened?" I patted the table for him to sit down on again. "Your ribs are bothering you, eh?"

Terence nodded. "Yard fight."

I gave him my best motherly smile, pressing two fingers to each rib, making my way down the row until he winced. "Well, we can't send you back out into the world all banged up. Can we get him an x-ray, Brenden? They're probably just bruised, but best double check."

Brenden huffed at Terence. "You can still come up

here. Just because Nurse Gracie's gone doesn't mean you won't get adequate medical care."

Terence didn't respond to this because it wasn't necessary. He didn't like talking unless there was no other option. "I can take Terence to x-ray," I offered, holding up my wrist. "Two birds with one stone."

Brenden nodded, glancing up at Jerry. My favorite nonintrusive guard escorted us to the x-ray room, which was just down the hall to the right. The machine took a minute to warm up, making its comforting whirring sound I'd missed. "You got any big plans for when you get your freedom back?" I asked kindly.

Terence nodded. "I'm staying with Darius." He pointed to my wrist that I hadn't realized I was cradling to my chest – a dead giveaway I was injured. "If your fiancé steps out of line, I'll take care of him for you." There was no hint of aggression or sleazy suggestion in his voice, just a promise between old friends.

Danny didn't like it. "My brother's not going to step out of line, yeah? You don't have to offer your services. She's well taken care of."

Terence's eyes zoomed in on my wrist. "I can see that."

I motioned to the chair behind the desk. "Go sit, *Henry*. Everything's fine. Terence is a good guy. He's an old friend, actually. Known me since I was a baby."

Danny let out a low groan that made it sound like my words pained him as he moved to the chair. "You drive me absolutely mad."

I ignored Danny, helping Terence get situated for the x-ray. "Hold still just like that," I instructed. I positioned his arms just how the machine needed them to best read his injury, and situated the heavy lead vest on his body. "And thanks for the offer. I'm glad I won't have to take you up on it. This wasn't from my fiancé. He's a good guy." I went to the machine and pressed the necessary buttons, turning him again to get a different angle. When he was finished, I took the lead vest off of him carefully with my one functioning hand, bestowing on him a quick hug that couldn't be detected by Jerry. I lowered my voice when Terence looked down at me as he stood. "Listen to me, Terence, I want good things for you. I want you to lay low and be careful. Stay out of trouble, okay? And I mean, if you see trouble, run *away* from it, not toward it. I don't want to ever see you back here."

Terence paused, and then bobbed his head twice.

My voice lowered with too much guilt. "I spoke with Judge on the way here. He said he wants you to lay low. You're almost out, and he doesn't want anything to set you back. So if you see a fight, walk the other way, okay?" I scratched my thigh, wincing when I grazed over the slash I kept forgetting was there. "He also wanted me to tell you that Javier stepped out of line. He said you'd know what to do." I looked up into his eyes, fear and heaviness weighing on me. "But don't do it, hun. Please don't hurt anyone."

Terence spoke slowly, his eyes narrowing. "You're delivering messages for Judge now?"

My eyes lowered with remorse. "I owe him a few favors. He's helping me with a security problem I'm having."

Terence's thick upper lip curled into a sneer. "You tell my big brother that for every message you deliver, that's another load I'll just happen to *not* deliver when I get out. He's down by one now."

I nodded, unable to speak for several seconds. "Be careful. I wish you could stay somewhere with people who won't get you into trouble." As I said it, I realized that I hadn't been taking my own advice. Since the Vandershots and Ezra's crew had walked into my life, there had been a steady stream of trouble. I hadn't been able to walk away, but I was expecting Terence to master the feat. "Please, Terence. I don't want to have to worry about you ending up back here. Be a good man. I know you want more than this."

"Okay, baby girl." We shared a sliver of a smile at the nickname usually only Judge used. Terence called me "Nurse Gracie" in lockup to keep my identity safe, but since it was just us, we spoke like the friends we were. He glanced down at my wrist. "You need to be more careful, too. Your security isn't cutting it. When I get out, I'll give your house a look to make sure everything's how it should be." Terence towered over me with his mouth in a tight line. "Plus, you never finished reading me that book. We were almost to the end."

I smiled up at him, unable to mask my affection for Terence. "Once you get settled, I'll have you over for dinner sometime. You can meet my guy, and I'll read to you until we finish *The Swiss Family Robinson*." I knew by this point that my story with the McCray brothers would never be finished, but perhaps it could have a happier ending.

"Will you make the applesauce like Mama used to?" The insecurity and longing for simpler times shone in his eyes, tugging on my heartstrings.

"Of course I will. I'll make a whole pot of it all for you. We can get Judge the store-bought kind if he starts being a pain," I teased, drawing out a smirk from Terence.

Danny stood across the way from behind the machine's controls, letting Terence know I was not alone. "Are you quite finished, then?"

Jerry watched the exchange with his hand touching the bat at his side, just in case. "Alright, Terence. Let's go back to the doc."

"Tell Brenden I'll be there in a minute," I said to Jerry.

Danny waited until the door closed before he spoke his mind. "We're leaving. Get your arm looked at, and we're out of here. You're never stepping a foot back inside this place, yeah?"

"Terence just looks scary, but he's a total puppy."

"That doesn't sound like a 'yes, Danny.'"

"Yes, Danny," I offered with a roll of my eyes. I positioned my wrist how I knew it needed to be, and instructed Danny which buttons to push. "Well done. You're almost ready for your medical degree. You've got that warm bedside manner about you," I kidded, trying to get him to loosen up. Unsurprisingly, it didn't work. "You know they can smell your fear, right? If you act like being here is no big deal, that's exactly how it is. If you act like you're looking for a fight, you'll find one, sure enough."

"Says the girl with the broken wrist. Spare me the finer points of your worldview."

We walked back to the infirmary with the x-rays, and even though I was down to one hand, I was still able to make myself useful helping Brenden tape Terence's ribs. Terence parted with a sweet bob of his head in my direction, mouthing "never come back here" to me like a prayer, before he was escorted out by Jerry.

45

STRIPPING FOR DANNY

I clipped my x-rays onto the light board to examine the bones that were immoveable. "Crap."

"What?" Danny asked, looking over my shoulder.

Brenden pointed to the problem bone in my wrist. "Just a small break, kid. It'll heal just fine after we set it. Easy enough."

"Yeah, okay. Danny, why don't you wait in the hallway?" I didn't feel the need to use his fake name, now that only Brenden was with us.

Danny snorted derisively, looking down his nose at me. "Are you having a laugh, or are you suicidal? Not out of my sight, kid."

"Brenden's going to have to reset my wrist, and I don't want you to hear me scream."

"I honestly don't have the patience for your pride today.

Set it, stitch it, and let's go. I mean it. Not a second longer than we have to be here."

Brenden chuckled as he motioned for me to sit down on the table. "Someone doesn't like that you play with the inmates?"

"Brothers are funny like that."

"Okay, now. Try to sit still. You know what's coming, but if you could try not to tense up, that would help me only to have to do this once."

I nodded, knowing relaxing was going to be out of reach. Danny seemed to know the right thing to do, though I hadn't had an inkling. He moved to my other side with a look that told me he had this whole thing under control. His arm wrapped around my back, tilting me toward him so I leaned into his chest from my seat on the table. Danny was bulkier than Von, which made him a good pillow to rest against. He cupped my face with his free hand so I only saw his eyes that were telling me to buck up when I wanted to run. Oh, how far and how long I wanted to run. For so many reasons, I wished for an infinite sprint that would carry me far, far away from Terraway, from broken bones, and from all of it.

When Brenden lifted my hand, I closed my eyes to brace myself through the pain I knew would snap a scream out of me. I'd reset quite a few bones myself, and the inmates always howled.

"Hey," Danny whispered. "Look at me. Don't go somewhere else in your mind."

"Relax your hand, Gracie. I'll make it quick," Brenden said in his calm doctor voice.

My lashes fluttered open, begging Danny silently to make the pain of Terraway go away from us. I felt his steady pull start to ramp up, peeling away my anxiety in layers until my hand was limp in Brenden's capable grip.

When the scream cracked out of me, Danny gripped me to his chest, cradling me. He kept my arm still, so Brenden could put it in a brace. I insisted I didn't need the song and dance of a brace for such a small bone, but Brenden overruled me with his handy MD. Danny was sweet to me the entire time, not calling me out on my yelpy cry. He didn't let go when I needed someone to stay with me. I would never admit to needing him there, but he was a good brother and read my mind, as only the best brothers can do.

"She's got a few deep cuts," Danny told Brenden when I was about to get off the table. When I tried to pass off Danny's concern as nothing, he said, "Do you really think you can stitch yourself up with one functioning hand? Let's get everything taken care of now. I don't want to bring you home with open wounds."

Brenden nodded with compassion in his kind eyes. "Of course, Gracie. Let's see what you've got. Where else do you need help?"

My cheeks flamed pink and I shot Brenden a look of chagrin. "For the record, I was going to try and fix this by myself. It's my... this area," I said, motioning to my chest.

For all my medical experience, I couldn't say the word breasts in front of my coworker. It was too embarrassing. I really, really didn't want to show him.

Brenden smirked at me, holding up his hands to display their innocence. "Why don't you show me? Maybe the cut won't be as deep as you're thinking." When I hesitated, he tilted his head to the side. "I've treated women before, remember. With you. It's your choice, of course, but you don't have to be uncomfortable."

I nodded, fiddling with the button on the flannel Danny had given me to wear. I couldn't move my fingers with the brace, and grew frustrated. "Just forget it. It's probably not that deep."

Danny moved to stand next to Brenden, motioning for me to look only into his eyes. With careful fingers, Danny undid the row of buttons, and then gently slid off the flannel. To his credit, he did not look down, but kept me locked into his gaze that told me not to worry.

To *my* credit, I did not punch him for partially undressing me. I only looked away from Danny's determined stare when Brenden gasped. "What happened to you? I'm serious, kid. What did this?"

Danny glanced down and swore, scrambling for a quick lie. "We were camping, her fiancé, and a few others of us. We came across a wolf who took a shine to her."

Okay, well that's not a total lie.

"A wolf?"

Danny cleared his throat. "You should treat her for an animal attack."

I looked down at my blood-soaked bra that had been teal and lacy once upon a time. It was now almost tie-dyed with the dried maroon that marred the perky original color. "Whoa. I guess it's a little worse than I thought."

Brenden laid me back on the table and started dabbing at my chest with a warm cloth to clean the skin around the wound. "It's nothing that's not fixable."

I covered my face with my good hand, wishing I'd taken my chances with the hospital and no ID. "I'm so sorry I'm making you do this. I really was just coming here for the wrist. This is so embarrassing."

Brenden chuckled as he set to cleaning me up so he could get a look at the source of the problem. "It's really fine. You're a far sight better than the usual patients I get. That you think this is a chore is too funny."

Danny picked up my good hand and moved to the other side of the table, making sure I looked only at him when Brenden disinfected the cut and then stitched me up. He wrote me a prescription to treat any lingering infection, while Danny buttoned the flannel shirt back on me, like a gentleman. I thought sliding my pants down for Brendan to clean up the slice on my thigh would bring me to a new level of mortification, but apparently, I'd already reached my max capacity for humiliation.

Brenden quirked an eyebrow at me while he washed his hands after he finished up. "Your fiancé let you go off injured like this? Not to speak out of turn, but no way would I send my brother with my wife if she'd broken her wrist."

Danny answered for me. "He ate something that was very bad for him, so he sent me until his sickness passes."

This seemed to make sense to Brenden, so there was nothing more said about it. There was only profuse thanks coming from me, and a polite smile emanating from Brendan before we left. After the brief glimpse into my former job, Danny clung tight to my hand as we made our way out into the fresh air.

46

MARIANG'S HEARTBURN

I stayed with Mariang and Danny in their hotel room that night to give Von some space from my blood. Mariang was good for what ailed me. She'd been super bored before I'd come, so she set to entertaining me with stories about her pregnancy, and the fun things she, Boston and Graham had gotten up to. I brushed her hair while she gossiped about the scandal of the mysterious man at the end of the hall who had a different woman with him every other night. I rubbed her sore ankles while she grinned at the brothers, as they argued about who could bench press more.

The five of us laughed, traded stories and palled around until Mariang started yawning. She offered me a pair of her short pink shorts and a tank top to sleep in. I wished I had the guts to ask her for something less revealing, but I didn't want to complain at the gift, especially when she was living out of her suitcase. I was a bit curvier than she, and knew I'd look not so classy in her clothes. But as Danny's flannel had bloodstains on it, I took her gift with a smile of gratitude.

Graham pulled down the covers for me, jerking his chin to the queen-sized bed near the window we were to share, while Boston and Danny did a double pull for Mariang in the other bed. I'd missed Graham's company in the way you miss an old neighbor you hadn't seen in too long. You missed him, but you didn't necessarily feel the need to sleep in the same bed with him. However, until my body had a little more time to heal, it was best for me to stay away from Von.

I got into the bed and twirled my ring around my finger. I watched the diamond sparkle in the dim lamplight Graham had on, so he could read his dusty historical biographies before he went to sleep. I don't know why, but there was something precious about his affinity for history nonfiction books. His hand reached out and found its way into my hair I'd taken down, absentmindedly tangling in the tresses as he lost himself in the affairs of people who lived centuries ago. When he finished, he turned off the lamp and slid down in the bed beside me, his arm bumping against mine as we lay on our backs with the sides of our heads pressed together. "Missed you, little sis," Graham admitted in a whisper.

"Missed you, too."

Graham opened his mouth to say something, but

Mariang let out a noise of discomfort from the next bed, turning on her side. My eyes landed on the clock, informing me that it was 11:05pm. It was the fourth time she'd tossed, and Boston apparently decided he'd had enough. "I'm jumping ship, mate," he said to Danny. "Must sleep." Boston slid into our bed on my other side, not bothering to ask if we had room for another. He cuddled up to me, his arm draping over my stomach, using me like a body pillow. "Much better." He nuzzled my cheek and let out a contented sigh. "I missed you."

"Well, make yourself comfortable," I chuckled, kissing Boston's forehead. The slight stretch made my stiches pull, and I winced as the twinge pricked at my skin.

Graham's eyes flicked down to my breasts, masking his sheepish smile with concern. "Does it still hurt?"

"It's not so bad."

Boston pinched my abdomen. "How about I kiss your sweet breasts to make them feel better?" I elbowed Boston, satisfied when a loud "oof!" expelled from his lips. "I was mostly kidding. Calm down. Am I really the first to offer that?" He made himself comfortable, closing his eyes as he rested his chin to my shoulder.

Graham went to open his mouth again, but Mariang let out another moan, turning to her other side with great clumsy effort. I sat up, ignoring Boston's frustration that no one would let him sleep. Making my way to Mariang, my eyes met Danny's as I touched Mariang's stomach. I climbed in bed with them and checked the clock to time when her next pains hit her. Four minutes later, Mariang's breaths picked up, and her hand tensed on the pillow while I rubbed her hard belly. "Hey, we should make a visit to the hospital. I think you're having contractions, and they're getting to be about four minutes apart."

Danny shot out of bed like he'd been spring-loaded, and waiting for this very moment. He whipped around the bedroom, throwing on clothes and getting out some for her, making sure her bag was packed as Graham and I slowly helped her out of the bed. "Wait, are you sure? I'm still two weeks early. I mean, maybe it's just heartburn."

I could hear Mariang's fear. I knew that fear; I had recently lived it. As much as you like to think that every mother in the world has done this, and hospitals are totally safe, there's still that blast of panic that grips you when the time comes for the actual searing pain to start. "Maybe, but let's go to the hospital, just to be safe."

We piled into the car, with Mariang in the front seat and Graham driving. Danny was a control freak, but Graham ganked the keys from his older brother when he noticed Danny's fingers were shaking.

Danny was in the middle of the backseat, leaning forward to hold Mariang's hand while she gritted her teeth through the contractions that were steadily getting more painful. When she let out a howl, I thought Danny was going to lose his mind. I squeezed the fingers on her other hand, leaning forward from the seat behind her in the back of the sedan to cheer her on. I had on a baggy undershirt of Graham's and borrowed leggings that clung to my scraped-up thighs as I leaned forward.

I called Ezra, letting him know it was D-day, and that we were on our way to the hospital. Boston dialed his mother's number and shoved the phone at me as soon as I hung up with Ezra. "Tell Mum. She'll want to know."

"Um, I, um..." But the phone was already ringing. I shifted my shirt and tried to sit up straighter, keeping my voice even and pleasant when the woman I didn't even know, but still feared, answered the phone. "Hello, Ms. Vandershot, Lavinia, um, Mama Vandershot. It's October, Von's friend?" I cringed and smacked my forehead with the phone when Boston sniggered. "Fiancée. Von's fiancée. Sorry."

"Oh! Hallow, dear. It's lovely to hear from you. How are the wedding plans going? Von never tells me anything."

"Oh, well there's nothing to tell just yet. We've been too busy with work to plan anything." I cleared my throat, cradling the phone on my shoulder so I could scratch my arm. "But that's not why I'm calling."

"Very well. What can I do for you?"

"I thought you'd like to know that Mariang's in labor."

Ms. Vandershot's voice went up an octave. "Mariang? Is she alright?"

"We're on our way to the hospital right now, Ma'am."

"Is Daniel there, perchance?"

"Yes, Ma'am." I gave the phone to Danny, my hand

shaking as I gusted out a breath of relief that I hadn't accidentally talked about Von naked, or cussed or something.

Boston reached behind Danny to muss my hair. "That was brilliant. Mum's nothing to be scared of, yeah? You don't have to do anything to impress her other than walk upright. She's just happy Von's settling down. You could look like Kabayo, and she'd still be excited her eldest is finally getting married."

"Thanks for that, you jag. Never ever spring your mama on me again!" I pulled out my phone and called Von, who answered on the second ring. "Hey, babe."

"You're talking to me," he gusted out with relief. "I'm so sorry, love. Tell me where I can send flowers to show you how worthless and wretched I am. I'll stay here until you come home, but give me an address I can tell the florist."

My nerves began to dissipate as a smile swept over my lips. "A florist? Do they sell unicorns at a florist? If you really want to say you're sorry, say it with a unicorn."

"I'll get on it straightaway."

"It's all fine, Von. It was my fault. I egged you on when you told me you were at your limit. There's nothing to be sorry for. Danny took me to the prison, and Doctor Brenden fixed me up, so I'm good as new."

"Danny took you where?" Von asked with a deadly threat to his tone. "Put him on the phone."

I winced at my slip. "I can't. I called to tell you that we're on our way to the hospital. Mariang's having her baby. Or heartburn. She's convinced it's heartburn that makes her scream every four minutes."

Von's voice swelled with emotion. "Tell my sister I'm on my way. Are you alright?"

"Of course. Brenden patched me up just fine."

"I don't mean that. I mean being around a woman in labor. Are you okay?"

My heart sank. I'd been trying to put my own labor and tragedy out of my head so I could be a team player for my sister. "It's all fine. We're almost to the hospital, so I'll see you there." I hung up before Von could make me feel things I knew I shouldn't. I reached forward and squeezed Mariang's hand when she screamed through her contraction. Graham and Danny were pulling for her, but it didn't seem to be making a dent. "You're doing so great, honey. Honestly, mother of the century right here." They were still four minutes apart, and I worried that the pain would only get worse, and she was nowhere near delivery.

47

THE COLD THAT SHOULDN'T BE

Watching Danny try to help Mariang would have been comedic gold if I'd been watching them on a sitcom. Every time she screamed, he jumped up from the chair next to her hospital bed, ran to the other side of the bed, then back again, tugging at his hair and shouting at her that it would all be okay. Then he shouted at the nurses to make her pain go away. Then he shouted at his brothers to get her more ice, though she had twelve cups of the stuff.

Every. Single. Time.

He'd tried to kiss her to give her a little bliss time in their happy place to take the edge off the pain, but the heartrate monitor blared that Mariang was dipping into the danger zone, so we ended that experiment right quick.

Then the heartrate monitor kept going off no matter

what we tried, making everyone panic. By the time the nurses came into the room to check it, her heart would be just at the bottom end of normal again, so they would leave. The whole thing was pretty frustrating.

Danny was in a world unto himself, and didn't temper his aggression when he yelled at the nurses. "Are you blind? Something's wrong! I can hear that insufferable machine beeping every few minutes! Have the doctor check her again!"

When the nurse looked like she might finally shout back at Danny, I intervened. I placed my hands on Danny's shoulders, making sure he took a full second to focus on me. "You need a break. You're stressing Mariang out, and she needs to calm down. It's a big deal, what she's about to do, and you freaking out isn't helping her." My tone turned syrupy when I checked Mariang's vitals. "Honey?"

"Yes?" Mariang's face was red and sweaty. Her pulse was weaker than I would've liked, but the baby's heartbeat was strong. I tried not to say anything that would make her worry.

"Is it okay if I take Danny out into the hall for a minute? Give you a little space to breathe?"

Mariang yanked me down by the front of my shirt and threw her arms around my neck, squeezing as tight as she could – which wasn't tight at all. "Thank you. You're a good sister. That you're here at all... I love you."

I kissed her cheek and smoothed her raven hair back. "I love you, too. Can I get you anything? I mean *anything*.

I'm pretty sure if you asked for the moon, Danny would lasso it for you. If you ever wanted a really nice piece of jewelry, now's the time to ask for it."

Mariang held her back, wincing. "Just do what you can to calm him down. Is Dad okay? He knows, right?"

"Of course. He was the first call. Alton's fitted the black tether bracelet to him so he can't leave the mansion, otherwise he'd be here with you." I couldn't imagine the carnage if Ezra showed up, what with Mariang's baby coming 'round the mountain. There'd be an elephant-sized lion roaming the hallways of the hospital for sure. I clicked my fingers to Boston for his phone and dialed Ezra, putting him on speaker. "Ezra? Mariang just wanted to hear your voice."

I set the phone on the nightstand, instructing the guys to watch her while I shoved Danny out the door into the hall. He grabbed his chest, breathing too sharply to actually get any useable oxygen. "I can't do this! She's not strong enough for any of it! What were we thinking?"

I didn't know the right words to say, so I pulled Danny in for a hug, his pulse racing in uneven thumps. His heart moved only for Mariang, and now that her heartrate was weakening, his was erratic as well. "Listen to me. They've got her hooked up to a heart monitor."

"And it keeps going off! They're looking like something's wrong, but they don't want to say it aloud. I know something's wrong!" His fist banged to the wall behind me, making me jump. "Don't bandy around the bush. Tell me straight what's happening to my wife!"

"First off, she needs to calm down. Thanks to you being amazing at keeping her safe, she's not used to being in a whole lot of prolonged physical pain. Labor is… rough, and it's long. So the more you freak out, the more she will. She needs to breathe and chill out as much as she can. You running around the room and barking like a lunatic isn't going to help with that."

"Okay. Yeah. I guess I am a bit stressed." Danny closed his eyes and leaned into my embrace. "Tell me the truth. It's bad, isn't it?"

I rubbed his back to soothe his worst fear. "Her heartrate is a little lower than it should be. I'm worried about her pushing with it low like that. I want to talk to the doctor about a C-section, but I know Mariang didn't want one."

Danny nodded, his cheek brushing mine. "Whatever gets the baby out safe and keeps Mariang healthy is fine by me. All we have to do is convince her."

"Good. Then come with me to talk to the doctor. Give Mariang five whole minutes of space. Then I promise you can hover all you want until she decks you."

"Thank you. I feel like no one's listening to me. The nurses just shrug at the monitor, and then leave when her heart goes back to normal. But I *know* my wife. I know when she's too weak for something, and she can't handle much more of this!"

"I know. I'm watching the whole thing." We walked to the nurse's station and requested the in-house doctor, since Mariang's wasn't there yet. It took only three minutes to get an audience with him, and he had many of the same concerns I did.

"Our first option is to do the cesarean, where we can control the circumstances a little more. The second option is that Mariang can try to deliver the baby, her heart gives out or she faints, and we have to rush the C-section. I'm worried about how weak she looks. The fetal monitor shows the baby's strong, but if we can't get her out safely, that won't matter."

"Do what you have to do to keep them both alive," Danny agreed, clutching my hand so hard, I thought he might break my only functioning one.

The doctor had salt and pepper colored hair, the beginnings of a pooched belly, and just the right amount of compassion in his voice as he explained the options to Mariang. He let her know she could still choose to try and deliver the baby naturally, and he'd let her go as long as her heart would allow her to try, but that there wasn't much hope for it, weak as she was.

"I want to wait a bit longer," she ruled, her face red and sweaty. "Am I close? Can we check again to see how much I'm dilated?"

The brothers were shooed out of the room, but Mariang insisted I stay with her and Danny. I held her hand through the examination and subsequent contractions, wishing I was anywhere else in the world. I tried not to feel the pain of losing my baby, but every now and then, the fresh memory coiled itself around my neck and squeezed, until I had barely any breath to speak with. Luckily, Mariang didn't need me to speak; she needed me to smile at her and stay by her side.

Mariang was closer to delivery than she'd been half an hour ago, but still wasn't dilated enough for the big moment. She screamed through yet another contraction, and try as he might to be her beacon of calm strength, Danny was at his wit's end. I pulled out a chair and sat him in it, and then helped Mariang to roll onto her side to keep her heartrate from dipping. I rubbed her back as I whispered encouraging things to her, and she cried through the pain I wished I could take on myself, so she didn't have to feel it. She had that certain quality about her – the kind that makes you want to move Heaven and earth to make sure she never stubbed her toe again. She pulled me down to lay in the bed next to her. There was barely enough room, but we made it work. She was scared, so I was there, making sure she didn't have to be afraid by herself. I spooned my sister, letting silent tears fall into her hair. I would endure any kind of emotional torment for her.

Ollie stopped by, but quickly darted out after a sweet kiss to Mariang's cheek and chuck to Danny's shoulder. He sat with the brothers in the hall to distance himself from Mariang's agony. I didn't much blame him. I wanted to be out there, too. But Mariang needed me, so I stayed by her side and muscled through my dread. "Just think," I said, rubbing circles into her back while she shook with pain, "in just a little bit, you'll have your girl in your arms. I think she'll have Danny's mouth and your eyes. Maybe Danny's ears and your hair. Super cute, right?"

"It hurts! It hurts so badly!"

"I know, babe. I'm here."

"And I'm here," Von announced, bolting into the room like friggin' Superman. He paused to kiss my cheek and then knelt on the other side of Mariang's bed, pressing a kiss to her wet nose. "You thought you'd start the party without me? For shame. You know how much I love a good party."

When Mariang opened her mouth to reply, a contraction hit, and the only thing she could do was howl. Von matched her cry with one of his own, smiling sympathetically and squeezing her hand when she worked out a short laugh at his dramatic antics after the pain subsided. "You came," she marveled. "You and October, you didn't have to be here. After everything you've been through, you still came?"

"Of course. You're my sister. I want to meet my niece. I was thinking of taking her horseback riding next week. Kabayo's wrapped around this one's finger," he said, jerking his thumb over at me. "I bet we could talk him into some shenanigans."

She reached out and touched Von's cheek with a trembling hand and tears in her eyes. "I love when you smile. I adore you, Von."

"Let me meet my niece, and I'll never stop smiling for you, darling." Von grinned when he kissed her palm, staying in her eye line until the next contraction. He started howling again to match her yells. "See? I'm so much better at this than you. My cries were more operatic, yeah? Let's let November decide. Who's better at being in labor, me or Mariang? I personally think she's faking it."

Mariang and I both laughed. Von was exactly what the room needed. "I'm glad you're here," I said, smiling at his handsome face as I rubbed Mariang's back.

"I am too, but perhaps you should take a break, yeah? This is all a little too fresh for you. Maybe Graham can take you down to the cafeteria."

I was about to say that I was okay to help Mariang, but Danny beat me to it. "No, she has to stay. The doctor listens to her. If something goes wrong, I want a medical professional in the room with Mariang."

Von stood, looking over us to stare at Danny in the chair. "You don't understand what you're asking her to do, being in here like this. She was just the one in labor, mate. It's cruel, asking her to stay."

Danny looked up, hopeless and lost. "Then I'm cruel. I don't care. All I know is that we need her to stay."

I rolled onto my back and reached out to hold Danny's hand for a brief moment. "It's alright. I'm not going anywhere."

After the twentieth contraction, Von decided he didn't want to scream anymore with Mariang, so he simply held her hand, shooting me looks of silent concern when the heartrate monitor kept beeping even after her contractions subsided.

"We have to reconsider the C-section, hun." Danny spoke into his hands, his nerves shot. "Your heartrate's taking longer to come back up."

"No, Danny. I want to try! Everyone thinks I can't do anything. I can do more than people give me credit for. I can do this! Don't you believe in me?"

Danny hesitated, and then nodded. "Okay, we can wait it out a little while longer. As long as the doctor lets you."

I held onto Mariang's hand, letting her squeeze it through her next contraction. Only this time, she barely put any pressure to the vice. "You alright? I barely felt you squeeze my hand that time," I asked in concern.

"I... I can't feel my fingers," she admitted, sounding drunk.

I barked over my shoulder, "Danny, get the doctor!"

"No," she whined, but she had been officially over-ruled. What had been just enough heartbeats a few minutes ago to keep the doctor on the fence, and let her decide her method of delivery, was now past the point of no return. Danny obeyed, knocking over his chair and shouting down the hallway for help.

It was at that exact moment I felt something familiar and cold shoot through me like a lightning bolt of ice in my veins. I'd just reaped someone, but knew it couldn't be. I couldn't have reaped. There weren't any humans in the room. The nurses were all out in the hallway, fearing Danny's wrath. I was the only partial human in the room.

That is, except for the other partial human I was currently wrapped around while she howled.

My mouth went dry, and all other noises in the universe faded from my mind, save for the sound of my own terrified heartbeat. My muscles went on lockdown as the ice stayed tight inside of me, my eyes widening as I tried to work out the panic that foreshadowed the thing that absolutely couldn't be.

I hadn't just reaped Mariang. I couldn't have. Mariang was strong. She'd dipped in the healing waters. There weren't any Terraway monsters clawing at her right now. We were Topside, safe from the drama.

I couldn't find my breath as the cold crept through me, freezing me around Mariang while I tried to reason with the ice, telling it that it didn't belong in me. There was no way Mariang was going to die today. It would be too soon. If she lived to be a hundred, it would be too soon. "No!" I worked out, my voice choked with tears that stung my face.

Von reached over Mariang to grip my shoulder in solidarity, no doubt assuming I was crying because of the baby emotions. When Mariang's soul leapt from me into him, he shot up from his kneeling position. "Was that... Did you just..."

Screw fate. I would fix this. I bolted out of the bed the

second the chill left me, and ran to fetch the doctor, who was already on his way in. "Something's wrong!" I told him, stating what he no doubt already knew. He checked her, frowning that she still hadn't dilated enough to deliver yet. Mariang's breath was shallow and her eyes kept fighting to stay open between contractions that didn't seem to hurt her anymore. Her pain was gone now, because I'd just ensured that she would have a peaceful death. It was the cruelest kind of tease, to give her a chance at everything she'd ever wanted, only to have it ripped away inches before the finish line. I couldn't work out words to warn the room at large that irreparable things were happening.

Surely not death. I couldn't have reaped Mariang. She has years left. Dozens and dozens of years! I've done everything, reaped more than I should, to make sure she lived. She's going to be a mother in just a few minutes!

With a kind but grave bedside manner, the doctor explained to Mariang that he wasn't willing to gamble on her heart being strong enough anymore. "I'm afraid we have to take your daughter out now if you want to live to see her."

"No! I... I can..."

Mariang struggled to sit up, but the second she did, her sweaty body fainted in my arms. Her heartrate plummeted to a dangerous low and stayed there. The monitor blared, yelling at us that we'd waited too long – listening to her when we should have been taking over.

Von scrambled to help me support her, lowering her

back into the bed while I started chest compressions. Nurses flooded the room, edging Von and me out and shoving scrubs at Danny, who looked like he might be the one passing out. They ran her bed down the hall, shouting instructions to each other and pumping her chest that ceased to move on its own.

48

ANASTASIA GRACE

I never learned the house doctor's name. Everything about the rest of that day turned to a blur of white noise in my ears. Though I was the only one who understood the medical terminology for what had happened, everyone understood the finality of the grave pronouncement.

I cast around for Ollie, but he'd left half an hour ago to sit with Allie, who was in a different wing of the hospital. Life was normal for him right now; he didn't know. I wanted him to stay in that bubble as long as possible.

Danny was taken into a room, shouting at the doctor and demanding they try harder. He cursed everyone and raged that they should've done more, that he had to see her because they were wrong. He'd given up everything so Mariang would be safe. They were surely wrong if they were saying she was dead.

Boston, Graham and Von wrestled with their brother in the hospital room, pulling in small doses until Danny stopped throwing punches at everything and everyone who had robbed him of the one beauty in his life. They lowered him to a chair, Boston and Graham sobbing uncontrollably as they tried to keep Danny upright. They tried gently to make him understand that sometimes life was death, and there was nothing to be done about it now.

The doctor was patient with our mess as he explained the other shoe that had to drop. "We weren't able to save Mariang, but we were able to deliver the baby. Your daughter's healthy and very much alive."

Danny had been blissed not completely out, but enough to where he couldn't comprehend what the doctor was saying, let alone get up to do anything about it. He stared listlessly ahead of him, unblinking as his jaw went slack and tears streamed down his red and forlorn face.

When the doctor realized he would get nowhere with Danny, he turned to me. "You're her sister? That's what I have here on her forms."

"Um, yes. I'm her sister." None of it felt real. It wasn't possible that Mariang was dead. It wasn't even Terraway that killed her.

I didn't pay attention to my steps as I followed the doctor down a few hallways, tears blurring my vision and making my feet stumble. Halfway there, I keeled over and let out a gut-wrenching cry, leaning on the doctor who supported my weight and had the decency to hold me while I wept in the stranger's arms. He led me slowly to the private room Mariang had been laboring in. Then he sat me in a rocking chair as I cried, unable to hear anything he was saying.

It wasn't until a pink blanket was placed in my arms that I realized the world was still turning, though it felt like with all the horror, it should've stopped long ago. Staring up at me was a squawking, round-faced angel. She had Mariang's hair, Danny's ears, Mariang's eyes and Danny's lips.

I don't know how I saw her that first time with so many tears marring my vision, but somehow I found her in the haze. A cry too horrible cracked out of my mouth, bubbling out and landing on the poor baby whose biggest crime was being born. The baby was the one who was supposed to be crying, but I was the one who couldn't control myself. I held her face to my cheek, rocking slowly as I felt her tiny baby breath on my skin.

Something in my gut stirred at the sweetness of her miniscule cry. Her insistence was so important to her, but still came out a high-pitched squeak. She needed her mother, and I was a poor substitute. I held little Baby Girl Manaul-Vandershot to my breast, falling more in love after every second I rocked her. She was perfect, and looked so much like Mariang, my heart could barely take it.

I don't know how long the nurses waited in the room with me, some of them crying softly as they watched me rock my niece. One brave nurse ventured forward, helping me hold the baby when my sobbing grew too erratic for me to see straight. She tried to arrest the baby from me, but I lashed out in desperation. "No! Her mama just died! She needs me." The poor nurse apologized and helped me hold the baby more securely, placing a pillow on my lap in case my arms grew too unstable.

I felt unstable, but I tucked it away because something inside of me was still a mama, so the baby's cries held the first and foremost importance in my mind.

When Von wandered in, agony slashed across his face at seeing me holding his niece. Tears cascaded down his angular cheeks as he pulled up a chair next to mine, holding his arms out for a turn. It was only to Von I could surrender her. She was too precious, too perfect. Anastasia Grace. That was what Mariang had wanted to name her.

A low, mournful sound erupted from Von's mouth. I heard the weeks of heartbreak in his cry, and the many more to come. "September! September, my heart." He moaned our daughter's name for a solid minute before he started to realize the baby in his arms had needs of her own. He rubbed her back, and started saying his niece's name over and over. "Anastasia. Anastasia, my beauty." Every time it came out, it was more loving, more grounded and slowly, it sounded less painful.

Von with a baby was a beautiful thing. He handed her to me with great reluctance, but had something on his mind he needed two hands for. "Okay. I don't know how to do this, and my brother's absolutely wrecked, so you lot get to stand there while I ask as many questions about babies as I can think of. I need something to write with."

The nurse near the door grabbed him a pen and paper, answering gently every intelligent and obvious question Von produced. He scribbled the answers on his paper with a trembling hand while I rocked poor Anastasia Grace.

It wasn't until Graham came into the room sometime later that I remembered there were others who might want to meet Ana. I couldn't surrender her, and Graham was too overwhelmed to hold her without potentially dropping the treasure. He stroked her cheek and then bent down to whisper to me, "Danny won't come. He doesn't want to see her. Boston and Ollie are taking him to see Mariang's body. Can you and Von stay with Anastasia? He's not... He can't... It's bad."

"Of course." I looked down at the beautiful girl who was calming down in my arms. Her squawking quieted when I offered her the bottle the nurse handed me. Mariang had wanted to breastfeed. So many plans Mariang had for her daughter, and this was the first one of many that would be sacrificed. "I can stay with her, no problem." I kept my eyes locked in on the perfect princess who totally owned me in the first two minutes. "I can stay with her forever."

Love the book?

Leave a review.

49

TRAP

**Enjoy a free preview of *Trap*,
book eight in the *Terraway* series.**

Though I'd seen an avalanche of deaths in the past year, I'd only been to one funeral in my life. It was for Mrs. Kitsa, when I was young. I could still smell the thick pancake makeup on her, marring the cookie smell she'd always traveled with. Mrs. Kitsa had been one of our neighbors a few trailers down. She loved to bake, and always had a smile for Ollie, Allie and me. When she'd passed at eighty-two, I'd been only nine. Ollie and Allie took me to the funeral, clothes washed, faces scrubbed and somber. We sat in the back, and I watched with fascination the ritual of a funeral. The praying, the hopeful message, and the mournful family who had never once come to the trailer park to visit their mother, grand-mother or great-grandmother. Yet they all cried quietly into handkerchiefs and sleeves, swearing they thought they'd have more time.

Mama McCray's funeral was when I was seven, but I hadn't been allowed to go.

Omen funerals in Terraway were... different. The grand affair was held at Kabayo's enormous stone castle. It somehow felt drafty and cold, despite the sunny ninety-degree weather that beat down on the expanse of grass covering the field. Last time I'd been in Silo, everything had been bone dry due to the drought, with barely a patch of green in sight. Now with regular rain coming, there were traces of emerald, jade and olive brushed through the woods, dotting the ground and filling out the mountains. It was beautiful, but I couldn't really appreciate it, being that we were there for Mariang's funeral. All six nations were gathered outside the castle. People from the furthest corners of Terraway came out to pay their respects to the woman who'd given everything to make sure they had a chance at survival. Mariang's body had been magi-cally preserved somehow, making her look like she was merely sleeping, though she'd been dead an entire month now. Each day felt like heaviness in my breast that I couldn't escape. Every passing hour that Mariang remained dead, I grew more weighted, the youth gone from me completely.

The council and kings had been given ornate chairs to

sit on, facing the crowd above the stone steps of the castle. The casket was before us, resting on the expansive dais between the royals and the people. I was on the council, and Mason as well, since he was the delegate from Sombi, so we were given chairs, but Von was made to stand behind me as my sentry, staring out at the crowd with a hollow expression.

The members of the council were dressed in their royal robes or their decorated military gear. I didn't put up a fuss about being given a long Renaissance-style dress to wear, but I couldn't stop fidgeting with the revealing neckline, the capped sleeves, or the heavy black and gold material that made me feel like I was wearing curtains or something. The black felt appropriate for a funeral, but the gold swirls that started at the hemline and crawled up like vines to cup and brush over my breasts did not. It wasn't until I saw Ezra's matching tie and Ana's black and gold baby gown that I realized the design must be a family thing. Ezra was seated at my left, his eyes bloodshot and expression vacant as he stared ahead at the millions his daughter had been sacrificed for over and over again. After all of it, she'd survived. It hadn't been Terraway that killed her, but our world, or nature perhaps. No one had expected her to die in childbirth – except Sama, perhaps, who had warned me in my dream back when I was pregnant that Omens had a higher mortality rate during pregnancy than other women. The shock of Mariang's death was still hitting us in waves. The world had left us bereft of her grace and kindness that only death itself could silence.

Von was behind me, wearing a fitted black suit, with a gold and black tie to match Ezra's. He was holding Anastasia Grace with bags under his eyes and a fatherly protective air to the way he cradled her. We hadn't slept much in the past month. Of course, no one slept well after Mariang passed, but we had been gifted the extra responsibility of taking care of Baby Ana. Danny could barely put one foot in front of the other, and couldn't comprehend that Ana was very much alive and in need of her parent. Von, Danny, Ana, Ollie and I had been living at my house, with the Vandershot boys rotating to pull for Danny as needed, which was often.

"Motherhood suits you," Finn whispered from his throne-like chair on my right. "You look lovely."

I responded with a polite, "Thank you, Captain." Everything I did was being scrutinized by the residents of Terraway, who were all sitting just a stone's throw away on the grass at the foot of the steps. I didn't feel the guilty thrill I usually did at being near Finn. My focus was on Von, Ezra, Danny and Anastasia. I hadn't even been to visit Allie in her coma in days. Ana had a penchant for screaming from midnight until around four in the morning, and intermittently throughout the day, so Von and I weren't sleeping much. Ollie had even bailed to spend a couple nights at Gabby's just to catch up on his rest. Apparently braving the "where is this going" talk with his on-again off-again girlfriend was less horrible than a nonstop screaming baby.

Mason was on the clear other end, sitting next to a man that could've been his twin. While the people were still milling about and finding their space on the grass, I got up from my chair and made my way over to my other Reaper, knowing he was afraid to get too near the baby – though Ana was now a month old, and supposedly in the safety zone to escape stirring the fetus hunger of Matruculans.

I knew I was supposed to be some queen or whatever, but I didn't care about decorum when it came to my Pullers. When Mason stood to greet me, I jogged forward after I passed the casket I didn't want to look at too closely. I threw my arms around him, squeezing tighter than anyone would have the tolerance for, were he not part The Hulk. Mason possessed a super strength that had a way of making me feel safe. Perched above the whole of Terraway for everyone to observe and comment on, I needed that feeling he instilled in me just by being there.

I could feel his smile against my cheek, his quarter-inch beard scratching my skin in a way that felt like home. "I missed you, *hani*. I know you've been busy taking care of Anastasia, but I'm worried about you. You're well? You're in one functioning piece?"

"I'm much better, now that you're here. This whole thing is horrible, and I'm sorry you're dealing with it all alone. I don't want that."

"Alton said he'd get me a phone, so I was thinking I'd

start calling you every night just to check in and make sure you're alive. We're not meant to be apart this long."

I could feel him pulling for me, and I breathed for the first time in a while. "Mason, I missed you."

"You're a ball of anxiety. Haven't Von and his brothers been pulling for you?" He ignored the millions of onlookers that were shifting around on the grass. He held me around the waist, moving his head back to examine my face. "You look exhausted."

"Aw, you say the sweetest things. You look beautiful, too," I crooned.

"I didn't mean it like that. You're lovely, as you always are. But you need more pulling than this."

I shook my head, making sure to keep my tears sucked back behind my eyeballs. "Danny's a wreck still, and Anastasia..." I gulped, fishing for the right way to word the issue. "Ana needs her mother. She's colicky, so she screams a lot. Von's pulling for her now just so we make it through the funeral. I don't want to overtax the guys, making them pull for me, on top of all that. I can deal the old-fashioned way."

"I see. Well, let's see what I can do while I have you in my arms." Mason hugged me tighter, kissing the top of my head and tucking me under his chin. Waves of peace shot through me, making my eyes flutter shut as I burrowed my cheek into his burly chest. I stiffened when I heard the "aw" and the whispers that broke out from the residents of Terraway, reminding me that I had an audience of millions. Mason was a feared and respected zombie killer, and I was cozying up to him like he was a precious bunny. Or maybe I was his bunny. It was hard to tell who took care of whom on any given day. "Better?" he asked, leaning down to peck my lips. He dropped his arms so he could offer me his elbow to hold like a gentleman.

"Much."

"Would you like to meet my younger brother? This is Carter, King of Hayop. Carter, allow me to introduce Lady October."

Mason's double stood, showing off his midnight-colored royal robe overtop his black tunic, and matching fitted pants that were tucked into his sturdy boots. He had dreads tied back with a leather string, looking like Mason used to, back when I first met him. Carter tilted his head to me and dipped his chin, and I did the same to him, thinking that was probably the right thing to do. I really had no idea about the proper politics of Terraway, and now was a bad time to ask Ezra at what times I was expected to bow. "Pleased to meet you, Lady October," Carter offered kindly. Carter had a boyish light to his caramel eyes that Mason just plain didn't. Mason had been all Viking from the get-go. Carter had the same build, but looked like he preferred the hard work being done from his throne. "My brother speaks very highly of you."

"Oh, well now I know you're lying. Mason hates me. I mean, one look at me and he starts ralphing." In hindsight, making jokes about puking the first time I met Mason's only living relative was probably not the queenly thing to do. But you know, whatever. It was either make playful banter or burst into tears. I batted my hand at Carter's grin. "But don't worry, the feeling's mutual. I mean, would you look at this guy? Barfalicious."

"Hey!" Mason bumped me with his hip, narrowing one eye down at me before his smile got the better of him.

Carter started to laugh, but then covered his mouth with his hand and faked a cough. "Excuse me. I didn't realize anyone on the council knew how to make a joke."

"Who said I was joking?" I motioned to Mason's perfect physique that shone even beneath his outfit that matched his brother's, but included gold cuffs around his wrists. "I mean, hit the gym once in a while, am I right?" The gold on his cuffs made it look like Mason belonged with me, with my family. It was a sweet assurance in the midst of the bleakness. I fished around for shtick, so I didn't plunge back into despair.

Carter's eyes were dancing with the light he seemed to travel with. "Oh, Mason. You said she was beautiful, but I didn't realize she was witty, too. Perhaps I won't avoid the council as much anymore."

"Yes, well." Mason smiled down at me, and I could feel the love beaming from him that I was making nice with his brother. "If you're finished bewitching Carter, perhaps you'd like to meet the other kings of Terraway who've been too busy to show up for council meetings."

I curtsied like I'd seen people do in movies and moved

on down the line, shaking hands, bowing and making as pleasant of chitchat as I could.

Mason gave me one more solid pull in his parting hug when we reached the midpoint of the stage. "This is as far as I can take you. Anastasia's still too young for me to be near."

"Oh, sorry. I'll talk to you after." I leaned up and blessed his lips with a closed-mouth kiss. "Love you, Mason."

"Love you, too. Now go shake hands, and tell Von not to listen to you when you say you don't need more pulling."

It was just my luck that Aranya's was the next throne I came to. Aranya was the jaggoff who'd helped his father, King Geon, lock me in their dungeon in Sakuna, trying to keep me as a prize for Sama. I wanted to punch him, but knew that would probably not be good politics. Lang rose to his feet beside Aranya, along with their sinister sister, Luna. They were dressed in matching brown royal outfits, and a smattering of bees circled almost pleasantly around Aranya's head. Lang was no doubt anxious I might throttle his tool of a brother right there with a whole sea of witnesses. The three bowed, but I refused to tilt my head to Aranya or Luna. Luna noticed the affront, but Aranya brushed aside the offense, extending his hand to me instead.

Boy, do I wish I would've passed on shaking it. I couldn't stifle the anger that flared in me. I gripped Aranya's hand and jerked him close, leaning up on my toes to whisper a threat to him and Luna. "Don't you think I've forgotten the stink of your daddy's dungeon. Make no mistake, as soon as things settle down for me, I'll make it my life's mission to make sure you're taken off that throne and hurled into your own prison. Then we'll have some real fun."

Luna was snide, not bothering to conceal her snarl. "Step foot in Sakuna again, and you'll see how fun things can really get when father's not holding me back."

Aranya's black eyes widened. His brown skin had been scrubbed of mud, but he still felt dirty to me. He kept his voice low, but I moved on after I heard, "Listen you little..."

I wasn't little, and I didn't have to listen.

Kabayo rose, his left hand on the small of my back as he shook Aranya's with his right, leaning in to whisper a threat of his own. He released Aranya with a look of horror on the man's face that matched his sister's. "Leave him to me," Kabayo whispered in my ear, releasing me with a light push away from the man who'd helped abduct me, and the woman who'd delighted in my degradation.

I gave a slight nod to Lang, which he returned. I tried to appear professional, and not like I wanted to hug him. It was important to his family that he remain loyal to their cause. It could make things sticky for him if they knew we were friends. My upper lip curled at Luna's pinched nose and waist-length curly brown hair, but I moved on down the line without further incident.

In the front row of the millions sat Ollie, Lynna,

Boston, Graham, Alton and Ms. Vandershot. It was the first time I'd ever seen Von's mother. I was afraid to look at her directly, though my eyes felt tethered to her face, bouncing back whenever they wandered too far. She'd come in for the funeral, and to meet her first grandchild. There was much of Von in her face, the angular cheekbones, the black hair that was thick and did what it felt like. Her long, dark waves were pulled back and pinned elegantly, making her look like a model for hairspray or something. She was beautiful, and second only to Sama was my fear of her.

The ceremony finally started a few minutes later. Some guy I didn't know gave the eulogy in a long black wizard's robe, performing several herb-centric rituals over Mari-ang's body. She lay like Sleeping Beauty inside her clear casket for all to admire, palms open and feet bare – as was the tradition in Terraway. Even in death, she was beautiful. I hated how lifelike she appeared, and gripped my fingers in my lap to keep them from clawing at my arms. I wanted to be there for Ezra and Danny, and knew I couldn't do that if I fell apart.

Danny was in a world unto himself, unable to speak, eat or make a decision unless someone helped him. The only time he slept was in my arms after Von pulled so hard, Danny had no choice but to go limp. I alternated between rocking Ana and holding Danny all the hours of the day I wasn't reaping. Now he stood at the head of Mari-ang's casket, facing the people with soulless eyes in a tailored black suit with gold cuffs that I knew he'd never wear again.

The service lasted two hours. Two whole hours I prayed Ana would sleep through. I didn't want her seeing any of this, and since she was a colicky baby, I worried about Von having to miss the funeral if she woke. Two whole hours I willed with everything in me that Mason and Ezra would have the strength not to shapeshift with a new baby so near them. Ezra was more controlled, his years giving me a little solace that he wouldn't lion out and try to eat my niece (I really hope that was the weirdest sentence I'd ever thought). Mason and Carter's chairs had been strategically placed at the far end by Kabayo, keeping as much distance as possible between the fresh newborn and my favorite Viking.

Finn had been assigned to watch Ana and me for the duration of my time in Terraway that day. The council worried that Sama's spirit or his whole friggin' army might make an appearance, since I was in Terraway, ripe for the abducting. It made for a tense funeral, as if we didn't have enough to stress about. Had I a solid two hours of consecutive sleep in the past month, I might've been able to be worried about Sama, but lucky for my sanity, I couldn't feel much.

I didn't understand the different steps of the ritual, but I managed to stand when the other council members did, and murmur the things I was told to say. Finn was my coach at my side, making sure I didn't embarrass Ezra or the council.

I was pretty sure I was blending in until the grand wizard in charge announced the procession of the *hiya*. I didn't know what that was, but I knew I was not all that comfortable around the silver-haired guy doing the funeral. Von had informed me he was Mangkukulam, which I knew was what Sama was. While this guy seemed on the up and up, I was positive I'd never be comfortable around any of the few warlocks of Terraway.

The Grand Mangkukulam in charge of the funeral raised his arms, allowing the last row of civilians to make their way past the casket to pay their respects first. I bowed my head and paced myself for the first of millions to make their way past Mariang in all of her sleeping ballerina beauty. What made my chin jerk up with sudden rage was when I heard the distinct sound of spitting in Danny's direction as they walked by.

Read *Trap* and continue with the *Terraway* series today.

ABOUT THE AUTHOR

USA Today bestselling author Mary E. Twomey lives in Michigan with her three adorable children. She enjoys reading, writing, vegetarian cooking, and telling her children fantastic stories about wombats.

While she loves writing fantasy, dystopian, and paranormal tales for her readers, Mary also writes romance under the name Tuesday Embers, and cozy mysteries under the name Molly Maple.

Visit her online at www.maryetwomey.com, and sign up for her newsletter, so you never miss a new release.

www.ingramcontent.com/pod-product-compliance
Lightning Source LLC
Chambersburg PA
CBHW010315100726
47906CB00006B/997